Chris Bohjalian is the critically acclaimed a̶u̶t̶h̶o̶r̶ ̶w̶h̶o̶s̶e̶ work has been translated into twenty-six languages. He lives with his wife and daughter in Vermont. Visit www.chrisbohjalian.com

Praise for Chris Bohjalian

'Superbly crafted and astonishingly powerful . . . It will thrill readers who cherish their worn copies of *To Kill a Mockingbird*' *People*

'The next *A Map of the World* . . . heartfelt . . . wrenching' *Glamour*

'The must-read of the season' *Woman's Own*

'Gripping, insightful . . . Readers will find themselves mesmerized by the irresistible momentum of the narrative' *Publishers Weekly*

'Astonishing . . . will keep readers up late at night until the last page is turned' *Washington Post*

'Few writers can manipulate a plot with Bohjalian's grace and power' *New York Times*

'A tragic but hugely uplifting tale of love, loss and friendship . . . Bohjalian has created a stunning, eminently readable piece of work' *Gay Times*

'It's the sort of book you want to read in one sitting, and it packs a twist at the end that leaves you speechless' Jodi Picoult

'A mystery anchored in sorrow, a harrowing and even haunting tale of literary influence, delusion, intervention. Chris Bohjalian has done it again' Gregory Maguire, author of *Wicked*

Also by Chris Bohjalian, available from Pocket Books

The Double Bind

Skeletons at the Feast

Midwives

Secrets
of Eden

CHRIS BOHJALIAN

POCKET
BOOKS

LONDON • SYDNEY • NEW YORK • TORONTO

F792,901 *€8.99*

First published in the United States by Shaye Areheart Books, 2010
An imprint of the Crown Publishing Group, a division of Random House, Inc.
First published in Great Britain by Simon & Schuster UK Ltd, 2010
This edition published by Pocket Books, 2010
An imprint of Simon & Schuster UK Ltd
A CBS COMPANY

1 3 5 7 9 10 8 6 4 2

Simon & Schuster UK Ltd
1st Floor
222 Gray's Inn Road
London WC1X 8HB

Simon & Schuster Australia
Sydney

www.simonandschuster.co.uk

A CIP catalogue record for this book
is available from the British Library

ISBN 978-1-84983-042-3

This book is a work of fiction. Names, characters, places and
incidents are either a product of the author's imagination or are used
fictitiously. Any resemblance to actual people living or dead,
events or locales, is entirely coincidental.

Printed in the UK by CPI Cox & Wyman, Reading, Berkshire RG1 8EX

For David Reed Wood
and, once more,
for Victoria

But for sorrow there is no remedy provided by nature; it is often occasioned by accidents irreparable, and dwells upon objects that have lost or changed their existence; it requires what it cannot hope, that the laws of the universe should be repealed; that the dead should return, or the past should be recalled.

—SAMUEL JOHNSON

Therefore shall a man leave his father and his mother, and shall cleave unto his wife: and they shall be one flesh. And they were both naked, the man and his wife, and were not ashamed.

—GENESIS 2:24–25

Secrets
of Eden

PART I

Stephen Drew

CHAPTER ONE

As a minister I rarely found the entirety of a Sunday service depressing. But some mornings disease and despair seemed to permeate the congregation like floodwaters in sandbags, and the only people who stood during the moment when we shared our joys and concerns were those souls who were intimately acquainted with nursing homes, ICUs, and the nearby hospice. Concerns invariably outnumbered joys, but there were some Sundays that were absolute routs, and it would seem that the only people rising up in their pews to speak needed Prozac considerably more than they needed prayer. Or yes, than they needed me.

On those sorts of Sundays, whenever someone would stand and ask for prayers for something relatively minor—a promotion, traveling mercies, a broken leg that surely would mend—I would find myself thinking as I stood in the pulpit, *Get a spine, you bloody ingrate! Buck up! That lady behind you is about to lose her husband to pancreatic cancer, and you're whining about your difficult boss? Oh, please!* I never said that sort of thing aloud, but I think that's only because I'm from a particularly mannered suburb of New York City, and so my family has to be drunk to be cutting. I did love my congregation, but I also knew that I had an inordinate number of whiners.

The Sunday service that preceded Alice Hayward's baptism and death was especially rich in genuine human tragedy, it was just jam-packed with the real McCoy—one long ballad of ceaseless lamentation and pain. Moreover, as a result of that morning's children's message and a choir member's solo, it was also unusually moving. The whiners knew that they couldn't compete with the legitimate, no-holds-barred sort of torment that was besieging much of the congregation, and so they kept their fannies in their seats and their prayer requests to themselves.

That day we heard from a thirty-four-year-old lawyer who had already endured twelve weeks of radiation for a brain tumor and was now in his second week of chemotherapy. He was on steroids, and so on top of everything else he had to endure the indignity of a sudden physical resemblance to a human blowfish. He gave the children's message that Sunday, and he told the children—toddlers and girls and boys as old as ten and eleven—who surrounded him at the front of the church how he'd learned in the last three months that while some angels might really have halos and wings, he'd met a great many more who looked an awful lot like regular people. When he started to describe the angels he'd seen—describing, in essence, the members of the church Women's Circle who drove him back and forth to the hospital, or the folks who filled his family's refrigerator with fresh vegetables and homemade carrot juice, or the people who barely knew him yet sent cards and letters—I saw eyes in the congregation grow dewy. And, of course, I knew how badly some of those half-blind old ladies in the Women's Circle drove, which seemed to me a further indication that there may indeed be angels among us.

Then, after the older children had returned to the pews where their parents were sitting while the younger ones had been escorted to the playroom in the church's addition so they would be spared the second half of the service (including my sermon), a fellow in the choir with a lush, robust tenor sang "It is well with my soul," and he sang it without the accompaniment of our organist. Spafford wrote that hymn after his four daughters had drowned when their ship, the *Ville de Havre,* collided with another vessel and sank. When the tenor's voice rose for the refrain for the last time, his hands before him and his long fingers steepling together before his chest, the congregation spontaneously joined him. There was a pause when they finished, followed by a great forward *whoosh* from the pews as the members of the church as one exhaled in wonder, "Amen. . . ."

And so when it came time for our moment together of caring and sharing (an expression I use without irony, though I admit it sounds vaguely like doggerel and more than a little New Age), the people were primed to pour out their hearts. And they did. I've looked back at the notes I scribbled from the pulpit that morning—the names of the people for whom we were supposed to pray and exactly what ailed them—and by any objective measure there really was a lot of horror that day. Cancer and cystic fibrosis and a disease that would cost a newborn her right eye. A car accident. A house fire. A truck bomb in a land far away. We prayed for people dying at home, in area hospitals, at the hospice in the next town. We prayed for healing, we prayed for death (though we used that great euphemism *relief*), we prayed for peace. We prayed for peace in souls that were turbulent and for peace in a corner of the world that was in the midst of a civil war.

By the time I began my sermon, I could have been as inspiring as a tax attorney and people would neither have noticed nor cared. I could have been awful—though the truth is, I wasn't; my words at the very least transcended hollow that morning—and still they would have been moved. They were craving inspiration the way I crave sunlight in January.

Nevertheless, that Sunday service offered a litany of the ways we can die and the catastrophes that can assail us. Who knew that the worst was yet to come? (In theory, I know the answer to that, but we won't go there. At least not yet.) The particular tragedy that would give our little village its grisly notoriety was still almost a dozen hours away and wouldn't begin to unfold until the warm front had arrived in the late afternoon and early evening and we had all begun to swelter over our dinners. There was so much still in between: the potluck, the baptism, the word.

Not *the* word, though I do see it as both the beginning and the end: In the beginning was the Word. . . .

There. That was the word in this case. *There.*

"There," Alice Hayward said to me after I had baptized her in the pond that Sunday, a smile on her face that I can only call grim. There.

The baptism immediately followed the Sunday service, a good old-fashioned, once-a-year Baptist dunking in the Brookners' pond. Behind me I heard the congregation clapping for Alice, including the members of the Women's Circle, at least one of whom, like me, was aware of what sometimes went on in the house the Haywards had built together on the ridge.

None of them, I know now, had heard what she'd said. But even if they had, I doubt they would have heard in that one word exactly what I did, because that single syllable hadn't been meant for them. It had been meant only for me.

"There," I said to Alice in response. Nodding. Agreeing. Affirming her faith. A single syllable uttered from my own lips. It was the word that gave Alice Hayward all the reassurance she needed to go forward into the death that her husband may have been envisioning for her—perhaps even for the two of them—for years.

THE NEXT MORNING a deputy state's attorney, a woman perhaps five years younger than me with that rare but fetching combination of blue eyes and raven-black hair, would try to convince me that I was reading too much into that single syllable. The lawyer was Catherine Benincasa, a name I would have remembered a long while even if our paths had not continued to converge throughout the late summer and autumn, because she was named after the saint who convinced Gregory XI to return the papacy to Rome in 1376, after three and a half generations of exile in Avignon. But I reminded Catherine that she had not been present at the baptism. If she had, if she had known all that I did about Alice's pilgrimage to the water—if she had spent the time that I had listening to her and offering what counsel I could—she would have understood I was right.

When Alice had emerged from the pond beside a wild rosebush with some of its delicate flowers still in bloom, she had fixed her eyes for a moment on the cluster of people in a half circle at the lip of the water. Their collective gaze was as bright as the sun. My parishioners were dressed for a picnic, and they were joyful. I watched Alice give her daughter a small wave. Katie had turned fifteen that summer and had suddenly, almost preternaturally, been transformed from a girl into a woman (or, as her mother had put it to me once when we were alone, her voice rich with love, "a tart with a heart"). The baseball caps, an affectation that had once been as much a requisite part of her clothing as her sneakers or shoes, were gone, and she had allowed her dark hair to grow long. She had replaced her overalls and T-shirts with skirts and short summer dresses and skinny jeans that seemed to cling to her long legs like Lycra. She wore flip-flops and ballet flats instead of the sneakers or the black patent leather shoes with neon spangles she had worn to church as a little girl and christened her "happy Janes." She had a small stud in her nose and great hoops in her ears. She looked nothing like the child I would recall eating a blue

Popsicle on the steps of the village's general store or the reserve out-fielder I had coached for two years on the town's Little League team, a player more likely to harvest dandelions in the grass than run down fly balls. She was disarmingly precocious and always had been. Now she wrote for the school newspaper and the school literary magazine, and she was one of those children who seem to defy the logic of genes: She was, in my opinion, smarter than both of her parents. She was a good kid who had become a good teen—too intelligent for drugs and too ambitious to get pregnant. She had survived the worst a man like her father could offer and moved on. In two years, I told myself, she would get out of Haverill, whether it was to a small state college in a remote corner of Vermont or to someplace more impressive in Massachusetts or Maine or New York. My money was on the latter. I hoped the child was thinking Ivy or Little Ivy.

She no longer came to church or to the church's teenage Youth Group meetings with any regularity, but she had come to her mother's baptism that morning, and I was pleased. She waved back at Alice, perhaps a little embarrassed, but I imagine also happy for her mother, since this was something that her mother clearly desired. As Katie had grown older—more mature, more confident—I sensed that she had begun to intercede on Alice's behalf when her father would threaten her mother. I knew of at least one punch she had prevented with her screams and her anger, and I assumed that Ginny O'Brien, Alice's best friend in the Women's Circle, knew of a good many more.

When Alice glanced back at me, she wiped the pond water from her eyes and used her thumbs like hooks to hoist back behind her ears the twin drapes of auburn mane that had fallen in front of her face. She then started from the pond, pulling at her long wet T-shirt the way all the women did, holding the material away from her chest so it wouldn't cling to her breasts as she returned to dry land. Beneath that shirt she was wearing a Speedo tank suit with a paisley pattern that reminded me vaguely of the upholstery on the couch in my mother's apartment in Bronxville, and her feet were bare. She had painted her toenails a cupcake-icing pink. Most women were baptized fully clothed in the baggiest pants and sweatshirts they could find, and—given the man to whom she was married—I found myself pondering the reality that she would never have worn only a bathing suit and a T-shirt had her husband been present. He wouldn't have allowed it, even though the T-shirt happened to fall to midthigh. But I also wondered if this was a rebellion of some sort, a challenge, because there was always the chance he would hear and there was always the likelihood he would see one of those photos that Ginny was taking. Had I not known the details of what she endured in her home, I would have found the image of Alice Hayward emerging wet like a sea nymph from the Brookners' pond an inappropriate, earthy, but inescapably erotic treat. She was thirty-eight when she died, the second-youngest member of the Women's Circle, and she had been blessed with eyes that were round and deep and that rested in her pale face like circles of melted chocolate.

When she reached the grass, almost neon green that morning after a week of midsummer rains, her friend Ginny hugged her. The clouds had finally rolled east in the night, and the sun shone down upon the two women, now sisters in Christ, as they embraced.

Years earlier Ginny had joined the church by a simple statement of faith. Not quite five minutes out of a Sunday service, a little paperwork, a handshake, some polite applause. No water.

Not Alice, not at that point in her life. She wanted to leave absolutely nothing to chance, and so she wanted baptism and she wanted it by immersion. Full immersion. She had come to Christ, and she wanted to be certain that she wouldn't be kept from the kingdom by an ecclesiastical technicality.

And so we went to the Brookners' pond after the regular worship service, the water high and clear that Sunday morning after all that late-July rain.

"Do you believe in the Lord Jesus Christ as your personal savior?" I asked her.

"I do."

"Do you intend to follow him all the days of your life?"

"I do," she said again.

I cradled the back of her head with my left hand and held her clasped fingers like the handles of a shopping bag with my right, and then leaned her backward beneath the surface of the cold, mountain-fed waters, baptizing her in the name of the Father, the Son, and the Holy Spirit.

There.

Like Christ, she had been buried and reborn. She had risen, been resurrected. The symbolism is unmistakable, as clear as any metaphor in the Bible. I wondered when I baptized Alice why so few members of the congregation chose immersion. The wetness means more than the words.

HER HUSBAND, GEORGE, hadn't set foot inside the church in at least four or five years, and he had not come to his wife's baptism. Later I would ask myself whether it would have made a difference if he had seen his wife baptized. I would see in my mind the deep, eggplant-colored bruises from his thumbs on her neck, as well as the marks on his face where she had gouged out whole chunks of his cheeks with her fingernails. (I had expected that the right side of his face would have been completely obliterated, but it wasn't. A little swollen, a little distorted, but not nearly the ruin I had imagined. We could all see the scratch marks there.) Alice may have walked into the water with resignation that Sunday morning, but she had fought hard for her life that Sunday night—if only reflexively. If only because she thought of her daughter and experienced one last, fierce pang of maternal protectiveness. If only because the way that he killed her was brutal and she couldn't help but battle back against the pain. And so the question of whether George's attendance at the spectacle (and, trust me, immersion *is* spectacle) would have saved Alice's life dogged me. That question, as well as the myriad others that followed it relentlessly like the rhythms of a sermon—would he have been transformed by his wife's faith? would he have given therapy a chance? would he have stopped pulling fistfuls of Alice's hair like black rope? would he have stopped yanking back her head like a church bell? would they both be alive today?—bobbed amid the waves of images that roll behind all of our eyes.

I followed Alice from the water, my own blue jeans heavy around my hips because they had sponged up so much of the Brookners' pond. Some of my fellow pastors, especially my peers in the South, wear weighted black robes that allow them to wade into the water without fear that the robe will float about them like algae. Not me. Weighting a robe in my mind transformed meaningful ritual into pretentious theatrics. Besides, I liked wearing blue jeans into the water, I liked the way they represented the ordinariness of our daily lives as we presented ourselves to God. And the fact is, I actually performed very few baptisms by immersion. This is Vermont. Our church, a union of the old Baptist and Congregational fellowships that had thrived in the nineteenth century when the community had been larger, didn't even have a baptismal tank, and Alice was the only person I baptized that summer by immersion, the sole parishioner to join the church in that manner.

"That was so powerful," Ginny said to her friend. "Aren't you glad you did it?" When they pulled apart, the front of Ginny's shirt was almost as damp as Alice's.

"I am," Alice said, and I saw that she'd begun to cry. Katie noticed, too, and did what she probably did often when she saw her mother's eyes fill with tears. She patted her on the back as if she were their family's springer spaniel, Lula, offering gentle taps that were about as close as a fifteen-year-old with a stud in her nose gets to an embrace in public with her mother.

The Brookners, the family whose pond we used, were summer people, a wealthy family who came north to Haverill from a suburb of Manhattan sometime around Memorial Day weekend and lived at the top of one of the hills that surrounded the village. Michelle Brookner and the three children did, anyway. Michelle's husband, Gordon, was an attorney who would drive up for weekends and a two-week vacation in August. From the Brookners' pond, it was impossible to see the town itself, not even the church steeple, but we could see the verdant hollow in which the village sat, as well as the cemetery at the top of the distant ridge. I looked that way to avert my eyes from Alice's tears.

Members of the Women's Circle gathered around Ginny and Alice, embracing Alice as Ginny had, and I found George's absence conspicuous in ways that it wasn't at a routine Sunday-morning service. I wondered briefly whether I should have visited him prior to the baptism and asked him to come. Convinced him. Later, of course, I would blame myself for not insisting that he attend, just as I would blame myself for not understanding the meaning of the ritual in Alice's mind—for denying in my head what I must have known in my heart.

When the medical examiner did the autopsies on the Haywards, he reported that Alice's rear end and her back were flecked with fresh contusions, which meant that George had beaten her the Friday or Saturday night before she was baptized and none of us knew. At least I didn't. Her kidneys were so badly bruised that she might very well have peed blood before she'd come to church that morning.

Nevertheless, I don't think it was that finding that set me off, because I wouldn't learn that particular detail until much later. In my mind at least, I was gone from the church the moment Ginny had called me the day after the baptism, that Monday morning, sobbing uncontrollably, with the news that George and Alice were dead and it looked like he had killed them both. In the midst of Ginny's wails—and she really was wailing, this was indeed a lament of biblical proportions—I somehow heard in my head the last word that Alice had addressed solely to me, that single word *there,* and the seeds of my estrangement from my calling had been sown.

There.

I'd nodded when Alice had said it; I'd echoed her word. I'd known exactly what she'd meant. She wasn't referring to Romans or Colossians, to the letters of Peter or Paul. She wasn't thinking of any of the passages in the Bible explaining baptism that we'd discussed at a table outside my church office or in the living room of her house as her immersion approached.

She was thinking of John, and of Christ's three words at the end of his torment on the cross; she was imagining that precise moment when he bows his head and gives up his spirit.

It is finished, said Christ. There.

And Alice Hayward was ready to die.

CHAPTER TWO

Vermont rarely has more than ten or fifteen homicides in any given year, and while the majority of them begin with domestic disputes, murder-suicides are blessedly uncommon: Usually a husband or ex-husband, boyfriend or ex-boyfriend, merely shoots or strangles the poor woman with whom he might have built a life and then goes to prison for the majority of what remains of his own. Frequently he turns himself in. We are conditioned to expect one dead at the scenes of our homicides, not two. And so the Haywards' story—a murder and a suicide together—was both horrific and exceptional.

George Hayward had come to southern Vermont from Buffalo as an ambitious young retailer who saw that Manchester could use more than high-end designer outlets and shops that sold maple syrup and quaint Green Mountain trinkets. He was the first to see that a clothing store for teens and young adults and modeled on Abercrombie & Fitch—but stressing natural fibers and stocking Vermont-made clothing—could anchor a corner of the block near the town's busiest intersection and thrive though surrounded by national chains that sold clothes sewn together in sweatshops for less. There were just enough tourists and just enough locals and—when word filtered south to Bennington, half an hour away by car—just enough college students to keep the store afloat through its first year, and by its second it was an institution. It actually would become a destination for young adults as far away as Albany, Rutland, and Pittsfield. Eventually his magic touch would extend to a southern-style rib restaurant (skiers in the winter particularly loved it) and an upscale toy store that used retro toys as the marketing bait for baby boomers, but electronic gadgets to ensnare their kids and make the serious money. For a long time, the formula worked. In addition to the house that he built in Haverill, he acquired what he and Alice referred to as a cottage on Lake Bomoseen—a svelte stretch of water perhaps nine miles long that over the years had numbered among its guests the Marx Brothers, Alexander Woollcott, and Rebecca West. Based on the photos, however, the cottage was actually rather elegant: a post-and-beam barn frame with a wall of glass windows facing west to savor the sunsets over the rippling pinewoods.

George had been a teen model in Buffalo, and he had grown into a dramatically handsome adult. He'd actually worn a wedding band before he was married to Alice to minimize the number of women who would hit on him on the streets and in the restaurants of first Buffalo and then Manchester and Bennington. Once when he was drunk, he told friends—famously, since this is Vermont, a state in which vanity and self-absorption are still viewed by the locals as character defects commensurate with gluttony, greed, and sloth—that his magnetism had helped to ensure that he found the requisite bankers and private investors to bankroll his big ideas before he had a track record. One of my parishioners said that he looked like Prince Valiant with a better haircut: His hair was a shade more terra-cotta than blond and was only beginning to thin now that he was on the far side of forty, and his skin barely showed the wear and tear of either retail risk or age. Some years he had a mustache that was the color of faded pumpkin pine, but he was clean-shaven the summer he murdered his wife. If he hadn't started drinking so heavily in his mid-thirties, I imagine his workout regimen would have kept even his slight, midlife paunch at bay. He was handsome and strong and could be charming and charismatic when he wanted. He had a chip on his shoulder (wholly unwarranted), and he was more savvy than smart, but he was far from humorless. He was a person of some renown in the southern Vermont business community. There were people who were firmly convinced that Alice, though pretty, was lucky to have him. Almost no one knew that she had gotten a temporary relief-from-abuse order against him that last winter of her life, and many people suspected that he had left her in those months they were separated.

Oh, but it was *she* who had risen up and kicked *him* out of the house, sending him to that cottage on the lake to see how life felt without her. He had attacked her once too often, and now she was going to try to make a go of it on her own.

She had been one of his salesclerks at the original clothing store while getting a degree in business administration, and it was there that they had met and fallen in love. They married soon after he had promoted her to manager at the restaurant. By the time he was embarking on the toy store, however, she was securely ensconced as a customer-service representative at a bank branch in Bennington. Given the reality that they had a young daughter, even the fanatically controlling George Hayward saw the advantages to another small but steady income stream when you were juggling local retail ventures in a world of mass merchandisers and chain stores with very deep pockets.

When she took him back as Memorial Day approached, believing him when he assured her that he was going to embark upon counseling and this time things would be different, some of our neighbors greeted his return to Haverill with relief: A family was reconciled, and a marriage had been preserved.

Imagine, then, their surprise when they heard that one disastrously drunken Sunday night he had strangled his wife and taken his handgun—not a thirty-gauge deer rifle, as the earliest rumors suggested—and shot himself.

Heather Laurent had arrived in Manchester for a day and a half of appearances that Sunday evening: the very night the Haywards would die and about twelve hours before their bodies would be discovered in our little village. Haverill is a small hill town roughly halfway between Bennington and Manchester; the general store is almost exactly eight miles east of the border with New York State. It was therefore Tuesday morning when Heather was able to read about the grim discovery in the newspaper while she ate breakfast in her hotel room at the Equinox and the line of admirers outside the bookstore in Manchester grew long as they waited for the store to open its doors for the day. She was going to be there that morning from ten to eleven, and then she was going to speak at lunchtime at a fund-raiser for the Southern Vermont Arts Center. The day before, Monday, she had visited the NPR affiliate in Albany and given a speech at Bennington College. As she read the story in the newspaper, the final touches were added to the displays of her books: a waterfall of pink satin ribbon cascading over the neat piles of her paperback, *Angels and Aurascapes,* and vases of blue irises and yellow daylilies surrounding her hardcover, *A Sacred While,* which had been published the month before.

There were two articles about the carnage in the newspaper, and it was in that second story that I appeared. The previous afternoon I had rambled on to the reporter—a woman I pegged at about twenty-five, a decade and a half younger than I and perhaps ten years the junior of Heather Laurent—about what C. S. Lewis had termed the problem of pain. From nearly fifteen minutes of the Reverend Stephen Drew's babbling, she had pulled two quotes.

"Sometimes it seems as if there's nothing guiding this world. Or if there is something out there, it's powerless or uninterested in us—or downright mean. Even evil," I'd said, paraphrasing what Lewis considered the pessimist's view of the cosmos. I may have gotten to Lewis's summary of the Christian's more optimistic perspective—I'd certainly planned to as a courtesy to my parishioners, even if it was a view I no longer shared—but it's very possible that I didn't. It's possible (perhaps even likely) that I became sidetracked and started addressing instead another of the questions she'd asked me: How was our town handling this awful tragedy?

"She was a member of our congregation," I'd said, referring to Alice. "She was a member of my church. I knew very well he was hurting her. I should have done more."

The reporter may or may not have noticed my transition from the plural to the personal, but Heather Laurent certainly did. And so after she had finished her speech at the arts center that Tuesday afternoon, she came to see me—she came to see us, to see me and Katie and our stunned little village—either a marionette moved by an omniscient god in a puppet show or merely an upright series of cells compelled forward by something inscrutably deep inside her DNA. A gene. A meme. Her one conscious thought? Someone had to help those poor, sad, pathetic people in Haverill. Someone had to help that pastor.

HEATHER LAURENT LOOKED very much as she did in the photographs that graced the backs of her books, though I would realize that only days later when I actually picked them up at the bookstore in Bronxville. She had a professional woman's short hair, manageable and fast in the morning, just a shade closer to blond than brown. A round, girlish face and a pixielike nose—though there was nothing spritelike about her stature. She was almost as tall as I am, and I am exactly six feet. Unlike my sister, however, who is also quite tall, she seemed comfortable with her height: She neither slouched nor averted her eyes, both tendencies I had noticed over the years in my sister. Later I would learn that she was a classically trained dancer. She was wearing a white button-down silk blouse with a gold chain suspending a modest cross against her collarbone and sunglasses that she removed as she first started speaking to me, sliding them onto the top of her head like a hair band. She seemed almost disconcertingly happy to meet me, an ease—given the pall that hung over Haverill that afternoon—that I ascribe to the fathomless hope that flourished inside her, her faith in (her words, not mine) angels and auras. Make no mistake: Heather Laurent believed every word that she wrote.

When she first appeared at the front door of the parsonage Tuesday afternoon, I assumed she was a television reporter from a network news program. I craned my head to see over her shoulder, expecting to see behind her a van and a young person with a heavy shoulder camera. Instead I saw simply a Saab that was ice blue, a little dried mud along the sides.

"Are you Reverend Drew?" she asked me as I pushed open the screen door. It was steaming, even for July, and I heard small children playing in the shade by the shallow river across the street.

"I am. And you're with . . . ?"

"No one."

"You're not with a magazine? A newspaper?"

"I'm Heather Laurent. I thought I would see if I could be of help."

I nodded. I wondered if I was supposed to know who she was. I imagined her as an E! network Katie Couric or a columnist for a glossy weekly I didn't read.

"May I come in?" she went on. "I don't want to be an imposition."

I shrugged and led her through the kitchen and the living room and out onto the back porch. Usually this late in the day on a Tuesday, I'd have finished the first draft of my Sunday sermon. That's what Tuesday afternoons were for. I would leave my church office about noon and wander to the general store, where I would buy a sandwich and eat it there, chatting with whoever happened to stroll by in the middle of the day. I might be there as long as an hour, especially if the lectionary suggested passages that weren't among my favorites and I was looking for inspiration. Often I've used that time to help people in ways that were more prosaic than profound, but utterly meaningful to them: Over the years in those lunch hours, I helped milk a llama, found the local septic-tank cleaner for the local excavator (a real emergency, trust me), and made urgent repairs to the swing set at the cooperative preschool before the children awoke from their naps. Then I would go home, since it was always easier for me to work uninterrupted at the parsonage than it was at my church office. In the summer I would take my laptop to the back porch and work there. By three-thirty or four, I would usually have fifteen to twenty minutes of reasonably uplifting biblical commentary. If it wasn't too late in the afternoon, I would visit the hospitals in Bennington and Rutland where my neighbors—members and nonmembers of the church alike—were recovering or dying or lying unsure on movable beds. Most weeks I went to the hospital two or three times. But Tuesday-afternoon hospital visits were always a balancing act, because I had to be back in town not too long after seven, since the trustees and the Board of Christian Education and the Pastoral-Relations Committee all had their monthly meetings on Tuesday nights (though, fortunately, not the same Tuesday nights), and I was expected to be present. I wanted to be present. Usually my deadline was three-thirty: If my sermon was in reasonable shape by then, I would go to one or the other of the hospitals. If not, I would forgo a hospital visit that afternoon and go instead the next day.

The Tuesday that Heather Laurent came to Haverill, however, I hadn't even tried to write a sermon. And I had no plans to go to a hospital. Somehow, instead of a sermon—which would have been trying enough that day, intellectually as well as emotionally—I had to find it inside me to pen some comforting remarks for Alice Hayward's funeral, scheduled for that Thursday morning at the church. (George's funeral was going to be a private family affair in upstate New York.) And I had failed: The comforting words had disappeared along with the uplifting ones.

When I realized that I was incapable, at least for the moment, of writing the eulogy, I had instead begun to tap out what was essentially a form e-mail that I thought I might—or might not—send to different friends across the country. Friends from seminary and friends from college. My friends who'd remained in the suburb of New York City in which I'd grown up and my friends from there who, like me, had chosen to build their lives in other, distant corners of the country. All but the second paragraph of each e-mail—that paragraph in which I dropped in select, idiosyncratic details about our joint histories—was identical. The letters were rich in anger and gloom and guilt. I told two of my friends that I was going to come see them soon. One was a friend from seminary with a parish in southern Illinois, and another was a friend from college who had grown rich in Dallas. I envisioned weeks alone in my car and all the scrambled eggs I could eat in places like Denny's, the counters sticky, the lighting dolorous. I told everyone that I was leaving the church—no sabbatical, this, no hiatus or retreat—because I could no longer bear to throw the drowning victims of reason and birth, my congregation, life preservers with long ropes attached to nothing.

Dave Sadler, the deacon with pancreatic cancer, now had a tumor so large he couldn't digest his food. He was starving to death in a hospice, and somehow I was supposed to reassure him that everything in the end would be all right. Caroline Pearce, three years old, had seen one of her little-girl legs sliced off by the metal that ripped through the side of her mother's car when a pickup plowed into it as she and her mother were returning home from day care. Beside her bed in the children's wing of the hospital—a room infinitely cheerier than the intensive-care unit where she had spent the first days after the accident, but still an awfully dark room for a toddler—I was supposed to smile. I was expected to console Nathan Bedard, a third-grader with a particularly virulent form of leukemia who'd be dead in two or three years, and I was supposed to inspirit his aunt and uncle, neither of whom had worked in almost a year and were in the process of selling the trailer in which they lived. Once the trailer was gone, they would bunk with friends and relatives—including Nathan's parents—for a while, but they had no idea how or where they would live for the long haul.

And I was supposed to find comforting words for fifteen-year-old Katie Hayward. I was supposed to help the little girl I'd watched grow into a young woman—a wise and pretty reasonable young woman, it seemed to me, in spite of all that she'd seen and suffered—make sense of the fact that her father's anger was boundless, and he was, in the end, capable of murdering her mother in a manner that was simultaneously intimate and violent.

From those letters I considered sending to my friends, mostly (but not all) discarded and deleted, I remember one paragraph perfectly: "I don't think I have ever had a predilection for depression, but at the moment I feel as if a friend who has always provided me comfort and counsel has gone away. I no longer know quite what I should be saying to others and have never before felt so personally and spiritually alone."

I tend to doubt that Heather Laurent ever saw that sentence, however, because the laptop was still on the porch when she appeared at my door, and though later we would stand beside it and listen to the murmur of the shallow river, she wasn't the sort who would have leaned over and tried to read the words that were at least partly shrouded by the glare from the muggy, overcast sky. And when she arrived, initially she sat down in the chair at the wrought-iron table that was across from the seat in which I had been composing my e-mails.

"This is a beautiful little village," she said.

"Thank you."

"The tragedy doesn't change that, you know. The tragedy doesn't make it any less lovely."

"Visit this place in mid-January. It gets pretty bleak."

She smiled and ran two fingers along the chain around her neck, resting them for a moment on the small cross. "You know what I mean," she said. "People understand the aura of a little place like this."

Briefly it crossed my mind that this woman was a nun. It was possible, I decided, that I had just mistaken a Catholic nun for a cable celebrity. "Are you with the church?" I asked.

"The church. Is there only one?"

"Oh, this afternoon they're all equally suspect."

"You sound awfully disillusioned."

"Maybe just awfully fed up."

"Well," she answered, "I'm not here with any church. I'm just a writer."

"And you're not with . . . anything?"

"I write books," she said, and it was clear in the gentleness of her tone that the fact that I hadn't a clue who she was didn't bother her.

"Are you going to write a book about our tragedy?"

"I hope not."

"That's not why you're here?"

She shrugged. "Maybe you're why I'm here. You. That girl. This town."

My anger then was still embryonic, it was still merely in utero fury—a hostility toward the universe conceived roughly twenty-nine hours earlier. Had Heather arrived at my home a few weeks or even days later, I might have been unable to hold my tongue. I might have thrown her out of the house. On the other hand, had she arrived a few weeks or even days later, I might have been gone. I've no idea for sure where I'd have wound up—Texas, most likely, or southern Illinois—but I think there's a good chance I would have pressed "send" on one (or more) of those e-mails and gotten the hell out of Vermont. Had Heather come even Saturday or Sunday of that week, she might have found an empty house and a stunned deacon or steward murmuring, "He left. He just up and left."

But that afternoon I was able to satisfy my anger with essentially harmless morsels of sarcasm.

"Well," I said evenly. "I guess I should be flattered."

"Don't be. Don't give me that much credit. Do you have any family, Reverend Drew?"

"No. I'm alone."

"No wife?"

"Nope."

"A partner?"

"I date." Usually I gave the inquisitive a bit more of a bone, but that afternoon I was in no mood to discuss the history and vagaries of my life choices. There were women in my past, but not a marriage.

"Are you from around here?" she asked.

"I'm not."

"Have you been in Vermont—with this congregation—a long time? Or are you an interim minister?"

I looked longingly through the screen door at the pitcher with iced coffee on the kitchen table. "Are these questions the preface to a more extended inquiry, Ms. Laurent, or merely an attempt at conversation?"

"Please, call me Heather. I'd like that."

"Next time I will," I agreed. The first Heather I had ever known had taken off all her clothes for me. I was five, she was seven. She lived two houses away. We were upstairs in her bedroom on a summer afternoon, and she promised me she would strip if I could find her red bathing suit. It wasn't a difficult search: I found it in the third dresser drawer I opened, wadded into a ball at the top of her underwear and T-shirts. She was the first female I ever saw naked. "And these questions?" I asked again.

"I haven't a clue. Really and truly. I'm just giving them voice as they come to me."

"In that case, I'm going to get some more iced coffee—though it's been sitting out so long by now it will merely be watered-down tepid coffee. Still, you are welcome to have some. In my current state of mind, this is an act of courtesy that has demanded a herculean resiliency. If I rise to that occasion, will you tell me why you've come to see me?"

"I drink tea."

"Then you're out of luck. I don't drink tea."

"Have I come at a bad time?"

I leaned forward in my chair and looked deep into her face. The edges of her lips, adorned with a lipstick so lustrous and red that I thought of the vestments I wore when I'd preach on Pentecost or Palm Sunday, were curled into a smile, and I realized that she had meant this as a joke. She understood there had been few worse times in my life.

"I think this counts as one, yes."

"Pour yourself that coffee," she said. "I don't need any. But I would like to stay and visit. May I?"

I rarely saw lipstick like that in Haverill. I rarely saw a silk blouse.

"I have nowhere to go," I answered.

"No meetings? No parishioners?"

"There are always meetings. There are always parishioners."

"But you have some time."

I nodded as I stood up and listened to her as I opened the screen door and retrieved the pitcher.

"I have nothing at all on my calendar this afternoon or evening," she said. "And I have a sense you can appreciate how liberating that sensation is. I just finished one of the world's longest book tours." Then she rose, too, and followed me inside.

"What's your book about?"

"My new one?"

"Yes. Your . . . new one."

"The world's aura and the way we are degrading it environmentally and ecologically."

"I suppose *aura,* in this case, isn't simply another word for icecap. Or rain forest."

"No, it's not. But certainly there's a connection."

"And your other books?"

"Other book. Singular. I've only written two."

"And it's about?"

She smiled as if she knew I couldn't possibly take seriously what she was about to tell me. "Angels. Auras. The quality of vibrations we emit and how they affect our relationship with the divine."

"I'm sure those vibrations really matter."

"You're not sure at all, but that's okay."

"Let me guess. You were at the bookstore in Manchester last night?"

"This morning, actually. Then I gave a talk at that beautiful arts center up on the hill. Yesterday I was at Bennington College and the NPR station in Albany."

"And now you're finishing your day with an appearance in scenic little Haverill."

"You're having a real hard time with that, aren't you?"

"Well, do you visit every village that achieves our sort of notoriety?"

"Nope."

"Just ours."

She nodded and then turned her gaze toward the open shelves and kitchen counters that were filled with the detritus of a single man's—a single pastor's—life. There were the odd, mismatched knickknacks given to me by dotty parishioners over the years: porcelain cookie jars (originally filled, of course, with freshly baked cookies with ridiculous names like snickerdoodles and choc-a-roos), one shaped like a potbellied elf and one like a plump, sitting beagle (that had, alas, lost an ear over the years); an earthenware butter dish I never used that resembled a submarine, a gift from a couple in the congregation after I gave a sermon with references to a 1960s television program I had seen that week on TV Land called *Voyage to the Bottom of the Sea*; a tin container for straws, empty, that was crafted from a Coca-Cola can; and a plastic paper-napkin holder that was shaped like a rather flat, two-dimensional log cabin. And then there were the pots and pans that once had belonged to my mother but now dangled—a little tarnished, a little dinged—like old meat from hooks above the stove, as well as the juice and water glasses from her bridal registry, not old enough yet to be interesting but still discolored with age. (When my father died, she had chosen to sell the house and move to a condominium apartment in a brick building in the village, and in her downsizing my sister and I had wound up with a sizable percentage of the contents from the pantry, the hutch, and the kitchen cabinets.) There were coffee mugs, two rows of them, many stained brown and some visibly cracked. And there were the four matching tins for flour and sugar and coffee and rice that were meant to look like miniatures of the sort of antique barrels one might have found once in a country store—or, at any rate, in a country store on a movie set—but each of them now looked only bulbous and bloated and tired. I was always a little embarrassed when a woman saw my kitchen for the first time. It wasn't often, but invariably I was left with the sensation that I had either remarkably bad taste or an awful lot to explain.

Moreover, I rarely cooked, since so much food came to me from parishioners and friends and since I was expected to attend so many meetings at night. Besides, I lived alone, and relatively few people actually like to cook for themselves. As a result there was an antiseptic odorlessness to the room, an aura of benign disuse. In a typical year, I must have prepared no more than two dozen dinners for myself in that kitchen.

Had she looked through the open door into the den, she would have seen an ironing board strategically placed before my television set and the pile of my shirts and pants that seemed always to be the size of a beanbag chair. I ironed just enough to keep up, but not frequently enough ever to shrink the mound. She would have seen the DVDs more appropriate in the bedroom of a fifth-grade boy than a minister flirting with middle age: an account of a Red Sox World Series championship, two-thirds of the *Star Wars* saga. She might have noticed the books I was reading, some on the floor and some on the coffee table and some on the television itself. There were books of inspiration and biblical interpretation, as well as the novels set in courtrooms and police stations and law offices—the mysteries that I savor the way some people appreciate science fiction.

It struck me, as it did always when a person saw the inside of my house, as rather pathetic. And while the homes of most single men are rather pathetic—testimonies in some cases to a stunted childhood, sad little museums of loneliness—mine seemed more so. I was, after all, a minister. It seemed to me that I should have transcended the pitiable curiosities of the single life. Usually I took comfort that at least my house wasn't rife with porn and NASCAR magazines, but that seemed like a small consolation that afternoon.

"How did you learn about us?" I asked. "The newspaper?"

"Initially. And then the television news. And then the Internet."

"Ah, Haverill's fifteen minutes of fame. Our chance to bask in the glow of the press. Lovely."

She picked up the butter dish in the shape of a science-fiction submarine. It looked vaguely like a stingray with a school bus behind it. "You sound so angry about the media," she murmured, her eyes scanning the vessel. "From the newspaper I would have guessed it was something else."

"And that was?"

She looked up at me, her mouth open the tiniest bit. "I'm really not that presumptuous," she answered. "And I hope not that arrogant."

"No, you can tell me. I'm interested."

"Really?"

"Really."

"I thought you blamed yourself for Alice and George Hayward's deaths."

"I do."

"And I thought you blamed your God."

"I would if I had one."

"That's what I thought," said Heather Laurent. "I think that's why I came."

FROM THE PREFACE TO *A SACRED WHILE*
BY HEATHER LAURENT (P. VI)

The host of a radio show once asked me point-blank, "Do you really believe in magic? Honestly?"

"Honestly," I said. "Really and truly."

"Do you think the people who have bought your book do, too?"

I told him I couldn't speak for the people who had bought my book. But it was clear both to me and to his listeners that this radio personality thought my extended discussions of magic in Angels and Aurascapes *were the ramblings of a lunatic. Most people, in his opinion, were smart enough not to believe in magic.*

And so I corrected him. "Most individuals on this planet have a religion they approach with some degree of earnestness," I said. "And what is a religion but a belief in the unseen and a faith in the impossible? Remember what Jesus says in Mark? 'For all things are possible with God.' Magic is about the endless ways in this world that the impossible becomes possible—just like religion. Religion, in essence, is ritualized magic."

I have lived a life with magic and without magic, and I can tell you with certainty that a life with magic is better. . . .

CHAPTER THREE

I went to Alice and George Hayward's house when Ginny O'Brien called that Monday morning, I saw the bodies myself. After the state's mobile crime lab had left, a number of us helped clean the place up—the blood on the wall, the fragments of skull and brain lodged in the mesh of the screen window beside the couch on which George had been sitting when he died—so neither Alice's nor George's families would have to. Everyone wanted to be sure that Katie would never have to see the piecemeal remains of her parents.

In the days immediately after the murder and the suicide, we learned small details about the couple's last hours that seemed to matter a great deal at the time. Ginny O'Brien, though shaken, was still a chronological font whose memory was precise.

Apparently she saw George Hayward drinking on his porch late Sunday afternoon, the day I had baptized his wife, and he was in all likelihood drunk during dinner. It was certainly clear he was drunk after dinner: We counted thirteen open, empty beer bottles in the kitchen and the living room, only a few of which had been rinsed, and the house—and George Hayward's corpse—reeked of alcohol. An investigator with the office of the medical examiner, a balding detective sergeant from the state police with a skull the shape of an egg, dusted each of the bottles for fingerprints. The Haywards' last meal on this earth included a salad with plump peas and tender string beans from their vegetable garden, chicken salad that Alice probably had prepared that afternoon, and ice-cream scoops of coleslaw that she had bought at the general store in the village seconds before it closed for the day: five o'clock on summer Sundays, three P.M. on Sundays the rest of the year. There were plates in the sink that suggested this had been their menu, as well as leftovers in the refrigerator and (we would learn later) recognizable, undigested remains in Alice's stomach.

Katie had left late that afternoon for a rock concert in Albany and then spent the night at the home of her friend, Tina Cousino, closer to the center of Haverill. Most people believed that if Katie had been home that night, it would not have prevented George from murdering Alice. The teen's presence would merely have increased the number of bodies that Ginny O'Brien would have discovered the next day.

At some point after the two corpses had been removed from the house and the mobile van from the state crime lab had left, when many of us were still there cleaning in our rubber gloves—a little sickened, a little numb—a thought crossed my mind. An image. George strangling Alice once she was no longer capable of fighting back. Did their eyes meet for a moment before she blacked out? I had read somewhere that to kill someone by strangulation, you needed to retain your grip on the neck long after the victim had lost consciousness and ceased struggling, otherwise he or she might resume breathing and eventually wake up. But what of these two who had been married so long? What did they see in each other's eyes as they grappled? Clearly George had kept his hands around her neck long after she had gone limp. Or had he? Was it possible that he had released her, presuming she was dead, but then she had started to come to and he actually had to go back to work? It seemed conceivable to me as I paused that afternoon in my blue gloves.

Regardless, before George would murder his wife, he would pass out himself for a time in front of the television set. This was around seven-thirty. The cordless telephone was pressed against Alice's ear as she carried George's and her dinner dishes to the kitchen sink and chatted with Ginny. Apparently it was not uncommon for Alice to wait for her husband to fall asleep before venturing a call to one of her friends—especially Ginny—though she was quick to insist that it was only a coincidence that more times than not George was either asleep or out when she spoke with the pastor or, far more frequently, with the various local women.

"Oh, somebody's dropped off," she'd said to her friend that evening, almost as if she were referring to a six-month-old baby who everyone agreed was really rather cute. Then the pair discussed George's toy store, which Alice said was struggling, as high gas prices were decreasing the usual summer tourist traffic. He was also worried about declining interest in his ribs restaurant—the novelty had long worn off—but he had been more quiet than antagonistic as they ate. According to Ginny, they had also talked about Alice's baptism that day, Ginny's own two middle-school-aged sons and the different summer day camps in which they were involved, and the reality that Ginny's mother, diagnosed with Alzheimer's two years earlier, seemed to have gotten much worse. Ironically, Ginny did not bring up her belief that either George should get counseling—hadn't he promised?—or Alice should leave him, or both. She did often. But not that night. They didn't discuss Ginny's frustration with her friend for never even showing up for the hearing after Alice had gotten a temporary relief-from-abuse order in February or her friend's decision to reconcile with her husband in May.

Later Ginny would tell the police that she'd planned on discussing her fears with Alice again the next morning—reminding her that she shouldn't fall under his sway just because he claimed he had changed—when she saw her friend at the Women's Circle.

People who knew the Haywards only casually would never have imagined that he beat her. Alice hid well her cuts and bruises, and only rarely did he touch her face. People might have sensed the strain between them, they might have felt what Heather Laurent might have described as an aura of unease (or outright unhappiness), but I'm sure they would have attributed the tension to the fact that George was juggling a variety of retail businesses in an uncertain economy.

The fact is, he had been abusive and controlling for years, blaming Alice for whatever small speed bumps he encountered on what he believed was his right to cruise unencumbered through life. From the moment they wed, he had begun to wean her away from her family in New Hampshire and, later, from her co-workers at the bank. He would savage her cooking and cleaning whenever he could, or her inability to stretch the budget he gave her as far as he liked. He would tell her what kinds of clothes she could wear and what kinds she couldn't: Stirrup pants and jeans that clung to her curves were out, as were Lycra bicycle shorts (even at her spin class at the gym), skimpy cotton dresses, and those camisole shirts with lingerie-like clasps that were popular that summer. Even though one of his stores sold inappropriately revealing tanks and tees and denim microskirts to teen girls, she was to dress like a schoolmarm.

When, once, she cataloged for me the clothes she was not allowed to wear, I sighed with a mixture of pastoral concern and libidinous longing: I would have been happy to have seen her in any of those things. Instead Alice was likely to be attired in dresses and skirts that were dowdy and sad. Still, when I saw her undressed for the first time, I was not surprised by what a prize she was. She was one year my junior; she had legs that were lithe and long, and a stomach as firm as a dancer's.

The Haywards had lived (and died) in a handsome Cape Cod they'd built on two acres of meadow that once had been a part of one of the village's larger dairy farms. The property was being sold just about the time that they were thinking of leaving their Bennington apartment, four rooms that had been fine even when Katie was a baby but was feeling cramped now that their daughter was six. Most of the property, including the largest parcels, went to the sons and daughters of the dairy farmer, but a substantial section was commandeered by a lawyer and his wife from Westchester—the Brookners—while a two-acre block with impressive views and a small ravine that tended to get a little swampy in April and May went to the Haywards. Theirs was a crisp and modern three-bedroom home, and George had done a fair amount of the work on it himself.

They would live there for not quite nine years.

ALICE WAS IN her nightgown when George wrapped his hands around her neck and crushed her windpipe and the strap muscles in the larynx, but she hadn't yet gotten into bed. The medical examiner estimated it was sometime between eight and nine P.M. when George pressed her against the wall beside a living-room window, in all likelihood lifting her off the floor and slamming the back of her head so hard against the wall as he worked that he dented the Sheetrock. And he killed her while she was slashing away at his own flesh with a ferocity that I suspected might have been there but had certainly never seen manifest myself.

Although no one other than Alice spent any time with George on the day that he died, we all assumed that the clothes in which he was found were the ones he had been wearing most of the day: Blue jeans and a navy blue T-shirt with a small chest pocket. He was barefoot when he was discovered on the couch, slumped back onto the cushions, one arm spread atop a throw pillow and the other hanging over the side of the armrest. George had been right-handed, and the bullet had entered his head just above his right ear, roughly three inches above where his jaw met his neck, and taken off a sizable chunk of his skull. Dangling from his fingers was a Smith & Wesson .357-caliber handgun with a square butt and a stainless-steel finish. The bullet had exited the head just left of the summit of the cranium and was embedded high in the wall near the window.

Nobody heard a gunshot, but the nearest house belonged to that lawyer's family from Westchester, and they hadn't been in Haverill that weekend. Likewise, no one heard the two of them fight, and so no one had any idea what precisely had set George off this last time. Ginny O'Brien conjectured the next morning that he'd probably hit Alice, and she'd either told him in some new fashion that he'd better not do that again, or—even more likely—said that she was kicking him out once more. This time for good. Perhaps she had straightened her spine and told him to pack a bag and be gone. But this also may have been merely an unachieved aspiration Ginny had had for her friend.

Nevertheless, in one of the days immediately after Alice was killed, a female minister I've known since seminary—a woman who counsels a great many victims (and perpetrators) of domestic abuse—tried to convince me that this was indeed what had occurred. George had probably hit Alice, and she had told him that was it, they were finished. She'd had it. George, in turn, had warned her that she'd better not even try to get dressed. And when she'd said that he couldn't stop her, he'd killed her. It was the classic pattern, my friend said.

Her point? Alice Hayward had wanted to live. She hadn't expected to die, and I hadn't missed some staggeringly obvious signal at the baptism. This wasn't my fault. Of course, my minister friend hadn't been at the pond that afternoon. Nor did she know Alice's and my—and I use this word with both guilelessness and guilt—history. Perhaps if Alice had left behind a suitcase, I might think otherwise. In my mind it is resting on her side of their bed, half filled and hastily packed. But there wasn't one. There wasn't even a small pile of clothes anywhere in the bedroom: No shirt, no jeans, no panties, no socks. I would not have needed a suitcase at the scene to have my faith resurrected, but I did need a sign that she had at least planned to leave the house that night.

AND THERE WAS this: Her mother would tell me when we met in my church on folding metal chairs that Monday night that her daughter had been planning to schedule appointments with a lawyer in Bennington and an advocate at the women's shelter. Alice, her mother insisted, wanted to understand what she needed to do to protect her daughter from George in the event that something like—and here her mother waved her arm once as if swatting at a fly and then collapsed in upon herself in sobs—*this* ever happened to her. Alice had even taught her parents a new expression: the termination or extinguishment of parental rights. She wanted, her mother insisted, to be sure that George wouldn't have control of Katie if somehow her husband got away with murder.

"I told her to get out of the house, but . . . but she wouldn't listen," she stammered through her tears, as her husband awkwardly rubbed her shoulders and the back of her neck from his own folding chair.

And if I needed any more proof of my suspicions, it resided in a red felt jewelry box that Katie had told us about that afternoon: Two days before she would die, that Friday, Alice had taken the ruby-and-diamond earrings and the pearl necklace that had belonged to her own grandmother—Katie's great-grandmother—and given them to her daughter, telling Katie to keep them close to her chest.

THE CHURCH WOMEN'S Circle included about fifteen members of the congregation. They met Monday mornings at seven to accommodate the half dozen members who had jobs outside the home, convening each time in a different woman's living room or terrace or kitchen. Rarely were all fifteen present; usually there were no more than eleven or twelve women there. The meetings usually lasted until nine-thirty or ten, with the members whose schedules demanded they leave sooner departing whenever they needed. During the school year, for instance, Ginny stayed most Mondays only until seven forty-five because she was due at the village school a little before eight. Alice's schedule at the bank was Tuesday through Saturday, however, and so she never left early. She was known for remaining till the very end, with the elderly women who were retired and whose children were grown and who had nowhere else they needed to be. When I had suggested the Women's Circle to Alice, offering the idea one evening when we were alone at the parsonage, I thought it would be weeks or even months before she might find the courage to contact one of the informal group leaders. I could see how thoroughly George had eroded her confidence and severed her ties with so many of her friends—with so much of the world. I contemplated having one of the members reach out to her. But I was mistaken. Within days Alice had contacted the woman nearest her age, Ginny O'Brien, and had asked if she could come to the next meeting. The fact that the group met on the very day Alice had off seemed like a good omen.

And I have no doubts that the women provided a necessary respite for Alice—and yes, a better shoulder than mine. Still, only Ginny knew the extent of George's violence, and Alice forbade her from ever bringing it up at the Women's Circle.

In the days after Alice's death, many adult members of the church took great comfort in Alice's involvement with the group. I was told often by parishioners in the four days before I left that if Alice had not been a part of the Circle, the Haywards' bodies would probably have been found by their daughter the next morning or afternoon, when she returned from Tina Cousino's house. Instead it was Ginny O'Brien who would alert the world that the couple was dead. That day Joanie Gaylord was hosting the group, and when Alice had failed to arrive by seven-thirty, Ginny called her friend. There was, of course, no answer at the Haywards'. And so when the meeting adjourned around nine-thirty, she decided to drop by her friend's house. She would tell me that afternoon that she'd had a bad feeling as she drove up the driveway to the usually immaculate yellow Cape and seen Lula the dog asleep on the porch. She had, in fact, known what had occurred before she even opened the unlocked front door.

She knew, she said, because the living room was right beside the entry hall, and so from the front steps of the house she had seen the flesh and bone and brain that had once been a part of George Hayward on the inside mesh of the screen window.

CHAPTER FOUR

There is no explanation for my decision to enter the clergy that is both quick and honest. They tend to be one or the other.

The quick answer—and it is a response I've given most often to especially avid or fundamental believers (of which there is no dearth, even among Baptists in northern New England)—is this, an anecdote I was told by one of my more erudite professors at seminary. When he was a young graduate being considered for a poor, rural parish in West Virginia, he gave a sermon at the church there one Sunday morning. It was, even in his own opinion, more intellectual than inspired, more long-winded than wise. It wasn't very good. After the service an old deacon—a coal miner who had somehow made it into his seventies without succumbing to any of the grotesque lung diseases that usually mark the end of a coal miner's life—approached him and asked with a voice rich in irony, "Was you sent or did you just went?" My professor understood instantly what the deacon was suggesting: He, the young pastor, seemed to lack passion and conviction. He seemed merely to be going through the motions. And so when people would ask me why

I'd become a minister and I could tell from the question that they wanted an answer singed with Pentecostal fires, I'd recount this story, always ending with a self-deprecating shrug and the remark, "All I can tell you is I believe I was sent."

The honest answer is more complex. On some level I was sent. Or inspired. Or called. But my calling, such as it was, wasn't a single booming invitation from above (really, is it ever?), or even one palpable experience of the living Christ in the here and now. When I was ten and eleven, I had a fairly common boy's interest in the horrific and the frightening, in whatever it was that caused one's heart to beat a little faster: chain-saw murderers, serial killers, and those nightmare ghouls who lurk under our beds. Nasty stuff, but pretty typical. And then, of course, there was the predictable array of werewolves, vampires, mummies, aliens, killer robots, psychotic cyborgs, and the assorted undead zombies and freaks that television shows and movies churned out for my entertainment and dreams (or, to be precise, for my disturbing, sheet-gripping nightmares). My friends in Bronxville and I would savor monster movies whenever they arrived for the summer at the theater across the street from the railroad station, and alone or together we would follow their computer-generated mayhem on what are now quaint and primitive video games. My fascination with this sort of carnage and violence was neither unusual nor a sign of a potentially dangerous personality disorder. Given the always precarious state of my parents' marriage, I wouldn't describe my childhood as flawless or serene. (Some years later, when I announced my decision to go to divinity school, my sister observed that I was moving from a bickerage to a vicarage.) But neither was my childhood inordinately painful or scarring. I played Little League baseball in the spring and Pop Warner football in the fall. In the winter I played ice hockey and skied. My father was head of personnel for a large investment bank and commuted with a great many of my friends' parents into lower

Manhattan, gathering like pigeons every morning at that train station by the movie theater. My mother was an editor at a travel magazine but left the publication in her early thirties to stay home and raise my sister and me. My father was ten years older than she was. Their marriage was certainly not exempt from the strangeness that marked the 1970s, but its strains had more to do with the idiosyncratic characters of my parents than with the nature of their friends. As far as I know, no one was swapping spouses at pool parties in July and August. And though I occasionally smelled marijuana, the drug of choice in that circle was clearly brown liquor: The adults encouraged one another to drink scotch the way they insisted their children drink milk.

As a teenager I listened to a lot of heavy-metal and punk music, and I papered my bedroom walls with posters of athletes and rock stars. I had girlfriends, but, in a pattern that would continue through college and into my adult life, I withdrew as soon as it became evident that the relationship was reaching what airline pilots call the V1 point, that point of decision: Either we lifted off and became a very serious couple or we aborted the takeoff and went our separate ways. Invariably I chose to slow the engines if my girlfriend showed no sign of decelerating first.

At some point in high school, when my history class was focused on the Roman Empire, my interest in all things Grand Guignol and sensational found a new fixation: the Crucifixion. My father had been raised a Baptist in southern Vermont—one of the reasons, I imagine, that I wound up here—and my mother was a Presbyterian from a nearby suburb in Westchester. I had gone to Sunday school at the local Baptist church along with my older sister until I was seven, but by the time I was in second grade, we stopped attending church with any regularity. My parents had been worn down by their bickering, their constant late nights on Fridays and Saturdays, my father's job, and the simple demands of raising their two children. We became

Easter and Christmas Christians, making it to church roughly twice a year, and my spiritual quest as a Christian was stalled somewhere between second grade and my adolescent desire to sleep till noon most Sunday mornings.

The Crucifixion changed that. The whole idea that an empire as seemingly civilized as Rome's—in the movies that formed my conception of the ancient world, the Romans were always extremely mannered and would have passed easily in Bronxville or Pelham—saw crucifixion as a reasonable and relatively common form of justice mesmerized me. I was appalled, but I was also fascinated. We'll never know exactly how many men were crucified when the revolt of Spartacus the slave was finally suppressed, but one account suggests that six thousand crosses lined the road between Capua and Rome. Of course, it wasn't the sheer numbers that made crucifixion at once abominable and hypnotic, it was the grotesque particulars of the execution. Nails as thick as Magic Markers and about five inches in length pounded through the bones in the palms of one's hands or—after the Romans had perfected their technique—through the bones in the wrists. Another, even longer nail, a shade under seven inches in the case of the crucified skeleton excavated at Giv'at ha-Mivtar—was banged through the heels of both feet. Or the ankles. Or the metatarsals traversing the arch. (Wander for even half an hour through the Uffizi in Florence: For nearly a millennium, the great artists in Europe were drawn to those nails.) Bodies would hang on a cross in the Mediterranean heat for hours or—not infrequently—two and three days, the criminal or the prisoner wide awake, in unspeakable agony.

And yet it wasn't usually those nails that killed the victim. It was asphyxiation. Eventually neither the victim's arms nor his legs could support his chest a moment longer, and the weight of his own body conspired with gravity to press shut his lungs.

This was torture of a most grisly sort, the kind of violence against the flesh that in my opinion novelists and filmmakers rarely have equaled. Only people (and by that I mean both individuals and groups of individuals working in concert as mobs and, alas, as nations) of a strikingly malevolent disposition are capable of such madness. Such cruelty. Such evil. The idea that someone, Jesus Christ, would subject himself to it willingly haunted me. I remember one Easter weekend I rented all the biblical epics the video store had in stock and watched them for hours on end. That month I pored over the different accounts I had found of the day Christ died. Bishop, Bouquet, and William; Morton and Zeitlin and the writers—four or forty or four hundred in number, we'll never know for sure—behind the Synoptic Gospels and that especially mystical fourth one, the Gospel According to John.

In college, the sort of small liberal-arts school where many of us from Bronxville would go, it was only natural that I would continue what had been my solitary and ill-defined studies in a more structured manner. I majored in religion. I started going to chapel. Then, when I pondered career choices as a senior, I kept coming back to the reality that what had interested me most for the past eight years had been religion, and why one man—a man who without a doubt in my mind had indeed walked this earth some two thousand years ago, regardless of whether he really was who he said he was—would be willing to die on the cross. I applied to a variety of divinity schools and seminaries and chose one known for its liberal theology and worldliness, just outside Boston. I wasn't notably zealous when I arrived at the seminary and for a time regretted that I hadn't simply joined the Peace Corps or become a schoolteacher in (pick one) an inner city or Appalachia or on a Navajo reservation: Either path, Peace Corps or public-school teacher, it seemed to me, would have been a far better way to make a meaningful difference in the world. This was especially true since initially I imagined that my studies in divinity school were most likely to result in my teaching religion someday at precisely the sort of college from which I had graduated. That, in a vague way, was my plan.

But I did believe that Christ had died on the cross and then risen. And with an increasingly warm feeling—not exactly ardor, but certainly absorption—I began to see the possibility of a life of service in the ministry. I envisioned a country parish in New England, a congregation not unlike the Baptist church that my grandparents had attended in Vermont. Toward the end of my third and final year, the expressed needs of the pulpit committee from a little church in Haverill, Vermont, were paired with my expressed desires. There was some concern from the committee that I was unmarried: Like many churches, they wanted their pastor to have a wife, if only because a minister's spouse actually does a good deal of the heavy lifting when it comes to running a church. But their instinct was that I would not cause them public scandal or betray their trust, and soon enough I would find a wife. The church was a little more than an hour from my grandparents', and the pastor there assured the deacons and stewards in Haverill that the Drews were good people, essentially vouching for my character though he knew me only in the most distant way: as the grandson of Foster and Amy Drew, both newly departed, and the son of Richard Drew, who had left Vermont some four and a half decades earlier.

Their instinct, of course, was wrong on both counts. But at the time it had looked like a reasonable match, and for fourteen years it had seemed to most of the world to have worked.

"WHERE IS KATIE now?" Heather Laurent asked me that Tuesday afternoon, as we sat on the porch. The sun was finally burning its way through the milky shroud above and was just starting its slow descent to the west. The shadows from the trees began spreading like moss across my backyard.

"She's with Alice's best friend, Ginny O'Brien. So are Alice's parents—Katie's grandparents. They drove here from Nashua on Monday morning as soon as they heard. They've been here ever since."

"They'll be in Haverill through the funeral?"

"Oh, most definitely. And probably beyond."

"And George's family?"

"They come from somewhere outside of Buffalo. They're staying in Albany."

"Keeping their distance."

"Yes."

"Have you spoken to the families?"

"I have: both families."

"You know, Alice's funeral service is going to be a circus," she murmured, and she noticed for the first time the swallows that were nesting under a porch eave over my shoulder. The mother bird seemed content to allow me to share the space with her—she had, after all, built her nest right here—but only rarely did the male remain beside her when I wandered out onto the deck. A deacon who loved animals had nicknamed them Lil and Phil.

"It will be large," I agreed. "But the worst will be the presence of Katie's friends. All those teenagers and the Youth Group. Though Alice's friends will be sobbing, it will be the tears of the teenagers that will be hardest for me to see from the pulpit. But I wouldn't expect it to be a circus."

"There will be media."

"True."

"It's going to be a hard one for you, isn't it?"

"Yes, I'd say it will be rather unpleasant."

"When is it?"

"Thursday. Day after tomorrow."

"I presume it will be at your church."

"Of course."

She took a breath and sighed. She rubbed her arms as if she were cold, but that wasn't likely the reason on this particular afternoon. I noticed for the first time that she had a pianist's fingers: slender and long, with impeccably manicured nails. She had coated them with a clear polish that picked up the sun when she held her hands the right way. "That poor child," she said softly. "That poor, poor child."

"Young woman," I corrected her. "She's fifteen."

"Do you know her well?"

"I do. She's smart. Funny. She's going places. She's not really active in the Youth Group anymore. I wish she were. But she's a good kid, a good student. She's usually in the school dramas and musicals. Right now her major form of adolescent defiance is a small stud in her right nostril."

"Her father let her do that?"

"It was a surprise to both parents. Her father did not take it well," I said, though I knew he had punished only Alice.

"I remember when I first pierced my ears."

"Rebellion?"

"Emancipation."

"Katie will do okay. She'll get through this."

"Yes, she will. But I still hate to see in my mind the things she's probably witnessed in that home over the years. Has she been back to the house yet?"

"No. Some of us—her friend Tina's mom, Ginny, me—packed the clothes that seemed most useful. Shoes. Sneakers. A nightgown. Cosmetics, some jewelry. But I have no idea if we brought the items that really mattered to her. The right hoodie, for instance. The right jeans. The right teddy bear. Think back to your adolescence and what your room was like when you were fifteen—how many outfits you probably tried on before you found what you really wanted to wear. The piles of stuff on the floor were just unbelievable. The mounds of clothes. The piles of DVDs and CDs and books. The cords for iPods and cell phones and her laptop, as well as her laptop itself. I had no idea which music mattered to her and which didn't—what she had already put on her iPod and what she was planning to download when she had some time to kill. She actually had a bureau drawer filled with nothing but trolls and tins of jewelry and rub-on tattoos. Maybe she hadn't touched it since she was seven. But maybe it was the most important thing in the room to her. I just had no idea. None of us did. So at some point Katie probably will go back to the house. She won't ever live there again, because she's only fifteen. But she will have to go back inside."

"Oh, I disagree. She may want to go back. But anyone in the world would understand if she didn't—if she refused to go back in there. I'm sure you or her friends or other parents would be more than willing to pack everything up for her."

"I guess you're right."

"Where will she live?" She seemed to ask the question with great care, perhaps because she was afraid I had been offended when she'd corrected me. Actually, I hadn't been bothered at all. She had made sense.

"There are options," I answered. "Her grandparents in Nashua are one possibility. But maybe she'll live here in Haverill with the Cousinos—with her friend's family. She might want to finish high school in Vermont and be with the kids she's known since she was six."

"And this Cousino family is okay with that?"

"So I gather."

"Have you talked with Katie?"

"Yes." This time I did find myself slightly affronted. As her pastor I had visited with Katie both yesterday and today, and so my answer may have sounded a little curt. Afterward I hoped I had sounded only surprised.

"How would you say she was doing?"

"She's devastated, of course. In shock. But she's doing what she needs to do," I answered. It was the first thought that came into my mind. "She's endured the questions the state police had about her parents, as well as the questions of a social worker and a therapist, and she's volunteered all the information they could possibly want."

"Is she incredibly angry with her father?"

"Wouldn't you be?"

She nodded. "But I'm sure she also feels some anger toward her mother."

"For not getting out?"

"For allowing it to happen. For being a victim."

"I imagine she's feeling some of that, too."

"I'd like to talk to her. She's one of the reasons I'm here. Do you think that would be possible?"

"It's certainly possible. But I'm not sure it's appropriate. She already has a small army of grief counselors—amateurs and professionals—at her disposal," I said.

"Is the house still a—what's the expression?—a crime scene?"

"No. The state police and the investigators from the crime lab were done by the end of Monday afternoon. It was pretty obvious what had happened. A lot of yesterday is already a blur, but I think most of the official people were gone by four-thirty or five."

"Ah, the official people."

"You know what I mean. The medical examiner. The detectives."

"Can I see the house? Or is that inappropriate, too?"

"The door's locked. But I think Ginny has the key, if you'd like."

"I don't think *like* is exactly the right word," she said. "But I do want to see the inside of the house."

"A visit to the Book Depository while in Dallas?"

"Something like that."

I shrugged. "I'll call Ginny. The two of us can go for a visit."

"Can I ask you something?"

"You've been asking me questions for the last half an hour."

"Just why do you blame yourself for George and Alice Hayward's deaths?"

"I don't blame myself precisely," I told her, careful to keep my voice even, a monotone of reasonability. "But I do fear that I gave Alice permission."

"To die."

"Yes."

"At the baptism you told me about."

"That's right."

"Did you marry them?"

"No. They were married in Bennington years before I met them."

"Did you want her to leave him? Just kick him out—or get the heck out of that house herself and never go back?"

Yes, I thought, *in hindsight I did want her to get out of that house. Briefly, perhaps, I even wanted her to move into mine. Into this parsonage.* But of course I didn't say that. Because no one knew. Because Alice and I had barely even tiptoed around such a notion, even when we were alone in her home and content in the fog of a postcoital torpor—when, usually, all things seem possible and all lovers are optimists.

"I did," I answered simply. "I kept hoping she would take Katie and run. Go anywhere. Move in with her parents in Nashua. Move in with Ginny right here. Perhaps get a place of her own in Bennington."

"It's not that easy. Not emotionally, not financially."

"I know. She was married to a reprehensible man. She would have needed someone willing to step up and protect her. Still, I wish . . ."

"What do you wish?"

"I never want to see a marriage go belly-up." It was not what I had planned to say, but I had to say something.

"Those whom God has joined together let no one put asunder?"

"Something like that. And sometimes I'm afraid that she tried to preserve the marriage for Katie."

"That's completely ridiculous, you know."

"I do. And sometimes I'm afraid that she clung to the marriage because she was afraid she didn't know what would become of her if she didn't."

"The devil she knew?"

"Precisely."

"What about her friends? What did they want?"

I understood what she was getting at, and she was correct. "I know Ginny wanted her to divorce him. She loathed George. Thought he was absolutely despicable. She was thrilled when Alice got a temporary relief-from-abuse order and he went to live in their cottage on Lake Bomoseen for a couple of months."

"When was that?"

"Just before Valentine's Day. He came back just before Memorial Day."

"Not all that long ago."

"No."

"So she got a restraining order—"

"A temporary restraining order. The police served it while George was at his office one Monday afternoon. There was a hearing scheduled a week later. Neither Alice nor George ever showed up."

"That's common."

"I gather. Tell me, are you married? I presume not, because you're not wearing a wedding ring." I think I inquired largely because I wanted a respite from her questions. But it's also possible that on some level

I still felt the need to be pastoral—to give her the chance to talk about herself for a moment. I may have been phoning it in by then—I may have been phoning it in for months—but old habits die hard.

"I'm not. But someday I will be, if only because I have a six-year-old girl's obsession with weddings," she said, and she shook her head as if she were in the midst of some small, odd moment of rapture. "Of all the rites of passage a culture creates for itself, weddings are perhaps the most beautiful. And, perhaps, the most mysterious."

"Well, I certainly preferred doing marriages to funerals."

"Preferred? Why the past tense? Isn't that a little melodramatic?"

"No."

"You really think you're finished?" She smiled. "Come on, your faith is that fragile?"

I sighed. Across the street the small river burbled and one of the children there squealed. The swallow adjusted herself on her eggs, using her beak to pick at something invisible to me on her wing. And somewhere not all that far away, a dog barked. Years earlier, I recalled, when I had been a junior in college and a member in good standing of what some students dismissively called the God Squad, I had been asked—challenged, more precisely—by a classmate who viewed himself as an atheist to explain Auschwitz and cancer and typhoons in Bangladesh that drowned tens of thousands of people. As I sat on my porch that first afternoon with Heather Laurent, I wondered what I'd said; my world had shrunk to such a degree that I honestly couldn't remember how I had responded. I wasn't sure what I'd felt—other, of course, than any sentient person's reasonable sadness—at all the funerals over which I had officiated and all the times I had sat beside beds in hospitals and homes and held people's hands as they died. As my own father had expired in a hospital room and spoke his last words before he sank into unconsciousness: "Go. Just . . . go." (I didn't. My mother, my sister, and I would stay till the end.) I had watched them all depart with what must have seemed to them as confidence and composure, my faith as solid and intact as the heavy pasta pot that hung on a hook above the parsonage stove. But something was different now: It was as if age or rust had worn a great hole in the bottom of that pot and my faith had trickled out like warm water. There were no answered prayers here. And so instead of addressing Heather's question, I observed, "With everything that must be going on in your life right now, you've come here."

"And that surprises you."

"It astonishes me."

"It shouldn't," she said.

"No?"

She shook her head. "Not at all. My father used to beat the living hell out of my mother."

My stomach lurched a little bit at the revelation, but years of pastoral hand-holding kept me from reacting in any visible way, and I mouthed the words I'd probably said hundreds of times every year of my ministerial life: "I'm sorry. I'm very, very sorry."

"Don't be. You weren't the one who hit her."

"Still . . . I'm sorry."

"No, no, no. *I'm* sorry. I shouldn't have dropped the bombshell on you like that. I'm used to most people knowing."

"Knowing?"

"A lot of their story is in *Angels and Aurascapes.*"

"Are they divorced?"

She gazed out at the maples behind my house and then looked me squarely in the eye. "They're dead. When I was fourteen, a few months after my sister and I were sent away to boarding school, my father killed my mother—and then killed himself."

FROM *ANGELS AND AURASCAPES*
BY HEATHER LAURENT (PP. 51–52)

. . . and then killed himself.

The head of the school, who had been deferring to the school psychiatrist for most of the past half hour, finally spoke. He asked my sister and me what we wanted to do, but neither of us answered him. We couldn't, because neither of us was capable of giving him the answers he needed. What did I want to do? My God, I was fourteen years old. I wanted to bring my mother back. I wanted to go back in time. I wanted to know where I was going to live— who was going to take care of me. I wanted to learn how to drive. Those were the things that crossed my mind in response to his question, those were the first desires that came to me. And what did my sister want? She was sixteen, she probably wanted pretty much the same things and to have the same sorts of answers. And the headmaster could grant us absolutely none of our desires or answer our most basic questions.

I understood, of course, that traveling back in time and getting my mother back were implausible wishes and never going to happen. But as we sat in the headmaster's office, I imagined quite concretely what I would do if I could drive—what, to go back to that initial question of his, I wanted.

And I understood I wanted this: I wanted to drive to my grandmother's house in upstate New York and explain to her that I was all finished with this fine school in New England. And then I wanted to go to one of the huge shopping malls near the old air force base in Plattsburgh, the ones kept in business by the Canadians, and buy all the clothes that my father had forbidden me from wearing and that my mother said I didn't dare bring into the house. I wanted, in essence, to wear a shirt with spaghetti straps that revealed my shoulders and tight-fitting shorts made from blue jeans that had been faded almost to a robin's egg blue. I wanted to get my ears pierced at the kiosk in the corridor by the poster-and-frame shop in the mall, and then I wanted to buy earrings. Lipstick. Mascara.

I wanted to drive my friends to my house, and I wanted them all to sit with me on the front porch without fearing that my father would embarrass me with his temper or my mother with her drinking.

That, I realized, was what I wanted to do.

And, fortunately, those images of not-unconventional teenage taste crowded out the reality of what had actually happened to my mother at the hands of my father.

Still, I hadn't spoken aloud any of this, I hadn't answered the head of the school's question. Finally, after the sort of conversational lull that's polite only after someone has died, he turned to my sister and asked Amanda what she wanted to do.

"I want to go home," I heard Amanda tell him, her voice appropriately subdued. She was an aspiring painter at the time and even then savored her solitude.

The head of the school nodded and smiled gently. This was the right response, even if home—technically still that cold and massive Victorian, which, despite the resources of both my parents' families, was in desperate need of a good scraping and painting—was about to become a pretty vague place.

"And you, Heather?" he asked again. "What would you like?"

"A shirt with spaghetti straps," I answered. "And pierced ears."

CHAPTER FIVE

That afternoon Heather shared with me an abbreviated but nonetheless harrowing account of her parents' sordid and, in the end, horrific marriage. In some ways its trajectory was eerily similar to the Haywards'. But, of course, in other ways it had its own idiosyncrasies and detours. Tolstoy was right about families. The most salient feature of her parents' marriage was money: Both Alex and Courtney Laurent came from what my mother would refer to as "families with means," though I am not sure that expression does justice to the veritable bank vaults that subsidized the Laurents. Apparently Alex and Courtney had grown accustomed to getting everything, needing nothing, and behaving in a fashion that suggested a complete uninterest in the responsibilities that came with all those advantages. The result, in Heather's opinion, is that her father was selfish and spoiled, while her mother was entitled and helpless. It was, in her mother's case, almost a learned helplessness. And so while Courtney Laurent had the fiscal resources at her disposal that most abused women lack, she would have needed someone to remind her of the reality that she had alternatives. Options. But Alex, in the tradition of most batterers, had seen to it by then that she was more or less entombed in the marriage: cut off from her family, out of touch with her closest friends. The Laurents had more money and more connections than the Haywards (though the Haywards were, by any fiscal barometer, extremely comfortable) and thus made a much bigger media splash when Alex Laurent shot his wife in the living room and then killed himself, but otherwise the scaffolding of the tragedy was not dissimilar.

Later Heather and I ventured to Ginny O'Brien's to retrieve the key to the Hayward house. Unlike me, Ginny knew exactly who Heather Laurent was, and in the woman's presence her demeanor was transformed from shaken and grieving to a little giddy. She was suddenly a bit like a hyperactive puppy, and I was reminded of the Haywards' affectionate but needy springer spaniel. Ginny had read *Angels and Aurascapes*, and when I introduced them, she told the author how much the book had meant to her—and how she had already marked *A Sacred While* as "to read" on all her online book forums and discussion groups, and suggested to the church book group that they tackle the new one together that autumn. (My sense, now having read both of Heather's books, is that Ginny most likely was made deeply uncomfortable by Heather's chapters on the "auras of death" but saw the logic and importance of, once in a while, taking a long walk in the woods with an angel.) We did not see either Katie or her grandparents, but I hadn't expected we would. I had spent a part of the morning with the three of them in my office at the church, and I knew they had a variety of errands that afternoon that ranged from the merely unpleasant to the downright ghoulish. They were seeing the mortician in Bennington, for instance, to pick out a casket, and deciding whether Alice should be buried in the cemetery in Haverill or with other members of her family in Nashua. I knew that her parents were going to choose Nashua soon enough and were simply trying to spare the feelings of

Alice's friends and her pastor in Vermont. But they were nonetheless taking the time to visit the cemetery, an act of due diligence that couldn't have been easy.

George's body—its eternal resting place was of great interest to Alice's mother and father—was going to be buried back in Buffalo, which mattered because Alice's family wanted to be sure that she was nowhere near the man who had killed her. Ginny, too. Ginny, however, had recommended cremating George Hayward, "since that vicious bastard's soul is already roasting in hell, anyway."

Still, I could tell by Ginny's puffy eyes that she had cried again that afternoon, suggesting to me that her anger was being subsumed by far healthier grief. She had found the strength to pull a comb through her hair and don a clean, creased polo shirt. Behind the house I could hear the growl of a lawn mower and the almost hypnotic way the noise waxed and waned like a wave.

"How are the boys?" I asked as we stood in the front hallway.

"Dan's doing a little better than Walter. I sent Walter to the movies with everyone else," she told me.

"That was a good idea." Both children were in middle school. Dan was eleven and Walter thirteen. I knew both boys well, and I wasn't surprised that Walter was taking the Hayward tragedy hard. He was a little closer to Katie's age and he was, by nature, more sensitive than most teenage males. I wondered how I would have responded at thirteen if my mother's best friend had been strangled by her husband.

"Yes. Anything to get him out of here for a while," said Ginny. Then she added, "That's Dan back there. He said he wanted to do something, so Walter showed him how to cut the grass. It's his first time."

After we had the key, Heather signed Ginny's copy of *Angels and Aurascapes*. The dust jacket was a carefully blurred photograph of a woman with windblown hair emerging nude from the sea, with what I presumed at first glance was a large beach umbrella behind her. It was only on the second look that I realized the umbrella was actually a seashell the size of a schooner sail and the sylph was a modern-day Venus. As we left, Heather told Ginny she would stop by later so she could chat with Katie and, if they were interested, her grandparents. I suppose I should have felt threatened. Mostly I was bemused.

Then Heather and I went to the house where not two full days earlier George and Alice had died. We had taken my car, an American-made compact with camel-colored seats that felt awfully shabby compared to her Saab, and we drove up into the hills that circle the village of Haverill like an amphitheater. We passed the library and the grange and the volunteer fire department, where a group of boys in knee pads and shorts were riding their in-line skates and skateboards on the sloping asphalt before the company's three-bay garage. We passed a sugarhouse, dormant since the first week in April, where two attractive but slightly dim yellow Labs that belonged to a family named McKenna were barking at the remnants of a fallen tree, as if the gnarled, rotting trunk were a crocodile. Occasionally, despite my frustration and grief, I found myself stealing a surreptitious glance at Heather's legs as she sat in the passenger seat beside me. Her skirt had ridden up high on her thigh. Her stockings were nude, the type Alice had worn to the bank in the spring and, I assumed, in the early autumn—though I had never watched Alice dress in the early autumn.

We even passed the Brookners' pond, where I had baptized Alice, a shallow bowl of brown water no more than forty or fifty yards from the road. Over the years the occasional car had driven by while I'd been in the midst of those infrequent baptisms. The vehicles always made the immersion more moving to me, because they made it such a powerfully public statement: strangers passing by behind glass, perhaps unbelievers, witnesses to the short but unfathomable statement each soul was making that moment in the water—*I believe.* Now joined with Christ Jesus by baptism, just as Christ was raised from the dead, someday so shall I.

There.

And we passed the cemetery at the top of the hill, with its markers and headstones and underground boxes of ash, the souls, it seemed to me that afternoon, gone not to heaven but merely to seed.

"This really is a pretty corner of New England," Heather said as I drove, and her voice pulled me from my little reverie of self-pity and gloom. I turned from the cemetery to her. Her earrings, I noticed, were gold studs with a small blue stone in each. "I hope you appreciate the aura of intimacy that envelops it."

I had absolutely no idea what to say to that and so I simply nodded and turned my eyes back to the road.

"AND YOU WERE here Monday morning?" Heather asked me. There was a slight torpor to her voice, but her eyes were moving like the pendulum on a metronome as she carefully surveyed the living room.

"Oh, I was here through early Monday evening." The investigators from the state's crime lab had taken what they needed and left. And while they had scrubbed away a good portion of the tumult in their work, there was still plenty left for those of us who wanted to help. Beside a window next to the couch where George's body was found, was a small china cabinet with beveled-glass doors. With my hands in thick rubber gloves, I had used a sponge to wipe skull and brain from one long pane of glass. Then I had pulled bone chips and hair from the screen window just above it. The bullet, after perforating the skull and traveling through the cranium, had been extracted from the wall not far from that window by a member of the crime lab.

"And this was the room where it happened?" she went on. The fact she had to ask was a testimony to our work.

"Indeed."

"You know," she said, "in books and movies, couples always fight in their bedrooms. Isn't that something? It's as if writers and film-makers want to vilify the domestic center of love. But, in my opinion, that's one of those great artistic conventions that's absolutely wrong."

"Is this wisdom gleaned from your parents' history or your conversations with readers?"

She picked up a small pile of compact discs that were lying on the floor beside a particleboard entertainment center. I recognized the artists that Alice liked best and presumed that the rest of the discs had been selected by George. I realized I knew which ones she had transferred onto her own iPod. "Both," Heather said as she flipped through the discs the way, once, I would have looked through a pack of baseball cards.

"If people don't fight in their bedrooms, where do they battle?"

As if they were delicate antique plates, Heather placed the discs back on the floor where she had found them. "You really have led a sheltered life. You've never lived with anyone, have you? Not ever?" She said it with good humor, as if she were making fun of a costume I might have chosen for a Halloween party or a souvenir T-shirt I had brought back from Cape Cod. It was as if she were commenting upon something that was really of little importance to me.

"Not ever," I said simply. Then, a bit defensively, I added, "As I re-call, my parents didn't have a special room to work out their issues. They bickered everywhere they felt like it."

A line of photo albums sat on a shelf like volumes from that most dispensable of books in the digital age, an encyclopedia. Heather stared at them for a long moment, clearly desirous of reaching for one and opening it.

"So where do most people fight?" I asked again.

"The kitchen. Followed by the rooms that have the television sets. In some homes that's a living room. In others it's a den."

"The TV's a bad influence?"

"Oh, I don't think TV is a good influence. But it's not the reason. It just happens to be in those rooms that people inhabit the most often." She finally gave in to her desire to see the pictures of George and Alice Hayward that were more revealing than the small head shots of each that had been in the newspapers, on television, and on the Web the past two days. She pulled the album that was most accessible from the shelf and began to flip through the pages. And then, much to my surprise, the smallest of whimpers—barely more than a sigh—escaped her lips, and she sat down in the chair opposite the couch where George's body had been found. Her knees almost seemed to buckle like the legs of a portable card table. She wiped at her eyes, but it was too late. She was crying, and it was obvious.

"I'm sorry," she said, shaking her head. "I don't know quite how this happened."

Usually I am fairly competent when it comes to crying women—or, for that matter, with crying men. A minister, even an unmarried one, embraces with impunity. But I wasn't myself those days; the truth was, even now I'm not wholly sure whom I had become. And so I allowed her to regain a semblance of her usual composure—a demeanor, I had concluded, that was at once so unflappably serene (I would say *ethereal*, but, given her interest in angels, that would suggest I attributed a layer of autobiography to her books that she never intended) and so completely earnest that I had begun to understand her popularity. Certainly she was beautiful, but there are lots of beautiful women in this world. It was that she was telegenic: an individual whose competence was manifest and whose sincerity was phosphorescent.

Her charisma was high-definition. She was the perfect pitchwoman for celestial guardians in the digital world.

Finally I leaned over and glanced at the pictures that had set her off. They were of Katie alone and of Katie and Alice together.

"She's going to be so pretty," she sniffled, referring to the now-orphaned fifteen-year-old.

"She already is," I said, but mostly I was focused on Heather. On how, despite my despair and my culpability and my innumerable failures as a minister and as a man, I could appreciate how lovely this woman was. I thought she might be a bit of a lunatic. But I also felt an undeniable attraction to her that managed to bob safely in the maelstrom of other emotions that would have taken precedence in a person of character—or at least in a person not unmoored—and sent it corkscrewing slowly but ceaselessly to the very bottom of the ocean.

She was studying a group of photos, some of which I had already seen on the Facebook and MySpace pages of teens in the Youth Group. (I should tell you that I only visited those pages with the teenagers themselves, when they wanted to share a digital album with me at Youth Group or, for one reason or another, after school.) There was Katie with some of her friends making faces beneath a Broadway marquee in Manhattan; there she and her mother were—again, making silly faces—in bathing suits somewhere near their cottage on Lake Bomoseen. There she was with her grandparents from Nashua, a whole page of photos taken the previous Christmas. There was a series of Katie on the church van: literally, sitting on top of it with some members of the Youth Group, a Red Sox cap shading much of her face. It was one of the last times I would recall her going anywhere with the Youth Group.

"You told me you've never been married," I said. "I assume you don't have any children."

"No, I don't. But I'd love to someday."

"Think it's in the cards?"

"If the right man is, maybe. But I have no interest in being a heroic single mother."

She flipped some more pages, and there was Katie beside her friend Tina Cousino's ancient gray Appaloosa. The horse had gone blind and lame and been euthanized a little over a year ago and was buried in a field by the Cousinos' house. Tina and Katie had choreographed a small service that had left me both moved and impressed. They had asked me to eulogize the animal, and I had. And there were Katie and Alice together approaching the summit of Mount Equinox, a hike they had taken with a woman from Alice's bank toward the very end of that period when Alice and George had been estranged. Mid-May, I recalled.

"There aren't very many of Alice and George together, are there?" she murmured.

"Well, not in this album, anyway."

"I'd wager there aren't many of George Hayward, period. If the pattern holds, he controlled the camera in the early years of the marriage, and so he took most of the pictures. Then, as their marriage deteriorated, they spent less time together in the sorts of situations that . . . someone would want to photograph."

"That's probably true. Most people rarely saw them together over the last few years. Maybe at a parade. Maybe at the volunteer firefighters' annual chicken barbecue. Maybe at a business fete of some sort in Manchester."

"George was a volunteer firefighter?"

"He was for a while. He quit a few years ago, when he opened his third business. But he was still friends with some of the guys."

The room smelled of cleanser and disinfectant. It was a bad smell to me at that moment, almost a little sickening, and so I opened another window.

"Who gardened?"

"Alice."

"These pictures of tomatoes should be on seed packets."

"She was a good gardener, no doubt about it. You should peek at her garden before you leave."

Heather started to nod and then stopped. She was staring at old Easter photos, and George was in these. He was sitting between Katie and Alice on the very couch on which he would die, and for the briefest of seconds I presumed she had paused simply because here, at last, was a photo of George Hayward. But that wasn't it, and I understood this almost instantly. It was, of course, the couch. She stared across the room at the wall where two days earlier there had been a couch. Now there was only a side table we had pressed against the Sheetrock to fill the void.

"You removed the couch," she said, and the idea seemed to horrify her.

"We couldn't clean it," I said. "And so Ginny suggested we just haul it in a pickup truck to the dump."

LATER I SHOWED her Alice and George's bedroom, a room with which I did have some familiarity, and Katie's room, with which I had almost none. I knew its location, little else, because Alice respected her daughter's privacy. The first time I really had been in there had been the day before, when that group of us had rounded up the sorts of things we thought Katie would want or would need.

And then I drove the two of us back to the parsonage, and she climbed into her Saab and returned to Ginny's house to wait for Katie. Later I would learn that she had stayed for dinner and she and Katie had taken one of those long walks at sunset that Heather claimed in her books were so healing. Ginny would tell me—realizing only when she was done speaking that such tidings might have been hurtful—that Heather's effect on Katie Hayward had been almost transformative. Apparently Heather had known precisely how to comfort the girl; she had said whatever it was that Katie needed to hear to be reassured that she would get through this, she would survive, she would never be alone. She would be held up by an angel, her sagging soul kept aloft by wings that might be invisible but were nonetheless as strong and tangible as an eagle's.

"Of course, you've helped Katie, too!" Ginny said when she was done, an afterthought that was awkward but still very well intentioned. "Heather has just . . . you know, lived through this. She can relate to what Katie is experiencing."

"I'm fine," I told Ginny, because I was. Ginny was right. Heather could provide Katie much better therapy than I, and not simply because—like Katie—she was an orphan whose father had murdered her mother. Unlike me, Heather still saw poetry in thunderheads and divinity in coincidence. The world, for her, still offered promise. "I'm glad Heather was here for Katie," I added. "And I'm glad she was here for you, too."

AFTER LEAVING GINNY'S, Heather returned to the loft in which she lived in Manhattan. It was, she had insisted earlier that afternoon, a pretty modest place, a condo she had chosen that offered little in the way of amenities or style but was rich in memory and aura. I had the sense she was being coy: I knew that part of SoHo. She must have gotten home after midnight.

I resolved that I would remain in Haverill through Alice's funeral. I would carry out my responsibilities as best I could for the next forty-eight hours, helping the town in the manner that was expected of me. I would talk more with Katie and her grandparents, as well as with

George's mother and father, who as far as I knew would be in Albany and southern Vermont at least one more night. I would greet people at the funeral home during the calling hours on Wednesday evening. I would pray with the people who wanted me to pray with them, and I would visit the sick and the dying and the parishioners who were confused by the carnage that had occurred in our midst. I would offer comfort and counsel.

As soon as Heather's car had disappeared down the road to Ginny's, I went to my office at the church and sat down with the church secretary, a remarkable woman named Betsy Storrs who had been working at the church a full decade before I arrived and had the demeanor of a grandmother (which she was) and the efficiency of a presidential secretary. At fifty-eight she learned to design websites, and our church's site was the envy of the Baptist churches in our corner of New England. Together Betsy and I determined which meetings I should attend in the coming days and which ones I could miss, as well as which parishioners were most needy at the moment—the most distraught at what had occurred, the most shaken—and which ones were merely whiners hoping to leverage a murder-suicide for a little extra TLC.

I should note that although Betsy helped with the triage, she never viewed her fellow parishioners in quite so misanthropic a fashion, especially in those days before I disappeared. I should also note that I was not always such a brooding, unsympathetic soul. Did I always have exactly the wrong constitution for a country pastor? Perhaps. Perhaps not. Though I had slid into my calling, that doesn't mean it wasn't the right path. At least initially. At least for a time. The fact is, it would be a very long while before I would view anyone in my flock as a whiner.

When I was about to leave the church, I peered into the sanctuary and saw Joanie Gaylord kneeling alone in prayer before the chancel rail. We don't kneel in prayer in my church, but Joanie—seventy-three that summer, an age and a birthday I knew well because Joanie was a prayer warrior and I never once missed one of her birthday parties—was on her knees that evening. I found this interesting and went to kneel beside her. The Women's Circle had met that week at her home.

"Would you pray with me?" she asked.

"Of course I will," I said softly, and I took her arthritic hand in mine while she prayed in silence beside me. We stayed like that for easily ten minutes, my mind straying into its more despairing alcoves despite my efforts to focus, before she cleared her throat and I opened my eyes.

"I wish I had known," she said.

"About George?"

"Yes. I wish she had told us. I wish Ginny had told us. I would have done something."

"Do you think it might have ended differently?"

She reached for the rail and with what looked like a great effort pushed herself to her feet, and so I stood up as well. "I do. I really do."

"You were there for her in more ways than you know," I reassured her. "You meant a lot to her."

"Do you think?"

"I know," I said, drawing the verb out with practiced pastoral emphasis. The last thing Joanie Gaylord either needed or deserved was to shoulder the sort of guilt that would be mine for as long as I lived.

TOWARD DINNERTIME, WHEN I thought Ron Dobson and Illa Gove would be back from their jobs in Bennington and Manchester, I phoned each of them. Ron chaired the Church Council and had been one of my closest friends since I'd come to Haverill. He had been my assistant coach those years I'd coached Little League, and his older son—now a shortstop on the high-school team and an active leader in the church Youth Group—had been our lone athletic bright spot. Good hitter, good fielder, good speed. Our team was never especially talented, and we never won more than four or five games a season, but I believe we always had massive amounts of fun. Illa was the leader of the Board of Deacons and Stewards that met at the church on Wednesday nights and a counselor by day at the shelter for teens at risk, in Bennington. I told Ron I'd like to drop by his house after supper, if it wouldn't be an inconvenience, and then I asked Illa if she'd mind leading her board meeting alone. I explained that I would be greeting guests at the funeral home about that time. She said she would be happy to.

Later, while Ron's wife was upstairs reading aloud to their young son and daughter, I told him without preamble that I was going to leave Haverill. I told him I was having a breakdown of sorts—not exactly a nervous breakdown, but a spiritual one. And in my profession a spiritual breakdown was every bit as debilitating as a nervous one. Maybe more. And so I was taking an emergency leave, I was going away. It might be for a week, it might be for a month. It might be forever. But I would be gone not long after the last of the mourners had left the sanctuary on Thursday.

At first Ron simply listened and nodded, occasionally rubbing his lantern of a jaw or adjusting the massive inner-tube-size doughnut that stretched tight the thin fabric of his short-sleeved summer shirt. He asked, more as my friend than as a trustee, whether I was planning to check myself into a hospital or a retreat, and then he wanted to know how to reach me when I told him I wasn't. It was clear that he was struggling with his dual role as friend and church leader, and he began to worry about the concrete logistics that affected the congregation.

"I'll make sure there's a substitute pastor in the pulpit on Sunday,"

I said. "And I'll make sure there's someone here in town on a more permanent basis by early next week."

"Permanent?"

"Interim, I guess. Someone who can be here for a . . . while."

"What about Ken?" he asked, referring to the deacon who was dying of cancer. "What if he dies when you're gone?"

"If there's a heaven, I'll see him there. If there isn't? Well, then, it doesn't matter, does it?"

"I meant the funeral. The family will need you to do it, not some substitute they don't know."

He was right, and I found myself wondering if, when that time came, I would have it in me to do what I had to do and not let down that kind and pious family. "We'll see," I said simply.

"That's not very helpful."

"I'm sorry. I'm more sorry than you know. But that's my point. I can't be very helpful right now. I can't be helpful at all."

"Look, I just don't want you to burn any bridges. I just don't want there to be any hard feelings when you decide to come back."

"And if I don't?"

"One return at a time," he said, shrugging. Dobson was an accountant with a small firm of his own. "One return at a time" was his mantra in March and April, when he and his partner were swamped by wave upon wave of returns. "My guess is we won't put anybody else in the parsonage while you're gone."

"I will understand if you do."

He shook his head. "This Hayward thing is tough on everyone. For all you know, you're just tired."

"Perhaps."

"I'll bet if you thought about it, you'd realize you felt a lot like this when some other people had died."

"You'd lose that bet," I said, and the moment the words were out there in the air between us—harsh words, needless and abrupt—I knew it was time to leave. I apologized, but it was too late. We stood almost at the same second, embraced awkwardly, and when I walked into the still-balmy night air, the only emotion I felt was relief.

IF, ON THE surface, I was not at my best the rest of that week, I was adequate. I did my job. I found time after the calling hours at the funeral home to meet with a half dozen teens in the Youth Group who wanted to talk, and though the group was somber and troubled, by the time they left my living room near eleven P.M., their faith was on considerably surer footing than mine. I had two breakfasts that Thursday morning, an early one with the deacons to make sure that the transition to the interim pastor would be smooth and then a later one with Katie Hayward, her grandparents, Ginny and Harry O'Brien, and the Cousino family. The purpose of that meal? Comfort and connection and communion of a more secular sort.

Alice's body was in its casket at the church that Thursday morning, though she was not going to be buried in Haverill. As I suspected, Alice went home to New Hampshire. And though the local mortician, an eccentric elderly gentleman whose funeral parlor was known for the exotic birds he kept, had been able to make her corpse presentable, Alice's family had decided upon a closed casket. (George's face, he would confess to me later, could have been reconstructed and made viewable, but he said he was just not inclined to do what he called his "best work" on it, and so that would be a closed casket, too.)

As Heather had predicted, Alice's funeral was so crowded that one of the stewards had to set up a video feed so the overflow of mourners in the common room below the sanctuary could watch, and we sat people in the choir loft behind me. The sanctuary was packed well beyond the capacity of our two sluggish ceiling fans, and I saw people sweating through their short-sleeved summer shirts (and others, undoubtedly, beneath their blazers), and I watched beads of perspiration run down some of their faces and mingle with tears. I think there must have been forty students from the high school alone in the church, many for the first time, and their faces—so guileless and sweet, despite the girls who were wearing too much eye shadow and lipstick and the boys who were struggling mightily to be too tough for tears—were the hardest for me to watch. Katie, of course, was a source of particular sadness for me. She wore a sleeveless, somewhat slinky black dress that might have been more appropriate at a cocktail party than at her mother's funeral, but how many black dresses does a teenage girl in rural Vermont own? I was surprised she had even one, and my sense was that in the past she had worn it surreptitiously. George Hayward probably hadn't even known it existed, though it was the sort of thing he sold without irony to teenage girls and college students at his store in Manchester Center. Her hair was pulled off her face, and she looked pale and a little blank to me. Numb. Her friends cried, but she didn't, and I realized later it was because Ginny had given her a tranquilizer. She sat impassively as I spoke and Alice's sister spoke and the choir sang and different people in the sanctuary stood up to offer their memories, mostly of Alice but twice of George. Alice's father, a sickly-looking old man with skin that struck me as fishlike and was riddled with age spots the size of dimes, flinched when one of the volunteer firefighters reminded us of the countless hours George had devoted to the company and how he hoped that the man's soul might, at last, find peace. George's secretary, a svelte and powerfully built young woman who could have moonlit as a fitness trainer, said he had always been a good boss and that no one in his small empire would ever have thought he was capable of such violence. (Instantly I was struck by the salacious and unfounded notion that she and George had been lovers.) No one, in my opinion, tried to grandstand for the media.

And among that great crowd of mourners in the church? Heather Laurent. Yes, she did return. She got home after midnight on Tuesday, yet still drove back to Vermont first thing Thursday morning.

But when I left Haverill on Thursday evening—not like a thief in the night, in all fairness, since the deacons and Ron Dobson and I had made sure that an interim pastor would be there to hold the hands of the congregation after their minister had ostensibly had a nervous breakdown—I did not leave with Heather. Though later there would be gossip to that effect, we most assuredly did not decamp together. I knew how that would look. And I hadn't known that she was coming back for the funeral. We did not meet up again until Saturday morning, when I showed up in the dark, warehouselike lobby of her building on Greene Street and pressed the ivory-colored call button beside her name. Upstairs she would tell me that she had hoped I would visit, but she hadn't expected it. She told me she honestly hadn't realized that I was still so willing to give myself over to my angel.

FROM *ANGELS AND AURASCAPES* BY HEATHER LAURENT (PP. 79–80)

My father shot my mother on the night of the day that he learned she had taken a lease on another house, one that would be large enough for my sister and me when we were home from school. This was as clear a signal as he needed that this time she really was going to leave him. And so, late that night, he shot her and then killed himself. But he didn't use the same gun. In fact, he didn't use a gun, period, when he took his own life. Instead, after murdering my mother, he walked next door to our neighbors' and left a note on the windshield of the car that the husband drove each morning to work. The note instructed the fellow to call the police immediately and to direct them to the Laurents' house. He wasn't to go there himself, and under no circumstances was he to call Heather or Amanda at boarding school. Then, after leaving the note pinned to the glass by the wiper blade, he went home, climbed the stairs to our attic, and hanged himself from an inner beam across the peak of our twelve-by-twelve-pitch roof.

CHAPTER SIX

Some months later that deputy state's attorney with those lovely blue eyes and the name of a saint would tell me that she had thought I was a pretty cold fish from the moment we'd met that Monday morning after I had baptized Alice Hayward. This might have been posturing to elicit some sort of reaction from me, but it may also have been an honest and legitimate first impression. Certainly I had been anesthetized that day by guilt and despair: guilt that I had not realized why baptism had been so important to Alice the previous morning and despair at her death. Make no mistake: I was grieving as her former lover as well as her minister.

But in all fairness to Catherine Benincasa, I know also that there were parishioners who thought I was distant. Or, perhaps, that I had secrets. Cards that I was loath to reveal. No one verbalized such things prior to my departure, of course. It was only after I left that people's secret doubts became rumor and gossip and innuendo.

I will be the first to admit that a pastor in a small town has enormous power over the people who come to church and even a fair amount over those who don't. The directors or coordinators of easily a dozen organizations across the county—the dental clinic for low-income Vermonters, for example, the hospice, the women's crisis center— would ask me to stand up for them at the town meeting the first Tuesday in March and thereby ensure that Haverill would vote to approve their budget requests.

And we have power in other, more invidious ways as well. There were temptations throughout the congregation, women—some half my age—whose eyes I would meet as I spoke Sunday mornings and whose gaze I would hold a second longer than was probably right. There were single women in the congregation who I know would have been happy to date me and married ones who would have risked the wrath of our small town had I shown any interest at all. Like any minister—not merely the Dimmesdales of fiction—in my little pond, I could have been either a big moral fish or a more complex sort of predator. Many of the parishioners I counseled were female and in a condition that could only be called vulnerable. And, because I am male, that ingrained desire to protect them invariably would kick in. Nevertheless, in most of my dealings, I strove for a moral compass that was sound. There were some women with whom I would flirt more shamelessly than with others, but they were always the parishioners who were happily married and understood that our flirations would never progress beyond vague intimations. In my fourteen years in Haverill, I had dated three women seriously, all of whom, it seemed to me, were unsuited to the life of a country pastor's wife. None of them were from Haverill: One was from Albany, one was from Manchester, and one lived far to the north in Burlington. The woman from Manchester grew close to my congregation, and I think they were hurt—and saddened for me—when we did not walk down the aisle of my church together.

Yes, I did ask her, despite my misgivings about whether her constitution was right for the role that would be demanded of her if she agreed. She declined, and it was the first time in my life that a woman ended our relationship before I did.

But the only member of the Haverill United Church I ever slept with was Alice Hayward, and that was mostly (though, in truth, not always) in the period when George had moved to the cottage on the lake, where he would reside for a little more than one hundred days: An adult man separated from his wife and his daughter, but living alone in a second house alive with their detritus and scent. I did not, as one newspaper later would put it, pounce upon Alice the moment her husband was gone. But it is an inarguable fact that I took advantage of her precarious emotional health. I massaged the lower back that had been left contused—stripes that changed like the leaves from scarlet to sulfur—with a leather belt. I brought my lips to the stomach that once had carried her husband's child and then would be beaten by that very man's fists, at least twice to the point that she was left retching into the toilet.

And yes, the illicit nature of our activities—the way one moment we might be sitting fully clothed, chatting languorously on the rug in her living room, but in the next we would be naked on that floor and my tongue would be buried between her legs with a hunger I had never before experienced—energized my otherwise distressingly placid life.

But it is also a fact that I had never planned to take advantage of Alice Hayward. For a time I had even thought we were in love.

IT IS A Monday afternoon in March, and Alice and I are lying in her bed as the snow blows fiercely against the western window and the howl of the wind is cut only by the occasional rumble of the town plow and sand truck. This storm is arriving a little earlier than any of us expected.

In another hour Katie will be coming home, and so in a moment Alice and I will rouse ourselves, shower together, and get dressed. I plan to be gone long before her daughter's bus will coast to a stop at the end of the Haywards' driveway.

"You know," Alice murmurs, her head resting on my chest, "he has his hurts, too."

I know who she means, but for a brief second I nonetheless have to spool back in my head the discussion we were having, because on afternoons like this we tend to allow ourselves long, sumptuous pauses in our conversations. Sometimes we will doze and pick up the strand of an exchange a full five or ten minutes later.

"George," I respond.

"His life was no picnic when he was growing up. All those brothers. My father-in-law can be horrible."

"Well, he hasn't made your life a picnic."

"No. But it wasn't always so . . . so troubled. And now . . ."

"Go on."

"I've taken away his daughter. He aches for her."

I want to say that he brought that loss upon himself. But instead I merely listen. I think I have an idea where this is going, but I want to be sure.

"You know I don't feel good about that," she continues. "But I didn't have a choice, did I?"

My arm is asleep, but still I am able to pull her against me. "No," I reassure her, "you had absolutely no choice." But as I had suspected—as I had feared—once more she is going to punish herself and recount things she feels she has done wrong in her marriage and the innumerable ways she drove her husband to hurt her. And this litany will end, as it does often, with her flagellating herself for being unfaithful. She will remind herself—and me—that George may have done some terrible things in this world, but he always, as far as she knows, was faithful.

I WENT TO visit my mother in Bronxville the Thursday night after the funeral, though she was sound asleep by the time I arrived. It was after midnight. But she had known I was coming, and so, as if I were nineteen rather than thirty-nine—a student returning home from college—she had stocked the refrigerator with beer and milk and Hostess cupcakes, which as a boy I had always preferred cold. Over breakfast on Friday morning, she asked me all the right questions about my future and whether (and here she was delicate) the deaths of two of my congregants were more of a personal or a pastoral crisis. I answered evasively by explaining that only one was a congregant and that I tended not to use that term in any event. On Friday the sky was a cerulean blue, and I walked alone for hours around the streets on which I had lived as a child and a teenage boy, loitering for a few moments before the slightly imposing Tudor in which I had grown up—a house not far from the swim and tennis club where my older sister would spend long summer days with her friends but that I always found less inviting and tended to avoid. I passed the school, an elegant, lengthy Georgian structure that looked like it belonged on a college campus, then the ball field and the library. That library and ball field and the village itself were far more likely to be my summer haunts than was the swim and tennis club. The town was a collection of hills, the roads laid out chaotically along the cow paths from the nineteenth century, the trees now tall and thick and statuesque, the houses substantial. Most of my neighbors, I would realize in high school, had money and advantages, but as a boy I had been largely oblivious to both. I was more aware of Mike Ferris's humongous baseball-card collection, for example, and how content and secure I would feel trading cards and arguing baseball with him in his family's screened porch as a thunderstorm would rumble in from the west.

That Friday as I walked along the sidewalk in the village, I detoured into the bookstore and bought *Angels and Aurascapes* and *A Sacred While*.

I had brought my laptop with me, and in the afternoon, as if I were consciously trying to give the investigation that soon would be launched interesting fodder, once again I surfed the Web for information about Alice Hayward (there was nothing I didn't already know) and about domestic abuse and death by strangulation and gunshot. Some of those sites would come back to haunt me during the investigation, but it was all very innocent. While online I read reviews of Heather's books and visited her website, and I found myself spending far more time with her blog than I would have anticipated. In the evening, after I took my mother to dinner at a French bistro in town that she had always enjoyed, I read from both of Heather's books.

And then on Saturday morning, I awoke and pondered my next destination. I had options other than Heather Laurent, including acquaintances who had remained in Westchester County. And there were my friends from seminary—one in Illinois, another in upstate New York, and a third in Pennsylvania. There was my friend in Texas. Instead, however, I found myself drawn toward lower Manhattan: I veered on to the Saw Mill River Parkway, then the Henry Hudson, and then the West Side Highway. I exited at Canal Street and turned on to Greene. I honestly wasn't sure whether I would ring the bell at Heather Laurent's building or just glance around her neighborhood for a few moments. There are fine lines between interest and obsession and stalking, but I think I was still well within the bounds of mere intellectual curiosity. And I may also have been experimenting on some level with a flirtatious quid pro quo: She had dropped in unexpectedly on me that Tuesday; now I was returning the favor on Saturday. I hadn't decided what I would do if she weren't home. Wait or leave a note or simply depart. For a few moments, they were all equal in my mind.

But I did press the call button, and she was home, and I felt a little rush of pleasure at the sound of her voice over the crackling intercom. She invited me up and said there would be doors to four lofts when the elevator doors parted, and hers would be the one farthest to the left. It turned out to be more information than I needed, because when the elevator reached her floor, she was there with her front door open, the loft behind her illuminated by the sun that was cascading in from the western-facing windows.

"I READ SOME of your books last night," I told her as I sipped the peppermint iced tea she had in a glass pitcher in her refrigerator. I couldn't remember the last time I had drunk tea, hot or cold. But just as I didn't keep tea around my kitchen, she didn't keep coffee in hers. This seemed very significant to me at the time, a further indication that there was no future between a pastor in the midst of a crisis of faith and a self-help writer with an apparent fixation on angels. "I enjoyed them," I said.

"But . . ." She was smiling.

"But there's a lot there about cherubs and seraphim. About luminescence and flashes of light."

"And prayer. And meditation."

"That, too."

Her loft, as she had told me, was really not all that extravagant: high tin ceilings, the original fleur-de-lis tile, but not the basketball arena I had seen in my mind. A soft wood floor, wide pine that I suspected had probably been there for generations, covered in sections with plush Oriental rugs. A row of tall windows faced out upon

Greene Street, each of them about half as large as the stained-glass windows of the church in Haverill, and there were four chandeliers dangling from the ceiling that initially left me confused and disturbed. I thought the bulbs of coiled glass were supposed to be the snakes that grew from Medusa's skull. But then I realized I was mistaken: The tentacles, I saw when I looked more closely, were merely the arms and trumpets and small, delicate feet of angels. The glass was white as cooked rice. And on a solid-looking pedestal on one side of a bookcase, positioned against a wall so a visitor couldn't help but feel he was being watched, was a carved bird the size of a preschooler. It was a bird of prey of some kind, an osprey perhaps, quite accurate, I thought, except that the wings—which were unfolded as if it were about to dive from a high perch—looked like they belonged on an angel. They ran parallel to the bird's body and were arched at the top like a harp.

"The reality is that I probably view angels in much the same way that you do," she said. "The fact you've come here suggests you don't believe I'm a complete phony." We were sitting on an elegant wrought-iron daybed with black bolsters. It was adjacent to the wall with the windows, near a row of hulking stainless-steel kitchen appliances: The refrigerator doors alone looked wide enough to be the entrance to a walk-in closet. There was another corner of the loft with a regular couch, a mirrored coffee table, and a pair of reupholstered easy chairs without arms that looked as if they were from the 1950s. She slept on a bed in an alcove ledge high above the corner in which— based on the desk and computer—she wrote. Along the wall opposite all those windows, broken only by the entryway, was a long line of modern wardrobe doors: the critical renovation she had made, she would tell me later, because the loft was wholly bereft of closets. I counted five wardrobes on each side of the entryway. And scattered along the walls that had neither windows nor wardrobes were framed dust jackets of her books beside specific bestseller lists, as well as a half dozen prints of angels: grown-up angels, I was happy to see, not pudgy child ones with naked ham hocks for thighs. There was a small painting of an angel in a copse of cedar trees that looked a bit like a Botticelli, but she had assured me that it was the work of a minor painter from Siena and it was barely two hundred years old.

"I don't believe you're a phony at all," I said.

"A bit loopy, maybe," she suggested. "But not phony."

"You're putting words in my mouth," I insisted. "Just last Sunday a fellow in my church who is five years younger than I am and dying of cancer gave the children's message, and he talked all about the angels among us. He told the kids angels don't always have wings."

"He's right."

"He said they were the women who drive him to and from his chemotherapy. Who make him his carrot juice."

She nodded. "I have readers, of course, who see angels in a pretty literal sense. When I was in Vermont the other day, I had one reader tell me that a particularly amazing angel had caught her husband's small plane in midair when the engine flamed out and stopped it from crashing."

"How?"

"You know, with his hands."

"Just brought it safely to earth?"

"Because the angel had wings," she said, as if this explained everything. I found myself imagining, no doubt as this reader had, an angel in a white robe flying atop a Cessna, holding the fuselage in his hands while flapping his wings to keep both him and the plane aloft. "As you might imagine, my books do better with some sorts of readers than with others."

She was wearing black jeans and a white linen top, which was untucked. Her feet were bare, and she had curled them beneath her on the couch. Her toenails were plum.

"What would you be doing if I hadn't appeared?" I asked.

"Going through the piles of mail my assistant prioritized in my absence. Reading e-mail. Grocery shopping. It was going to be a pretty glamorous Saturday."

"How long have you lived here?"

"Oh, let's see. Today's the first day of August. A little less than two years. I call this the Loft That *Angels* Built," and I understood she was referring to her first book.

"And you've always lived here alone?"

"I have."

"May I ask you something?"

"You seem to be asking me a great many somethings. Go ahead."

"Do you pray?" I hadn't meant it to be an especially challenging or antagonistic inquiry—though I did hear in my head the homonym, *prey,* and that part of me that I have discovered is capable of unexpected bouts of savagery and anger may have lent an edge to my voice—and she sat back and seemed to be contemplating the question, her eyes growing a little stern, her forehead slightly creased. I imagined her suddenly as a child struggling with a math equation that was beyond her ken. "Everyone prays," she said finally, "even if they don't use that verb. Even if they're not completely sure who or what they're imploring. Why? Have you stopped praying?"

"So it seems," I answered, and I told her how hard I had tried that past week to connect with a living God—and how I had even faked it late Tuesday afternoon before the altar with Joanie Gaylord. I had, in truth, spent a good part of Wednesday afternoon at the church. I was either alone in my office in the wing by the Sunday-school classrooms or in the sanctuary itself trying to pray. I let Betsy or the answering machine handle the usual sorts of calls that came in—a request to give the invocation at a special Masonic gathering at the lodge in Bennington, a change in the date of an upcoming Church Council meeting, the increasingly urgent need as September approached to find a Sunday-school teacher for the third- and fourth-graders—as well as the barrage that was linked directly to the Haywards' deaths and up-coming funeral: The mortician. A deacon. The high-school principal. Ginny.

In theory I knew a very great deal about prayer, so praying shouldn't have been all that difficult. I had studied it at seminary, I had read all the right books. I'd led prayer groups in my little church, I'd conducted seminars for pastors and lay people in our region. And though I never had expectations of a miracle when someone was ac-tively dying, there had been a period in my life when I had believed fervently in the healing powers of prayer. For over two decades, I had prayed every single day of my life.

Yet when I'd fall on my knees in the days immediately after Alice and George Hayward had died, praying in different measures for for-giveness and healing and understanding, I'd come to realize that I didn't know a bloody thing about prayer—at least not anything useful. When I needed to find the Lord most desperately, I hadn't a clue where to begin.

"Can you tell me why?" Heather was asking. "A minister must have a reason to stop praying."

"I was no longer confident that anyone was listening."

"In that case you sure put on one hell of a good show on Thurs-day morning."

"At the funeral service?"

"Yup."

"Thank you."

She shook her head—bemused, incredulous, I couldn't say for sure—and a lock of her hair fell over one of her eyes. It was, perhaps, the most arousing thing I had seen since the last time I'd been alone with Alice Hayward and I'd allowed myself to savor the sight of the small of her back when she rose from the bed to get dressed. The sense that no one was listening—no one was watching, no one cared—had begun to feel unexpectedly liberating since I had climbed into my car and left Vermont. Originally I had felt only loneliness and despair at the realization that there might be nobody out there. No more.

"Did you always know that your faith was so weak?" she asked.

"No. I actually thought it was rather strong for most of the last two decades. Trust me, it withstood plenty of sickness. Plenty of death. I have prayed with parents who have lost children, I have knelt before the very old in the moments before they would die. I've done funerals for teenagers and young mothers. I know the inside of the hospice as well as anyone who works there."

"But your faith couldn't withstand the deaths of the Haywards." It was a statement, not a question.

"Apparently not."

"What made their deaths so different?"

"Guilt. Anger."

"I understand the guilt. What is the anger?"

"Isn't it obvious?"

"No."

"It's George. It's the fact that he killed her. It seems that faith—at least my faith—is perfectly comfortable with benign disgust but absolutely no match for rage."

"Come with me," she said, and she stood and brought her glass of iced tea to the kitchen island with the black marble countertop. "We're going out."

"Okay."

"You need to do something completely different. You need a change of pace."

"We're going dancing?" I asked playfully.

"Oh, I doubt you could dance with me. I used to be a pretty serious dancer."

"So I read in *Angels*," I said. "And you're right, I couldn't keep up with you. I would embarrass myself rather badly."

"Stephen, I was kidding," she said patiently. "You wouldn't embarrass yourself at all."

"I would. Trust me. It wouldn't be pretty."

She was already slipping into a pair of black lace ballet flats and motioning for me to leave my iced tea on the table beside the daybed. "I want to show you something," she said.

"Nearby?"

"In the city."

"Are you going to tell me what it is, or am I supposed to be surprised?"

She shrugged. "Nothing mysterious. I'm going to show you an angel."

"I thought you were my angel," I said. It was the first optimistic remark that had occurred to me in nearly a week, and I found myself smiling.

"I am," she said. Then she took me by surprise and stood on her toes and kissed me softly on the lips.

LATER THAT DAY a colossal thunderstorm would rumble over Manhattan and raindrops the size of dimes would dance upon the sidewalk. The air was electric and the sky the color of slate. We stood in nothing but T-shirts before the windows of her loft and watched the pedestrians below us race across Greene Street, leaping like long jumpers across the rivers that suddenly lapped at the side of each curb while trying to avoid the spray from the yellow cabs and delivery trucks. Earlier that afternoon, however, the clouds had been far to the west, and we had gone to Central Park, where she had showed me an angel: a tall, confident bronze woman with wings who, Heather told me, had looked out upon the terrace since the nineteenth century. She was striding purposefully atop a fountain, the water cascading from her feet into a bluestone basin below her, the sheets a precursor to the soaking rains that would fall from the heavens in hours.

The bronze statue was Heather's favorite angel in Manhattan, but I would learn that there were others she liked a good deal in Brooklyn and the Bronx. Though angels were easy to find in cemeteries, she said that she didn't especially care for funereal angels and tombstone cherubs—she wanted her angels among the living, not watching over the already dead—and thus she scoured parks and gardens for the angels with whom, on some level, she seemed to want to commune.

At the park we ate ice-cream sandwiches on a bench just beyond the shade, and we ate quickly because we were hungry and the ice cream was melting fast in the sun. We were surrounded by softball players and sunbathers and people picnicking on the grass who, I imagined, were falling in love, and I felt at once a part of them all, a select member of a club of people who were happy—unencumbered with doubt and despair—and completely separate from them. I never forgot that Alice was dead and Katie was an orphan and there was a congregation in Vermont that I had deserted. That afternoon, on the bench in the park and then in the bed in the loft above her writing desk, Heather told me more about her parents' marriage and deaths, and we talked about our siblings—including her sister, Amanda, and the strange ways that the girl had responded to their mother's death at the hands of their father. Some of this I knew from Heather's books, but some she had kept from the world as a courtesy to Amanda.

"It's why I wanted to meet Katie," she said as we stood in her window frame and watched the rain fall with a Polynesian intensity. "It's why I worry about that girl."

Amanda was living in a moldy log cabin in the woods in upstate New York with a circumspect—possibly agoraphobic—bird carver, and the two of them went weeks without so much as venturing even to the general store in some dot on the map called Statler. She was an alcoholic who no longer drank, but she no longer attended AA meetings, either. And once she stopped drinking, she shed weight the way a snake sheds its skin. She wasn't strictly speaking an anorexic in Heather's opinion, but the woman was five-four and couldn't have weighed more than a hundred pounds when they had seen each other just after Memorial Day. She smoked relentlessly, and her skin looked as fragile as papyrus. And yet, Heather said, her sister was still wise and funny and capable of parlaying her badly socialized lover into an artist of some cachet among curators and collectors. She was, despite her outwardly brittle façade, a formidable business presence. She was appealing and charismatic when she needed to turn it on for a well-heeled dealer at a Spring Street gallery.

And as Saturday night turned to Sunday morning, we talked of the lovers we had had in the past, though I did leave one name conspicuously absent from my short but deeply personal inventory, and, like so much else that I did and said that week, this would come back to haunt me.

I found it interesting that just as I had asked one woman to marry me and she had declined, Heather had been asked once to get married and she had said no. She had loved this fellow, she said, but she hadn't wanted the life that would have come from marrying a bookish religion professor at a small college in Pennsylvania. The fact that this was precisely the path I almost had taken was an irony that was not lost on either of us, since by then she knew this part of my history. I realized as we chatted and dozed and made love that I was not merely a reclamation project for Heather—a notion that had crossed my mind the first time I entered her, though it had not diminished my ardor at all—but was more precisely a much-needed respite. She did, as I had suspected, need to be needed, though it would be a while before I would begin to realize how literally she had meant it when she had agreed that she was my angel. But she also saw in me someone who hadn't had the slightest idea who she was when we first met and then hadn't given a damn when she'd told him.

When we awoke Sunday morning, she asked me if I wanted to go to church. It wasn't quite eight, and if I'd been in Vermont I would have been making last-minute changes to the service or chatting with the choir director about a hymn or checking my props for the children's moment. I might have been making sure there were candles on the Communion table or, perhaps, simply listening as a few members of the choir rehearsed. There was an energy then that I can liken to the sensations an actor or a stage manager must savor in the half hour before the house opens and the audience starts filing in for the eight-o'clock curtain.

"No," I answered. "I'd rather not. But I don't want to stop you from going. I should . . ."

"You should what?"

"Well, I was going to say I should be leaving. You do have a life, after all."

"Where would you go?"

"I don't know. Somewhere. I do have options."

She sat upright in bed on her knees, and her head almost touched the ceiling. "I had fun yesterday. I had fun last night. I hope you know that."

"I do."

"Did you?"

"Though I feel guilty saying so, yes. Yes, I did."

"And you feel guilty because you should be in Vermont? Or because you couldn't prevent Alice Hayward from dying?"

"Not couldn't. Didn't. There's a difference. And I think I feel guilty for both reasons—though I do feel far worse about the reality that Alice Hayward is dead than I do about the fact that I'm AWOL."

What I did not feel bad about—then or now—was my attraction to Heather Laurent. People would vilify me further that autumn by suggesting I was some sort of immoral, overly libidinous Casanova. How could I have gotten involved with another woman so soon after Alice's death? they seemed to ask. My response—had anyone had the decency to inquire to my face—would have been rather straight-forward (assuming I even deigned to proffer a response). I would have pointed out to them that Alice's and my affair, such as it was, had lasted but six months; that the affair had been over for two and a half months when I allowed myself to fall into bed with Heather Laurent; and that Alice's and my separation had been amicable. I was devastated by the fact that Alice was dead and her daughter was an orphan. But sleeping with Heather Laurent was neither an act of disloyalty nor a barometer of my callousness as a person. I needed comfort, too. If there is a grimoire for grief, why should it not include romance? The bereft have taken solace in vices far worse.

"Have you ever preached on remorse?" she asked.

She slept in a T-shirt and old dance shorts with a drawstring, and abstractedly she fiddled with the cord. When she asked the question, she had the slightly puzzled look on her face that I was finding more and more appealing. It was the face she made when she was deep in thought, and it was unguarded and childlike, and it made me want to sit up in bed and kiss her. (Imagine the sorts of monstrous names I would have been called had I ever suggested during the investigation that I found something childlike in a woman to be appealing. The aspersions upon my character would have been far worse. And while my mother wouldn't have believed that such a thing was possible, my attorney and I took dark comfort in the reality that I was a Baptist and not a Catholic, and the crimes of which I was accused, thank heavens, at least did not involve altar boys.)

"Yes, I've preached on remorse," I answered. "I've preached on guilt and I've preached on shame. I've preached easily seven hundred and twenty-five sermons in my life. There isn't a lot I haven't preached on."

"If you could make amends—"

"But I can't make amends," I said, cutting her off. Quickly I softened my voice, because I feared in that instant that I had hurt her feelings with my abruptness. "That's the problem. I can't bring Alice back. There is simply no way to make this sort of horror right."

She fell back on the pillow and lay on her side, resting her head on her hand. I was still flat on my back. Her T-shirt was black with a pair of pink ballet shoes on it, and I liked looking up at her. Her hair was still a little wild with sleep. "You told me you never believed in angels in a literal sense," she said after a moment.

"That's right. Not ever."

"'For he shall give his angels charge over thee, to keep thee in all thy ways,'" she said, quoting the ninety-first psalm. "'They shall bear thee up in their hands, lest thou dash thy foot against a stone. Thou shalt tread upon the lion and adder: the young lion and the dragon shalt thou trample under feet.'" I recognized that the three verses were from the King James Version.

"Can you do that with every angel reference in the Bible?" I asked.

"No way. But some."

"Still, I'm impressed."

"Don't be. I'm sure you know considerably more passages by heart than I do."

"You'd be surprised at how little I know—about anything."

"And you've never, ever believed in angels. Really?"

I could have given her any number of glib responses, but she deserved better than that. "For a time," I confessed, "I believed in angelic presence: God's light in the people around us. People behaving angelically. And sometimes I met people whose demeanor seemed angelic to me. There was a fellow in the congregation when I arrived, an old farmer. A deacon. He was seventy-seven when I got there, and I was a twenty-five-year-old pastoral novice. He was frail, but very kind, very wise. He took me under his wing and taught me all about Haverill, about the history of the church. About the ministers who had come before me. He made sure that the transition was smooth. And—and this is no small *and*—he taught me how to use most power tools. That deck where we sat the day we met? He and I built it together. But no, I've never believed in a genus or species of creature you might call an angel."

"Nothing with halos?"

"No. Nothing with halos—or wings."

"'Hope is the thing with feathers,'" she said.

"Emily Dickinson?"

"That's right."

"She was referring to birds."

"I've always found some voices angelic," Heather said.

I thought about this. "I had one parishioner who told me he heard the voice of God in his daughter's singing voice," I admitted. "And there were certainly some Sunday mornings when I hated to have to follow the choir's anthem with a sermon."

"I didn't actually mean singing—though I know what you're talking about."

"Ah, you meant a plain speaking voice."

"I did. Some voices are more angelic than others," she said, and for a moment I tried to recall that elderly deacon's voice. He'd been dead seven years by then, and so it took me a moment to recapture the euphonious fusion of words that marked his speech—that marked so many of my most rural neighbors. His voice was gravelly and soft, and he laughed lightly but often. Supposedly a toddler laughs four hundred times every day and an adult barely fourteen. That deacon was an exception. Once I even preached a sermon on that—on laughter as a gift from God.

"I guess I can recall voices that were saintly and beatific," I agreed.

"I had a feeling you could."

"Of course, I can also recall voices that, by comparison, were downright evil."

"You are in a dark place."

"Apparently."

"I suppose you're thinking of George Hayward's voice?"

"Actually, I was just being ornery."

"George Hayward's voice wasn't demonic?"

"It wasn't around me. But before he would hurt Alice, she said he would grow condescending. He would start talking like a law-school professor. Old-school. Socratic. He'd start asking her questions, and whatever answer she gave was going to get her in trouble. *Do you think it behooves Katie's mother to dress like a whore? Did you think you were being helpful doing a load of darks without checking with me to see if I had something—a turtleneck, maybe, a pair of jeans—I might want laundered? How did you expect me to respond when you chose to be with Ginny O'Brien instead of your husband? Are you a lesbian?* He never raised his voice before he would hit her, and even when he was drunk as a sailor, he spoke like Henry Higgins. Alice always knew she was in trouble when he began doing his *My Fair Lady* thing."

When George Hayward died, his entrepreneurial metabolism may have finally begun to slow. He was, according to Alice, spending increasing amounts of time at his desk and in meetings, rather than on his feet in either of his stores or his restaurant, and I wondered what effect those changes had had on his temper. Moreover, the bigger and more diverse his retail kingdom had become, the more difficult it must have been to manage. To rule. To control. He had three very different enterprises. And so, perhaps, over the years he had grown more determined to have absolute sway over Alice. I tried to hear in my head what sort of voice he had used with his employees and how it might have differed in tone from when he was alone with his wife. Publicly he had always seemed rather likable. But in point of fact he was—and even ministers have these sorts of thoughts, though we seldom verbalize them—petty and cruel and thoroughly nasty. I am honestly not sure in whose image he was made.

"And Alice's voice? What do you recall about hers?" Heather asked.

There is much that I could have told her about Alice Hayward's voice. I could have described how silky and low it would become in a murmur in bed, or the vibrato it took on when she cried. One of the times when she was in my office—this was before I had crossed the Rubicon into her bed—her voice grew eerily even, almost clinical, when she was explaining to me the source of the chiaroscuro of yellow and hyacinth on her cheek. Most of the congregation accepted her claim that she had walked into an open medicine-cabinet door in the bathroom in the night. She had a swimmer's body, and sometimes, when we were alone, she would sound to me like she had a swimmer's voice: a bit throaty, occasionally hoarse, always a little more fragile than her lovely physique. *Remind me who I am,* she said to me one of our first mornings together in her and her husband's bed. *Sometimes I can't believe I'm the sort of woman who gets to have a lover.* I found the word *gets* powerfully endearing, as if I were a prize and adultery a privilege. She was blossoming, and I soaked in her every word.

With Heather, however, I shared none of that. I wasn't yet prepared to reveal the secrets I knew of my most recent lover. Instead

I answered with an evasiveness that people later would say marked so much of my behavior that summer and was emblematic of a dangerous character flaw. A desiccated soul, an arctic heart. In hindsight, I should have told Heather something. Anything. I would have been better off that moment and, I imagine, in the months that followed. But I said nothing.

And when I look back on that Sunday, I should have seen the parallels between that elderly deacon and Heather Laurent—or, for that matter, between Heather and any of the people I had met in my life who had had about them the penumbra of an angel. But on that morning, a week to the day since the Haywards had died, I was far more focused on the dark of the world than I was on the light. I knew what had occurred seven days earlier in the Cape on the hill, and it seemed to me that if there was an otherworldly element residing somewhere deep inside each of our spirits or cores, it was far more likely to be demonic.

THE IDEA THAT I was fleeing was ridiculous. It was absurd in that I answered my cell phone each and every time it rang—at least when I had it with me—and it was absurd in that I was traveling with a reasonably recognizable woman. (Yes, I know a writer is seldom as famous as a movie star: If Angelina Jolie wanders into a library, the fans and the media will swarm; if Margaret Atwood wanders into a cineplex, the lines for the popcorn barely will waver.)

I hadn't told my mother where I was going, because I honestly hadn't known myself when I left Bronxville. The same is true in regard to the Pastoral-Relations Committee and the deacons at the church in Haverill. Likewise, Heather hadn't known at the time that she would go visit her sister in upstate New York, bringing with her in tow a minister who wasn't sure what he should be doing with his life or what it had meant that he had baptized a woman a half day before she would be strangled. I was quite content in Heather's bed in her loft. She was, too, I believe, after all the traveling she had done in the preceding months. But whatever need she had to cocoon and replenish her (and I will use one of her words here) aura, it was subsumed by her worry about Amanda and her concern for that basket case of a pastor from Vermont. And so we disappeared into the Adirondacks.

And while it is tempting to express some understanding for the appalling ways that Catherine Benincasa or reporters or bloggers would misinterpret my movements—to begin a sentence with *Still* or *Nevertheless*—that would be disingenuous. The truth is, I don't understand it. And though many people believe I am anything but forthright, in the end I was more candid than I wanted to be or expected to be or was even obliged to be. I know my crimes and I know my mistakes. I live with them.

But I also know that whatever else I may have done (or, worse, failed to do), I positively did not flee. It honestly hadn't crossed my mind that there might be a need.

Of course, none of us ever knows as much as we think we do. None of us. If there is a lesson to be learned from my fall—notice I did not say my rise and fall, because it's not as if the ascent to the pulpit of a country church represents an especially glorious accomplishment— it is this: Believe no one. Trust no one. Assume no one really knows anything that matters at all. Because, alas, we don't. All of our stories are suspect.

PART II

Catherine Benincasa

CHAPTER SEVEN

My husband is a great guy. It doesn't take a dirtball like George Hayward or Stephen Drew for me to see that. I think those two have a lot more in common than the reverend ever would be willing to admit.

But that's the thing about men like that. Total denial. Everyone talks about how a battered woman has a complete unwillingness to admit to herself what's really going on in her life, and I can tell you that the river Denial is indeed pretty freaking wide in the minds of a lot of those victims. The worst, for me, are those cases where some boyfriend or stepfather is abusing the woman's daughters, and when we finally charge the bastard—when the daughter finally comes forward—the woman defends the guy! Takes his side! Insists her own kid must be making this up or exaggerating. Trust me: No twelve-year-old girl exaggerates when Mom's boyfriend makes her do things to him with her mouth.

And, clearly, Alice Hayward was no stranger to denial herself. When I returned to my office that Monday after viewing the mess up in Haverill, I learned that Alice had gotten a temporary relief-from-abuse order that winter. Had managed to kick her husband's ornery ass out of the house and—somehow—gotten him to go live for a couple of months at their place on Lake Bomoseen. And then, like so many battered women, had taken him back. Hadn't even shown up for the hearing a week after the papers were served.

But the men's rationalizations are even worse. They'll curl your hair.

Now, Stephen Drew wasn't using some poor woman's face as a floor sander, and he wasn't inflicting himself on some defenseless middle-school girl. (Note I am not being catty and adding "as far as we know." Because, in my opinion, we do know: He wasn't.) But he certainly abused his place and his power, and he sure as hell took advantage of women in his congregation. For a minister, the guy had ice in his veins. Lived completely alone, didn't even have a dog or a cat. He really creeped me out once when he went off on this riff about the Crucifixion as a form of execution. Very scholarly, but later it was clear that even his lawyer had wished he'd dialed down the serial-killer vibe.

And he was, like a lot of the real wife beaters, a great self-deluder.

And, perhaps, a great actor.

That morning I met him, he told me how he'd baptized Alice Hayward the day before and how he should have seen this coming from something she'd said when she came out of the water. I couldn't decide whether he was overintellectualizing the fact that there was a dead woman in her nightgown on the floor and a dead guy with half a face on the couch, or whether he was so completely in shock that he was finding reasons to feel guilty himself. It wasn't like *he* had strangled the woman. It wasn't like *he* had shot the creep on the sofa.

Shows you what I know.

It was one of my associates, David Dennison, who first questioned what really had occurred at the Haywards' the night they both died.

David is the medical examiner. He's tall and scholarly-looking, and his hair is almost translucently white. His eyes are sunken, a little sad even, but he's a very funny guy. I've worked with three pathologists in two states, and I've learned that most MEs are pretty witty. I think if you're going to do that for a living, you have to appreciate black humor. He's also an excellent witness, and as a prosecutor I need that in an ME. Cop shows on TV have ruined me: I don't dare put a dull guy on the stand if I want to keep a jury awake.

In addition, David is a total control freak, and I want that, too. I have seen him go up to a person at a crime scene who is clearly there for the first time and politely take their hands and put their fingers together as if they're praying. The last thing he wants—the last thing any of us want—is for someone to accidentally screw up a key piece of evidence by touching it.

David didn't say much to any of us that Monday morning we all converged on Haverill. His office is up in Burlington, a good two and a half hours away, but he got to the crime scene by lunchtime. Everyone from the village was either somber or stunned, but the few words I overheard him exchange with Drew were collegial and about as pleasant as one could hope for. Drew, like many of the people who eventually wind up as suspects, was very, very helpful. He told us lots about the Haywards—about both George and Alice. After all, he'd been providing some counsel for Alice. (That was actually what he said to me: "I offered her some counsel." It was only later that we'd figure out that a hell of a lot of that "counsel" had been between the sheets.) And he was a real scrubber. He donned those rubber gloves and just went to town on the gore in one corner of the room. (In the days that followed, this also would strike me as a tad suspicious.) He was a cool customer, not the sort of person I would have expected to panic suddenly and flee.

In any case, it was David's preliminary autopsy report that caused me to sit up in my office chair and reassess in my mind what had occurred. According to David, the cause of death for Alice was precisely what we all had assumed: strangulation. The manner was homicide. Aspects of George's death, however, were a little murky: Though the cause was still that gunshot wound to the head, David had not cited the manner as suicide. Instead he had typed in that single word that would help trigger the whole investigation: *pending*. In his opinion there were factors in George's death that left him wondering, and his report suggested that homicide was a possibility. In other words, it was conceivable that someone other than George had pulled the trigger of the gun that Sunday night—and, likewise, that someone other than George could have strangled Alice. It wasn't likely, in that bits of George's skin were under Alice's fingernails and it was clear that she had scratched the hell out of his face. But people are bizarre. For a time I kept open the possibility that George and Alice had fought violently but it was a third (or fourth) person who had murdered Alice.

The first red flag for the ME was George Hayward's head wound. When a person decides to put a bullet into his brain, he tends to press the barrel against the temple. At the hairline, usually. Or, if the gun is not actually touching the skin, it's still pretty close: A suicide is either a contact or a near-contact wound. Besides, a person's forearm is only so long; you really can't aim a gun at your temple from a distance of greater than six or seven inches, and most suicides bring the gun a lot closer than that. The result is that most of the powder is driven into the skin and there is a dense deposit of soot. When a pathologist washes away that soot, he is likely to find abrasions and stippling, all those burning bits of powder embedding themselves into the flesh. The farther the gun is held from the bullet's point of entry, the less pronounced those marks will be. In David's opinion the bullet that killed George Hayward was certainly not a contact wound and—based on the negligible amounts of powder and stippling and soot—not even particularly close. The gun might have been fired from as much as a few feet away.

Second, there was the pattern of the blood and bone and brain that had sprayed the living room: the remains that people like the Reverend Drew and Alice's best friend had cleaned up on the screen and the china cabinet, and had tried and failed to remove from the couch. David thought it was possible that the spatter was the result of a bullet pulverizing the skull in a suicide. But from the moment he had entered that room, he told me later, a part of him had wondered at the angle.

Finally there was George Hayward's right hand. There was residue on it from the gunshot, but not a lot. And while no one puts a great deal of stock in gunshot residue these days, he still thought there might have been more if Hayward had indeed pulled the trigger. (The fact that there were traces meant nothing: In a small room, residue can be anywhere once a gun is discharged.)

Toxicology—the blood and urine tests—would take two or three weeks, but David suggested that a lot more could be inferred right now with another look at the gun. Just how severe was the blowback? Or, to be blunt, how much of the bastard's brains were up the gun barrel? (Make no mistake: Though it seemed possible now that George Hayward was a murder victim, he was still a complete and total bastard.) David also suggested that after the weapon had been examined, someone in the crime lab should conduct a series of test fires with the same load to offer a baseline on the stippling it was likely to elicit. Once we did that, we could get a fairly precise sense of the distance the gun had been from Hayward's temple.

Now, none of this would have led me to start wondering what sort of involvement Stephen Drew might have had with the deaths of either George or Alice Hayward if the guy hadn't gotten out of Dodge the second the bodies had been shipped to New York and New Hampshire for burial. Had he stuck around, it might have taken considerably longer before any of us in the state's attorney's office would have turned our eyes upon the local pastor. One of my associates, for instance, conjectured that the murders might have been an attempt to cover up a robbery and the burglar had known of George's history of domestic abuse. In other words, someone had murdered the pair of them and then made it look like it was George's handiwork. And there was also the possibility this was all some sort of horrible thrill killing, not unlike the 2001 murders of two Dartmouth College professors in their own home: Perhaps someone had strangled Alice while George had watched and then offed him. But why make that look like something it wasn't? And when the house once more was viewed as a crime scene and thoroughly investigated, there was no indication that anything had been stolen and no reason to believe that either of the Haywards or their teenage daughter had had some sort of secret life as a drug dealer.

What we did find, however, were a variety of clues that Alice Hayward had been receiving more than mere pastoral counsel from that minister who'd fled Haverill hours after conducting her funeral service.

AFTER I READ the autopsy report for the first time, I rang David Dennison. He was expecting the call.

"I had a feeling the word *pending* would pique your interest," he said.

"Are you just trying to make my caseload completely suck? The Hayward mess wasn't supposed to have any effing complications."

"Has anyone told you that you have the mouth of a teenager?"

"Teenagers don't say *effing*. No censorship there. And Paul says

I sound more like a sailor, thank you very much. And he spends his life around teenagers: I think if I sounded like one, he would have told me by now."

"So what do you think?"

"I think it all seemed so simple when we were at the house that day."

"It did look nice and neat."

I glimpsed once more the photos of Alice Hayward that had been taken at the scene. Her eyes, starved for air, were bulging, the whites dotted with burst blood vessels, and her mouth was forever fixed in a rictus of agony and fear. "No it didn't, David. It looked horrible."

"You know what I mean," he said, his voice not really defensive. Then he shared with me his suspicions about what might in fact have occurred, given the way portions of George Hayward's brain were sprinkled liberally across the wall and the couch. When he was done, he added, "And I expect more serious questions when we get back the blood and urine work in another week or two."

"What do you think the lab will find?"

"That George Hayward was too drunk to kill himself. This is all preliminary, of course, but I wouldn't be surprised if as many as four hours separated the two deaths."

"You're kidding."

"Good God, did you count the beer bottles?"

"I did."

"The guy smelled like a frat basement on a Saturday morning."

"I tried to avoid fraternity basements, thank you very much."

"And his dinner was all but digested. Mush. Hers? I could have counted the string beans and peas. So here's one scenario. He strangles her around eight or eight-thirty. Then, filled with remorse or panic, he drinks. Well, drinks some more. A lot more. And finally he passes out. Then, around midnight, someone shoots him."

"Sounds a little far-fetched."

"Wait till we have the blood-alcohol numbers. I wouldn't be surprised if we're talking the neighborhood of point-three or more. Alcohol poisoning. I wouldn't be surprised if it turns out he was flirting with lethal."

"But you can't be that precise on the times of death. Plus or minus two hours, they both could have died around ten," I said.

"Possible. But gastric emptying time is about four hours. People lie, but stomachs don't. Assuming they ate dinner together—say, seven or seven-fifteen—she's dead before eight-thirty. Him? Could be closer to midnight."

"Of course, if Hayward was that drunk, it's also possible that he didn't kill Alice, either."

"Well, yes," he agreed, and I didn't have to verbalize what both of us were thinking. Sometimes none of us has the slightest idea what really goes on in a house when the shades are drawn and the doors are closed. There are the postmortem realities—how a body decomposes or cools to room temperature, how it stiffens or putrefies or lets loose with one last bowel movement—but what that body was doing in the moments before it died is often unfathomable. And, in the case of a homicide, often freakish and weird. There might have been things going on in that Cape that were emphatically beyond our wildest conjectures and people passing through whose presence would have astonished the neighbors.

And passing through with the Haywards' welcome complicity: There had been no indications of forced entry at the house on the hill. The doors were unlocked, and the windows—though filled with screens—were open.

Yet we did know this: George Hayward would beat the living crap out of his wife when the spirit moved him. That pastor had said so, that pal named Ginny had said so, and the couple's one kid, the teenage girl, had said so. And this meant that whoever had killed the one or the both of them had been aware of George Hayward's nasty little hobby. When we found Alice's body, her rear end and lower back were flecked with two- and three-day-old contusions and welts, which meant that George had beaten her the weekend she was baptized. David said her kidneys were so badly bruised that she'd probably been peeing blood on the day that she died.

"Had she had sex that day?" I asked. "Consenting or otherwise?"

"No indications. No semen in the vagina."

"Well. At least it isn't a rape."

"Small consolation when you've been strangled."

"True."

"And I do think George murdered Alice."

"You do?"

"Absolutely. His skin was under her fingernails. Those are her scratch marks on the left side of his face."

"Well, then," I said, "I think I should send an investigator to Haverill, don't you? I think I should have someone go shake some trees."

"I agree."

A few days later, we would all be wondering where the pastor had gone and why he wasn't answering his cell phone.

JIM HAAS HAD been the state's attorney for the county before I arrived, and my sense was that he would be the state's attorney after I had moved on. He was no longer the prodigy he'd been ten years ago, when, in his mid-thirties, he had rooted out the drug dealers from Albany and the Bronx who were snaking their way into the county high schools, and convicted the Arlington novelist who had murdered his wife and tried to make it appear as if it had been a random home robbery and slaying. I had just arrived after working for two years in the prosecutor's office in Concord, New Hampshire, and I had been impressed as hell with Jim's first accomplishment. But the second? Oh, please. I can count on one hand the number of women in northern New England who were killed in my lifetime in random home robberies. We all know women are often murdered by the men who profess to love them the most. But Jim really enjoyed leading our small office and mentoring younger lawyers like me, and he savored the strange currents that seemed to waft through Bennington and southwestern Vermont. We had our extremely funky, always-a-little-goth college just outside the city; there was that great New England world-weariness that comes from being a mill town that no longer has a whole lot of industry—which made us a bit like Pittsfield and Albany, our urban neighbors across the state lines; and there was the reality that we were surrounded by iconic little Green Mountain hamlets filled with longtime locals and second-home interlopers from Manhattan, Westchester, and Fairfield County.

When I went by Jim's office to brief him on the Hayward case, the mayor had just left and I could tell that Jim was basking in the reality that the mayor had come here rather than expecting Jim to come to him. I considered reminding him that Mayor Peter Grafton liked meeting the people at the Blue Benn Diner while chowing down on the corned beef hash, and our office was between the Blue Benn and his. Peter had probably met with Jim on his way into town and still had egg on his breath.

That morning Jim was wearing the sort of microfiber blazer that looks very good on razor-thin male models but was stretched a bit like Saran Wrap on a guy as stocky as Jim. He isn't overweight—he's actually pretty handsome, with clear green eyes that I've seen him use to great effect on female jurors and a mane of dark brown hair that has only recently started to thin—but if I were to guess, I'd say he carried around close to 220 pounds on a frame of roughly six feet.

"You know," he said, sitting down behind an Empire desk the size of a mini golf green and motioning me toward the chair beside it rather than opposite it, "already I'm hearing from politicians who see an opportunity in this nightmare. City councilors. State legislators. I hate politicians."

"No you don't. You love them, Jim. You are one."

"Let me rephrase that: I hate it when politicians try to exploit something tragic for their own gain. I hate it when they try to grandstand."

"Me, too."

"Already there are people planning to campaign on this. Use violence against women as part of their platform—but with absolutely no specifics, no program, no plan."

"At least they'll be against it."

"How can you joke like that? You're a woman!"

"That's precisely how I can. Because I am a woman."

"It's like when that patient hanged himself at the state psychiatric hospital. Suddenly every politician wanted a new director. A new hospital. New ways of caring for the mentally ill. There was chaos and noise, and in the end absolutely nothing changed."

"I remember."

"Now they'll make it sound like it's the state's attorney's job to prevent domestic abuse."

"Jim—"

"They'll want to set up task forces. They'll want hearings. Legislation. At least this one is easy for us. Cut and dried—and I promise you, I would not have used that expression just now if George Hayward had used a knife."

"Jim?"

"Go ahead."

"David doesn't think George Hayward killed himself."

He rocked forward in the great palm of his leather chair. "What?"

And so I told him about the head wound and the ME's conjecture. I shared with him the possibility that if George Hayward had not shot himself, then it was—at least for the moment—conceivable that he had not strangled Alice, either.

"There's someone else?" he asked, a slight catch of dryness in his throat. That was it.

"Apparently. But at this point all I'm telling you is that George Hayward may not have been a suicide."

He sighed, and I imagined he was contemplating all of the ways I had just complicated his life, and how so much of his small office's resources were about to be committed to what had seemed, just a few minutes ago, a relatively simple domestic cataclysm.

MY HUSBAND TEACHES earth science and chemistry at the high school in Bennington, and he is worshipped by his students. Every third graduating class seems to dedicate the yearbook to him, and he is constantly lampooned in their variety shows—but in ways that make it clear he is more beloved than spring break. Once when I was helping him chaperone a dance, half the senior girls viewed me as some haglike interloper. One literally asked me who I was and what I was doing there. She asked me how I knew Mr. Ribner. *Well, he's my husband,* I answered politely. *How do you know Paul?* The boys revere him, too, especially the soccer players. He played soccer through college, and the high-school soccer team now has something of a reputation as a powerhouse in the state. They've been state champs four times in the six years that he's coached the team.

Sometimes after our own boys are in bed (which is always a major production, because one is three and one is six, and they are both relentlessly energetic), we will be comparing notes on our day. He will be talking about some refugee kid—a student with nothing—who's raised some incredible sum of money in the walkathon for the local homeless shelter and also happens to be a spectacular forward, and I will be telling him about (for example) some minister in Haverill who was fucking some battered woman he was supposed to be counseling and then took justice into his own hands and shot her husband.

I'm no biblical scholar, but even I know who has the final say when it comes to justice and revenge, and it isn't the local pastor. Weeks later one of the Vermont newspapers would christen Drew the "Vigilante Reverend," but I always thought that implied there was more fire in the guy's soul than was actually there. It also, it seemed to me, gave the guy a veneer of likability he didn't deserve.

Of course, I seem to be an exception among women. Obviously Alice Hayward saw something in him. So did Heather Laurent. And I'm confident there were other women in Haverill, too, and someday they'll come forward. Even now there are rumors and suspicions and no small amount of whispering. But he's certainly not my type: He's almost too pretty. His hair is too perfect. And the camera just loves him. Those first pictures of him in the newspaper that Tuesday morning? We're talking the dad in a J. Crew catalog.

Still, I honestly didn't see Drew as a suspect at first, even when David suggested that George Hayward might have been murdered. It was only when one of the original investigators, Emmet Walker, went back to nose around Haverill the week after the funeral and learned that Drew had left town that I began to wonder. Emmet, along with a younger trooper named Andy Sullivan, stopped by the church. The secretary there introduced them to some old fellow named Gavin who said he was filling in as pastor until Drew either returned or decided that he would never be able to. Both Gavin—whose full name was Gavin Muir Maxwell, as solid a name as you can find, in my opinion, for a retired Baptist minister who works now as a sort of substitute teacher for shepherdless flocks—and the church secretary were talkative. They reported that Drew had left Thursday evening, the night of Alice Hayward's funeral, and that he had said he wasn't sure where he was going. But the secretary, a lovely woman named Betsy Storrs, who I practically want to make my new godmother (my actual godmother is long dead), told Emmet that she saw the reverend's passport on his desk before he went into the sanctuary to conduct Alice Hayward's service, and the day before that she had heard him on the phone trying to find out the limits on his Visa and MasterCard.

"Did you see him remove any papers from his office?" Emmet had asked.

"We have a lot of state secrets here," Betsy had replied solemnly. "Next to Los Alamos, there are more important documents here than anywhere in the country."

"So he didn't take anything?"

"Of course he took things," she said, shaking her head, and she showed him how the pastor's personal drawer in the gray metal filing cabinet was now only half full. "The fact he took his passport and so many of his personal papers is why I don't expect him back anytime soon. I am telling you, he was very, very shaken by this. This hit him in a way that caught all of us completely off guard. I thought I knew Stephen well—at least as well as anyone in this town—but I'm telling you, I never saw this one coming."

Emmet didn't think she was angry. But he was confident that she thought the minister held his cards very, very close to his chest.

FROM *ANGELS AND AURASCAPES*
BY HEATHER LAURENT (P. 119)

My sense is that angels come to us: We don't come to them. We don't so-licit them, we don't ask for them—though, certainly, we may address prayers in their direction. But we don't knock, because, after all, we would be knock-ing on air—on aura. Their presence, however, is undeniable in my mind, and when we need them, they may appear without fanfare at our front doors. They are watching. And it will always be a source of wonder to me how often we miss the obviousness of their arrival, mistaking them for a neighbor or family or friend.

Or stranger.

Too often we presume that the unexpected strangers in our lives bode ill, or we are skeptical of their designs. We think we know more.

And while I am well aware that there is indeed all manner of malevo-lence in the ether, there is benevolence there, too. And just as there is random horror—murder, suicide, child abuse, car accidents, disease, famine, war, ethnic cleansing—there is also indiscriminate kindness. Not merely miracles, though I have experienced them. But simple human connection, either bro-kered by an angel or sourced by one. That is why I try to encourage people to be receptive to that new person who seems to have appeared in their life out of nowhere.

CHAPTER EIGHT

When I was a kid, I used to pull down a trapdoor in the ceiling hallway along the second floor of my grandparents' house and climb up into the attic. I did it all the time when I was seven and eight years old, because my grandparents lived only about fifteen miles away, and so my family was visiting them all the time. I wasn't supposed to be up there, but when my parents were having coffee with them after dinner or brunch or sitting in their backyard on these ancient wooden lawn chairs that must have weighed as much as a small car, it's where I would go. My brother and sister never joined me. When they were there, too, they'd park themselves in front of the TV. What was up there that interested me so much? Old magazines. My grandfather— my mom's father—had been an editor for *Vermont Life,* and he had boxes of dusty copies of that magazine, as well as plenty of *Time* and *Life* and *True Detective.* Sometimes I would try to entice my brother to join me by making a very big deal about some vaguely provocative photos of Marilyn Monroe I'd found in an old *Life* and some even more suggestive photos of female hippies at Woodstock in an issue of *Time*. But he never took the bait, and so I was always up there alone.

By dragging a small upholstered easy chair from my grandparents' bedroom to a spot just below the trapdoor, I was able to stretch just enough to reach the cord that opened it. Attached to the door were a series of clunky wooden steps, and they always reminded me of the basement stairs at my own family's house. The attic had windows along three of its walls, and so even though there was no electricity up there, there was enough light to thumb through the old magazines and look at the pictures. I would usually sit on an old rocking horse with pretend stirrups because I was afraid there were mice up there and I didn't want my feet touching the floor, and I would read what I could understand and simply study the pictures beside those articles that either bored me or were way over my head. Obviously, most of what I came across was way over my head.

But the articles that I believe I spent the most time with—and the ones that have stayed with me ever since—were the ones about violent crime in New York and San Francisco and Miami, Florida. Stories about husbands who murdered their wives, drug dealers who machine-gunned federal agents, serial killers who had children buried in their basements and backyards. Scared the crap out of me—but I was totally fascinated. My grandfather's *Vermont Life*s with their pictures of bright red barns and rustic sugarhouses? Those stories about apple orchards and fiddlers and ice fishing? They were of less interest to me at that age. So there I was some Sunday afternoons in a velvet dress and crimson tights, my hair no doubt in a ponytail, studying black-and-white photos that would have made Weegee proud. Who can say what drew me to that sort of thing so early on, but I couldn't keep away. When I'd had enough—when I was almost *too* scared—I'd run like a racehorse out of there. I couldn't wait to rejoin my siblings by the TV or my parents outside in the sun.

Later, when Paul and I were dating and the relationship was growing serious, I brought him to that house to meet my grandmother. (My grandfather had passed away years earlier.) While we were there, I brought him upstairs to the attic and showed him the magazines—ostensibly so he could see the issues of *Vermont Life* that my grandfather had worked on. My grandmother was going to be selling the house soon, and she surprised me by asking me if I wanted the magazines. Not the *Vermont Life*s, which she said were going to the state historical society. The issues of *Time* and *Life* and *True Detective*. I passed. But to this day I have no idea how she knew that I was attracted to them.

AT BREAKFAST MY boys can be holy freaking terrors. Not every day, but often enough that Paul once put a shower curtain on the kitchen floor beneath their chairs to try to make a point. Another time I made them eat their cereal without milk—no fluids at all in the bowls—for a week. Yup, I'm the mom who punished her kids by denying them milk. Very nice, I know. I can just see the headlines when the Department for Children and Families comes to take them away. The problem is that Lionel, my three-year-old, drives Marcus, my first-grader, crazy because he doesn't understand why the other males in the house get to go to school and he doesn't.

"Toddler Town is just like a school," Marcus will tell him patiently, a real little diplomat, but Lionel somehow sees a big difference between his day care and his brother's elementary school and Paul's high school. And so either he will take his cereal spoon and smash it into Marcus's bowl so it catapults the Cocoa Fobs or Pepperoni Clusters (or whatever presweetened nightmare we're feeding them that day) into the air or he will use his fingers like a shovel and start scooping the stuff out onto the table as if he's trying to build a sand castle with his bare hands on Cape Cod. And, of course, Paul and I are trying to get out the door—and get the two boys out the door—and that only adds to the chaos.

The Haywards were murdered at the end of July, and so in the days when the investigation was starting to ramp up, Lionel had his usual Toddler Town, Marcus had a summer day camp called Kid-Friendly Arts or (I swear, I am not making this up) K-FARTS for short. No one officially associated with the organization ever calls it that, and the letterhead and materials never use that acronym, but all of the parents refer to it with that enticing little shorthand. Apparently the organization is in the process of changing its name. In any case, the timing of the murder of the Haywards meant that Paul and I didn't have to get the boys to school, but most mornings we still had to move things along at breakfast. Usually Paul would drop the boys off at Toddler Town and K-FARTS, since he didn't have to be anywhere ever in the summer (no, I'm not bitter). One morning in August when Emmet called, I was in the midst of sponging off the kitchen table and making sure there wasn't visual evidence of the crap I feed my kids on their mouths. He was on his cell, and he wanted to know if I had reviewed the papers and the materials he'd left at my office the day before. I hadn't, because I'd left work a little early to take a deposition in a case involving a drunken speedboat driver and a water-skier who—as a result of the driver's recklessly downing margaritas on the dock—was never going to water-ski or walk again.

When I think about how I spend most of each day, it's a wonder I ever let my kids out of my sight.

"Well, it's all pretty interesting," Emmet said.

"Oh?"

"We brought back a carton of stuff for the crime lab. But the main thing I wanted to tell you is this: Alice Hayward kept a journal. It's one of those books with blank pages that really isn't much bigger than an address book. As a matter of fact, that's what I thought it was when

I found it—though I didn't understand at first why an address book would be way in the back of the woman's underwear drawer. But as soon as I opened it up, I knew what it was."

"She talks about her husband?"

"She does, and it's fascinating. Once in a while, you can almost see what she saw in him. I mean, he was a louse. A complete and total louse. But he wasn't always bashing her around the house. And after he did, man, was he contrite."

"That is the pattern. He might have been a nice guy some of the time, but I promise you, it was only after he'd whacked her somewhere."

"He wrote her poetry. Not my cup of tea, and I have no idea if it's any good. But it sounds very loving. I can see how he convinced her to take him back. But here's the really interesting part: George Hayward isn't the only man in it. You know who else she writes about?"

"Tell me."

"That minister who lit out of town. Stephen Drew. At least I think it's Stephen. There was something going on there."

"You *think* it's Stephen?"

"There's no name, just a code. She draws a little cross where you'd expect to find a name. So the journal is like, 'cross said this' or 'cross and I did that.'"

"And it's not a *t*?"

"Definitely not. The first time she used it, she made it pretty ornate."

"Well, he was her minister. He told us they would talk a lot. It's why he was so broken up about her death."

"I think there was more to it than that."

"How much more?"

"A lot."

"As in they were sleeping together?"

"I got that vibe. To wit, here's one of the passages from the diary I scribbled in my notes: 'Cross's hair reminds me these days of Christmas. It always has the aroma of evergreen.'"

"But she never comes right out and says they were sleeping together."

"Not in the pages I skimmed. But she was probably afraid that her husband might find the book, and so there's nothing definitively incriminating in it."

"A cross isn't real subtle. If she had something to hide, she wasn't real clever."

"I agree. But listen to this one: 'Day off, Katie with friends. Cross and I spent hours together today. Very peaceful, very quiet. What to do?'"

For a long second, I thought about that one. "What's the date?"

"March twenty-ninth."

"That was long after she had gotten the relief-from-abuse order and George was living on the lake."

"Take a look at the journal. You'll see what I mean," Emmet said. "Here's another one I wrote down: 'Cross here. Didn't leave the house for hours and hours. Heavenly.'"

Paul was in the kitchen, too, but he didn't know who I was on the phone with. Still, he would tell me later that my eyes went very wide and for a moment the tip of my tongue rested just at the edge of my lips. He has mimicked the look for me before and calls it my "savanna glare." He says it's the look I get when I'm seriously into the hunt and the prey has just stumbled big-time in the grass.

IT HAD THE potential to be a fascinating case to construct. On the one hand, it was going to be embarrassingly easy—a slam dunk—to show that Stephen Drew and his hair with the aroma of the church

Christmas tree was sleeping with Alice Hayward. Later, when we dusted the whole Hayward house for fingerprints, we found what would turn out to be Drew's all over the bedroom, including the very top of the headboard. We found them on the nightstand and in the kitchen on wineglasses. We found his DNA in body hair in the shower drain in the master bathroom, and we determined that a piece of pubic hair in the bottom of the hamper belonged to the reverend. We found fibers from his living-room throw rug in the carpet of the Haywards' bedroom.

On the other hand, it was going to take some serious investigation to prove that he had gone to the Cape on the hill that Sunday night in July and shot George Hayward in the head.

Drew had had his weekly meeting with the church Youth Group that evening, and the gathering had lasted until a few minutes after nine. When he finally reemerged after fleeing, he told us that he had gone home to the parsonage as soon as that meeting was over. He insisted he hadn't gone anywhere near the Haywards' house that night— and we had nothing to link him to the murder itself. The only prints on the gun, the load, or the gun cabinet were George's—though some on the handle and one on the trigger were badly smudged, which was important, because it thus seemed possible that a second person had handled the firearm after George. There was no indication that Drew's car had been in the gravel driveway that night and no tracks that matched any of his shoes on the lawn—at least none that remained by the time we realized that Drew should be considered a suspect. We could see from Drew's Internet service provider that he'd been on-line from nine-fifteen until ten-thirty, answering e-mails and surfing the Web, but we would need a court order—or his laptop, which later we would subpoena—to learn the sites and Web pages he had visited. Then, he insisted, he had gone to bed. I was hoping that Alice might have called him earlier in the evening—battered women often seem to phone someone close to them just before their boyfriend or husband blows for the last time—but there was no evidence that she had.

And yet he had disappeared a few days after what was looking more and more like two homicides, rather than a suicide and a single murder. That was what kept coming back to me. The guy was a friggin' minister, and he'd jumped ship at the time when the town needed him most. That really got to me—that and the teeny-tiny detail that he was boffing a parishioner who would be murdered.

FOR NEARLY A week, from a Wednesday till the following Monday, none of us had the slightest idea where the good reverend had gone. No one in Haverill knew, and his own mother said that she hadn't seen him since the previous Saturday morning. We left messages everywhere, including on his cell phone. I'd been thinking all along about the fact that the church secretary had noticed his passport on his desk the morning of the funeral, and so on Friday I sent a fax to the State Department to see if he had left the country. He wasn't officially a suspect at that point—though unofficially in my mind he sure as hell was—but we certainly wanted to talk to him.

And he hadn't left the country. Hadn't even boarded an airplane and flown anywhere domestically.

Which meant, if he was on the move, that he was probably traveling somewhere in his car. (I didn't completely discount the idea that he might have paid cash for a bus ticket, but somehow the patrician Pastor Drew didn't strike me as the sort who would mingle with the bus-station crowd.) And while this is a big country, it's really not that difficult to find someone on wheels. There are the credit-card receipts at gas stations or the cash withdrawals from ATMs or the reality that there are a lot of cops and troopers out there on the road. I had heard back from the State Department on Monday and was wondering if it was time to put out a bulletin on the reverend when, lo and behold, he finally returned one of Emmet's calls. And as soon as Emmet hung up with Drew, he called me. It was midafternoon, and I was in my office.

"We have contact," he said, his voice so deep and refined that he always sounded oddly plumy to me for a Vermonter. I attributed that to the reality that Emmet was all business. Some people mistook the crispness that was a part of his demeanor as a state trooper for coldness. Usually that served him well, but not always. The reality is that he was tall and lean, his nose was a wedge, and his close-cropped hair was the dark gray of ash in a woodstove: He could be an intimidating presence when he wanted.

"Really?"

"I just got off the phone with him."

"And? Did he have an explanation for why he fell off the radar—or why he wouldn't call back?"

"He said he hoped we didn't think he was avoiding us."

"Now, why would we think that? Because no one in the world had the slightest idea where he was—"

"He was in—"

"Because he didn't return any of the messages you left at his home, his church, or on his cell phone?"

"He was in the Adirondacks. That was his explanation. He said he went with a friend to upstate New York for a couple of days and he was in some rugged corner of the mountains without cell-phone coverage."

"He was camping? He didn't strike me as the type."

"No, he wasn't camping. But he was in what he described as a relatively primitive log cabin."

"In the Adirondacks . . ."

"Near Statler."

"Never heard of it."

"No reason you would have," he said. "It's a general store and a billboard, apparently."

"And there's no cell coverage there?"

"Nope."

"He didn't check his messages at home? He didn't call in to the church?"

"No, he did not. He said he was calling me back from the interstate, an hour or so from Albany—though he wasn't coming home. He was heading to New York City. His cell showed he had messages, and so he was returning the calls from the highway."

I sat back in my chair and took a sip from the water bottle on my desk. I raised my eyebrows to try to relax. "Is he alone? I don't recall him having any personal Adirondack connections."

"He says he's with that friend. He added that she was driving."

"So you knew he was a responsible driver, I suppose."

"I suppose."

"What's her name?"

He paused for a moment, and in my mind I saw him looking down at his notes. "Heather Laurent," he answered finally.

"You're kidding."

"Why? Should I know that name?"

"Well, *you* shouldn't. You have a penis. But women love her books. She writes bestsellers about angels. Frankly, I think she's a complete and total lunatic. Remember when I was so sick last month with bronchitis and I stayed home? I saw her on one of the morning talk shows going on and on about her latest book. And maybe it was because I was oxygen-deprived and half delusional from the medication, but I swear I thought she was talking about angels like they were our freaking neighbors."

"Well, he's a minister. I would think angels would give them something to talk about."

"Yeah, I'm thinking no. My sense is her take on angels isn't exactly going to mesh with his. She's somewhere between New Age and wack job. Her angels, I have a feeling, find you parking spaces when you need one. What did he say about her?"

"Really very little."

"I think she was in Vermont a couple weeks ago. I vaguely remember something in the newspaper."

"Mostly I asked Drew about his relationship with Alice and George Hayward," he said, and then he told me in detail what he had learned—and what Drew wouldn't reveal. Emmet is a pro, and so he didn't let on that we had reason to believe from Alice's journal that either she had one hell of a fantasy life or she and Drew were more intimately involved than anyone knew. And Drew stuck to a pretty simple story: Alice was one of his parishioners, George was not, and he'd offered Alice pastoral counseling.

"Would you say you two were friends?" Emmet said he had asked, and Drew had replied, "Absolutely. We were very good friends." The detective then inquired whether the minister could recall the last time he'd been to the Haywards' house, and Emmet said there was a pause and he had wondered whether Drew was deciding whether to admit he'd ever been there. In the end he told the detective he'd been there most recently in, Drew believed, May—other, of course, than the Monday after the Haywards had been murdered. At that point he had asked Emmet why we were looking for him.

"Oh, we're just tying up loose ends," Emmet had replied. But he did ask the minister whether he was returning to Haverill anytime soon and where he could be reached if he wasn't. The answer was Heather Laurent's loft in Manhattan for at least a few more days and then, maybe, with a couple of different friends around the country. But Drew also said he might simply return to Vermont after leaving Manhattan and get some things from his home before taking that longer road trip. Either way, Drew added, he'd most likely be in areas with cell coverage.

"Did he ask you if he needed a lawyer?" I asked Emmet.

"No."

"He sounds very accommodating."

"I said I'd call him if I had any other questions."

"Do we have something that we know has his fingerprints on it—or even his DNA?"

"We don't."

"What about when we were at the Haywards' the day after their murder? Remember what a scrubber Drew was? How helpful he was?" I said, and it seemed possible now that he had been working like mad to make sure that he'd left behind no evidence of his involvement at the scene Sunday night. Perhaps inadvertently he had left us a lead.

"I vaguely recall him Windexing the windows, but he would have been wearing rubber gloves by the time he grabbed the spray bottle."

"He moved the coffee table."

"That's right. But he was probably wearing the gloves by then, too."

"And I recall him drinking some kind of diet soda from a bottle," I said, hoping, if he was implicated, he had gotten sloppy.

"If so, it may still be under the sink. They had a recycling tub under there."

"Good. And if Drew does come back to Vermont, let's drop in on him or see if he wants to stop by the barracks. Perhaps we can ask him some more questions before he realizes he needs an attorney and winds up in custodial care."

"Will do," Emmet agreed. Then: "And you said Heather Laurent was a bestselling writer?"

"Yup."

"I wonder how she and Drew became friends. Think they went to school together?"

"It's possible."

"Let me look into her, too. Maybe she fits in here somewhere."

"But don't talk to her until you've talked to Drew again—if possible."

"I understand."

I couldn't imagine Drew traveling with the Queen of the Angels, and so as soon as Emmet and I hung up, I Googled her. I saw she was as pretty as she had struck me on television. And I learned that her father had murdered her mother and then killed himself. I decided then that the two were something more than friends, which made me ponder further the motives that drove the Reverend Drew. I began to wonder whether this Heather Laurent had been involved in the Haywards' murder as well. A love triangle? Possible. I saw online that she had appeared in Vermont on the Monday the bodies were found, which meant that she might have been here on Sunday night. And absolutely anyone is capable of absolutely anything. I know that. It is, for better or worse, the fallout from my job.

SOMETIMES LATE AT night, I will peer into each of my boys' bedrooms. Most nights they sleep in their own beds in their own rooms, their doors open, but that summer it wasn't uncommon for Lionel to grab his pillows and a blanket and curl up either at the foot of Marcus's bed or in the beanbag chair beside it. He had only been out of a crib for a year and a half. And though he was potty trained, he still slept in pull-ups—just in case. Paul says I will stand there for long minutes in my nightgown, just staring. Intellectually I know there's a connection between what I see at work most days and the time I spend watching my boys sleep: The weirder my caseload, the more likely I am to act like a sentinel.

They are both very deep sleepers. Their pediatrician once said she believed that little boys sleep more deeply than little girls. I've no idea if that's true, but I know that my sister and I never seemed to slumber the way our brother did. My father would wake me up when it was time to start getting ready for school, and I would hear him the moment he started turning the knob on my bedroom door. In the months when we were investigating the murders up in Haverill, I found myself standing with obsessive frequency over my boys' beds or that beanbag chair and watching the two of them. When Lionel was in Marcus's bedroom, the air would be filled with the aroma of baby shampoo, and I would just stand there and study how my three-year-old would curl his small body into the beanbag chair as if he were back in the womb, his knees against his chest, while Marcus would sleep flat on his stomach, his legs as straight as an Olympic diver's as he entered the water. They were often in matching pajamas, though I have actually tried to discourage that. It's Lionel who insists on being a Mini Marcus and dressing as much like his older brother as his older brother will allow. Marcus, it seems, is much more tolerant in that regard than I would be. That summer the boys were sleeping in pajamas with a montage of comic-book superheroes, men and women who sort of do what I do, but without needing a judge's permission or a jury's agreement. And both boys would be sleeping so soundly that I would have to watch very carefully to detect the slightest rise in either Lionel's slender shoulders or Marcus's back. It's as if all that energy they start to expend from the moment they open their eyes—Exhibit A, breakfast—has completely drained their tanks by bedtime.

Occasionally that August and September, I would find myself wondering what sorts of things Katie Hayward had fallen asleep to— or what sorts of noises had woken her up in the small hours of the morning—and as I learned about Heather Laurent's history, I would find myself contemplating the fights and screams that had kept her awake in the night, too. What do you do if you're a girl and your father is beating the crap out of your mother? Or what if he's simply one of those fiendish monsters who knows how to twist the dagger verbally—knows just what barbs will hurt the most and really get under his wife's skin? I knew that at some point soon we would be interviewing Katie again, and I didn't relish the prospect. She was only fifteen, now an orphan, and I had been told that she was doing about as well as one could expect. She was living with her pal Tina Cousino's family in Haverill so she could remain in the same high school and retain the same friends. But teenagers are always funky to interview. Often they're not trying to mislead you, but still their answers are all over the place. *We weren't home Friday night, we were at the movies. No wait, that was, like, Saturday. We got back around ten. No, maybe midnight. I don't remember. But it was after dinner. At least I think it was. Like, why does it matter, anyway?*

Sometimes I would be pulled from my reverie by Paul. I remember one night in late August, he came up behind me and wrapped his arms around my stomach. I was already in the summer nightshirt in which I slept, a man's Red Sox jersey that falls almost to my knees, and he whispered, "They never move." It was true. When one of us would go get them in the morning, there was a reasonable chance that Lionel would still be a crab in the beanbag chair and Marcus would still be about to crack the plane of the water. But what of Katie when she had been the age of either of my boys, when she had been six or three? Or even that lunatic Heather Laurent? How had they slept? Had they pulled pillows over their heads so they wouldn't hear their parents' fights or the names that their father would reserve for their mother? At what age do you figure out that your dad is a bastard? That your mom's life is a train wreck and she's keeping it together with makeup and lies? We had a photo from the murder scene of the impression that the back of Alice Hayward's head had left in the Sheetrock in the living-room wall the night George had killed her. If we went back to the house and ran our fingers behind the framed prints and photos on the walls, would we find other indentations? The idea crossed my mind. Even then we knew a fair amount about how George's anger would smolder before bursting into one sudden burn and then abruptly flame out. Until the night he killed Alice, he tended not to hit her anywhere that was visible. This wasn't an absolute rule, of course. There had been bruises before on her face. But usually he would smack her in the ass or on the lower back. The back of her head. Based on the details that Alice had shared with Ginny O'Brien, he may even have deluded himself on occasion that this was creepy but interesting sex play—though it doesn't appear to have had a damn thing to do with sex. Just because he never broke a bone and only once or twice blackened an eye, just because she only went to the ER one time, didn't mean that George Hayward wasn't violent or that the violence hadn't been escalating. Ginny herself told us that she should have seen this coming. Alice had made it clear to her friend that it had been an extremely rocky July, but somehow she thought she could handle it.

It seemed like what sometimes occurred was that George would manufacture an accident: He would drive her backward into the massive hutch in the dining room. He would push her into the triangular point where two lengths of kitchen counter merged. He would knock her into the banister at the foot of the stairs. He was totally capable of calling her a cunt—a useless cunt, a stupid cunt, a pathetic cunt—and later he would write her long letters of apology. Now and then he would write her poems. And he wasn't without talent. No one did remorse the way George Hayward could, which may have had something to do with why Alice tolerated him for as long as she did.

That, of course, and the fact that once she had loved him. They had loved each other. Still, if George had read the wife-beater's manual—and somewhere there really must be a how-to book that all these pricks read—it wasn't long after they were married that he hauled off and hit her that first time.

OFTEN I FOUND myself wondering this: What precisely was Drew thinking after the crime lab had left, when his hands were in the blue gloves and he was cleaning up the remnants of George Hayward's brains late Monday afternoon? Had he expected the night before that he would be doing precisely this? Given how much thought he'd put into making Hayward's death look like a suicide, had his mind wandered to the chance that he would be the one who would quite literally clean up the mess? Was this his way of punishing himself? Or was he simply doing all that he could to make sure that he had left no trace of his crime behind?

The idea that Alice's choice in men ran to guys like George Hayward and Stephen Drew made me very, very sad. One afternoon at the office, I watched some video of her at Katie's ninth birthday party. The theme was "fun at the beach," which interested me because the snowdrifts climbed partway up one of the windows of the Hayward house and there were icicles hanging like stalactites from the hydrangea outside their living room. There must have been eight or nine girls and a couple of boys there, all looking to be third- and fourth-graders, and I saw a few of their moms hovering in the background or herding the kids the way you herd cats: energetically, but not with any sense that you're really going to accomplish a whole hell of a lot. Everyone was in shorts and sandals, and there were several Hawaiian shirts. A few kids were in bathing suits. There was a clown in big beach trunks, a muscle T-shirt, and gigantic flippers. As I watched Alice manage the chaos and a kind of Nerf volleyball, I could understand completely what guys saw in her: She was pretty and sweet and efficient. Part banker, but also part cruise director. There was one string bean of a boy who was scared to death of the clown and had wedged himself between the couch and the wall, and the camera caught Alice reassuring the child that the clown was harmless and friendly and was there to make people laugh—and then, when the boy wasn't convinced, taking him by the hand and leading him up the stairs to Katie's room, where she said he could play until the clown had gone home. I found the moment a little chilling, because I was pretty sure that it was George who was manning the camera, and at one point, as she was showing the kid which of Katie's toys were the least girlish—some trolls and board games like Monopoly Junior—she turned and said right into the lens, "He'll be safe in here. If we close the door, he won't hear anything at all that might scare him."

It was times like that when I would think how incredibly lucky I was.

EMMET CALLED DREW again and asked him if he had decided yet whether he was going to return to Vermont. The reverend took no umbrage at the question and said he thought it was likely. He was, at the time, still playing house in Manhattan with the Queen of the Angels. By then I had read her books. And though I didn't see how she might be involved with this nightmare, neither could I discount her involvement.

Still, my suspicions remained pretty simple: Drew had gone to the Haywards' that July night, either by coincidence or because he feared that George was going to hurt Alice. Although there was no record that she had called him, perhaps she had said something to him that day. Perhaps she had even said something to him at the baptism. Who knows? And so he goes to the house and finds Alice dead and George passed out drunk on the couch. The guy has his handgun out, either because he's been threatening Alice with it before he strangled her or because he was planning to kill himself. And Drew is furious—no, not furious. Drew isn't the sort who gets furious. Fury is beneath him. Instead he is disgusted. Appalled. So he takes the gun from the coffee table or a cushion or perhaps even from George's limp hand and shoots him. Kills him right there on the couch. He believes if he discharges the gun close enough to the guy's head, it will look like a suicide. Perhaps he had gotten the idea from Heather Laurent's tragic family history. I thought it was possible that he and Heather had been pals a long while, and so the idea of making it look like George had killed himself after killing his wife was already in his head. I might even get murder one on this theory.

A longer shot, but one I had not yet written off, was the possibility that Drew had done in both of the Haywards. Or, perhaps, Drew and the Angel Advocate together: *The angels will come for her, Stephen. She's so very unhappy. She'll be much better off as an angel!* Again, this wasn't likely given the public persona of Heather Laurent. From her books and the clips of her I had watched on YouTube, she didn't strike me as the type who looked real favorably on homicide. But I've been wrong about people before, and I will be again. You just never know.

In any case, when Emmet spoke with Drew that second time, the minister realized that we had begun to suspect his involvement.

"I'm beginning to think you have some serious questions about me," he told the detective sergeant, his voice in Emmet's opinion suggesting only bemusement.

"Well, sir, we would like to sit down with you and talk to you a bit more about your relationship with Alice Hayward."

"I already told you everything there is to know. I was her pastor."

"I understand."

"There's really nothing more worth sharing."

"We would like to know what she told you about her relationship with her husband."

"Isn't whatever she told me private? Isn't it protected by some sort of ministerial confidentiality?"

"We're not worried that Alice confessed some horrible crime to you in the confessional," Emmet replied.

"Then what could I possibly tell you that might be of value?"

Emmet said he was deciding precisely how much to reveal about our suspicions, or whether he should mislead the reverend a little bit to get him talking, when Drew made our lives awfully easy. He suggested, "Look, why don't I stop by your barracks? There you can ask me whatever your hearts desire."

Emmet was shocked but agreed. Happily. Drew said he was returning to Vermont the next week and would clear up whatever was bothering us.

When we were discussing his second phone call with the pastor, Emmet asked me if I still thought that Drew had fled.

"Absolutely."

"Then why do you think he's so comfortable coming in now?"

"He panicked," I said. "But now he's regained his equilibrium. His arrogance."

"Think he'll really show up?"

"Versus?"

"Versus you getting a phone call from a lawyer in the next couple of days telling us that he isn't going to talk after all."

"I don't know. We'll see."

Eventually Drew would get a lawyer. But it wouldn't be until after he had met with two state troopers at the Shaftsbury barracks and—much to the frustration of his attorney in the weeks that followed—given us a rather lengthy statement.

CHAPTER NINE

Paul and I view the last days of August very differently. For me—for most of the parents in this world—there is incredible relief. You're no longer cobbling together a schedule of day care and day camps and baby-sitters to make sure that one of your kids isn't pretending he's Batman and jumping from a second-story balcony or taking his pedal-powered fire truck and driving it down the stairs and through the plate-glass living-room window. (No, my kids never did either of those things. But my brother did both. It's amazing to me that he's alive today.) But for Paul it's the end of vacation. Summer's over, and he has to go back to work. And while he seriously enjoys teaching—I love him dearly, but he just laps up all that attention he gets when he stands and talks at the front of a classroom—he is also the first one to take the back-to-school circulars that start coming in the mail in July and getting them the hell out of the house and into the recycling bin in the garage. It's like they have the Ebola virus on them or they're radioactive. If it comes from Staples in July, it's gone within seconds.

I remember Paul was savoring one of his very last days of freedom when David Dennison called me with the news that George and Alice

Hayward's urine and blood workups had finally arrived. As he'd suspected, there were no traces of drugs. Also as he'd expected, Alice had been sober and George had been very, very drunk at the end. His blood-alcohol count was .37, high enough to cause a coma in most individuals. Dennison said that people metabolize alcohol differently, and this guy clearly had a pretty high tolerance. But it was almost inconceivable that he'd been capable of shooting himself in the end. In Dennison's opinion it was likely that Hayward had been passed out when someone else had come into the house and shot him in the head. I did ask the obvious: Might Hayward have tried to shoot himself but been so many sheets to the wind that he'd nearly botched the job? Aimed so high on his temple that it looked more like a homicide than a suicide? Dennison said it was possible but not probable. In the ME's mind, it was now clearer than ever that George Hayward had been murdered.

THE PAPERWORK FOR Alice Hayward's temporary relief-from-abuse order was no more chilling than most. Horrifying, but not extraordinary. To wit: He wasn't holding the palm of her hand down on the burners on the electric stove when they were on, he wasn't torturing (or killing) a beloved cat or dog, and he wasn't sodomizing her with a beer bottle. I had seen all of that in restraining orders in the past. The last straw for Alice? The night before she had gone to the courthouse, George had pushed her down the stairs and she feared that he had broken her arm. She cited a history of violence, and given the litany of abuse she was sharing, the biggest surprise was that this was the first time she'd gone to the hospital for an X-ray. Once, she thought, George had broken a finger when he'd held her hand in a drawer and slammed it shut, but she reported that she had managed to free her other fingers and it was only a pinkie. But he had been getting worse, especially now that Katie was older and more frequently out of the house. Twice in the past ten months, he had hit her in the face; prior to that, he had tended not to risk hurting her in places that were easily noticeable.

She had come to the courthouse on a Monday, the judge had approved the temporary order that afternoon, and the papers had been served while George had been at work. The hearing to make the order final had been scheduled for the following Tuesday, a week and a day later, but neither George nor Alice had shown up. Usually that suggests the couple is back together, which only means we will probably see the woman again and the circumstances will be even more dire. In this case, however, I would learn that the Haywards had not reconciled. At least not yet. George Hayward accepted the papers the afternoon they were filed and retreated to the family cottage with his tail between his legs.

Nevertheless the court clerk had called the women's shelter the Monday that Alice had arrived at his office to link her with an advocate there, and so I asked Emmet to see whether an advocate and Alice had ever connected. I also asked him to check in with George's parents in Buffalo and Alice's in Nashua. I wasn't expecting to learn much from either exploration, but you just never know.

WHEN THE RIGHT Reverend Drew met with our investigators at the state police barracks, Emmet found him merely mystified at first and then—when he realized what kind of mountain of shit he had willingly walked into—defensive and guarded. Then angry and more than a little scared. He went from suggesting we had to have better things to do than ask him lots of questions about the tragedy in Haverill to the outrage we see pretty often from the educated and the entitled. They think they can bluster their way through this, or that a little righteous indignation will make a fingerprint or DNA evidence irrelevant. Yeah, like that's going to happen.

DETECTIVE SERGEANT EMMET WALKER: So you left the church just after nine P.M. that Sunday night.

STEPHEN DREW: Yes.

WALKER: Where did you go?

DREW: I told you, I went home.

WALKER: Alone?

DREW: Absolutely. With whom would I have gone?

WALKER: Did you leave your house again that night?

DREW: No.

WALKER: You were in the house until Monday morning.

DREW: That's right.

WALKER: Did you speak to anyone on the phone Sunday night? Did anyone come by?

DREW: Are you looking for proof that I was at the parsonage? Do I need an alibi?

WALKER: Sir, I am just filling in the details of the investigation.

DREW: Please, there is no need to call me sir.

WALKER: Okay.

DREW: If you want to be formal, then call me Reverend.

WALKER: Yes, Reverend. Did you speak to anybody on the phone on Sunday night? Did anybody come by? A neighbor? A parishioner?

DREW: You must have checked the phone records by now. You must know that I called nobody and nobody called me.

WALKER: And visitors?

DREW: None, again. It seems I have no alibi, doesn't it?

WALKER: When was the last time you saw Alice Hayward?

DREW: I presume you mean alive.

WALKER: Yes, sir.

DREW: At the potluck following her baptism on Sunday morning.

WALKER: Did she say anything that suggested she thought she might be in danger?

DREW: Yes, but I didn't understand at the time that it was a cry for help. Actually, it wasn't a cry for help. It was . . .

WALKER: Go on.

DREW: She said "There." I don't know. Maybe it was nothing. She said it after she was baptized. After she came up from the water. When I was at the house and I saw that George had killed her, the word came back to me, and it seemed to me that she must have known he was going to do it and that's why baptism was so important to her.

WALKER: And when was that?

DREW: When was I at the house?

WALKER: Yes.

DREW: It was Monday. Obviously.

WALKER: When she was estranged from her husband this past winter and spring, do you know who she was seeing? Or whether she was involved with anyone other than her husband at the time of her death?

DREW: Well, that's quite the UFO of a question.

WALKER: Sir?

DREW: Reverend. Please. I asked you to call me Reverend—that is, if you won't call me Stephen.

WALKER: My apologies. Who was Alice Hayward seeing when she and her husband were separated?

DREW: What makes you think she was seeing anybody at all?

WALKER: She wasn't?

DREW: Why would I know?

WALKER: You told us you were offering her pastoral counseling. Perhaps she told you something.

DREW: I see.

WALKER: So was she seeing someone other than her husband— perhaps even sleeping with someone other than her husband?

DREW: Why is that relevant?

WALKER: This is a murder investigation.

DREW: I think it's pretty obvious who killed Alice Hayward. You were there Monday morning. George Hayward killed his wife and then killed himself. Do you honestly doubt that's what happened?

WALKER: Maybe. Hard to say right now. Did she ever mention another man to you in your . . . counseling?

DREW: Do I need a lawyer?

WALKER: That would be up to you, Reverend.

DREW: Okay, tell me. What do you want to know?

WALKER: Do you know if Alice Hayward had a relationship at any point this year with a person other than her husband?

DREW: No.

WALKER: No you don't know, or no she had no relationship?

DREW: As far as I know, she wasn't seeing anyone.

WALKER: No one.

DREW: No one. She was not having an extramarital affair. She was not sleeping with anyone other than her husband.

WALKER: When was the last time you spoke with George Hayward?

DREW: I can't remember. It wouldn't have been in the days before he killed himself.

WALKER: When would it have been?

DREW: I don't know. Late May or early June, maybe. We may have run into each other at the general store.

WALKER: In Haverill.

DREW: Yes.

WALKER: What did you two discuss?

DREW: It was small talk, if it was anything. I was not likely to have a meaningful conversation with George Hayward. I know ministers aren't supposed to think like this, but we're human: He was a malevolent presence, and I never found that praying for him changed him very much.

WALKER: Were you aware that he was abusive toward his wife?

DREW: Of course.

WALKER: How angry did that make you?

DREW: That's a ridiculous question. Obviously it left me sickened. It left me enraged.

WALKER: How enraged? Mad enough to do something about it?

DREW: What are you implying?

WALKER: Nothing. I am merely conducting an investigation.

DREW: Because if you think I killed George Hayward . . . well, that's preposterous.

WALKER: I understand.

DREW: Really, is that what you think?

WALKER: No one is accusing you of anything, Reverend.

DREW: And would you please just call me Stephen? The way you say Reverend . . . it sounds almost sarcastic.

WALKER: I meant no offense.

DREW: This is all completely ridiculous. Do you want me to take a lie-detector test? I will, you know. Will that put this outrageous notion to rest?

He never would take that polygraph test. His attorney would see to that.

But his lie that Alice wasn't seeing anyone or having an extramarital affair would soon come back to haunt him.

THINGS BEGAN TO move quickly after that. We went back to the Haywards' house and found that the fingerprints on the diet-soda bottle we had seen in the hands of the preacher man matched those on the headboard in the master bedroom. They matched prints in the bathroom off that bedroom and on a little blue bottle of massage oil in Alice's nightstand. I now had all I needed for a judge to approve my affidavit to get an official set of Drew's prints and a swab of DNA from his mouth. I could subpoena his laptop. I might have a while to go before I could connect him to George Hayward's murder, but it wasn't going to be hard to prove that he had been intimate with his parishioner.

Emmet put in another call to Drew, but this time the reverend didn't call back. Instead it was his lawyer who rang, and he didn't call my detective sergeant, he called me directly. His attorney was a guy named Aaron Lamb. I like Aaron, though he has represented some real scum. And, invariably, real rich scum. Aaron's the guy who the head of the power company will call when he accidentally runs over a bicyclist on Route 7A while passing in a no-passing zone. Aaron's the attorney you want if you were just snagged for embezzling a few hundred thousand dollars from the hospital or if you're a psychiatrist who's found it easier to sleep with your sexy young patients once you've drugged them. And, clearly, he was the lawyer you wanted if you were an aristocrat from Westchester who had chosen to go slumming as a country pastor in Vermont and then went ballistic one night and de-cided you would take vengeance into your own hands and shoot your now-dead lover's husband.

"I hear you and Detective Emmet Walker are thinking of joining the Haverill United Church," Aaron said, his voice its usual silky-smooth icing with just a dollop of boredom tossed in. He was a tall man who had thinning dark hair and rimless eyeglasses with titanium earpieces. He always moved in my mind like a diplomat: His posture was extraordinary, and the world seemed to part before him. He was one of the few men I knew in Vermont who could get away with a ventless Armani suit—no small accomplishment, since a lot of the guys here dress like farmers at a funeral. My sense is that when we beat him—and with the sorts of cases he handled, his clients were convicted as often as they were acquitted—his principal emotion was frustration: He knew that most of his clients were guilty as hell, and he really didn't care that at least half the time they were going to wind up in prison. Mostly he wanted to win because winning was such a fundamental part of who he was.

And when we lost to him? At least his clients weren't likely to be repeat offenders.

"Well, I can't speak for Emmet," I said, "but Haverill's too friggin' long a drive from my house. I try not to spend that much time in the car on a Sunday morning."

"So then why in the world would you want to talk to Reverend Stephen Drew? This can't possibly have anything to do with that Hayward fiasco."

"I know, I know: I just love my dead ends. But I am nothing if not thorough. And Drew was one tough guy to reach for a while there."

"You know, he helped clean up the Hayward house. That's the kind of man he is."

"Yeah, I saw him. I was there, too."

"Of course you were."

"I gather you're going to be his lawyer?"

"Yes indeed. Frankly, you seem to be hanging a lot on a pastor's crisis of faith and his decision to take a break from the pulpit. The minister—and understand I am using this word sarcastically—fled about three and a half hours from Haverill. He was in the Adirondacks, across the lake from Vermont."

"He's not going to be dropping by the barracks again anytime soon, is he?"

"Nope."

"Nor take that polygraph."

"I think not."

"But you know what he *is* going to do? He's going to give us a fingerprint and a mouth swab."

"Not without a nontestimonial order from a judge."

"Which shouldn't be a problem," I said, because I knew I had Alice Hayward's journal. I would've loved to have told him about it that moment on the phone, but it wouldn't have made sense to share its existence with the guy's defense attorney at that point in the investigation. All I needed to do then was share the material with the judge. Still, I'm human, and that was one of those times when I wish I could have dropped that little IED at his feet and seen his face when it exploded. In my mind I could see Aaron actually recoiling in the massive, ergonomically perfect Herman Miller that he called a desk chair but I thought, the one time I visited his office, looked more like something he'd wrestled from the Cathay Pacific first-class cabin. I was pretty confident that the reverend either hadn't known that Alice Hayward kept a journal or hadn't yet told his attorney. Either way, it was going to be very bad news for Aaron.

Besides, soon enough he would get to see the journal for himself. But by then Stephen Drew would be what we tell the press, when they ask, is "a person of interest." Not yet a suspect. But someone we need to spend a little quality time with.

ALMOST OVERNIGHT, IT seemed, everyone was aware that Stephen Drew had been sleeping with Alice Hayward. I spent my life telling reporters from three states that I couldn't possibly comment on an ongoing investigation. But the more folks we interviewed in Haverill and at the bank where Alice worked, the more our suspicions got out. People would had to have had their heads in the sand or been schoolmates of Marcus or Lionel not to have figured out what we believed had most likely occurred that awful night at the Haywards'. Some parishioners, I imagine, clung to the possibility that there was a killer (or killers) out there who had murdered both Alice and George—preferring, apparently, random horror to the idea that their pastor was capable of sleeping with a part of his flock and then murdering a neighbor. And, I guess, indiscriminate savagery was still a not-inconceivable option—as was some weird love triangle involving Mother Seraphim. But the laws of reasonable inference suggested that George had strangled Alice and then Stephen had shot her husband. Let's face it: It might be sunny when you wake up in the morning, but if the lawn is sopping wet and there are puddles in the driveway, it's pretty likely that it rained in the night.

And those parishioners were in the minority: The absolute last thing that most people wanted—especially the fine, upstanding citizens of Haverill, Bennington, and Manchester—was for this to have been some arbitrary slaughter committed by a third party who was still lurking undiscovered in the lengthening shadows of the Green Mountains. The local chambers of commerce and the state representatives grew real antsy at that prospect, and I could see early on that they were going to make my boss Jim's life hard if it turned out that George Hayward had been murdered by anyone other than the local pastor in Haverill.

I FELT ESPECIALLY bad for Katie Hayward. The amount of crap she was having to shoulder just boggled the mind. She hadn't been at the house on Monday morning, and so I hadn't met her, but it was clear this poor girl's nightmare was only getting worse. She wasn't merely an orphan now whose father had probably killed her mother; her mother was sleeping with the town pastor, and the newspaper, TV, and Web stories just kept coming. A couple of times, I called the social worker who was assigned to the girl to check in, and it sounded like Katie was doing about as well as could be expected. So far there had been relatively little (and I honestly don't know what to make of this expression) "acting out." But there had been a few days of near catatonia. And she'd gotten a tattoo (illegal, but harmless), which didn't surprise me because her social worker was known for her tattoos. Katie's was an open rose on her left shoulder that she had gotten in honor of her mother; Alice loved roses and had bushes of salmon-colored wild ones along the wall of the house that faced the vegetable garden. School had finally started, and everyone seemed to think that this was a good thing for Katie. The teenager had gotten over the awkward—now, there is an understatement of a word—moments that had surrounded her like a fog her first days back in the classroom.

Still, Emmet had to go back and talk to her some more, and as a mother I felt like a ghoul asking him to do that. But I had to. I also had him talk to some of Katie's friends, including Tina Cousino. Katie said she knew that her mom kept a journal, but she had never read it. She wasn't even sure where her mom kept it. And she said she didn't believe that her mom was involved with Stephen Drew:

K. HAYWARD: I know some people think there was, like, something going on between my mom and Stephen. But that just seems too weird.

WALKER: By Stephen, you mean Reverend Drew?

K. HAYWARD: Yeah. He likes us to call him Stephen. I think the only time I ever heard him called Reverend was when there was some visiting minister in the church who was all weird and formal. He kept saying Reverend Drew this and Pastor Drew that.

WALKER: What do you mean by "something going on" between your mother and Stephen?

K. HAYWARD: You know. Like having an affair.

WALKER: Was Stephen ever at your house that you know of?

K. HAYWARD: I guess. I know he helped my mom with my dad.

WALKER: Counseling her.

K. HAYWARD: Uh-huh.

WALKER: When was he there?

K. HAYWARD: I don't know.

WALKER: Did you ever come home from school and find him there?

K. HAYWARD: No.

WALKER: Did he ever have dinner at your house?

K. HAYWARD: I think so.

WALKER: You think so?

K. HAYWARD: It was a long time ago.

WALKER: So he did?

K. HAYWARD: I guess.

WALKER: Just the one time?

K. HAYWARD: Yes.

WALKER: When was this?

K. HAYWARD: Winter, maybe? Or, like, spring.

WALKER: Can you be more specific as to a month?

K. HAYWARD: No. I'm pretty sure it was after Valentine's Day and there was still some snow. But not much.

WALKER: But it was definitely when your father was living out at the lake?

K. HAYWARD: Uh-huh.

WALKER: Were there other times he was at the house?

K. HAYWARD: Probably. But I don't remember any.

WALKER: Then why do you think that?

K. HAYWARD: Maybe because everyone says he was there now. I don't know.

WALKER: But you do not recall ever seeing him at the house other than that time he was there for dinner.

K. HAYWARD: No.

According to Alice's journal, it had been a Monday night in early March when Drew had had dinner with her and her daughter. This is what I mean about teenagers being harder to interview than spies. It's not necessarily that they're trying to mislead you or withhold a key piece of evidence. It's just that their hardwiring is so freaking different from a grown-up's or a child's.

WALKER: So he never came by for . . . I don't know . . . a quick bite to eat after church? A lunch, maybe?

K. HAYWARD: Definitely not after church. While the kids are in Sunday school, the adults have this thing called Second Hour. They're supposed to sit around and talk about Stephen's sermon in the big common room, but whenever I would pass through there to get juice or something when I was in Sunday school, they were, like, talking about muffins and stuff.

WALKER: Muffins?

K. HAYWARD: You know, stuff that isn't important. They'd be talking about the muffins that some old person had baked for the Second Hour. Grown-ups like snacks, too.

WALKER: What was it like when he had dinner that night with you and your mother?

K. HAYWARD: Awkward. Totally awkward.

WALKER: Why?

K. HAYWARD: Because I sort of don't go to Youth Group anymore. And I did when I was in middle school and for part of ninth grade.

WALKER: And you felt guilty about no longer going?

K. HAYWARD: Well, yeah!

WALKER: Why else was it awkward?

K. HAYWARD: Look, it wasn't awkward because my mom and Stephen were together. Okay? That wasn't it. My mom and Stephen hooking up? Too weird, I don't want to go there. Besides, my dad . . .

WALKER: Go on.

K. HAYWARD: I hoped things would get better between them.

WALKER: Between your mother and father.

K. HAYWARD: Yes.

WALKER: Get better in what way?

K. HAYWARD: Not fighting.

WALKER: But we're discussing a period when your father was away.

K. HAYWARD: I just don't think my mom and Stephen were . . . you know.

WALKER: Okay. And when your father returned, they were fighting less?

K. HAYWARD: I don't know. Maybe. Something happened the Friday night before they died.

WALKER: Your parents had a fight?

K. HAYWARD: Yes. But maybe it was Saturday. It's kind of a blur.

WALKER: Do you know why they fought?

K. HAYWARD: I wasn't home.

WALKER: Then how do you know they had a fight?

K. HAYWARD: I just do. You can tell. Dad must have hit Mom.

WALKER: There was a bruise? A mark?

K. HAYWARD: Not one I could see. But there almost never was. I think only a couple of times he hit her on the face. He was, like, a businessman. He was careful. But . . .

WALKER: Go ahead.

K. HAYWARD [*starting to cry*]: But he felt terrible about it afterward. He always felt horrible. That's the thing. Until that night . . . until the night they died . . . I thought things would get better between them. Between my mom and dad. He came home from the lake, and I didn't know if things would ever be totally normal. But except for a few bad nights, like that Friday or Saturday, I was sure they were working stuff out. My mom thought so, too! That's why I don't think she would have wrecked it by getting involved with Stephen!

WALKER: Not even before your father came home?

K. HAYWARD: No! No, no, no. Things were getting better until that night, and I guess that's why . . .

WALKER: What?

K. HAYWARD [*crying harder*]: I guess that's why he killed himself after he killed her. Because, like, things had been getting better.

Later Emmet would ask her if she had any familiarity with Heather Laurent before her parents had died—whether her mother or Stephen had ever mentioned her—but it was clear that the girl hadn't met her until that last Tuesday in July. Before then she'd never heard of the pastor's new squeeze, and her mother had never spoken the woman's name. And neither of Laurent's books were anywhere in the Hayward house. Prior to her parents' murders, Katie Hayward knew as much about Heather Laurent as she did about the medieval popes.

I PORED OVER a photocopy of Alice Hayward's journal. Even as a teenage girl, I never kept a diary. It wasn't that I was afraid someone would read it and something might come back to haunt me. It was, to be totally honest, that I've just never been all that introspective. And so the idea that this customer-service representative of a community bank kept a diary fascinated me, and I studied every entry for clues.

Alice had begun keeping the journal almost a year before she would get the relief-from-abuse order, and so altogether the diary lasted close to eighteen months. None of the entries were more than a paragraph or two, and sometimes she would seem to go weeks without cracking the little book's spine. What intrigued me as much as anything was how her handwriting changed in the course of that year and a half. At first, when she was largely chronicling the latest time that the bastard she called her husband had smacked her hard in the back or called her a cunt, the penmanship was tiny and cramped, almost no space between the letters of each word. Five times, Stephen Drew—as Stephen Drew—appeared in the diary before Alice got the court order that kicked her husband's sorry ass out of the house. She wrote that she had seen the reverend at his church office on three occasions and at an unspecified locale on two others, and though she wrote that she and Stephen were discussing her husband, she didn't offer much detail. An entry from late October was pretty typical:

OCTOBER 25: *Met with Stephen for over an hour. Told him about George's threat last night and how much he had drunk. Stephen thinks like Ginny. I should get out. When George gets like he did last night, I think they're right. I know they're right.*

> *But last Friday he was so different. It was like St. Croix. So I*
> *think of St. Croix on the one hand and how much my stomach*
> *hurt when he knocked the wind out of me last night on the other.*

St. Croix was a reference to a vacation just the two of them had taken the previous winter. And the threat? No idea. Katie Hayward had no recollection of a particular warning toward the end of October or even a memorably violent fight. Nor was she aware that her father had punched her mother so hard in the gut as Halloween neared that she'd had the wind knocked out of her.

It was in November that the cross would first appear. It was less than three months before Alice would request and receive the relief-from-abuse order, which of course led me to wonder: Why was the reverend lobbying for Alice to leave George? Was it because she would be safer or because he wanted to have her to himself? And it was right about this time that her penmanship went from letters that were invariably small and crowded together to more florid curlicues and swoops. A few great sweeping *P*'s and *M*'s and *O*'s. A lot of capital letters. I imagine the penmanship looked a little bit like mine had when I'd been in middle school. If this not-so-mysterious "cross" was indeed Stephen Drew, there were seven entries that the prurient mind—or the prosecutor's—could interpret as chronicling an intimate afternoon or evening with the pastor. Three were in that period before George Hayward was sent packing, and four were between late February and early May. None, alas, was explicit enough to confirm that Drew and Alice were lovers. But all of them had the feel of a schoolgirl crush:

DECEMBER 14: †*'s hair reminds me these days of Christmas. It*
always has the aroma of evergreen. We were alone, and we talked
about my situation. Our situation. I view everything differently

when I see it through his eyes. Suddenly the things that I thought were my fault aren't. All those things that I had viewed as my mistakes? Not my mistakes at all. I always come away a little hopeful, a little confident that there is a plan and things will get better. He is the gentlest person I know. And he opens up to me in a way he doesn't with other people, in the same way that I can open up to him.

MARCH 11: *The whole house was ours tonight. Unimaginable happiness. The day was good, too. Katie and I had breakfast together, which we usually don't because she is so busy with makeup and figuring out her clothes and trying to find her math homework. And I'm busy getting ready for work. But I made waffles. I woke up before my alarm, and I surprised her with waffles. Such a good time. And then there was* †. *At one point, when I saw* † *in the afternoon, he said together we should make some decisions about my future. He's right. It is time. And then there was the night. Heavenly.*

The March 11 entry certainly implied that Alice Hayward and Reverend Drew were romantically involved, but I had spent enough time with Aaron Lamb in the courtroom to know this: Before a jury he was capable of arguing convincingly that on March 11 Alice and her pastor had had a discussion about her estrangement from her husband during the day, and then later Alice had had a cozy evening at home with her daughter—capitalizing upon the mother-daughter bonding she had initiated with waffles at breakfast.

Likewise, the short passage that Alice added on December 14 didn't exactly have the two of them rolling around the floor together beside a Christmas tree. The fact that she says they were alone wasn't proof of anything, since Drew obviously was going to be counseling her in private. I knew even as I reviewed the diary that I was going to need a lot more evidence to charge him with murder.

What I found most interesting as the State's resident cynic was this: Drew had become a cross in the diary long before George Hayward had left. If the pair had been playing Hester and Dimmesdale, it seemed possible that the affair had commenced as long as eight weeks before George Hayward had been ordered to keep his distance. I would have loved to have been a fly on the wall in their counseling sessions. I could just hear that Waspy, clipped voice of Drew's as, perhaps, he urged her to leave George—which obviously was exactly the right advice, unless his ulterior motive was inside his own khaki pants. And I couldn't help but wonder whether the fight between Alice and George that finally led her to get the relief-from-abuse order had been triggered by her involvement with her minister. Either Drew had given her the confidence to get rid of her pathetic excuse for a husband (a very good thing) or he was manipulating his way into her bedroom (a pretty despicable misuse of power). There was no entry until little more than a week after she had kicked George out of the house, which wasn't illogical, since Alice clearly wasn't an inveterate diary keeper and she must have been busy reorganizing her life once her husband was gone:

FEBRUARY 17: *George still at the lake, Katie and me holding down the fort. She is okay.*

I don't feel like a single mom, but I guess I am. House is quiet since Katie's out a lot. Funny: Not sure I feel safer not having George around in the night. I know I am. But now it's just us girls, Katie and me and Lula. I still keep the gun in the tubs with my clothes in the closet. I don't want it around.

Back is still sore, but arm and elbow less swollen.

The sore back and swollen elbow were the only references to the violence that had led her to finally get that restraining order.

Still, I did learn more about Alice Hayward, and it was evident that she really wasn't the self-help-magazine poster child for battered wives everywhere. She wasn't a perfect fit with the profile. Sure, George was the primary breadwinner and clearly subsidized an outwardly very nice lifestyle for them, but she wasn't totally dependent upon him financially. She had a job and an income. Moreover, she wasn't the daughter of an abused wife.

I did, however, wonder if her self-esteem wasn't so low that it had started to burrow underground—and that did fit the sketch. The brute she was married to was quite capable of undermining her faith in herself. He might not have been using her skull as a piñata, but he still knew that he could inflict pain anytime he opened his mouth:

Obviously I wasn't trying to burn the pork chops. But I did. I ruined them just like he said. I ruined dinner. If he'd just left me alone.

He says it was my fault Katie stayed out too late with Tina and a boy named Martin we've never met. He's probably right. But I tried to reach her on her cell, I did my best. I did!

I can't make a plumber appear like magic. Maybe other people can.

When did I get so wrinkled? When did I get so fat? He's right. Sometimes I just hate myself. I even hate my hair.

Called me a cunt, and I asked him what he meant by that. He got red in the face, and I got scared, and he reminded me that I had been flirting with Katie's English teacher. Was I? I thought I was just trying to be nice because Katie is so talented and he's shown so much interest in her writing. But maybe I did cross a line. Maybe I did go too far. So embarrassed now. So angry at myself. He didn't hit me.

Said I looked like a slut. A fat slut. Not even a pretty slut. He said I humiliated us both.

How could I have picked exactly the wrong drapes? I did. I am such a jerk sometimes. Such a jerk.

It didn't seem to me from her diary that she was staying with George for the sake of their daughter. The girl by then was a fifteen-year-old with a stud in her nose. If anything, Alice had the common sense to see that getting smacked around and verbally abused by her man wasn't precisely the sort of role-model behavior a teenage girl ever should see. But she did understand this about her marriage: George was better to her when Katie was around—and she herself was safer.

George is different when Katie's in the house. Not always. But sometimes. It's like he's on his best behavior. I know Katie has seen us fight, and lately she's gotten in the middle (which somehow I can't let happen ever again). But I also know George is less likely to hit me when she's home. So maybe she tells herself all parents fight. He drinks less when she's here, and that means he's really more himself. The man I know he can be and the way he used to be all the time. Not perfect. But not mean.

I wish I knew how to talk to her about this. I wish I was smarter. I wish I wasn't so embarrassed. But her father and I just have so much history. It's weird. She doesn't know the best of her dad, and I don't think she knows the worst. But I'm sure she knows a lot more than she would ever admit.

One more thing about Alice was textbook: She would defend George's behavior by blaming it on alcohol. The idea that when he was steering clear of beer, things were better seemed to reinforce the connection in her mind that it was barley and hops that were bruising her, not her spouse. I thought it was notable that he didn't drink on their wedding anniversary:

> Flowers, chocolates, a massage with those soft hands of his—the whole deal. It's been a really excellent week. Made love tonight, and it was good.

There were two separate sheets of heavy, granite-colored résumé-bond paper folded into the diary, and each one held a poem George had written to her in blue ink. They were both fourteen-line sonnets. One included an indictment of his own behavior:

> Of all the things I've broken,
> Of all the things I've seen come apart,
> The moments I'd wish you'd spoken
> Were the moments I'd broken your heart.

The other suggested the remorse he felt after he'd hurt her:

> And so, trust me, I know what I have.
> What I don't see is where the anger begins.
> But when I come for you with roses and salve,
> Know at least I am aware of my sins.

The diary included no mention of Heather Laurent: not as an author whose books Alice was reading and not as a presence in either her life or the life of her pastor. I hadn't really expected to find the Queen of the Angels in the journal, but so much of the investigation was proving a source of surprise that I wouldn't have been left breathless if she'd had a small cameo.

I WAS CONVINCED that Alice was kidding herself when she wondered in her diary how much Katie knew. I was confident that the kid knew plenty, and I was sure of that well before she'd even been interviewed again. You can clean up a wife beater and dress him up nice, but he's still a wife beater, and eventually his true colors will come out.

When I was growing up, people who only knew my family casually would have been quick to award my parents the marriage blue ribbon for best in show. And given the sorry state of a lot of marriages out there, I've come to the conclusion that it really was pretty good. But much of their marriage *was* show, an excellent façade they offered to the world—and, sadly, to each other. In reality their marriage was a far cry from storybook. Sometimes, however, I think it could have had a little magic to it if they'd been the sort who talked more. They almost never fought, which may actually have been a part of the problem. They died married, my dad first from lung cancer and my mom next from Alzheimer's. There was a six-month period when my brother and my sister and I were practically commuting via airplane from our homes in Bennington, Boston, and Manhattan to Fort Myers, Florida, where our parents had moved after our dad had retired. My dad was in excruciating pain, and my mom was getting lost in the bathroom. Getting old? Not for the faint of heart. You really need a spine when it's time to check out.

My parents' big problem was that they weren't especially compatible, and then they rarely talked about how to bridge their differences. I have no idea what they saw in each other at first, and it may have been as simple as the idea that they both were settling. They *thought* they were in love, they *wanted* to be in love, and they worked hard all their lives to fake it. My dad was thirty-five when they married, and my mom was thirty-two. She wanted kids badly, so her biological clock must have sounded in her head like a car alarm. But the thing is, they never quite figured how to say what they really wanted, either to communicate their desires or to be comfortable with what the other was asking. The few times they may have tried, it didn't seem to have a real happy outcome. Once I remember hearing through the bedroom walls the sort of conversation that creeped me out then and makes me a little sad even now. I was twelve, old enough that I knew more than the basics of procreation and recreation between the sheets, but not old enough to have tried anything at all. It was near midnight, and I had been in bed for at least an hour. I'm not sure why I woke up. But I did. My mom was clearly trying to convince my dad to try something a little out of the ordinary in the sack, and he was clearly resisting. He was forty-eight then, and my mom was forty-five. And I got the sense that sex wasn't hugely satisfying for her and that she wanted it to be before she was ninety (an age she wouldn't even approach in the end) and it was too late. She was alternately pleading and wheedling with my dad, and my mind was awash with lurid possibilities, which was making me more than a little queasy since these were my parents. I was just about to pull the pillow over my head when my dad said, raising his voice so that I could hear clearly the panic and the disgust and the fear, "You know I can't *perform* that way!"

Perform. It's a pretty harmless, pretty antiseptic word. I know that the word *performance,* especially when it's linked with *review,* can be a little unnerving. But I don't think it freaks out most people the way it does me. Whenever one of my associates refers to an opening or closing argument as a *performance* or suggests that he or she didn't *perform* well, I'm catapulted back to my seventh-grade bedroom and the sheets with sunflowers muted by laundry detergent and days drying on a rope line in the sun. I've told my husband that he has to strike the very word from his vocabulary around me.

In any case, I'm confident that there are any number of nouns and verbs that Katie Hayward will hear over the course of her life that will instantly bring her back to the Cape on the hill and the horrific things she overheard there.

ALICE'S PARENTS IN Nashua, New Hampshire, had a pretty good idea that George occasionally whacked their daughter around. They knew the details in the relief-from-abuse order, and one time with her mother Alice had brought up the term *extinguishment of parental rights,* suggesting that she feared someday her husband would do the absolute worst. She told her mother that she had researched George's rights to Katie if "something" ever happened to her and she was planning to see a lawyer in the autumn—that is, if things grew nasty again. (As far as we could tell, she never had gotten around to contacting an attorney.) George's parents in upstate New York knew considerably less, and it seemed that the four in-laws never spoke. When I read the reports of the interviews, it didn't seem implausible that Fred and Gail Malcomb would raise a daughter who might tolerate a certain amount of abuse: an only child who clearly wasn't spoiled, a father who was distant and believed in corporal punishment ("within reason," Fred stressed), and a mother who was submissive to the point that she would often look to her husband for approval before she answered a question. Likewise, Don and Patrice Hayward were not improbable candidates to bring up a boy who would grow into a man capable of hitting his wife. Theirs was a family of boys: five of them. No girls. Don didn't even allow female pets, so every one of the dogs that paraded through George's life when he was young was male, and there never were any cats. Seemed inevitable that sometimes all that male bonding or all that testosterone left over from ice-hockey practices or games ("ice warriors," Don called his sons) would result in a little brawling in the house. But, Don insisted, he never hit Patrice, and Patrice didn't disagree. He also said it was unbelievable to him that his son would ever have hit Alice, "no matter what she did to deserve it," and that the relief-from-abuse order was based on trumped-up accusations. He said the only reason his son returned to Haverill from the lake house and tried to salvage the marriage was for the sake of his daughter.

I made a note to myself about the reality that when George was grown he had both a daughter and a female dog: Was that a source of frustration for him? Disappointment? Why had he allowed his family to bring a female home from the animal shelter? Ginny would tell us that Alice had lost a baby boy to a miscarriage not long after she and George had arrived in Haverill. Alice believed that if the baby had lived, things might have been different. Ginny doubted that, and I did, too. But it was at least conceivable that George's longing for a son might occasionally have made him even more of a thug.

The fathers of both victims worked, the mothers stayed at home. Fred Malcomb was employed as a manager at an ice-cream factory. Don Hayward owned a small insurance company. Neither had retired at the time of their children's deaths.

The most interesting—and, perhaps, the most revealing—remark volunteered by Don Hayward? In the follow-up interview, after the Haywards had been informed that it appeared George had been murdered, Don grew a little combative and asked, "So how do you know she didn't kill him? Alice? How can you be so sure that little you-know-what didn't shoot him herself—you know, before someone else came in and strangled her? She never much liked him, you know. That's the truth. Even after all he did for her and all he gave her, she never much liked him."

Emmet considered explaining the details of gastric emptying times and how the contents of the stomachs of the deceased suggested that Alice had been dead for hours before someone shot George. But in the end he didn't bother, since by then Don was rattling on about all the remarkable things George had accomplished in his life as a businessman and Patrice was sobbing.

FROM *ANGELS AND AURASCAPES*
BY HEATHER LAURENT (P. 311)

I've always assumed that for most people there is great comfort in being home and—more important than that—a profound, almost visceral sensation of safety. And by home I mean quite literally inside the house. Certainly this is the impression I have gotten from my friends who are married or partnered, as well as from my friends who had childhoods that were more normal than mine. You come home and metaphorically (or actually) you start the fire. You hang up your jacket in the hall closet. You run the baths for your children, you watch your cat groom herself on the bar stool nearest the radiator. You cook. You eat. You hold someone you love. And the whole world with all of its dangers and troubles—its savagery and its pettiness—becomes something other, something beyond your front door. In theory, no one hurts you at home.

For my mother, however, I have always assumed that when she would shut that front door for the night, she felt far from secure. It was like being in the cage with a sleeping tiger, which I presume is at least part of the reason why she drank. She never knew what might awaken the animal. Even at the end of her life, I am not sure whether she knew what specifically might set her husband off, what might cause him to hiss at her or rage at her or destroy something small that she cherished: A plate. A wineglass. A photograph. Once he took one of her favorite black-and-white prints from their wedding album—an image of her with her grandfather—and tore it into long strips of confetti while she cried and begged him not to. I assume she was never completely sure what might lead him to hit her.

And then, of course, there were all those nights when, drunk, she would taunt him. Challenge him with a derision that was self-destructive and could lead only to an escalation in their cycle of violence.

Nevertheless, I would have liked to have seen my father's face at his funeral. My mother's at hers, too. The desire had a different motivation in each instance: In the case of my father, I wanted to see whether he was peaceful in death. Did all the anger and frustration that caused him to scowl—that left his eyebrows knitted in so many of those frayed snapshots—die with his flesh and body and blood? He had been a handsome man, with cheekbones as pronounced as a ledge: But was it the darkness that actually made him attractive? As for my mother, I wondered what her countenance was like when her eyes weren't darting nervously like a rabbit's or shrunken by scotch to mere slits— when she wasn't anxiously trying to anticipate her husband's moods. Would she, finally, have a face that allowed the beauty that had been subsumed by all that disappointment and fear shine through?

The last time I had seen either of them alive had been over Christmas. The only angels I had been conscious of back then had been the porcelain ones that decorated the fireplace mantel and the glass ones that my sister and my mother and I hung on the balsam we stood every year in the bay window in the living room. (It would only be later that I would become aware of the angels among us, the sentient and beatific with wings.) At one point when my sister and I were standing in our kitchen after our mother's funeral, when we were surrounded by all those grown-ups and all the food that neighbors had brought that neither of us had any interest in eating, Amanda turned to me and asked me what I thought the morticians had done to our parents' bodies between their deaths and their funerals. It was a good question. In hindsight, we both needed more closure than either of us had been offered. Anybody in our situation would.

A few years later, when I was taking a course in college on aberrant psychology, I would come to understand that it was not merely the morticians who had worked upon my parents' bodies in the period between the murder and the suicide and when their bodies were lowered in mahogany caskets into the earth. It had been the medical examiner who had, in all likelihood, peeled back their faces and weighed their hearts and swabbed the inside of my mother's vagina.

CHAPTER TEN

I t's not easy to weird out a pathologist, but Heather Laurent succeeded. I already had a meeting with the crime lab on another case, and so I drove up to David Dennison's office the day after he called so he could tell me precisely what Heather had said and, apparently, done. By then we had checked out the basics of Heather's history—though we hadn't interviewed her yet—and pretty much all that she had written in her books about her parents' deaths was true: Her father had indeed shot her mother and then hanged himself in the family attic, leaving behind two teenage daughters. Nice. What a guy.

David's office was a first-floor corner just off the mortuary (and he always preferred that we call it a mortuary instead of a morgue, since the word *mortuary,* he believed, conveyed a greater respect for the dead), and the mortuary was a sprawling series of rooms you entered via the ER at the hospital in Burlington. Convenient, no? If you wound up in the ER and made it, you went upstairs to the hospital; if not, they wheeled you on a gurney through the double doors marked AUTOPSY SERVICES.

The resources were impressive for a state as small as Vermont, because for over a decade we had a governor who'd been a physician. Eventually he was able to secure the funds for a first-rate facility, the sort of place where you really can treat the dead with the honor they deserve. When the legislature was debating the funds for the new space, David testified famously (famously in Montpelier, anyway) that he wanted a kinder and gentler mortuary. We only have a dozen or so homicides a year here, but for one reason or another—usually what we call an untimely death—David and his staff still autopsy about 10 percent of the people who die. And since we usually lose about five thousand people, the pathologists autopsy close to five hundred Vermonters annually. And then there are the corpses with organs and tissue to harvest. David is adamant in his belief that the tissue donation room has the best air in the state.

And the day before, Heather Laurent had showed up out of the blue at Autopsy Services about four o'clock in the afternoon. David had had me paged, but I was in court, and Emmet was in Haverill interviewing Ginny O'Brien and Tina Cousino.

"I have to assume that Heather Laurent is a suspect," David said when I arrived.

"She may be involved somehow, but I wouldn't say she's the lead horse. Not by a long shot. Why would she be at the top of your list?"

"Because she's insane."

"You think?"

"Well, not literally. But she is a kook. And I'm not saying she should be the lead candidate, either."

"She's loaded, you know."

"I'm not surprised."

"She comes from buckets of money and has made a boatload more with her books. Why did she come here? And what did you do when she did?"

We were sitting in his office, and he motioned at the chair in which I was sitting. "Mostly we talked."

"Here. In your office."

"I went out to reception when Vivian said Heather Laurent was here to see me. I told the woman it was inappropriate for us to speak."

"But you did anyway."

"She wanted a tour."

"Why?"

"Because she had never seen the inside of a mortuary. She asked to see the bodies."

"Bodies . . . generally. Right? She had to know that the Haywards have been in the ground in New York and New Hampshire for a good long time."

"Yes. Bodies generally. She told me about her parents, which I already knew. But it seems she never got to see their bodies after they had died. The last she saw of them, they were alive. It had been over Christmas. Next thing she knew, they were in caskets. She wanted to know what had probably happened to them in between."

"Other than being shot in the one case and hanged in the other."

"Yes. Other than that."

"I didn't even know she was in Vermont."

The shelf on the wall behind his desk was awash in Beanie Babies, small plush animals filled with plastic pellets instead of traditional stuffing. His two daughters, when they had been little girls, insisted on giving him the creatures because they had a vague idea that the office of a man who spent his life taking cadavers apart and putting them back together could use a little cheer. For the first time I noticed that two of them—a zebra and a lavender dachshund—were each wearing a doctor's white coat. The dachshund even had a stethoscope, which struck me as ironic only because I didn't imagine that David listened to a lot of beating hearts most days. I wanted to pick one up and throw it at him.

"Don't worry: The tour I gave her was seriously abridged."

"I can't effing believe you gave her any tour at all. You're the one who's the lunatic—not her. Are you embarrassed? I sure as shit hope you are."

His face was a little square and usually rather regal—especially given how early he'd grayed. But now he looked like a scolded child, and his eyes, always a bit drawn, grew small. "I think you're making too much of this," he said defensively.

"Emmet hasn't even interviewed her yet! We didn't even know she was here!"

"Well, now we know."

"Where is she?"

He paused. "She went home. To Manhattan."

"Lovely. Did she say why she was here?"

"I told you, she wanted to learn what had probably happened to her parents' bodies."

"I mean in Vermont: Why was she in Vermont?"

"I don't know."

"You didn't ask?"

"We were too busy talking about why she had dropped by my office—though she did say she had just come from seeing Katie Hayward at the high school."

"Oh, for God's sake."

"I know—"

"Did she say what she and Katie had talked about?"

"No."

I was irked and felt a little flushed. I took a deep breath. "So: How extensive was this tour you gave her?"

"Not extensive at all. It's not like I was going to walk her through the chain of custody for the Haywards—for any of the bodies that arrive here. I showed her my office, an autopsy room, and the tissue donation room. Since it was the reason she'd come here, I told her what I presumed had been done with her parents."

"And then she left."

"That's right."

"What did she say about the Haywards?"

"She was saddened."

"Oh, please."

"And she wanted to know about the nightgown Alice Hayward had been wearing when she'd been killed."

"Did she say why?"

"She said she was curious and caught me off guard. So I told her."

"You told her?"

"I did, I'm sorry. I was walking her to the door and it just slipped out. Later it crossed my mind that she wanted an alibi: You know, a moment when someone—i.e., yours truly—could testify that she had asked him what color it was. But I'm being paranoid, right?"

"One can hope."

"I really am sorry."

"Her buddy, Pastor Drew? Did she say anything about him?"

"Not her buddy any longer."

I sat forward in my chair. "Really?"

He shook his head. "No. You didn't know?"

"We're not exactly girls in the hood, David. No. I did not know. What did she say?"

"I was talking to her about her own parents and what sorts of things the medical examiner—and, I added, the mortician—had probably done with them. I was being very vague."

"Sensitive," I said sarcastically. "That's you."

"Thank you. I really was telling her only the basics, but she kept wanting to know things about how her own parents had died. The physiological specifics. It was, in her opinion, the exact reverse of the Haywards. In the Haywards' case, it was the male who was shot and the female who was strangled; in the case of her own mom and dad, it was the female who was shot and the male who was strangled."

I nodded, simultaneously interested and a little disappointed in myself that I hadn't made this association on my own. I wasn't sure if it mattered, but it was a connection of some sort. "Go on."

"So I was explaining to her the differences between ligature strangulation—you know, with a scarf or a rope—and manual strangulation. I was babbling on about strap-muscle hemorrhages and the likely calcification of bone in her father's neck—"

"All things she needed to know."

He raised an eyebrow but otherwise ignored me and continued, "—and Heather interrupted me. 'Manual strangulation is much more personal,' she said. 'You're staring into your victim's eyes. You have to be very angry.' I thought that was a wee bit of an understatement. Very angry? You have to be a fuel tank that just exploded! But I was polite and agreed. And that's when she said, 'I just don't see how Stephen Drew could have missed the rage that must have been consuming George Hayward.'"

"And you said?"

He shrugged. "I was evasive. I said people are human. They miss things. And that's when she let on that she and the minister weren't real tight. Her response? 'And some people only see what they want to see. Some people's hearts are harder and more selfish than others'. They resist the more virtuous angels among us.'"

"Wow. Does that mean there are angels that aren't virtuous?"

"Possibly."

"Did you press her on what she meant?"

"I asked her if she meant Pastor Drew, and she said she did. Then she looked away. Right out that window. And she looked totally disgusted—which wasn't a look I had seen on her face until that very second."

"But she didn't say anything more. She didn't elaborate."

"Nope. Maybe just as well. Most of the things she said were pretty loopy. At one point when I was showing her the autopsy room, one of the lab techs happened to come in with a Tupperware container full of hearts for the medical school. The lid was off. They were old and had bleached out over time, and so they looked more like headless chickens than human hearts. Heather didn't recognize what they were and asked. I told her. And her response? 'Why is it we always want the heart of a lion—and not the heart of an angel? An angel's heart is as strong as a lion's but has the benefits of acumen and history.' I didn't tell her that the only history in most of the hearts I see is too little exercise and too many Quarter Pounders with cheese. Then, a few minutes later, she noticed the bags of bones." Reflexively he glanced down at his shoes when he said that. No one wants to talk about the bags of bones: They are the human remains—the femurs like clubs and the mandibles that remind one of scoops, the occasional pelvic girdle—that have been unearthed at construction sites or excavations around the state. Most of them, we presume, are Abenaki remains from the nineteenth and early twentieth centuries, and we will never attach a name to any one of them. But we have no precedent about how or where to reinter them, and the last thing we want to do is dispose of them with the hazardous waste that is part and parcel of any mortuary (or morgue). And so they sit in massive, Ziploc plastic bags on a couple of shelves in a far corner of one of the autopsy rooms.

"And what did she have to say about the bones?" I asked.

"They're why humans can't fly."

"Because we have bones."

"Yes. We need bones more like birds'."

"Or angels'?"

"Uh-huh."

"Really?"

"Yup. We need bones like the angels'. She said we'd fear dying so much less if we allowed ourselves to feel the presence of the angels among us."

"And you said?"

"I said absolutely nothing. It was a straight line with far too many responses. And she was so completely sincere. But you know what expression did cross my mind after she left?"

I waited.

And he said, his voice at once troubled and bemused, "Angel of death. I'm telling you: That woman is as stable as a three-legged chair."

THE TEST FIRE of George Hayward's handgun would show that it had been discharged at about two and a half feet from his skull: in all likelihood too far for a self-inflicted head wound. The lab used a bullet with a full metal jacket, as had Hayward, rather than one with a hollow point that is designed to remain inside the body and—not incidentally—expand as it penetrates its target, causing considerably more internal damage. Certainly we were aware of suicides where the victim had held the gun at arm's length, aimed the barrel back at his head, and used his thumb to pull the trigger. But it was rare. After all, if you're trying to kill yourself, why risk missing? And given how drunk George Hayward had been that night, it didn't seem likely to anyone in my office that he would have had the cognitive capabilities to figure out that he could hold the gun so far away and use his thumb to fire the weapon.

WE SEARCHED THE parsonage in Haverill, but we found nothing that was going to link the Reverend Drew to the Haywards' murders. I'm not sure any of us actually expected to find a flannel shirt with George Hayward's brains on the pocket, but we had to check. Alice Hayward's prints were on the kitchen table and on one of the ladder-back chairs beside it, but that was the only trace of her we found in the house. Nothing in the bedroom, nothing in the bathroom. And there was nothing on the reverend's computer that indicated definitively either that he was having an affair with the woman or, later, that he had murdered one or both of the Haywards—though there was plenty that suggested an interest in the crime that he and his lawyer had to know could be made to look incriminating as hell if we ever presented it to a jury. In the days after the bodies were discovered, he was Googling sites with general forensic information about murder by strangulation and murder by a gunshot to the head. He had spent hours clicking through sites on crime-scene investigations and how a suspect might try to eliminate evidence of his presence at a homicide. He was also searching for anything he could unearth about Alice. High-school photos. College-yearbook appearances. There was little there, but he had seemed to have found what there was. What we discovered also corroborated a part of his story: On the Sunday night that the Haywards had been killed, he had frequently visited the website for Major League Baseball and followed the progress of a ball game between the Boston Red Sox and the New York Yankees. And in the following days, he had indeed written e-mails to friends, as he had told us, some of which he had sent but most of which were sitting in the drafts folder in his mail program. All of them suggested he was merely a minister enduring a profound crisis of faith; none of them intimated that he just might have gone postal and shot George Hayward in the head.

Certainly the DNA swab he had given us, as well as his finger-prints, was damning as hell if we were trying to convict him of adultery. His presence was all over the Haywards' house, especially the master bedroom and bathroom and the kitchen. Unfortunately, this wasn't seventeenth-century Boston. We needed more than adultery. And, still, nothing that we had linked him to the house that awful night.

GORDON AND MICHELLE Brookner, the neighbors closest in proximity to the Haywards and the owners of the little pond where Alice had been baptized on the day she would die, had seen the pastor's car visit the Hayward house a number of times the previous winter when they had come north to go skiing. The timing, they thought, had been February and March. They knew that Alice and George had what Michelle referred to as "a troubled marriage," because of the winter months when George had been exiled to Lake Bomoseen. But they hadn't known until Alice was dead that George was physically abusive, and they had been surprised. They had rather liked him. Thought he was an impressive young entrepreneur. They had liked both Alice and George. It also hadn't crossed their minds that Stephen Drew might have been romantically involved with Alice; that, too, was a story they would hear first only after the Haywards were dead. "He was the minister. Why wouldn't he have come by their house?" Michelle observed.

When Emmet returned to speak once again with Betsy Storrs, the church secretary who I wanted managing my life and, if possible, coordinating the food and decoration for every major family holiday that was my responsibility—especially Thanksgiving—she was uncharacteristically evasive when asked about the minister's relationship with Alice Hayward. Had she ever seen Alice's car at the parsonage? Yes, but she had seen lots of people's cars at the parsonage. How often was Alice in Stephen's office? Most frequently in the months immediately before

"George and Alice decided to take a marital breather," and then only occasionally in the late winter and spring. The only times she could recall Alice there after George had returned were two instances in July when she and Stephen were discussing the significance and specifics of her desired baptism. Did she think that Stephen and Alice had been more than mere friends? "No friendship is mere, is it?" Well, then, did she believe that it had gone beyond the traditional bounds of a pastor's relationship with one of his flock? Perhaps, but that was between two consenting adults, and she certainly couldn't testify under oath that she had ever seen anything inappropriate; besides, "if there was something tawdry there, Stephen and Alice can answer for that when the time comes in heaven. And yes, I do think Alice is in heaven right now, and when Stephen dies—which I hope isn't for a great many years—he will be, too."

AND WHAT OF the business associates George had had in his retail ventures over the years? What of the bank loan officers and store managers and waitresses and clerks who had known George? Altogether he had a small empire, with twenty full- or part-time employees in two shops and a restaurant, plus three staffers in his headquarters office on the floor above the toy store. Might one of those workers have had a bone to pick with the man? Likewise, what of Alice's associates at the retail branch of the bank where she worked? Was it possible that there was a teller or customer-service rep who was a killer? Or might Alice have told them something that would illuminate in some way what had happened to her and her husband that July night?

In the end we interviewed nearly thirty women and men who were acquaintances of the Haywards and might have known something— anything—about why the two of them had come to such a tragic end.

When we were finished, we knew that Alice was a customer-service representative for a community bank who was more alone than anyone realized and that George was a businessman who was starting to grow tired of what he did. (Without his supervision, by the end of September the toy store and the rib joint had closed. The original clothing store was still in business, but it was unclear whether it would last even through the December holidays.) No one expressed a particular closeness to George, but no one seemed likely to want to kill him. At the same time, everyone was saddened by Alice's death, but George had done such a first-rate job of isolating her from possible friends that no one at the bank seemed especially devastated by her murder, either. They were distressed, naturally, perhaps a little troubled by their proximity to murder, but they had moved on. And none of the people we spoke with seemed to have any motive for killing either of the Haywards or any information that was going to bring us nearer to indicting someone who might.

PAUL'S AND MY wedding anniversary fell on a Saturday that autumn, and the two of us had dinner plans that evening. But the day began when all three of the men in my life brought me waffles in bed and cards that each of them had made. Lionel's was a wobbly amoeba created from pink and red construction paper that in his mind was undoubtedly a heart. Marcus's was a painting of Cupid that he had downloaded from the Web, printed, and pasted into the background of a photo of Paul and me in the backyard. (It actually looked to me like the little Roman was drawing back his bow to murder one of us, but I reminded myself that only I would see a killer in Cupid.) And Paul's was a cute card from the drugstore, but the best part was the coupons for "romantic dinner for two" and "afternoon at the spa" that he typed up and folded inside it.

"I made the waffle batter, and Lionel picked out what would go in them," Marcus informed me with great earnestness and pride, while behind him Paul raised his eyebrows and nodded a little warily. Clearly my breakfast didn't need a warning from the surgeon general, but these might not be Food Network–quality waffles. I looked at the white, brown, and dark black flecks scattered along the grid.

"Coconut, chocolate, and burned coconut," Paul offered helpfully. "But not badly burned."

"And peanuts," Marcus said.

"Walnuts," Paul gently corrected him.

I pushed the pillows against the headboard and patted the mattress so my little boys knew to join me on either side of the bed, which they did in an instant. Outside, the sun was up, and there was the reassuring thump I heard many autumn Saturdays, the sound of our neighbor Rudy, an architect, tossing wood into the shed that later that day he would stack with mathematical precision. I poured a little maple syrup—which I discovered Paul had warmed in the microwave—onto the waffles and took a bite. Then I smiled at my boys and at Paul, and I don't think I thought for a moment the rest of that weekend about all of the disappointing marriages and broken families there are in this world, and the myriad ways love seems to go bad.

WHEN WE INTERVIEWED Ginny O'Brien the second time, journalists and bloggers already were convicting Stephen Drew. Consequently, Ginny was more forthcoming than she had been initially. It seemed less important to protect the confidences that Alice had offered, since they were no longer secrets shared between friends. And, of course, we knew more, and so we knew which questions to ask.

EMMET WALKER: Alice told you that she and the reverend had an intimate relationship?

VIRGINIA "GINNY" O'BRIEN: Yes.

WALKER: They were sleeping together?

O'BRIEN: Yes.

WALKER: When did she tell you this?

O'BRIEN: Last winter.

WALKER: Can you be more precise?

O'BRIEN: It was before Christmas. I don't know how long she and Stephen had had a relationship then, but she first told me about it a few weeks before Christmas. She was all giddy, and so I got all giddy. George was just too dangerous. I understand what she had first seen in him—Lord, I know what lots of people had first seen in him—but underneath it all he was just plain despicable. Horrible. I would have been so happy if she had just left him and married Stephen. Stephen's not perfect, but everyone would have been better off, and she'd still be alive today. Can't you just see her as a pastor's wife?

WALKER: I never met her, ma'am.

O'BRIEN: Of course.

WALKER: Did Alice come right out and say that she and the reverend were having intercourse, or did she simply imply it?

O'BRIEN: She said it. They were having sex. But I'm sure she only told me.

WALKER: And this started before she got the temporary relief-from-abuse order?

O'BRIEN: Long before. Like two or three months before. I don't know this for a fact, but I always assumed it was Stephen who had talked her into getting the restraining order. She wasn't listening to me, so she must have been listening to him.

WALKER: How long did the affair continue?

O'BRIEN: Until sometime late in the spring. She got the restraining order, and George left. I was sure that she would start divorce proceedings and soon enough she and Stephen would be living happily ever after.

WALKER: Why didn't that happen?

O'BRIEN: Stephen.

WALKER: What do you mean, "Stephen"?

O'BRIEN: He didn't want to get married.

WALKER: Did Alice tell you that she and Stephen had actually discussed marriage?

O'BRIEN: Not exactly. It never went that far. She just had the sense that . . .

WALKER: That what?

O'BRIEN: That she wasn't good enough for him. Isn't that sad? Isn't that ridiculous and sad?

WALKER: Yes, it is.

O'BRIEN: Of course, Stephen probably didn't help matters in that regard: He's a little . . . I don't know . . . aristocratic. At least he thinks he is. And he never seemed to want to move the relationship along. Maybe he felt guilty.

WALKER: Guilty because he was having an affair with a married woman?

O'BRIEN: And a parishioner. I mean, one of his sermons this spring was really interesting and—given what I knew about Alice and him—pretty darn revealing.

WALKER: What did he say?

O'BRIEN: He went on and on about how awful he was. He even used that word: awful. He said he was the worst of the sinners. I mean, we all knew he wasn't. This was pulpit stuff, I figured, to make a point that God loved even him.

WALKER: That was the point in the end?

O'BRIEN: I think so. I just remember that it made some people in the congregation love him even more.

WALKER: But not you.

O'BRIEN: Oh, I like Stephen. I just thought in that sermon he was a bit of a hypocrite. So what if you're sleeping with Alice Hayward? She shouldn't have been with a monster like George. Just announce to the world that you two are in love and be done with it. Marry her! Move on! Instead they broke up soon after that sermon. Well, they stopped sleeping together. It's not as if they were ever really a public item. It's not like there was something to "break up."

WALKER: Who initiated it?

O'BRIEN: The breakup? I think it just faded. George wanted to come back, and he vowed he had changed. He'd probably done such a job on her head over the years that she really didn't believe she deserved anyone better than him. And maybe Stephen really did think he was a sinner to be sleeping with Alice and that's why he didn't pursue something more. And Alice certainly wasn't going to press him. She didn't have that kind of confidence.

WALKER: She didn't have the confidence to press Stephen for a commitment?

O'BRIEN: That's right.

WALKER: Where would they rendezvous?

O'BRIEN: You mean for sex?

WALKER: Yes.

O'BRIEN: At her house.

WALKER: Not the parsonage.

O'BRIEN: I don't think so. It was too close to the church. It's in the middle of town. And anyone could drop by.

WALKER: Did Alice ever mention anywhere else?

O'BRIEN: Once when Katie was with a school trip to Montreal—an overnight for French class—they went to the hotel on the waterfront in Burlington. It was all very clandestine. She checked in, just in case he was recognized by some Burlington pastor or something. Sometimes his photo was in the Baptist newsletter. But he insisted on paying for it. They had a good time. Ordered room service and never left the hotel room.

Sure enough, on the second Thursday in March, Alice Hayward had stayed for a night at the Hilton in downtown Burlington. Her room was on the top floor, and it faced Lake Champlain. Had a lovely sunset over the Adirondacks. And the charges had been paid for with Stephen Drew's MasterCard.

TINA COUSINO, KATIE Hayward's best friend, was a very cool customer. Emmet said he had no idea that eyelids could hold the weight of so much shadow and liner or that there were parents in this world who would allow their sixteen-year-old daughters to wear so much mascara. The result was a pair of eyes that belonged, he said, to a clown that either wanted to look very scary or happened to be very sleepy. Her hair had been dyed the color of root beer and fell in a single flat wave halfway down her back. She had dozens of bracelets on each arm between her wrist and her elbow, some made of silver and some made of rubber and some made of tin. She had a sickle moon of metal studs running along the helix of each ear. Most of her answers were monosyllabic, but eventually Emmet was able to get what he needed. According to Tina, Katie knew well that her father had abused her mother and she didn't have especially fond feelings toward the man. But she also didn't talk about her parents all that much. From the few times she had, Tina had gotten the impression that Katie viewed her father as far more pathetic than terrifying. Katie was aware of the contrition that followed his bouts of violence and had even seen some of her father's poetry. One night she had made fun of it with Tina. But she had never given her friend the impression that her mother was capable of sleeping with someone other than George, and the idea that Alice Hayward had been involved with Stephen Drew came as a complete shock to Tina. Among her longer responses? She found it "totally weird, totally disturbing" that her friend's parents had died while she and Katie had been thirty-nine miles away at a Fray concert in Albany. She knew the mileage, she volunteered, because the next day when she heard what had happened, she'd gone to MapQuest. The distance, she said, seemed to matter.

STEPHEN'S MOTHER AND his sister had no idea that he'd been involved with a parishioner named Alice Hayward. They had never heard of most of the women he'd dated in Vermont. The only name that rang a bell was the name of the woman he had asked to marry him, but no one in Stephen's family realized that the relationship had progressed so far. No one, it seemed, even suspected that it was more than a friendship.

"I always thought he was gay and just didn't want to tell me," his mother said. "I wouldn't have been upset."

His sister had disagreed. "Gay? Stephen? No, he's into women. He's just not into relationships. He's really not into people. What he's doing as a minister is a complete mystery to me."

I KNOW THE difference between mourning and grief. I have seen enough of death—in my own life and professionally—to know that the differences aren't subtle at all. My brother-in-law, who in some ways I was as close to as my own brother, died when he was only thirty-one. He was commuting to work on his bicycle. He was at the very end of his training as a cardiologist. According to a witness, he was riding his bicycle on the shoulder of the two-lane road that linked his small house with the four-lane road that led to the hospital and adjacent medical school where he worked, when he was nipped by the wide side mirror of a pickup truck. The truck never stopped, and the witness, another physician in a car behind the pickup who was also commuting to work, was too focused on my brother-in-law's body as it careened through the air like a crash-test dummy to register the license plate. He was thrown from the bike into the trunk of a thick maple tree and then back onto the pavement. His skull slammed into both, shattering his helmet like a ripe pumpkin rind, and he died from massive head trauma. In hindsight this was clearly for the best, because his neck had also been broken and in all likelihood he would have been paralyzed from the chin down if somehow he had survived. My brother-in-law would not have done well as a quadriplegic.

And my college roommate died of cancer as a relatively young mother, leaving behind two daughters, each of whom is only a year or so older than each of my boys. For months I saved the last message she left on my cell phone when she had tried to reach me in her final days in the hospital: *Hi, Catherine, it's me. They can't do anything more. I love you.* She sounded tired, but in no way relieved. I was in a conference in San Francisco, and she was dying in Maryland. I went right away, but she deteriorated so quickly that she never made it to the hospice. By the time I arrived, she was already so doped up on morphine that she never even had a clue I was in the room.

And, of course, I have seen the children of women who were murdered by their boyfriends and husbands, and the parents of women who were slaughtered by strangers, their bodies left unceremoniously in the woods. I have seen the mothers of little girls who were raped and smothered. (Smothering seems to be the method preferred by uncles and stepfathers when they want to kill the elementary- or middle-school girl they have just sodomized. They seem to desire plastic bags.)

Sometimes you just expect the waves and waves of sorrow to wash over you. Swamp you completely. That, in my mind, is real grief. And mourning? That's when you've reached the stage where you can build a stout seawall against those colossal breakers and go about your life. You might be sprayed by the surf, but you are not incapacitated. In the days after my brother-in-law died, my sister and her in-laws were grieving. They were shell-shocked and disconsolate and incapable of doing little more than getting dressed in the morning. My roommate's husband hadn't that luxury because of his daughters. He wasn't allowed to grieve. And so he had to make do with mere slow-motion mourning.

On the other hand, he'd had time to prepare for what was coming. My sister and her in-laws hadn't.

That's the thing about the families who lose someone to a homicide or a violent accident: There's no time to build that seawall. There's no time even for sandbags.

I thought about this whenever my mind wandered to poor Katie Hayward. I wondered what it must be like suddenly to be so completely and utterly alone. The kid didn't even have siblings. Sometimes I wish I could do the interviewing myself. I can't, for the simple reason that it could result in my having to testify in court, which would compromise the prosecution. But Katie was one of those people I would have wanted to speak with as a parent as well as a prosecutor. Do it myself so I could talk to her as a mom. Apparently she was continuing to hold up reasonably well. There had been a few sleepless nights in September and some long days when she ate little and spoke less. Once a teacher found her sobbing in a school bathroom stall. But she was doing her schoolwork, melding well with the Cousino family, and she had auditioned for and been cast in the school musical. She had written an op-ed for the school newspaper condemning what she called the administration's cavalier energy policy.

All of this meant that I couldn't wait to find out what Heather Laurent had said to Katie when she had returned to Vermont in September. I wanted to know what Mother Angel had been doing in Haverill before she had decided to drop in on David. In two days Emmet and another trooper were taking an overnight road trip: first to meet Amanda Laurent in Statler, New York, and then to Manhattan to formally interview Heather herself. But that afternoon Emmet had gone back to the Cousino house in Haverill with Katie's social worker, Josie, a powerhouse of a woman with dreadlocks and tats, to speak to the teenager about her most recent chat with the Queen of the Seraphim. I didn't want us to push too hard after what the poor kid had been through—and I doubt that Josie would have let us—but I had to know what Heather had said to the teenager and what the woman had asked.

EMMET WALKER: And so Ms. Laurent came by your school.

K. HAYWARD: Uh-huh. She came to my lunch table with Mrs. Degraff.

WALKER: Who is that?

K. HAYWARD: My guidance counselor. Heather—it's, like, okay if I call her Heather, right?

WALKER: Yes.

K. HAYWARD: Because she wants me to.

WALKER: Did Mrs. Degraff know Ms. Laurent?

K. HAYWARD: No. But she had heard of her. Heather writes books. Anyway, you have to get a visitor's pass to walk around the school, and you get those at the front office. That's so some crazy doesn't walk around with a gun and get all Columbine on us.

WALKER: I understand.

K. HAYWARD: And Mrs. Degraff was called in when Heather said she had come to see me. She told Mrs. Degraff she was good friends with Ginny O'Brien—which, if Ginny had heard, would have caused her to, like, totally soak through her pan—

WALKER: Go ahead.

K. HAYWARD: It would have made Ginny crazy happy.

WALKER: And so you and Heather and Mrs. Degraff chatted.

K. HAYWARD: Uh-huh. But Mrs. Degraff wasn't there most of the time.

JOSIE MORRISON: I would have been present, but no one called me. And I think Heather Laurent was probably very helpful. I've read her books.

WALKER: What did you talk about?

K. HAYWARD: I don't know. Stuff.

WALKER: No specific recollections?

K. HAYWARD: Mostly just how my life totally sucks, I guess. And how it's okay to feel that way. She's been through this, you know. She knows better than most people what I'm going through.

WALKER: What did she ask you?

K. HAYWARD: You know. The usual. Like, how was I doing? What was I feeling? She asked what everyone asks. And she gave me her cell-phone number, so I can call her if I'm about to wig out.

MORRISON: And remember, Katie: You have plenty of support right here, too. You can always call me, too. Daytime. Nighttime.

K. HAYWARD: I know.

WALKER: How *are* you doing?

K. HAYWARD: Okay. I guess.

WALKER: What did you tell her—Ms. Laurent?

K. HAYWARD: Look, do I have to talk about this? It was one thing to talk to Heather. She knows what I'm going through. It's one thing to talk to Josie. If everyone else would just leave me alone . . .

WALKER: I'm sorry. Did Heather tell you why she was in Haverill?

K. HAYWARD: Well, at first I thought she had been with Stephen.

WALKER: Your pastor.

K. HAYWARD: Well, the pastor. I don't know if he's my pastor. I guess he's back in Vermont, but he's not back in church. And it's not like I'm real involved with the church these days, anyway.

WALKER: Did she say what she was doing with the minister?

K. HAYWARD: The rumor is she was doing the minister.

WALKER: Pardon me, ma'am?

MORRISON: Katie, you really need to save that tone for me. That was a joke, Sergeant.

WALKER: I see.

K. HAYWARD: No, she didn't say much. And she wasn't there to see him, anyway. I'd thought she was, but I was wrong.

WALKER: Did she say anything?

K. HAYWARD: She used to like him. That's what the rumor is. But she doesn't anymore.

WALKER: How do you know that?

K. HAYWARD: Well, I don't know it. Not for sure, anyway.

WALKER: But why would you suspect it—that she and Stephen are no longer seeing each other?

K. HAYWARD: Because she is totally into angels and she said he isn't.

WALKER: She told you that Stephen Drew doesn't like angels?

K. HAYWARD: Sort of. She said he had built a wall against angels.

WALKER: Do you know what she meant by that?

K. HAYWARD: No idea. But look. Everyone says he was sleeping with my mom. Everyone. Then everyone says he was sleeping with Heather. That's probably what she meant.

WALKER: You told me the first time we spoke that you didn't believe that your mother and Reverend Drew were intimate. Have you changed your mind?

K. HAYWARD: Intimate?

MORRISON: Sleeping together, Sweetie.

K. HAYWARD: Oh, I get it. Yeah, I've been following what people are saying. You can't help it, you know? And I guess I was wrong. Way wrong. Maybe they were sleeping together. Everyone in the whole world seems to think so.

WALKER: What else did Heather say?

K. HAYWARD: She told me to keep my heart open to angels. To take care of myself. And to be careful.

WALKER: Be careful?

K. HAYWARD: Uh-huh. That's why she came to the school. Don't you think? To warn me and to, like, let me know I could call her whenever.

WALKER: It felt like a warning?

K. HAYWARD: Uh-huh. It definitely felt like a warning.

WALKER: A warning about what? Or whom?

K. HAYWARD: I don't know. Maybe some evil angel—if there is such a thing. Maybe grown men in general. It's not like she and my mom have had great success with your gender. I'm just saying . . .

WALKER: Just saying what?

K. HAYWARD: I don't know. Look, this is all totally confusing. But you know what? If my mom did have an affair with Stephen, I'm glad. She needed something nice in her life. At least I think I'm glad.

WALKER: Why the doubt?

K. HAYWARD: Well, we'll never know if that's why my dad . . . um, you know.

WALKER: No, I don't know.

MORRISON: Killed her mother, Sergeant. We'll never know if that's why Katie's dad killed her mom.

FROM *A SACRED WHILE*
BY HEATHER LAURENT (P. 129)

In 2006, Florida lawmakers passed a law that protected the billboard from one of the great environmental threats to its existence: the tree. During the debate a state representative in favor of the bill testified, "Tourism depends on billboards, not on trees."

This is one of the biggest differences between the Northeast, where I grew up, and Florida. Our tourism depends on trees. Vermont, for example, doesn't even allow billboards.

Roughly 4 million tourists descend upon the Green Mountains alone each and every autumn to peep at the leaves and savor what poets like to call "the fire in the trees." There are a great many reasons people celebrate the fall foliage, not the least of which is that it is indeed very pretty. For a few weeks in late September and early October, the New England maple blushes a shade of cherry far more vibrant than a preschooler's most colorful Magic Marker, the ash glows as purple as the billboards on Broadway, and the birch trees bloom into a neon that's downright phosphorescent. The woods grow more scenic, more lush, and more visually arresting—especially when the sky above is Wedgwood and the vista is framed by the rising wisps of our own autumnal breath.

But here's a reality that fascinated me as a young adult: Fall foliage is not the Grand Canyon. Or Yosemite. Or even Niagara Falls. It's not jaw-dropping, pull-me-away-from-the-edge-of-the-cliff, never-seen-anything-like-it spectacular.

So why the attraction? Why the cars, the crowds, the buses lumbering like moose up and over each mountain gap? At least part of what draws us is this: death. Not all of it, certainly. Some of the pull is romance in a four-poster bed *and an inn with a dog and a fireplace. The leaves are a pretext to escape an urban condo with a view of another urban condo.*

But we also understand that the phantasmagoric colors we see in the trees are millions (billions?) of leaves slowly dying. We might not know the biology behind the change, but we realize that the leaf is turning from green to red because imminently it will fall to the ground, where it will sink into the forest floor on its way to becoming humus.

The science is actually pretty simple: The tree is aware that the cold is coming and the leaves haven't a prayer. Consequently it produces a wall of cells at the base of the leaf, precisely where the stem meets the twig, thus preventing fluids from reaching the leaf. At the same time, the leaf stops producing chlorophyll, the chemical behind photosynthesis and the reason leaves are green. Without the chlorophyll, the leaf's other chemicals become obvious, such as the maple's red carotenoids. Soon the leaf withers and dies.

But what a handsome death it is. No dementia, no incontinence, no children or loved ones bickering over whether to pull the plug or order one last round of chemo cocktails. Humans should be so lucky as to turn the kaleidoscopic colors of the forest when we pass.

Of course, the whole of autumn is about transience. The entire natural world seems to be shutting down, moldering, growing still. The days are short, the nights are long, and everything looks a little bleak—except for those leaves. Those kaleidoscopically lovely maples and birches and oaks allow us to gaze for a moment at the wonder of nature and to accept the inevitable quiescence of our own aura. Like so much else around us, it's not the leaves' beauty that moves us: It's the fact their beauty won't last.

CHAPTER ELEVEN

There were a couple of reporters who expected an indictment any day now as the last of the leaves fell from the trees, and they were confident that when the time came, we would be arresting Stephen Drew. They called my office often that autumn and were constantly nosing through court papers. They were convinced that what had occurred that night in July was really pretty simple. Somehow Alice Hayward had gotten word to the parsonage that her husband was going ballistic, but by the time her ex-lover arrived, she was dead and her husband was passed out drunk. So Drew killed him.

Other reporters wouldn't guess at a timetable for an indictment but groused that it was taking so long. And the longer it took, the more bizarre were the theories their readers started posting on their newspaper or television websites. The Haywards had been murdered by a Charlie Manson–like group of teens, a small cult whose leader was so brilliant that he had been able to cover up all traces of their presence. The Haywards had been manufacturing crystal meth at a sugarhouse in the woods and were killed by a customer. George Hayward's retail ventures were fronts to launder money, and George and his wife had been murdered by some connection from Albany or the Bronx. Alice had shot George, and then later someone had—for reasons no one could conjure—strangled her.

I, of course, kept coming back to the simpler realities. There was Stephen Drew, and there was Heather Laurent. Though I thought it unlikely that Heather was involved, as a result of her admitted visit to the house the Tuesday after the Haywards' deaths her prints and tracks were everywhere when we returned to gather more evidence. She had also been in Vermont the Sunday night the pair was killed and had some sort of connection to the venerable Pastor Drew. And oh, by the way, she was a total nut job. So I couldn't write her off completely.

Still, I read the stories in the papers and on the Web, and I watched the drama unfold on the local news. And when reporters called, I told them—as I did all the time with all sorts of cases—that I really had nothing to say.

EMMET WALKER AND Andy Sullivan with the Vermont State Police were joined by a detective from their New York State comrades when they ventured to Statler and by a detective from the NYPD when they descended upon SoHo. They returned to Vermont late on a Wednesday night and came to my office in Bennington first thing Thursday morning to tell me what they'd learned. I had something that resembled a small feast waiting for them to thank them for their very long days—and nearly fourteen hours in the car—earlier that week. Not too far from our office is the sort of mom-and-pop bakery that specializes in angioplasty-inducing cinnamon buns and cake doughnuts. It always has the heavenly aroma of a confectionery sugar explosion. Somehow the place has survived both the economic ruts that a city like Bennington is prone to as well as the periodic bouts of gentrification. I brought back a basket of goodies for the boys, because cops of all kinds really do like doughnuts. It's not a myth.

"The place was a horror-movie set," Emmet said, chuckling a little bit and licking the sugar from a doughnut off his fingers. "I could just see the opening credits before my eyes as we walked around the cabin."

"And was it an actual log cabin?" I asked. We were talking about Amanda Laurent's home in the Adirondacks.

"Well, from a kit," he said. "And it wasn't the fact it was made of logs that disturbed me. It was dark, but lots of homes are dark. It was the carvings. Her partner—"

"They're not married?"

"She said no. But they've been together a long time. Name is Norman Beckwith. He's a bird carver."

"And not real talkative," said Andy. His chin was in the palm of his hand. Andy was a year or two shy of thirty, a nice young guy whose head was perfectly shaped for his buzz cut. His face was wholly without lines, and he looked a bit like a little boy from the Kennedy era who was playing dress-up in his dad's trooper duds. Hard to imagine him actually needing to shave. Even at a traffic stop in his Ray-Bans, he couldn't have been very intimidating.

"No?"

Emmet shook his head. "No. Really only came out of his studio under duress. Tall. Gaunt. Pale. He had one of those thin beards that followed the line of his jaw. It was just starting to turn white. Hair was a little greasy, but combed back. Dark brown and, like his beard, also starting to go gray."

"And Amanda?"

"If you saw her on a city street, you would have said either heroin addict or over-the-hill runway model. Skeletal. Sunken eyes. Cheekbones that looked like razor ridge. Flat hair. A honey blond. But she's very smart and very funny. Nothing like Norman. She's his agent. He makes these birds, and she sells them. She smokes like a coal plant."

"But it was the carvings that really gave me the shivers," Andy volunteered.

"How so?"

"There must have been twenty-five or thirty of them," the younger trooper said. "Eagles. Falcons. Kestrels. All birds of prey and all looking really pissed. And they were perfect. Most of them, anyway. Amanda sells them for him to these high-end galleries that focus on decoys and wooden animals, and to regulars who actually drive to his studio in Statler. At first I thought they were taxidermied birds. They were on shelves and tables, and a few were on the floor because there wasn't enough shelf space on the walls. But what was weird was that their beaks were open. Wide open. And they looked sharp enough to cut glass."

"Andy's right," Emmet said, and he raised his eyebrows in agreement. "They had attitude. They looked like they thought we were field mice. They wanted to eat us."

"And only kill us after they'd started eating," Andy added.

"You said most of them were perfect. Which ones weren't?" I asked.

The two troopers glanced briefly at each other and then rolled their eyes almost simultaneously. "There was a wall with what I thought might have been ospreys, but the wings were wrong," Emmet said.

"I didn't know you knew so much about birds."

He shrugged. "I know a bit. Anyway, the wings seemed fluffier. And they were shaped more like a harp and clearly weren't going to offer the raptor the sort of wingspan a bird like that needs for a glide. So I asked Norman about them. And he said I was right, the wings weren't really right for a raptor."

"Very nice. Extra points for Emmet Walker on *Name That Bird*!"

"Go ahead and joke. But here's what else he said. Well, mumbled. He said he had given those birds angel wings in honor of Amanda and Heather Laurent. Each of those ospreys has—and this is a quote—'the wings of an avenger.'"

"And this is in honor of Amanda and Heather?"

"So he said."

"Why are they avengers?"

Emmet smiled a little wryly. "He didn't have a good answer. He said that some angels are just meant to be avengers. That's their assigned task."

"He didn't say what they were avenging?"

"Nope."

"Any ideas?"

"No again. Sorry."

Outside the window I saw storm clouds the slate gray of autumn. "So what else did you crazy kids talk about?" I asked.

"Well, the key thing is this: The basics of Stephen Drew's story check out—or at least Amanda corroborated the basics of his story. She says that Drew and Heather Laurent were there for almost a week, and when we got out a calendar, she picked the right six days. She also said she had no idea that her sister had been involved with Stephen Drew until they showed up there."

"Was her visit a surprise?"

"No. She had called them ahead of time. But she hadn't told them she was bringing her new boyfriend."

"So they hadn't met him before."

"That's correct. I got no indication from them that they were aware of any relationship between Stephen Drew and Heather prior to the deaths of the Haywards."

"Had they heard about the Haywards before Heather and Drew got there?"

"They'd seen the story on the news. They still assumed it was a murder-suicide."

"Your cell phones work there?"

"No, they didn't. That part of Drew's story checks out, too."

"She say anything about her father's history of abuse or her parents' deaths?"

"Finally, but only after I had pushed her a bit."

"And?"

"We'll have to go through the transcript carefully once it's typed up, but nothing that suggested she saw anything except the most obvious parallels to the Haywards' deaths. She worried about the teenage daughter, mostly. Said the girl is in for a world of pain. But I think we already knew that."

I'm really not a stress eater, but I found myself reaching for a maple-crème doughnut. I had hoped for something more helpful from the long road trip to Statler. "What about her sister? Heather? Anything interesting emerge from your time in Manhattan?"

"We saw Anne Hathaway—the movie star." This was Andy.

"Well, that must have made it all worthwhile."

"She was shopping," he went on. "Seems to have been visiting someone in the building across the street from Ms. Laurent. I recognized her before Emmet."

"Good for you, Andy."

"Well, you asked," he said, his tone a little hurt.

"Our escort was an NYPD detective named Adrian Christie," Emmet continued. "He was from Jamaica, and he knew who Heather Laurent was going in. His wife had just read *A Sacred While* in their book group this month. He made all the introductions. He was really very helpful."

"What did you think of Heather?"

"She's pretty. I thought she was actually prettier than her dust jacket. And to go back to your first question: Yes, some interesting things did emerge. First of all, she won't admit that she and Stephen were lovers, but she is quite clear about this: They are no longer friends. She says that she met him on the Tuesday after the murders—"

"But she was in town that Sunday night. We have records that she had checked in to the Equinox about four-thirty that Sunday afternoon."

"Doesn't deny it. Had to be in Albany for a public radio taping Monday morning and an appearance at Bennington College in the evening. It all checks out. She says it was Tuesday when she went to Haverill for the first time, and that was when she met Stephen Drew for the first time. She says their *friendship*"—and he emphasized the word with an uncharacteristically facetious pop—"really didn't last all that long. A little more than a month—though when you piece together Drew's whereabouts, they were together almost all of that time in either Statler or Manhattan. As far as we can tell, they spent a couple of days in SoHo, about a week in Statler, and then another week in Manhattan. Drew then returned to Vermont, but only briefly. Pretty quickly he rejoined Heather Laurent at her place in the city and stayed for another week or so."

"Why the breakup?"

"He hadn't told her that he'd had an affair with Alice Hayward. He only 'fessed up to her after his attorney told him that Alice kept a journal and he was going to have to give us a mouth swab."

"And this made her mad."

"Well, it angered her as much as anything can anger her. She's not a person with what you might call anger-management issues. She's pretty serene. On the surface she actually comes across as a bit of an airhead—but, in fact, I believe she is very, very smart. She said Drew was more of a son of the morning star than he liked to admit."

"The 'Son of the Morning Star' was George Armstrong Custer,"

I said. "He got that nickname because he used to attack at dawn. The Crows gave it to him. I only know that trivia because Paul is a bit of an American-history geek."

"That's not what she meant."

"Too bad."

"She was referring to Lucifer: Isaiah, chapter fourteen, verse twelve."

"Satan?"

"A fallen angel. It was Dante and Milton who made him Satan."

"Emmet, you are a source of unending wonder to me. Have you read Dante and Milton?"

"No. I just did a little research before coming here this morning."

"So what do you think? Was Heather Laurent involved in some way? You trust her?"

"I think she's a strange one. But her strangeness moderates against manual strangulation and shooting someone in the head. It moderates against conspiracy."

"So your money is on Stephen Drew?"

Before he could respond, Andy piped in. "That guy is ice."

"I take that as an affirmative, Detective Sullivan?"

He nodded. "Emmet and I talked about this on the way home from New York City. Unless George Hayward has a freakishly long arm and was able to hold the gun real far away, we both put our money on the pastor."

IT IS LARGELY a coincidence that I have the name of a medieval saint from Siena. My Italian mother—whose last name was Brusa—was vaguely aware that there was a St. Catherine, but my great-grandparents had emigrated to Barre, Vermont, in 1901 so my great-grandfather could work in the granite quarries there, and by the time I was born in 1975, my family was deeply Americanized. My great-grandfather was a stone carver, and though he spent the better part of his adult life blasting great blocks of rock from the ground—a job that would, eventually, cause him to die slowly and painfully of silicosis—he nonetheless left behind a poignant legacy in the Hope Cemetery just outside of the town. Three of the most photographed tombstones are his: the little girl nuzzling two sheep that marks the spot where a nine-year-old victim of influenza named Marissa was buried in 1919; the lion with a mane that looks like a halo, his mouth open in a full-throated roar, that sits atop the decomposing body of one of the mayors of Barre; and the graceful young woman on bent knee, her eyes turned up toward the heavens with a look of beatific comfort on her face, who marks the patch of earth where my great-grandmother was buried, far too young, in 1927. Yes, Antonio Benincasa had chiseled the monument for his own wife when she predeceased him. It was, my older relatives insisted when I was a child, one of the world's truly great, genuinely tragic love affairs.

But by the time I arrived, the granite dust was long gone from the clothes and the lungs of the Benincasas. My father and my grandfather (the one who didn't edit *Vermont Life*) were both lawyers, and I know I made my family happy by taking the LSATs and going to law school. It gave my younger sister clearance to become a wedding planner and my younger brother the freedom to go to New York City to make his fortune—my grandparents and great-uncles actually used expressions like that—as an art director in an ad agency. I certainly have no regrets.

And I do feel an undeniable pride in the fact that I am named—if only inadvertently—for a Sienese saint. Although my grandparents never visited their mother and father's homeland, my parents returned for visits, and so have Paul and I. The year before Marcus was born, we spent two weeks in Tuscany, and while we were in Siena, I felt a bit like a rock star whenever I whipped out my credit card and people saw my name. In some ways St. Catherine was one of those great medieval lunatics: Visions of Christ with his apostles when she was six, scourging herself with an iron chain and fasting as an adolescent, lopping off her gorgeous brown hair as a young woman. Hair shirts. The works. Religious fanaticism at its absolute fourteenth-century best. But she also nursed and buried victims of the plague, had one-on-ones with the city's most reviled criminals, and talked a pope (whom she called "Papa" or "Daddy" in some of her letters) into putting the papacy back where it belonged. She worked hard for peace among the small Italian republics and fiefdoms. This was not a shabby CV. And she was one hell of a writer—or, as was likely the case, she was capable of dictating one hell of a letter. Let's not forget that she was a woman in the fourteenth century and one of twenty-four children. Both realities lobbied against literacy. Some biographers believe that she learned to write only at the end of her life. Still, she left behind three hundred letters and *The Dialogue of Divine Providence,* a chronicle of her religious raptures.

In any case, I have always viewed my name and its connection to St. Catherine as an unexpected, undeserved gift, even if the closest I have come to a religious vision is falling asleep in a catechism class when I was in the fifth grade and dreaming of the sand dunes on Cape Cod. While my work pales compared to hers—you don't see me nursing neighbors about to succumb to the Black Death or advising the Vatican on policy—I hope that my efforts bring a measure of justice to some of the victims in my small corner of the globe.

When Paul and I were in Tuscany, we went to the San Gimignano Museum of Torture. San Gimignano is a spectacularly beautiful medieval village built on a hill, which pretty much describes seven hundred other villages in Tuscany. If you look at a map of the region, you'll see that every other village is Montesomething. Paul and I had rented bicycles, and if we'd been a little more energetic in a single day, we could have biked in a circle from Montisi to Montefollonico to Montepulciano to Montalcino and then back to Montisi. The difference between San Gimignano and most villages is that it has seven massive medieval towers looming over the town and more tourists per cobblestone than the Ben & Jerry's factory in Waterbury, Vermont. It's a sort of Disneyland for the Chianti-and-pecorino-cheese crowd. And, of course, it has that torture museum: a three-story collection of antiquarian torture devices, most of which involve wrought iron, ropes, or very sharp points. Its ostensible message, if it has one, is that humans once had little regard for human life and were capable of inflicting truly appalling pain on one another in the name of religion or country or mere self-righteousness. There are the basics, such as the rack and the iron maiden and a functioning guillotine (which was, ironically, supposed to end torture by killing the victim instantly). There is a dungeon. And there are displays of devices that only a real psychopath could have come up with, a disproportionate number of which seemed to involve impaling people. Everything is explained in five languages, and the diagrams can only be called grisly. I had seen my share of disturbing images in the magazines in my grandparents' attic growing up, and I had visited some pretty despicable crime scenes—but still I grew a little nauseous inside the museum. And yet I also wasn't oblivious to the reality that I was, in some ways, the twenty-first-century version of those guys who thought, six hundred years ago, that a bone-crunching manacle or a good old-fashioned pair of rib-cage-ripping tongs had their place in the judicial system. I know that my anger at certain kinds of criminals—the stepfathers who molest and murder their stepdaughters, the husbands who batter and murder their wives—is pretty near boundless. But I view myself as civilized. Moreover, an awful lot of the time—perhaps most of the time—the self-proclaimed arms of justice in the Middle Ages were torturing the innocent, not punishing the guilty. It wasn't about a specific crime, it was about a specific belief.

Nevertheless, I wondered that day in the museum and I speculate sometimes even now what I will do if I ever have before me a capital offense. In Vermont that would demand something like a kidnapping across state lines with a death resulting. Or using the Internet as part of the abduction. At the moment I work for the county, so I won't face this dilemma unless my career takes me to the U.S. Attorney's office in Burlington. But someday I might wind up there. And when I thought about the blood and the bodies I had seen in the Haywards' living room and the kid who was transformed overnight into an orphan, I would find myself angry and appalled and a little unnerved at the pain and the violence that we still inflict on one another daily.

IN ADDITION TO a variety of reporters wanting an indictment, there was my boss, Jim Haas. When I was throwing papers into my attaché and preparing to leave for the day, he knocked gently on my door. It was open, but Jim was feigning deference—which meant, as it did always, that he wanted something. And while I might have assumed it would have something to do with the death of the Haywards, I did have other cases, and so I honestly didn't know which of the dead victims or breathing criminals—the sex offenders, the embezzlers, the drug dealers—was about to postpone my picking up Marcus and Lionel at their after-school programs. Paul had a soccer game at a high school twenty-five miles distant, and so I was getting the boys that afternoon. Jim looked tired and aggravated, and he had loosened his necktie. He paused in the frame after tapping the door's hollow metal with his knuckles.

I was already on my feet, and so I murmured a greeting but didn't stop scanning the papers I was retrieving and the folders I was collecting from different corners of my desk.

"Got a minute?" he asked.

"Barely."

"I want to talk about the Haywards."

I grunted something that could have been interpreted as a willingness to listen.

"Are we any closer?" he asked.

"Than when we talked on Monday? Nope."

"But you still believe it's the pastor."

"Yes, but only because I don't have anyone better."

"What can I do to help? What would it take to get an indictment?"

"Against Stephen Drew?"

"That's right."

I thought about this for a brief moment. "Well, evidence would be good," I said finally.

"You have none. . . ."

"None that says he murdered either George or Alice. I have plenty that says he was having an affair with Alice. I have a motive for killing George. But nothing to link him either to the murder of his lover or, more likely, the murder of his lover's husband. Any special reason for the sudden urgency? It's not like we're in an election year."

"Very funny."

I smiled, but I honestly hadn't meant it as a joke.

"Really, it's not sudden," he went on. "But I just got off the phone with Sondra Norton, and she says that people are scared. Some are beyond scared. They're mad. No one likes an unsolved murder—or, in this case, two unsolved murders. It makes folks edgy, especially now that Stephen Drew lives in the neighborhood."

Sondra ran the shelter for battered women and their children. She was also one of our representatives in the Vermont House. And Stephen Drew, for reasons of his own, had now left the parsonage in Haverill and was living like a three-dimensional wanted poster in an apartment in downtown Bennington.

"We all know there isn't a killer on the loose who's preying on people he doesn't know," I said. "Whoever killed the Haywards knew them and had a clear motive. Sondra must know that, too. She's grandstanding. After all, it is an election year for her."

"Sondra doesn't grandstand. You know that."

"She does great work. She's a great person. But I don't think she has to worry about the safety of her constituents. Whoever killed the Haywards isn't about to strike somewhere in downtown Bennington."

"You're not worried about the reverend?"

"I think he had a concrete motive."

"You snap once, it's much easier to snap a second time."

"I really don't believe anyone needs to add extra locks to their doors."

"That's not the point. I've also heard from both county senators. I've heard from our mayor. And I seem to be hearing from the media far more often than I would like."

"Is that the point, Jim? Is that what this is about? People are frustrated? You're frustrated? You're spending more time than you want to holding people's hands on the telephone?" Immediately I knew I had sounded more exasperated than I should have. He stood a little more erect, and his eyes narrowed.

"Alice Hayward was a battered wife who was murdered. Strangled. Someone wrapped his hands around her throat and crushed her larynx, broke the bones in her neck, compressed the carotid arteries, and caused her to asphyxiate. And that someone was almost certainly her husband. *Almost* certainly. But it also might not have been her husband, because another person—and it sure as hell wasn't Alice—took his gun and discharged the weapon into the right side of his skull, splintering bone, causing brain trauma, hemorrhaging, and a serious mess on the family's living-room windows, walls, and couch. *That* is the point."

"I'm sorry," I said.

"Sometime this week or next, when we can clear everyone's calendars, I'd like us to sit down with the folks at Criminal Investigation and see exactly what we have and what avenues we haven't pursued."

"I have a gut feeling you'd like me to be there."

"Go with your gut," he said, and then he turned on his heel and left.

PERHAPS A DOZEN times in my life, I've run into people while we're investigating them. Bennington County is like that: It's a deceptively small corner of Vermont. I've run into suspects and perps out on bail while squeezing chickens at the supermarket, while getting gas at the convenience store (with Marcus in his car seat in the back), and at the annual colonial fair over Father's Day weekend in June (with, thank you very much, my whole family present). Of those dozen or so encounters, all but once the individual knew exactly who I was. And of those times when it was clear that the suspect and I knew precisely where we stood with each other, only twice have I felt the hairs rise up along the back of my neck. One time was when I was having new brake pads put on my car and the wagon tuned up for winter. One of the mechanics, I realized, was an angry young guy charged with aggravated assault and felony unlawful mischief: He had walked into a downtown bar with a steel pipe in his hands and beaten the crap out of some poor dude who'd smiled at his girlfriend. He ended up breaking the guy's arm. Then, on his way out, he smashed the bar's plate-glass window for good measure. With his grandparents' help, he had managed to post 10 percent of the twenty-five-thousand-dollar bail. (It never ceases to amaze me how many people are out on bail and shouldn't be. Presume this guy was innocent? Yeah, right. I could have filled a dinner party with witnesses. I was also convinced that he was the person who'd been burglarizing vehicles for weeks in a city parking lot and robbed an older couple one night as they unlocked their minivan using—surprise!—a steel pipe as a weapon. And yes, later we would charge him with those crimes, too.) We saw each other at the car dealer just after I'd arrived at the service counter, while I was waiting for them to sign me out a loaner for the day, and our eyes met. He looked seriously pissed at me: His bangs were plastered to his forehead, and he glowered like a petulant schoolboy. Then he motioned with his head out toward my car, which was in the lot just outside the service-garage window.

"That yours?" he asked.

"It is."

He studied it for a moment as if he were checking out a girl in a bar and then wrinkled his nose dismissively as if it didn't measure up in some way. Finally he turned back to me and smirked. "We're gonna get some ice tonight, I hear," he said. "A lotta ice." Then he disappeared back into the shop. That night, after I had picked up the car, I was sure my brakes weren't going to work when I needed them most. For almost a week, I found myself braking long before I normally would have—just in case.

The other suspect who unnerved me when I ran into him outside the safe confines of court was none other than the Reverend Stephen Drew. I knew he was living in Bennington, and I knew he was renting an apartment not far from the courthouse. Nevertheless, it took me a moment to put a name to his face when I came across him on the sidewalk about fifty yards from the courthouse entrance. It was almost six o'clock in the evening, and there was a chill wind blowing in from the west. There were still another two weeks of daylight saving time, but it was overcast, damp, and dusky outside—and there was almost no one on the street. I was racing to the bookstore, which I knew was about to close, because I wanted to pick up a couple of picture books for a pal of Lionel's who was having a birthday party that coming Saturday.

And there the minister was. He was leaning against the brick side of a recessed doorway, and he had the collar turned up on a gray jacket that fell to midthigh. He pushed himself off the wall and blocked my path.

"You're Catherine Benincasa," he said. "We met the last Monday in July. I'd recognize you anywhere." It is always a tad alarming when a suspect in a murder investigation calls you by name on a deserted street at twilight, and his tone was somewhere between menacing and weary. The nearest people were either the security guards back inside the double doors at the metal detectors of the courthouse or the patrons at a bar shut tight against the cold nearly a block away.

"I am," I said warily. "Hello, Reverend Drew."

"Stephen. Please. I was just about to give up."

For a split second, I misconstrued what he'd said, misinterpreting "give up" for "give myself up," and I thought he wanted to turn himself in. But his demeanor was too chilly, too confrontational for that. I realized then what he had actually meant. "You've been waiting for me?"

He nodded. It was just cold enough that I could see his breath. "I waited yesterday, too, but I never saw you leave the building."

I had to restrain myself from saying something catty about how I'd never before met a pastor who was also a stalker, because I honestly didn't know yet whether I was in danger. Instead I said simply, "I wasn't in court yesterday afternoon."

"Ah."

"You know I can't talk to you."

"Why?"

"And your lawyer would be furious if he knew you were trying to talk to me."

"My lawyer does not tell me what to do. I think we should chat."

"I'm sorry," I told him. "I am not going to speak to you without your lawyer present."

"But you will if Aaron joins us?"

"Aaron Lamb won't let you talk to me. I promise."

His hands were burrowed deep inside his jacket pockets, and when he removed them suddenly, I must have flinched. He shook his head and said, smiling, "You really believe I killed both of them, don't you?"

"We're not having this conversation," I reiterated simply.

And it was then that he started to tell me about crucifixion. The connection, in his mind, was injustice. At least that's what he said. But he started talking about injustice and execution and the barbarity that always marks the human condition. It was erudite and hypnotic and deeply disturbing. If I lived alone, that night I would have pushed furniture against the front and back doors of my house. I was able to extricate myself only when another lawyer, one of the public defenders who had spent that afternoon at court coping with calendar calls before a judge, came up beside us. It was a friend of mine named Rosemary, and I immediately introduced her to Drew and then allowed myself to be led by her down the block until we had reached the bookstore and the reverend was behind us in the distance. Still, that evening I would insist that she walk with me to my car, and the following night I was careful to leave my office with another lawyer in the state's attorney's office.

When Aaron called me the next day, he tried to feign fury that I had spoken with his client, but it was clear Drew had told him that he had initiated the conversation. I could also tell that Aaron wished that his client hadn't decided to share with me in visceral detail what it must have been like to die on the cross.

THE FOLLOWING MONDAY, Jim Haas, Emmet Walker, and I spent nearly four hours in Waterbury with BCI—the Bureau of Criminal Investigations. David Dennison joined us from Burlington. We examined all of the evidence we had amassed and we analyzed all of the interviews we had conducted. And when Jim and Emmet and I sped back to Bennington in Emmet's freakishly clean unmarked detective sedan, we were no closer to indicting Stephen Drew than we had been the day before. At the same time, we were no closer to finding a new direction—a new suspect—worth pursuing.

We were on Route 7 in Wallingford when Emmet abruptly chuckled from behind the wheel. I was sitting in the backseat behind Jim and Emmet, and so I caught Emmet's eye in the rearview mirror.

"What's funny?" I asked.

"You know, maybe this Stephen Drew did us all a favor," he said. He was driving with one hand, and he shrugged. "Maybe we should just stop spending the taxpayers' money."

"Yeah, it's crossed my mind, too," I admitted, and I didn't have to glance at Jim to know he was glaring at us both from the corner of his eye.

"I mean, think about it. If Drew hadn't shot George Hayward, we really would have to try the bastard and jail him—and jail him for at least twenty years. Maybe longer. And a trial and two decades of incarceration doesn't come cheap."

Jim wasn't completely sure how serious the state trooper was. "There is a principle here, Emmet," he said, his tone his professorial best. It was the voice he used when he was making his opening statement or closing remarks to a jury: patient and avuncular and wise.

"Oh, I know, I know. George Hayward may have been the O. J. Simpson of Green Mountain batterers, but that still doesn't mean someone had the right to shoot him in the head. But think about it: not a bad death, especially given what he did. He passes out drunk and never wakes up. And justice is done. Frankly, I think we should send the reverend a thank-you card and move on."

We wouldn't move on, of course. At least not completely. For me it was always going to be a bit like the gnawing frustration we all experience when we misplace something and know it's somewhere in the house—but where, we haven't a clue. The cell-phone charger, the car keys, the cap to the felt-tip marker that will dry up if we don't find it soon. It's annoying as hell. But I think I knew at that moment in Emmet's car, as he flipped on the directional and accelerated into the passing lane to get ahead of a lumbering milk tanker, that if we solved either of the homicides in Haverill—found something to link Stephen Drew definitively to the murder of George Hayward—it would be more the result of very good luck than very good work. We had done our best, and, it seemed, we'd been outdone by a country pastor.

PART III

Heather Laurent

CHAPTER TWELVE

The cosmology of angels is neither problematic nor puzzling. Nor is it sectarian. Virtually all religions have spiritual messengers or escorts. Someone to take our hands when we need their grasp most, someone to pull us hard and fast from the fire. Someone to yank us off the pavement as that oncoming pickup truck whizzes past while we are strolling at dusk, so that the vehicle may transform our windbreakers into sails but we continue on unscathed. Or, just maybe, someone to yank from our fingers that orange vial of pills because it has become too painful to live. My father's brother and an older cousin of mine had both spent time in McLean, and so depression had never been a taboo subject at the breakfast table in my home growing up.

In my case it was indeed going to be a prescription drug that I was contemplating for my last act. My roommate my first year at college had a prescription for sleeping pills, and between Thanksgiving and Christmas I fell into a funk deeper than any I had known since my parents had died. (And those initial months after their deaths had been a fog; I was so buffered by large dollops of shock and small ones of relief—yes, relief—that the first year had been considerably easier than the ones that immediately followed.) I had been deteriorating all semester, but it had begun to accelerate as the days grew precariously short. I had gone to my aunt and uncle's home in Fairfield for Thanksgiving, and the four days there had been more dispiriting than usual, and already I could see the changes in Amanda—how caustic her humor had become, how dark. How she was intent, it seemed, on starving herself to death. So many of the things I cared for most or associated with moments of comfort in my childhood—dolls, a couch, my childhood bed, a teakettle my mother had cherished—were scattered to the attics of relatives and friends or had been sold in the estate sale. There was just no more debris from the sinking ship that had once been my life that I could cling to. And I was miserable at college. I was lonely, I was doing poorly in class, and I was grappling with the reality that I was enrolled in a university rather than a conservatory. Unfortunately, I was five-ten—at least two inches too tall for even the more statuesque dancers—and I had never completely recovered from a series of ankle and toe injuries that had dogged me as a junior and senior in high school. It had been clear for a couple of years that I was never going to be a ballerina. And though I was in the dance program at the school, I had begun to realize that my voice was going to be my undoing when I began to audition for Broadway shows. It was adequate at best, and that was after four years of work with vocal coaches and voice teachers. What did that leave? The Rockettes. And no one, in truth, makes a living as a Rockette. Perhaps I could be a choreographer. Or a dance teacher. But I was never going to be a performer.

My depression, of course, was being fueled by far more than a fear that my professional dreams were starting to evaporate. I was eighteen, and the sad fact was that I was essentially alone in the world. I had been an orphan since high school, and my sister was falling apart even faster than I was. I simply didn't see anything that gave me hope or confidence that tomorrow just might be better than today.

Now, the separation between depression and suicide is more crevasse than chasm. For months I had been working my way gingerly over the rocks along the ledge on the near side but studying how easy it would be to throw some ropes across the fissure and cross over. That whole autumn I was eating less and less, not consciously trying to starve myself the way Amanda was but simply incapable of making the effort most meals to pull myself together and go to the dining hall. I can recall lunches and dinners when I would just cry in my bed with the sheets pulled over my face. I wasn't sleeping, but I wasn't getting up, either. I would often just lie there, and my mind would drift to very dark places. On one occasion my roommate found me shivering in my parka on the floor by my bed at about three in the afternoon, naked other than that down jacket, and murmuring that I just couldn't do this—though I wasn't forthcoming about what "this" was, because even I wasn't sure whether I meant getting dressed or breathing with purpose. I couldn't explain to her quite what had happened, and I imagine if she had been more self-aware (and less self-absorbed), she would have reported me to the school's health services. But she attributed my funk (her word) either to boys or to the fact that I was the kid at college whose parents had died in that murder-suicide. I think she expected me always to be on the verge of a nervous breakdown. That autumn I would lose twenty-five pounds. There were classes where I would sit in the back row of the lecture hall and look around, oblivious to anything the professor was saying, and suddenly my eyes would be bleary and tears would bounce off the yellow pad on which I was supposed to be taking notes. (Invariably the page would be blank.) I would look at myself in the dorm's bathroom mirror, and even I could see that I was terrified and despairing and utterly lost.

Some days I would sit at a library carrel and in my mind walk myself carefully through my aunt and uncle's home or across the university campus and try to imagine precisely the tools or the manner in which I might kill myself. There was that beam running across the steep twelve-by-twelve-pitch roof in my relatives' attic, a perfect spot to loop a rope if I decided to follow my father's lead and hang myself. There was their car and their garage. Or the antique bathtub with the lion-paw feet in the guest bathroom, where I could lie in soothing warm water with a paring or carving knife beside me and watch the clouds of my blood turn the bathwater pink. At the college there were tall buildings with glass windows, most locked but all easy to smash with those heavy wooden chairs, and I gazed out from the highest floors all the time. There was the bell tower in the chapel, and one day I went so far as to walk to the hardware store in the village beside the campus and finger the meticulously bundled lengths of clothesline. There was the train that passed along the edge of the college near the physical plant, just far enough away that only when our windows had been wide open in September had we heard its occasional whistle. One afternoon I clawed my way through the wild tangle of bushes and shrubs beside those tracks and crouched for long moments, awaiting the train and envisioning in my head the passage from *Anna Karenina* when that heroine throws herself under the shrieking metal wheels. At night when I was incapable of studying for a French test or writing a paper on the literature of the Great War, I would read what I could about what was euphemistically referred to as "self-deliverance." I saw that if I was going to kill myself, I seemed to be on the right path: Toy with the idea first. Touch the materials. Grow accustomed to your plan.

I would contemplate who might find my body, and at first I would worry how it would affect them, but soon I was beyond caring. When you are as far down that path toward self-destruction as I was, you grow oblivious: not selfish, precisely, but insensible. Still, I decided finally that the best thing I could do was to choose a method that would make it likely that I was found by someone who did not know me well (if at all) and that my body would not be left in a condition that might leave that person with memories it would be hard to expunge. Consequently, I never seriously contemplated using a gun.

And so the night before the first day of exams, while everyone was hunkering down in dorm rooms or the various libraries scattered across the campus, I dropped the small bottle of my roommate's sleeping pills into the dance bag that doubled as my book bag and slipped unnoticed into the basement of our dorm. I also packed a water bottle and some antihistamine tablets I had gotten from the infirmary to ensure that I wouldn't vomit back up the great handfuls of sleeping pills I was planning to ingest. I had caught a glimpse of myself in the bedroom mirror on my way out the door, and I was struck by how drawn my face seemed, even by the standards of that miserable autumn, and how my hair looked a bit like a crazy woman's: I hadn't washed it in four or five days—hygiene falls by the wayside when you're depressed—and it was hanging in strands that were long and oily and flat.

The dormitory was a Georgian monolith from the turn of the century, and the basement was a maze of thin corridors created by the rows of empty trunks and stacked cardboard boxes that belonged to the eighty of us who lived on the four floors above. There was a corner with our bicycles and a few pieces of decrepit furniture that not even a college student would use. I wanted no one to know I was in the basement, and so I navigated the stairs and the labyrinthine chaos on the cement floor by flashlight. I had pulled the door shut behind me. What I found most interesting as I searched for my own trunk was how the basement, which previously had been a source of terror—the abode of spiders and mice and demented men who lurked in the shadows—seemed now to be merely a cold room jam-packed with the detritus of young adults. It wasn't frightening at all.

And, soon enough, I found my trunk. It was wedged vertically between another first-year student's chest and some supermarket cartons still filled with sheets. The trunk smelled a little mustier than when I had arrived back in late August, but otherwise it was downright comforting to find it. I dragged it to the corner of the basement nearest the massive closet with the dorm boilers, the warmest section of the room, and then took some of the sheets from one of those boxes. The chest was big, but I was still far too lanky to fit inside it, even curled up pathetically in the fetal position. But I could make myself comfortable if I viewed the trunk as a tub and dangled my legs over the edge and used those sheets as a pillow and a mattress. That was my plan. Reclining in the dark in the trunk of a dorm basement, I was going to find that great undiscovered country. I thought—and I know now this isn't necessarily the case—that overdosing on sleeping pills would be a painless way to die. I would doze off and either never wake or wake to a reality I had never imagined.

I turned off the flashlight, but there were basement windows facing the road, and the streetlights allowed me to see reasonably well once my eyes had adjusted to the room.

For perhaps five or ten minutes, I procrastinated. I counted the sleeping pills (there were plenty), I lined them up like candy Pez in my palm or along the upside-down top of the trunk. I eyed the antihistamine tablets and took small sips from my water bottle, but only very small sips because I wanted to make sure that I had plenty remaining to wash down the pills. I listened to the sounds of my dormmates and fellow students, occasionally running along the corridors and stairs above me; I heard their laughter and bellowed greetings. I heard rock music from somewhere in the building, but I couldn't pinpoint the source. Generally, however, the campus was quieter than on most nights, because everyone was uncharacteristically focused. And as I listened, I cried. These were not sobs and wails but a steady stream of sniffles and tears as I wondered who the unlucky soul would be who would find me (an inevitability that did cause me to hesitate, but only briefly, and in the end was not the reason I am alive today), and I thought again of what a pathetic and tragic footnote to the world the whole Laurent family was. I was awash in self-loathing and self-pity and no small amount of anger toward my father (a murderer) and my mother (a victim) and even poor, troubled Amanda (like me, a deserter, a person who it seemed was also planning to escape this world soon enough). I clutched perhaps a half dozen pills in each of my hands, and slowly I lost myself in a memory of a moment when I had been a little girl in, I believed, the second grade. My mother was braiding my hair, which meant this was the one afternoon each week when I wouldn't have had dance, because it was required that my hair was up when I was at the studio—we were not permitted to allow it to swing free in a braid. I was sitting at the kitchen table with a small ramekin of her homemade chocolate pudding (what she called with great affectation her *pot de crème*), and I was aglow with serenity and composure. Say what you will about aggressive dance training, it does wonders for a little girl's poise. The sun was cascading in through the western window, brightening the whole room, and I was very, very content.

Still, it only made the fact that now I was crying in a trunk I was imagining as my coffin all the more pathetic—and me all the more likely to finally go through with my suicide. Really, I was not hoping to be discovered and saved. And so I brought my right hand to my mouth, wondering how many of the pills I could swallow at once. Two? Three? Perhaps even four? And it was as I looked down at my hand that I saw my hair had fallen across my breasts—in a braid. An absolutely perfect, elegant, tangle-free French braid. I dropped the pills and patted the crown of my head to be sure. Then I brought the braid to my face and savored the aroma of the rose-scented shampoo my mother had used on my hair when I'd been a little girl.

I reached for the flashlight so I could be sure of what I was seeing. Indeed, I wasn't making this up or seeing something that wasn't there in the gloaming light of the basement. My hair was clean and had been arranged in a French braid that was faultless. And then I felt the most unimaginable calmness envelop me. I closed my eyes and breathed in the perfume of the soap that had magically cleansed my hair, and I allowed myself to relive the quietude and peacefulness that had marked those moments when my mother had braided it. When I finally opened my eyes, for a fleeting second I saw a woman there in the basement. I saw her beatific smile, and I saw, just over her shoulders, the tips of her luminescent wings. And then she was gone.

I gathered my roommate's pills from the floor of the trunk and from the creases in the sheets, and I gathered myself. I was, I realized, laughing, and I wouldn't stop for a long time that night. I laughed and I smiled as I packed up the trunk and the sheets and then started up the steps to the first floor of the dormitory.

And while it is possible to doubt or explain away so much of my first encounter with an angel, here is one absolute that I have never lost sight of and that has reinforced in my mind the concrete stolidity of this vision: My mother had never taught me how to French-braid my own hair. I had never done it myself. And I hadn't had a French braid since at least two years before my mother had died.

THE FIRST DINNER that Stephen and I had together was a warm caponata salad in my loft: roasted eggplant and peppers and onions tossed on a bed of mesclun and served with perfectly round medallions of goat cheese. The man, it was clear, had usually eaten badly, both because he was single and because the parishioners who wanted to feed him were allergic to vegetables. While I was sautéing the egg-plant in olive oil, he insisted on putting together a tray of hors d'oeuvres he had bought, and it was an angioplasty-inducing array of chips and cheeses and dips that seemed to belong in a frat house on Super Bowl Sunday. I didn't really need it or want it, but it was very well inten-tioned. We drank a bottle of wine from Bordeaux that he had purchased on the walk around Manhattan we had taken that afternoon and that he said had always been a favorite vineyard of his father's. I thought that was very sweet. Food is a gift and should be treated reverentially—romanced and ritualized and seasoned with memory. It was why I had wanted us to eat in rather than go to a restaurant or order something that someone else had made delivered to my home in greasy cardboard containers.

Stephen had arrived outside my apartment building around lunch-time that Saturday, and while he felt he was just dropping in out of the blue, I had suspected he would come. And yes, I had expected him that very day.

I almost told him that, but he would have thought I was mad—rather than merely eccentric, which I could see early on was the way he had pegged me. (He wasn't the first.)

And I knew he was coming because I knew by then how much he needed me and I, in turn, needed him. I understood what my respon-sibilities were. I had known for almost a week, since I had arrived in Vermont. I was drawn to the Haywards' story, but I was drawn as well to the newspaper photos of a young pastor whose eyes were them-selves somber verse.

Certainly there were variables; there always are. I hadn't planned on taking Stephen with me to Amanda's home in the Adirondacks, I hadn't anticipated introducing him to Norman's wooden birds. But as I have matured, I have become increasingly comfortable with my place in God's world and with my sense that I don't have to understand everything—though, obviously, I am not perfect at this, and doubts find their way into my aura. I couldn't save Stephen, as much as I wished that I could and wanted to try.

But that Saturday night when Stephen and I dined in my loft, eating by candlelight on the daybed with our plates in our laps, my mind was open and receptive to whatever was needed of me. I cannot always subsume my ego the way I know that I should, but that evening I did. I shouldered my wings and waited. For a month we were happy and in love. At least I was. I shouldn't speak for him.

"HIT ME AGAIN, you drunken fool! Hit me again!"

Of all the things my parents hissed and screamed and snarled at each other over the years, it is the way my mother sneered those words at my father one Christmas Eve when Amanda and I were in elementary school that comes back to haunt me most often and compels me to pray to my angel for solace and peace. I was ten and Amanda was twelve, and neither of us believed any longer in Santa Claus. The four of us had been with friends of my parents' for Christmas Eve, an annual gathering of four distant families that always involved massive amounts of drinking among the parents and desperately awkward silences among the children because we all went to different schools. Shortly after midnight my family left, and we were, as usual, the last to leave. In hindsight I have come to realize, my parents were always the last to leave because they were terrified of being alone together in that rambling house and especially in the confined space of the bedroom they were compelled to share.

Our drive home took about an hour, which was how long it would have taken if my father had traveled the two-lane roads at a steady, reasonable speed. Instead, however, as inevitably occurred when he was far too drunk to drive, he would creep along perhaps ten or fifteen miles below the posted speed limit and then accelerate wildly when my mother would say—her breath a nauseating and perhaps flammable blowtorch of Johnnie Walker scotch and Eve cigarettes—that he drove like a granny. A ninny. Or she would goad him on by telling him that she had to pee. And so he would accelerate. He would show her. He would drive like a wild man for the next three or four miles, the car careening across the double yellow line in the center of the black pavement or swerving off the shoulder so the side panels or the roof of the car would be brushed (or scratched) by the leafless tree branches. He would race at sixty and seventy miles an hour on those tortuous roads, decelerating abruptly only when he had narrowly avoided a collision with an oncoming car or he had navigated a turn with only the barest of clearances. That Christmas Eve we lost a hubcap from the right rear tire when he grazed a farmer's old stone wall a good ten feet off the road—our white Cutlass Supreme traversing in a blink the frozen ground with its patches of rock-hard ice and snow—and I think only Amanda and I understood how close the call had been. (The next day it would be my grandmother, a guest at our house for Christmas, who would inform my parents that the hubcap was gone when she innocently asked them where it was. They were, as they were most Christmas days, enduring such excruciating hangovers that they didn't even bother to venture outside to the driveway to take a look.) All the while Amanda prayed beside me in the backseat, her eyes squeezed shut and her lips silently moving. It has crossed my mind numerous times over the years that the only reason we survived that night was my sister's terrified entreaties to either an angel or God.

When we got home, I presumed that the worst was over. Given my parents' relationship, there was absolutely no reason to make that assumption. But I did. Amanda went directly to her room, and I went to the den to see if there was anything at all on television other than the Yule log: essentially a televised fireplace with Christmas carols in the background. My mother sat down with me on the couch and tried to wrap her arm around my shoulders, but that night I was resistant to her embraces. She tried to win me over with a remark about how only a year or two earlier I might have been putting out cookies for Santa and then racing upstairs to bed so I would be asleep when he arrived with his reindeer. But I was in no mood to try to add a patina to what had always been a childhood of Christmas Eves marked by my parents' verbal and, on occasion, physical brawls. Quickly my mother sensed my frame of mind, and even though she was still very drunk, she left. She kissed me on the forehead and stumbled to her feet on shaky legs. She had kicked off her boots as soon as she had walked in the door, but even in her stocking feet she was having trouble negotiating the plush living-room carpet. And then, all alone, I clicked back and forth among the four or five television stations we had.

It was perhaps fifteen minutes later that my parents began to argue. I will never know precisely what triggered that one, but it really doesn't matter. What matters is that soon after they started, I heard the sound of a great amount of glass shattering, and I knew it was the beveled mirror that was suspended by two oak arms above my mother's dresser—a Victorian piece that I know now was well over one hundred years old. Then my father emerged from the bedroom and stomped toward the top of the stairs, where he paused for a moment at the balcony that ran perhaps fifteen feet along the corridor, his hands in fists at his sides as he surveyed the first floor. I gazed up at him, but our eyes never met and I wasn't altogether sure that he had registered I was there on the living-room couch. He was still in the clothes he had worn that evening, though his shirt was untucked and the top three or four buttons were open. His T-shirt was the color of a peach. His wonderful, creosote-black hair, which had been slicked back at the party, looked now as if he had teased it with spaghetti tongs.

My mother appeared behind him in only her panties and blouse, barefoot, and her own hair—a great flaxen mane—was also in disarray. Her lipstick was smeared like a clown's, and her mascara was dripping in rivulets down the right side of her face. (It's possible, I imagine, that it was running from her left eye as well, but I recall noticing at the time that for some reason only her right cheek was streaked with makeup.) She was sobbing and she was furious and she threw herself at him, pounding her fists into his back and shoulders with such force that it looked for a split second as if he would hurtle over the side of the balustrade and fall either one flight into the living room or—worse—a full two flights if he tumbled over the section of balcony that was above the stairs that linked the living room with the finished basement.

"Stop it!" he yelled, grabbing her fists in his hands. "Settle the fuck down! You nearly fucking killed me!"

"You stop it, just stop everything!" she screamed back, a demand that, as unreasonable as it was, might have accomplished its intent if she hadn't added, "You are pathetic. You are just the most pathetic loser."

"Pathetic? I'm not so fucking drunk I—"

"'Fucking'? Why don't you swear some more in front of your children? Why don't you tell them what you just called me? Heather, do you want to know what your father just called me?" I hadn't any idea how to respond to this appeal, and so I murmured—not loud enough for them to hear over the din of the television and their own verbal pyrotechnics—"Don't fight. Please. Don't fight." In my mind I see myself curled up on the couch in the red Christmas skirt from Saks Fifth Avenue and the turtleneck dotted with silver snowflakes I had worn that evening, a throw pillow clutched in my arms as if it were a stuffed animal. I'm sure I was crying, too.

"You're a drunk, you know that?" my father told her, and he released her fingers as if they were a fish he was tossing with two hands into a lake, his arms upraised when the movement was done. "You're a fucking drunk and the poorest fucking excuse for a mother I've ever seen. You're a shrew and—"

He never finished the sentence, because my mother, her hands newly freed, slapped him, and the stinging *thwap* was so loud that his ears must have been ringing. He brought his palm to his cheek and held it there for a moment. And then he slapped her back, so hard that she toppled backward and landed on the carpet near the top step of the stairway, one of her legs beneath her and the other splayed out as if she were a dancer trying and failing to perform a split. Her panties, I saw, were soaked through with her blood, and for a second I was terrified she was badly hurt. But then I remembered: My older sister had just started menstruating and our mother had hoped to demystify the notion of a monthly cycle for both of her girls by telling us that she, too, was in the midst of her period. That night she was so profoundly inebriated that when she had removed her tampon when we'd gotten home, she had forgotten to put in a fresh one.

"You're drunk," my father scolded her.

"You're drunk!" she shouted back. "And you're a drunk, too! You're a wretched and feeble excuse for a man! Your own father knows it, your mother knows it, your daughters know it. They know. They know."

She pushed off against the wall and stood to face him. "They know," she mocked him one more time, and she glanced down at me for the merest of seconds. And so my father smacked her again, but this time she was prepared for the blow and remained on her feet, though her body fell hard against the wall, her head bouncing like a basketball off the Sheetrock and causing the small framed print of a rosebush near her to quiver.

"They know their mother's a shrew!" he yelled. "That's what they know! She's a fucking, bleeding, harpy shrew who can't even keep her goddamn underwear clean!"

She dropped her hands to her sides in a posture of absolute submissiveness and hissed, "Hit me again, you drunken fool! Hit me again."

And so he did.

CHAPTER THIRTEEN

Initially Stephen didn't tell me why the deputy state's attorney or those state troopers from Vermont seemed to suspect him of some involvement in that tragic murder and suicide in his community. He had shared with me a very great deal about Alice our first days together in Manhattan, but somehow he had missed that one small detail that they'd been lovers. He had had many opportunities when it would have made sense to tell me, beginning with the day we met right up until the day that we left Statler—especially when we reached the highway on our way back to New York City and he discovered that his cell phone had a series of messages from the Vermont State Police. Weeks later his defense would be that I would have misconstrued what had happened in those months and who he was as a person. Likewise, he said, I wouldn't understand what had really occurred that July night in Haverill and why it had ended so horribly.

The reality is that had he told me at any point in those first days we were together, I wouldn't have felt the need later on to withdraw. He could have told me in Haverill, and he could have told me in Manhattan. He could have told me in the hours and hours we spent in the car driving to and from the Adirondacks. He could have told me on our hikes in the mountains or after we had made love in the woods, in those moments of postcoital intimacy when we shared so much of our personal histories. We spoke of so many of our lovers, I wouldn't have minded. I would have understood. I had felt that the angels were with us those days.

I was, quite obviously, mistaken. I had allowed my mortal judgment to cloud my celestial instincts.

FOR YEARS I had worn a small gold cross around my neck. It really wasn't much bigger than a thumbnail. It was a gift I had been given by my aunt when I was born, with the assumption that I would grow into it. When my mother finally shared it with me, I must have been seven, and I had little regard for it. It sat in the bottom of my elementary-school jewelry box, along with plastic hoops and clip-on seashell earrings and pretend pearl necklaces. And this was fine with my mother. The cross wasn't costly, and the church played virtually no role in our household (which, looking back, might have been precisely why my aunt gave me that piece of jewelry).

Years later, when my parents were dead and I was sifting through the rubble that remained of my childhood, I found the cross and brought it with me to college. But I only started wearing it after my angel saved me from death in the dormitory basement. It was never in my mind an amulet, but its aura was numinous and its presence was comforting. I have been told that I touch it on occasion when I seem to be lost in thought.

An indication of how quickly and how deeply I was beguiled by Stephen is this: Of all the gifts I have been given by lovers over the years, the only time I replaced that cross around my neck was when

Stephen gave me a gold chain with a gold angel. He found it in the estate case of a jewelry store in the Village when he was walking alone on the day before we would leave for my sister's in Statler. It was an art nouveau design and perhaps twice as large as the cross—which meant it was still rather delicate. The angel was female and typically eroticized for the period. Her hair was a long and luscious waterfall, her breasts were exposed, and her wings had been tapered more for seduction than flight. She was absolutely beautiful, and it was clear that when she moved, she moved like a ballerina. She was gazing up at a pigeon's blood ruby balanced at the end of her fingers.

It was a striking piece with an aura that was as alluring as it was inspiriting, and as long as Stephen and I were together, I wore it and cherished it. I have it even now. The fact that it was given to me by Stephen affects the associations but not the aura that was a part of the angel before she came into my life and will be an element of the angel when she is a part of someone else's. I keep it because it reminds me both of the wonder and the wistfulness of being bewitched. But I can't bear to wear it.

IT SEEMED TO matter greatly to the state troopers from Vermont whose idea it had been to go to Statler the week after Stephen Drew had arrived at my home. I told them that I had been planning to visit Amanda for a while. The truth is that Amanda and I see each other at least every other month, either because I venture to Statler or she is in Manhattan meeting with galleries. I am confident that on one of these visits my angel will reach hers and my wounded but no less remarkable sister will begin to heal. Ah, but whose idea had it been for Stephen to come along with me, the troopers kept asking? I could see how pleased they were when I admitted that it had been Stephen's. I had proffered the invitation, I said, but he had been hinting. He had been fascinated by Norman's osprey when he'd been at my loft in Manhattan; he had wondered about how Amanda had handled the deaths of our parents. He had remarked on the beauty of the Adirondacks and how—despite his proximity—he rarely seemed to visit those rugged mountains. He even told me how he could go for a Michigan, a Plattsburgh, New York–based concoction consisting of a steamed hot dog on a steamed bun smothered in meat sauce and onions. And so I suggested that he join me, and he agreed without hesitation. He didn't offer even token resistance, not a single "Oh, I couldn't," just to be polite.

And I was thrilled. It was important to me that we were together. His aura was in total disrepair, and he needed to be in a world that was wholly new to him—a place where his aura might be free of memory and association and thus could heal. Moreover, our bodies were absolute canyons of want that week. Certainly the aura hungers, but so does the flesh. I used to dance; I know the pleasure the body can offer. And so yes, I wanted Stephen Drew with me.

"THAT'S AN OSPREY," Norman was mumbling, and I looked up from my tea at the picnic table that served as my sister and brother-in-law's dining-room table in their log cabin. Stephen was staring at Norman's shelves of ospreys with angel wings and the way the morning sun gave them an elysian glaze as it poured in through the wide, eastern-facing windows. Stephen had recognized right away the similarities to the raptor I had insisted on buying from my brother-in-law for my loft in the city.

"It's very good," he said to Norman. The two men were standing together. Stephen's hands were folded behind him, and Norman's were jammed into the pockets of his ragged blue jeans. "Heather explained to me about the wings, how you allowed yourself to imagine what an angel's wings might look like. It's haunting. Very creative." I don't believe he had meant to sound condescending, but he had. And I knew instantly what was coming.

"I didn't have to imagine the wings," Norman said, his voice low and curt. Then, his body hunched over, he stalked from the log cabin, and I knew he was going to find Amanda in the vegetable garden, where she was weeding.

Stephen turned to me, trying to gauge either my reaction or the magnitude of his offense. He sat down beside me, his legs straddling the bench.

"What was that about?" he asked.

I slid my mug of tea toward him and offered him a sip. A little grudgingly he took one. "You came across a bit patronizing," I said.

"I didn't mean to. Last night he seemed fragile to me, but not especially temperamental."

"Oh, I think you diagnosed that right. He is fragile. And I can tell he's worried about Amanda. But he also takes his work seriously," I said. I took back the mug and placed it on the picnic table and then wrapped his fingers in mine. "And he really didn't need to imagine the wings," I explained.

"I do hope you're going to tell me he had a beautiful painting as a model," he said. "Something from the Renaissance, maybe." By then he knew of my first face-to-face experience with an angel in the basement of my dormitory at college. He knew of the other times I had been blessed with encounters with angels as well. He was skeptical but patient.

"Nope."

"If Norman has seen an angel, too, then why is he so . . ."

"Damaged?"

"That's a good word."

"We're all mortal. We're all damaged. We still need to be able to welcome the angel into our realm. We must be hospitable. We need to return the angel's love and be willing to live our lives accordingly. He's not there yet. He's still too guarded. Too solitary. Angels are sociable. They rather like showboats."

"Where was he?"

"When he saw the angel?"

"Uh-huh."

"In Ray Brook."

"The correctional facility?"

"That's right. It's about sixty miles from here. He was in for robbery. He needed money for drugs, and over the course of five days he hit a half dozen liquor stores and convenience stores in Albany. It was quite a visible rampage, and I still find it appalling that it took nearly a week before he was rounded up. He didn't hurt anyone. He's not the type who wants to hurt anyone. Nevertheless, he had a pretty violent method, and it could have ended very badly for someone behind those counters—or for Norman or a police officer. He would go in and smash a bottle on the counter in front of the kid at the register. That would be his weapon. It was, I gather, extremely intimidating, especially since it was evident that Norman was seriously strung out."

In the trees that bordered the yard, I saw a chickadee light on a branch and I watched a brown creeper spiraling up the side of a maple. I had told Stephen before we left Manhattan that Norman was bipolar, which was why as a younger man he had wound up on illegal drugs. There had been no one to diagnose and treat him and so he had treated himself in the only way he could imagine. Now, however, he was properly medicated.

"And he saw this angel in prison?" Stephen was asking me.

"Uh-huh. He came to his cell while the other prisoner was sound asleep. Lights were out, but still the small room grew brighter by far than it ever did during the day. I gather the one window they had was very small. And Norman saw perfectly the rows of feathers on the angel's wings, as well as their shape."

"What did the angel say to him?"

I thought for a long moment before answering. "In all of the things I have shared with you about angels, have I ever described a verbal exchange with one?"

"I guess not."

"We can no more hear the voice of an angel—at least in a literal way—than we can see the face of God."

"Ah, but the angels spoke in the Bible. Think of Gabriel's comforting words to Mary in Luke."

"Mary shared Gabriel's visitation with the disciples many years later. I have no doubts that an angel came to her when she was a very young woman. But it has always seemed more likely to me either that Mary remembered the comforting presence in a fashion that grew more conventional as she grew older or that the men who wrote the Gospel put words into the angel's mouth."

"There are a lot of Christians in this world who would seriously question that interpretation."

"And there are a lot of Christians in this world who nonetheless buy my books," I told him, and he chuckled loudly. I hadn't meant this as a joke, and I hadn't meant to convey with it the sort of edge that he would tell me later he had heard in the remark and had caused him to laugh. I had simply meant that the historiography of Christianity is a subject worth discussing and there is a continuum of belief among Christians. I tried to rein in his smirk by reminding him that Baptists think very differently from Episcopalians and more people in this country believe in angels than in evolution.

"Touché," he agreed. Then: "So the angel said nothing to Norman."

"Not a word."

"What did Norman do?"

"He fell asleep. This was his very first night in Ray Brook. Before that, he had been in either a psychiatric hospital or a county jail. But now his mental health had been stabilized and he had been convicted and sent to prison. A real prison. And he was going to be there for a while, and so he was scared. Absolutely petrified. And completely alone. And the angel came to him and knelt on the cement floor beside his cot and took his hand. Just held it. And Norman felt warm and, for the first time in a very long time, at peace. He felt comforted. He knew he would be fine, and he fell asleep with his fingers in the angel's hands. When he awoke in the morning, he felt more serene than he ever had in his life. To this day he has never forgotten the details of that angel's wings. Sometimes he has to work hard to recover that sense of well-being. He is still withdrawn, he still snaps at people. You saw that. But the wings? He's a visual artist. They're with him always."

Stephen seemed to think about this, to be imagining the angel in Norman's cell.

"Had he met you by then?" he asked me, and I had the sense that this man would have made a better lawyer than a minister. I didn't mind, but I felt as if I were being cross-examined.

"Nope."

"Amanda?"

"No again. He wouldn't meet her until after he was released. They were in the same halfway house together. That's where they met," I explained. I had told Stephen on one of our walks in Manhattan about Amanda's history as a young adult. Despite a trust fund that was identical to mine, she was often living crammed into two-room apartments with nine or ten other people, sleeping on floors, depleting her assets, and taking jobs for a day—motel housekeeper, most often—to scrounge up extra money for cocaine, methadone substitutes, and antianxiety drugs. "How's that for an odd place to fall in love? Two basket cases holding each other together. But it's also rather beautiful, isn't it? They became friends when Amanda made a joke about her sister and angels and he told her the story of his prison-cell visitation."

"So Amanda has never met an angel."

"No, she hasn't. Not yet. She doubts both Norman and me when we compare notes about our winged guardians. I am confident that her angel has tried to reach her—and will keep on trying. But as a mortal you have to be willing to meet them partway. Not necessarily halfway. But you have to be receptive. To know that you can't do it all and be willing to open your mind to seraphic healing."

"Versus sexual healing?"

"Come again?"

"It's an old Marvin Gaye song."

"You are such a cynic," I told him, and I punched him lightly on the arm. "Sometimes I just can't believe there was someone willing to ordain you."

"My sister would agree with you—as would, these days, a great many of my former parishioners."

"Don't say 'former.' Really, I know you'll go back," I said, and at the time I honestly believed that. But he disagreed with me.

"No. There's too much blood on my hands."

"There's no blood on your hands! You have to stop saying such things."

His head was bowed, and when he raised it, he raised an eyebrow as well. Then he stood and went to the window, where, with his back turned to me, he said—and it was the first time I had ever heard such daggers of condescension in his voice—"I can't abide those people any longer. The whole congregation. The whole community. I know that's horrible to admit, but it's the truth. I'm sorry. We're not really a very good fit. We never were. And, unfortunately, I know what used to go on at the Haywards' house. I also know what I did and didn't do, I know what Ginny O'Brien did and didn't do, and I know what the whole congregation did and didn't do. That's the problem. And so I think it's in my own best interests to steer clear. My health, mental and otherwise, depends upon it."

At the time I had thought he was being either melodramatic or, just maybe, metaphoric. It would be weeks later that I would recall this exchange and first contemplate the notion that he had meant every word.

I LIKED TO check in with Amanda and Norman because they had nobody else—no mortals, that is—and they were both so profoundly wounded. Moreover, Amanda was unable to open her mind to the angels in our midst. Early one afternoon that week, when the sun was still high above the copse of evergreens to the west of their log cabin, I went skinny-dipping with Amanda in a secluded section of a nearby river we called the funnel. Amanda took pride in the fact that she lived in a spot that allowed her to swim naked whenever she pleased, and she had so few visitors who might want to swim that she didn't even own a bathing suit. In truth, I think skinny-dipping was also her way of flaunting to Norman and me the state of her mental health: Either her weight was stable and she was fine or she was again shedding pounds and slowly killing herself. That week Stephen and I made love there twice.

The water at the funnel cascaded through a flume of boulders the size of trailers, falling perhaps twenty-five feet, before emptying into a basin that was carved out of the earth like a gigantic cereal bowl. Occasionally Amanda and I would snowshoe there in the winter, and it always felt to the two of us as if we had just walked through the wardrobe into Narnia. The trees along the path from the log cabin to the river would form a silvery canopy, the boughs bending beneath the weight of the ice and snow like frosted palm fronds. Others would become elegant black-and-crystal sculptures: Willowy raven frames, layered with sky-blown glass. The forest that is filled with the music of the wood thrush and the warbler in June is almost preternaturally quiet in January, and even the falling water seems to have grown still. The icicles dangle like earrings.

Nevertheless, it was obviously only in the summer when we would spend whole afternoons at the funnel. Soon after my sister had bought the log cabin and the surrounding property, Norman had taken his chain saw and cut down a swath of the westernmost maples and cedar and pine at the swimming hole so the water would be warmed as much as possible by the afternoon sun. Still, it was never going to be more than sixty-six or sixty-seven degrees, and I wondered how my wraithlike sister could handle the temperature with absolutely no body fat under her skin. That day as we floated on our backs in the shallow pool—the water there was no more than four feet deep—or sat on the boulders that had been warmed by the sun, I stared at my sister's reedy physique: The sharp tips of her collarbone and shoulder blades, the brittle rods that passed for her arms. When she reclined on her towel on the rock, I counted the ribs along the sides of her chest and the points on the hard square of her hip bones. Her breasts were the small hillocks of a middle-school girl.

She was in a bad phase, I saw, and whatever progress she had made in the spring had been undone by days in which she would consume nothing but diet soda and carrot coins from her garden. She was smoking once more like a chimney and had brought her cigarettes with her to the funnel.

"Are you seeing Karen?" I asked her, referring to her therapist perhaps an hour distant in Watertown.

"I am."

"And the nutritionist?" I couldn't remember that woman's name.

"Nope."

"How come?"

"She seemed to know how to get under my skin."

It was always a balancing act with Amanda. I knew the questions I didn't dare ask as well as the things I didn't dare say. *You really can't afford to lose any more weight. You look fine now—don't drop another ounce. For God's sake, Amanda, you have to eat!* What further complicated our conversations when she was in one of these periods was my knowledge that it really wasn't about body image in my sister's case: It was about suicide. She believed much more deeply than I ever had—even when I was curled up in that trunk that night in my first-year dorm—in the utter meaninglessness of life. And as much as I might have wanted her hospitalized, I knew that she would never have stood for it. Once, four years earlier, Norman and I had tried and failed.

"So tell me about your new man," she said to me after a moment. She was smiling, but I knew there was a serrated edge to her question.

"What's to say? What do you want to know?"

"Oh, I don't know. Is the plan to pull him back from the abyss, too? Help him see some angelic meaning in the way his parishioners imitated Mom and Dad?"

It always struck me that Amanda could still refer to those two individuals as Mom and Dad. It was a linguistic nearness that now evaded me. They would, at best, be my parents. My mother. My father. I saw them largely through the formal prism of how they had fought and died or (on good days) the ways they had seemed so glamorous when I was young.

"I think that's how it started," I admitted. "That *is* why I first went to Haverill. I went for him. The girl. The town."

"But now it's just him."

"We have a connection."

"The angels have whispered in each of your ears?"

"They have in mine. I can't speak for him."

"Interesting choice in people to help," she murmured, and she draped one of her skeletal arms over her eyes.

"Meaning?"

"He seems pretty damn self-sufficient."

"Maybe that's his problem."

"I'd focus on the girl. The teenager. She's the one who could end up like us," said my sister.

"Katie."

"Uh-huh."

I considered correcting her: I didn't think that Amanda and I had wound up similarly. But so much of life is about forgiveness and healing—restraining that urge to tweak or lash out or get in the last word—that I said simply, "I don't think it's an either/or proposition. At least I hope it isn't."

"How much do you like him?"

"So far? Plenty."

"Do you trust him?"

"Excuse me?"

She yawned, and I noticed when she went to cover her mouth that she was no longer wearing either of the two silver bracelets that usually adorned her wrists. I feared that either they no longer fit or they hurt. My sister was disappearing once again into a wisp of a woman, frightening in her calculated emaciation, and I made a mental note to call her doctors as soon as Stephen and I had left.

"I said, do you trust him? Don't you worry that this country pastor sees you as his new meal ticket? All of a sudden, a rich, pretty lady drops into his life like an angel—and, please, sis, I only used that word because the simile was irresistible—and he sees in her an opportunity. A retirement plan, if you will."

"He clearly has assets of his own."

"Not like yours, I promise. One of these days, you will branch out into angel merchandise. Angel baubles and angel jewelry boxes. Angel note cards. Angel figurines and Christmas ornaments. Angel rainbow catchers for kitchen windows. Angel vacation cruises."

The sun had warmed the rock beneath me, and I gingerly rolled off my towel so I could feel the heat on all of my skin. My sister was enjoying herself, having a little fun at my expense. "What would occur on an angel cruise?" I asked, in part to change the subject but also in some way to indulge her.

"Oh, you'd give your lectures," she said. "Everyone would watch the stars from the middle of the ocean. They'd tell stories of the angels who had saved their lives. There would be yoga. Meditation. Angel food cake at all the buffets."

"You've really thought this through."

"No I haven't. I was just being glib."

I smiled at her, but she couldn't see me because her eyes were still covered by her arm. I said a silent prayer that either she would open her heart to an angel or that an angel would do for my sister what clearly I could not: encourage her to save her own life.

THERE WERE A half dozen boxes of familial history that wouldn't be sold in the estate sale that followed my parents' deaths. There was their wedding album and a long shelf of college and high-school yearbooks. There were scrapbooks and photo albums. And there were the long trays of slides, many of which had belonged originally to my grandparents: my father's mother and father. These cartons, after the house in upstate New York had been sold, were stored in the attic in my aunt and uncle's home in Fairfield, Connecticut.

I had been out of college and living alone in a small studio in a corner of Brooklyn not quite a dozen subway stops from lower Manhattan when I came across a Bell & Howell slide projector with a carousel in the window of an antique shop in Bay Ridge. It was twenty-five dollars, which seemed like a lot of money for a piece of technology so profoundly useless in the advent of the digital age. But I recalled those yellow-and-blue cartons of slides in the attic in Fairfield, some holding thirty images and some holding forty, and how I hadn't looked at any of them since one New Year's Eve when I'd been in the sixth grade. It had been at a dinner party, and my mother had decided in the period between dessert and the moment when the grown-ups would all stand in front of the television with champagne flutes in their hands to watch the ball drop in Times Square that it might be fun to savor the fading Kodachrome images. In all fairness, a great many of the slides would include my parents' friends who were with them that evening, so the idea wasn't as self-absorbed and egocentric as it might sound.

And it proved to be a lovely idea. The grown-ups were just tipsy enough to be moved, but not so drunk that they would pass out in the dark. My father set up the white screen in front of the bay window, and we—a dozen grown-ups and the two Laurent daughters—positioned ourselves on the couch and the floor and the dining-room chairs that we carried into the living room. We stopped watching a few minutes before midnight only because the adults felt a moral obligation to bear witness to the precise second that the New Year was commemorated on Broadway.

And so I decided there on the street in Brooklyn to buy the projector and carry it back to my studio. It must have weighed twenty-five pounds, and my apartment was on the fifth floor of a five-story walk-up. The five flights were, in my mind, a great gift: They helped keep me in shape, and the apartment that awaited me at the top was high enough that I could see a part of the bay (though not the Statue of Liberty) through a sliver between two taller buildings to the west.

A few weeks after I bought the slide projector, I went to my aunt and uncle's for Thanksgiving. When I returned that evening to Brooklyn, I brought with me a dozen trays of slides in a canvas bag. Amanda, who was living in Boston at the time, hadn't come to Connecticut that year. None of the slide trays had been labeled, but my selection hadn't been entirely random. I'd made sure that I had images that covered the early years of my parents' marriage as well as ones highlighting Amanda and me as little girls. (By the time we were in elementary school, even my father—who had savored his use of slides as the family documentarian—had boxed away his slide camera and was using only film.) And then the next evening, completely alone, I allowed myself to study for long moments the man who had murdered my mother and then killed himself; the woman who would die at the hands of a man whom, I have to assume, she had once loved and with whom she had expected to grow old; and their two little girls, each of whom was transformed by their parents' deaths in ways it would take years to fully comprehend. That night I used a white bedsheet for a screen.

What struck me most as I sipped a glass of wine and studied the images was how charismatic and elegant my parents had been. The colors were faded, which gave the two of them an even more retro sort of allure: Rock Hudson and Doris Day. My father was more robust than I usually thought of him, though my mother was exactly as beautiful. In some of the slides, when she was just about my age then, she was decked out in dresses with pointed collars and cuffed sleeves. In others, as the 1960s became the 1970s, she was in gold-sequined bathing suits on the white sands of Palm Beach and the farthest tip of Long Island, her skin nearly the red of a lobster. Meanwhile my father, who appeared in considerably fewer photos than my mother, would be decked out in beige trench coats and black wing tips, in charcoal gray business suits, or in tennis shorts and navy blue sweaters. In one shot, years before I was born, he was wearing a salmon-colored Nehru shirt and a peace medallion the size of a coaster, and my sense was that he was at a Halloween costume party. My father with a peace medallion? Had to be his idea of irony.

And there were the cars with their fins and the convertible my mother had loved when I'd been so very small and remembered now only in terms of its inviting red leather seats and how invigorating the breeze had felt in my hair in the summer. And there were my sister and me. In prams. In matching bathing suits (but never gold-sequined). On, I have to assume, Amanda's first day of school: I am beside her, looking up at her, and my face is a combination of longing and awe. She has a lunch box and a small backpack that is shaped like a monkey. Curious George? Perhaps, though I have never had any recollection of either of us having had a special fondness for those yellow books, and when I asked Amanda about it, she was characteristically evasive, clutching her memories close to her heart. I was pleased that her hair had been brushed before school. Our mother was mercurial, and some mornings she simply couldn't cope—all the energy she had expended the night before battling with our father would leave her a rag doll—and our hair had been rats' nests.

Ah, but in the evenings? That was when both of our parents would experience their strange and unpredictable transformations—their all-too-frequent transmogrifications. They were vampires. Were-wolves. The night changed them. But they didn't instantly become monstrous. Often there was, first, those long hours of celebrity-like glamour. That night in Brooklyn, I held the stem of my wineglass between my fingers and gazed at a slide of my parents arm in arm on their way to a black-tie dinner, my father in a tuxedo and my mother in a strapless gown that shadowed her collarbone. They were in control—of their lives and of their emotions. They were in charge. They could have been movie stars.

In that image they were standing in front of our house on a summer evening, the convertible with red leather seats parked in the portico just to their left. One of our magnificent weeping willows is over their shoulders. When we sold the house, my aunt told me, the roots of those trees were just starting to burst through the cement floor of the cellar. She thought this was rather funny, an indication in her mind that Amanda and I were getting out of the house just in time. Although in hindsight the violation of the structure from the inside out and the bottom up can only be viewed as a metaphorical sledge-hammer, it is nonetheless telling.

But there was one more detail to that aging Kodachrome slide that caused me to sit forward on my couch and then, a moment later, to put the wine on the floor and approach the sheet. To actually run my fingers over the cotton. To press it flat, to understand if what I was seeing was merely a wrinkle in the fabric or an illusion caused by something behind the sheet. A picture hook in the wall, maybe, or a dimple in the Sheetrock. What was there? What was drawing me to the makeshift screen I had hung on a wall in my tiny apartment? There in the window of my childhood bedroom, standing in profile and gazing down at the corner of the room in which I knew had once sat my small white bed—absolutely oblivious to the slide picture being taken outside the house—was an angel. I could see the tips of the wings, her shoulders (and she was a female angel), and the hair the color of corn silk. I could not see her face because of the angle.

Angels demand nothing from us but faith, and I should have known then that there was no reason to doubt the image on the wall. I had been saved by an angel five years earlier: What grounds had I to mistrust what I was seeing now? Why should I have wondered that she had been looking out for me even then, when I was a small child? But I did wonder, I did doubt. And that was my mistake. I took the slide from the carousel to see if I could see the angel on the actual slide. I turned on the lamp by the table, pulled off the shade, and held the slide near the bulb. Of course the angel was gone. Evaporated like a splash of water from the concrete lip of a swimming pool under a hot summer sun at midday. When I placed the slide back in the carousel, there was no longer a trace of her. The window was dark, and that little girl I had been long ago was, once again, all alone in that bedroom.

THERE WERE MOMENTS when I was fascinated by the way Stephen's fertile mind worked. One morning when I awoke, he was still beside me in bed, but I could tell that he had been awake for a while. It wasn't quite seven-thirty, and the sun was turning the seraphim in my chandeliers the color of pearl. I burrowed into his chest and asked him what he was thinking, expecting perhaps an account of a dream or an analysis of the independent film we had seen the night before at the Angelika. He pulled me against him and said simply, "There were no secrets in Eden."

I liked the idea that we were alone in my bed and he was contemplating Eden.

"No," I agreed, "there weren't. What made you think of that?"

"Eden? Isn't it enough that I have a beautiful woman curled up beside me?"

"Thank you. And I'll accept that my presence was a part of the inspiration."

"But only a part."

"Yes."

I rested my hand on his heart and watched it rise and fall on his chest.

"Genesis is a blunt instrument," he said after a moment. "Especially the story of Adam and Eve. The symbolism is pretty heavy-handed. Obvious."

"Is a sermon forming in your mind?"

He shook his head. "No. I was just contemplating what an arduous burden a secret is. If I were the storyteller, I would have spent more time in what had to have been that nightmarishly stressful period between when Adam and Eve ate from the tree of knowledge and when God confronted them with what they had done. Just imagine how oppressive the wait must have been. There the two of them are, cowering in the garden, just waiting to be discovered."

"Genesis isn't known for character development."

"No. But the beauty of Adam and Eve's nakedness? It's that they haven't any secrets at all. Not a one. And maybe that's the magic of Eden—and what we've lost forever."

There was a ruefulness to his tone that was endearing. It made me want to hold him—and be held by him—forever.

I HAD THE sense that the investigators wanted to find parallels between the ways my parents and the Haywards had died. Why not? It was, in part, those rudimentary similarities that had drawn me to Haverill that first July afternoon. But as I learned more and more about the Haywards' marriage, I was reminded that even batterers and drunks have their distinctions and quirks. The biggest difference, it seemed to me, was that although my father's behavior was indefensible—and I am not even referring to the reality that in the end he would murder the woman he'd married—my mother was no picnic to live with. She drank too much and had a tongue that was poisonous. She could be desperately loving with Amanda and me, but she seemed to take pleasure in the ways she could verbally emasculate our father. I remember the first time I saw *Who's Afraid of Virginia Woolf?*, I thought it was a home movie.

From what I learned about the Haywards, Alice had spent her

life trying her best not to antagonize the beast that was her husband. My mother, on the other hand, was poking hers with a sharp stick. That doesn't excuse the fact that my father would hit her. It isn't a justification for homicide. But the auras of both of my parents were sad and grim in ways that were unlike the auras that must have shrouded George and Alice Hayward and kept their particular angels at bay.

I WAS IN a vintage-clothing shop on lower Broadway when Stephen called me on my cell phone. I was in the dressing room—a dark and musty little cubicle with a fraying curtain the color of subway-track muck—wondering if I was still young enough to pull off a sleeveless black sheath from the 1960s or whether it made me look like an amazon. I was in a very good mood, a little giddy even. It was late afternoon, and when I saw that it was Stephen causing my phone to chirp, I may even have allowed myself a little extra sigh of contentment. We hadn't been apart long, but already I missed him madly, and our tentative plan was that he would return to Manhattan that weekend and stay with me. We had ruled out my coming to Vermont until he had a better sense of whether he was capable of resuming his duties in the pulpit. The idea that he was continuing to live in the parsonage though he was no longer serving as the minister was a source of great consternation to him. I don't think his parishioners cared then—though they would soon—but he did. It was one more thing, it seemed to me at the time, over which he felt needless and unreasonable guilt. Already he was looking for a place he could rent in Bennington.

"Hi, stranger," I said, and I leaned against the wall of the dressing room. I turned up the volume on my phone so I could hear him over the throbbing bass of the store's sound system. "How are you doing?"

"We need to talk."

There was an urgency to his voice that I had never heard before. I was aware of the way his mood could vacillate between brooding and playful; I had seen him despairing to the point where there was an edge of meanness to his tone. But the insistence I noted in those four words was new to me.

"Okay," I said. "What's up?"

"Where are you?"

"In a stall that could seriously use some Febreze." He went silent, and I realized that my lame little joke had given him the wrong idea of where I was. "I'm in a dressing room in a clothing store. A shop that has some great dresses. I think I'm too old for the one I'm wearing, but it was still fun to try it on. I—"

"When can I call you so we can talk?"

"Well, we're talking now. But it sounds like this is serious."

"It is."

I thought about the things he might want to discuss that would make him sound so grim, and the obvious one was that he wanted to—as he might have put it—break up with me. That he wasn't going to come back to New York after all. I wasn't precisely sure how far along our relationship was, but I did know that I wanted it to continue. Initially I had presumed that I'd been dropped into his life by his angel because he needed me after the Haywards had died, but as we spent more and more time together, I had begun to wonder if, perhaps, our angels—mine and his—had been in collusion and had consciously brought us together.

"We can't talk now?" I asked. He was, quite obviously, stalling. Whatever he wanted to discuss, he was hoping he wouldn't have to broach the subject while I was in a slightly rank dressing room in clothes I didn't own.

"I'd rather you were alone."

"I am alone."

"I'd rather you were home."

"Do I need to be sitting down?" I asked, teasing him.

"Please," he said, and his voice softened the tiniest bit. "I need to tell you something, and it's important you understand that this isn't a moment to be light."

" 'Angels can fly because they can take themselves lightly.' "

"What?"

"That's a quote from G. K. Chesterton."

"Heather, I just came from a state police barracks. For the last forty-five minutes, I was interrogated by two very curt troopers."

I realized I had misread the signals in his voice. This was not urgency so much as it was outrage. He was indignant. "Go on," I said.

"Now?"

"Now. It's fine."

"They think I killed them. Maybe just him. George."

I slid down onto the thin wooden board that served as a seat and went completely still. I actually did need to sit down. "Why would they think that?" I asked. "That's ridiculous."

"It is ridiculous. Completely ridiculous. And appalling. Obviously I didn't kill the two of them. I offered to take a lie-detector test. But they're serious enough about this that I'm going to have to get a lawyer."

"Where did they get this idea? They certainly didn't think you'd had anything to do with this tragedy when it first happened."

"I know."

"Why, then?"

"I don't know. I just know I'm furious."

"It does sound a little absurd."

"Trust me: It is."

From the corner of my eye, I saw the feet of teen girls and women younger than me walking beneath the drape, but the world went eerily silent. I was no longer aware of the pulsating music the store had been playing or the conversations between customers just outside the dressing room. I stared down at the black wool of the dress, bunched up a little bit in my lap, and rested my forehead in my hand. My ears were ringing. On the floor of the dressing room was a torn sliver of bathroom tissue, and I couldn't imagine why it was there.

"Heather?"

"I'm here," I said. Then: "So you're getting a lawyer?"

"I am."

"Well, if you've done nothing wrong, then you have nothing to worry about. I know that's not universally true. But have a little faith in your angel," I said, and a memory came to me. *I thought you were my angel.* It was what he had said that first Saturday morning when he'd come to my loft and I'd told him that I wanted to show him an angel. He had called me his angel at least three times since then, and I expected him to say those words to me now. But he didn't.

"I expect I'll depend mostly on my lawyer," he said instead. "But thank you very much."

"You're still coming to New York?" I asked.

"Yes, of course. I just might be a day later than planned. It depends on who is representing me and when he or she can get together with me."

I was relieved, though not completely. From the other side of the drape, I heard teen girls giggling about the scatological drawing and the sexual double entendre on a T-shirt. They sounded too young to be so knowledgeable, and that only unnerved me further. I was engulfed in an aura of demonstrable unease.

"When you know when you're coming," I said, "please call."

"You sound annoyed."

"No. *Anxious* would be a better word."

"I didn't know you got anxious," he said, and I wondered if I had heard a ripple of challenge in his tone or whether he had meant this only as a small jest.

"Oh, I get anxious," I told him. "As you get to know me, you'll see I have a whole cauldron of emotions." Still, I don't believe I expected at the time that he would see hurt and anger and, worst of all, betrayal.

AS SOON AS Stephen returned to Manhattan, I insisted we stroll into the West Village and stretch our legs along the narrow, oddly angled streets bordered by manicured brownstones. He had arrived near dinnertime because he'd met with a lawyer in Vermont over lunch. Eventually, I thought, we might get as far as the Hudson, where we could watch the late-summer sun descend in the horizon beyond the river, and on the way there I might show him an angel that warmed me near St. Luke's Church. But mostly I just wanted to talk and savor the first small wisps of autumn in the air.

Initially he was guarded and resistant to my inquiries. It was as if we were back on his porch in Haverill the Tuesday just after the tragedy. The conversation was unsatisfying, and I felt a stab of apprehension that we might not be able to recover what we had had. But that didn't seem reasonable to me that evening since—then—I believed everything he had told me and thus the inquiries of the police were unfounded. Ludicrous. A strange comet that would streak across the night sky, cause a little disconcerting befuddlement, and be gone. And eventually his resentment and pique did fade and the distance between us narrowed. When we left my loft, we might have been mistaken on the street for a brother and sister who were not especially close: We walked without touching, and our eyes never met. But by the time we reached St. Luke's, we were holding hands. And when we returned to Greene Street later that night, I was burrowed against him and his arm was around my shoulders. We would be fine, I decided. We were laughing, and his wit had lost that caustic bite that dogged him when he was irritated.

And for a week we *were* fine. Occasionally after talking to his lawyer—with whom he seemed to speak daily—he would breathe deeply through his nose and sigh and stare for long moments at either my osprey or my angels or the passersby on the street below us. Never would he tell me what he and his lawyer had discussed, and usually the conversations were brief. Still, it was clear he was exasperated, and one time I said to him, "Those little phone consultations with your lawyer can't be cheap. This is a nonissue—he'll make it disappear. Let it go." And after a few minutes he would, and our vacation from real life would resume. We would walk and read and eat and make love. I did a radio interview with a program that broadcast from Manhattan's City Hall, and he made faces at me through the glass when the host wasn't looking. I wrote a bit, did a few online q&a's, and responded to the occasional request from my publisher. But I did little else that week that could possibly have been construed as work. We saw no movies and no shows, because we were content—at least I was— to bask in a world that wasn't much bigger than the alcove and daybed in my loft.

WE HAD BEEN together again for a week, and as far as I was concerned, nothing in our world needed to change. I knew it would, of course. But I was very, very happy. Sometimes when I look back at the period when Stephen and I were involved, I find myself doubting that we could ever have been so perfectly mated, so finely attuned to each other's cravings and desires. It is as if that varied collection of memories we store—some precisely rendered and accurate, others modified by the caprices and needs of an aura, some gifts from an angel—in my case has a series embedded there that is more fiction than fact. That is, perhaps, all fiction. A string of pearls that turn out to be bath beads when you squeeze them.

And a part of my later sadness would stem from the reality that so many of our long talks together had been total fiction. I discovered I had been lied to for nearly five weeks.

But for those five weeks I had been as content as I have ever been in my life.

It all came apart after one more of his conversations with his attorney. As he did always when he spoke to this Aaron Lamb, he took his cell phone and stood at the corner window, retreating to the section of my loft I lived in least. He spoke softly, and while I might hear an occasional word—*investigation, allegations, evidence, office*—I never knew precisely what they were talking about. I heard no specifics. And that last phone call was really no different, though I did hear two words that struck me in a way that none had in any of their previous conversations: *diary*. And *DNA*. I honestly think I knew before Stephen had ended the call that something different and new had transpired, and it boded ill for our affair.

After he slipped his phone into his pants pocket, he folded one arm around his chest and rubbed at his chin with the other. He hadn't shaved yet—that week he tended to shave just before lunch—and he seemed to be toying with the stubble along his jawline. It was obvious that this call had agitated him more than most.

I pushed my chair away from my desk and turned to him. "Anything interesting?" I asked softly, though it was evident to me that there was.

He cleared his throat before speaking. "I'm not sure *interesting* is the right word," he said carefully. "It may be interesting for uninvolved parties. The prurient who have followed one family's nightmare in the media. But for me? I'm not sure I would use the word *interesting*."

"What word would you use?"

He had remained on his feet, and his fingers were still at his face. "Let's see. *Disturbing,* perhaps. *Disquieting. Problematic.*"

"Sit down. Tell me: What did he have to say this time?"

He didn't sit, and so I stood and went to him. I pulled his arms from his body to mine and rested them on my hips. For the briefest of seconds, he seemed to resist. I noticed the room wasn't as bright this time of the morning as it had been only days earlier, and I realized we had reached a stage in the season when the sun no longer rose quite as high over the surrounding buildings.

"Tell me," I said again.

"Well, where to begin . . ." He was frowning.

"Aaron told you something. Begin there."

"He did."

I was growing restless at the protracted way he was sharing his news. I wanted to know what he had learned so I could offer comfort and counsel. And though I no longer presumed it would be essentially nothing and he would need from me only reassurance, still I hoped. As we stood together in silence, I sent a short, brief petition to my angel that my misgivings were unwarranted. That nothing had changed. "Are you going to tell me?" I asked finally, careful to keep my voice light.

He took a breath and looked out the window over my shoulder. "Alice kept a journal," he said, his voice a little clipped.

Instantly my anxiety was transformed into dread, and I felt as if I were sliding underwater. For the rest of that conversation, his voice would sound slightly muffled to me, as if my ears were beneath the smooth plane of a very still lake. I understood from the moment he had said there was a journal that we were moving inexorably toward separation. If I didn't know precisely what he was about to tell me, I had a feeling. The gifts of prophecy and fear? Trifles compared to the insight an angel will give a receptive mind. I didn't yet remove his hands from my body, but only because I clung to the tiniest strip of kindling that I was mistaken.

"Go on," I said.

"In all likelihood I am in that journal."

"As her pastor?"

"As her . . ."

"For God's sake, Stephen, just tell me."

He sighed. "There is an element to the story—a little background, if you will—that I didn't share with you. Arguably, I should have. But I made the calculated decision that it would only distress you if I did. I think, in some way, I thought I was shielding you."

"From what? The idea you're a killer? I think you have grave demons, Stephen, but I promise you: I don't see you as a killer."

"I'm glad. Thank you," he said, and I am convinced he added that only because it gave him an extra second to stall. To frame his thoughts. Then he continued, "For a time Alice and I were lovers." He looked into my eyes, but I looked away, and after a brief second I pushed myself off him. I may have seen something like this coming, but the sensation of betrayal was nonetheless palpable, and I could hear my heart thrumming in the back of my head.

"We were lovers, and—"

"I heard you the first time."

"And I should have told you."

"When were you two together?" I asked. It seemed the first of a great many pieces of very basic information I needed to gather.

"Late last year. Early this year."

"How early? It's currently September. Was this two nights? Two weeks? Two months?" Outside my window I watched a double-decker tour bus lurch to a stop at the traffic light.

"Two seasons."

"Winter and spring."

"Yes. Through the second week in May."

"And in all of our conversations about the murder and the suicide and your guilt, you never told me this . . . why?"

"I don't know. I thought I was protecting you. And it didn't seem relevant."

"I think the fact you fucked her is as relevant as the fact you baptized her," I said, though I was able to restrain myself from raising my voice.

"I deserved that."

I tried to remind myself that hostility invariably boomerangs back. In the end we wound ourselves, too, when we lash out.

"I imagine I was concerned that you would get the wrong idea about Alice's and my relationship," he went on when I remained silent. "Or, perhaps, that you might presume I was at her house that evening."

"The evening they were killed?"

"Yes."

"Is there anything else you haven't told me?" I asked him.

"About Alice?"

"About anything."

"No. But things are changing. I am going to have to return to Vermont and give them what they call a DNA swab. I am going to have to give them some fingerprints and turn over my laptop."

"Are you being arrested?"

"No. Not yet, anyway."

I took a deep breath and then exhaled slowly. "Are you scared?"

"Of?"

"Oh, I don't know. I would think being a suspect in a murder investigation just might unnerve a person."

"I can't tell: Are you being sarcastic?"

"Yes, Stephen. I am being sarcastic."

"That doesn't seem like you."

"I just asked you if you were frightened, and you asked me what of. The moment seemed to call for sarcasm."

"You have every right to be angry with me. I should have told you about Alice."

"Were you two in love?"

He went quiet, and I couldn't decide whether it was because they had been and for some reason he didn't want to admit this or whether he honestly couldn't decide. Finally: "I'm not completely sure what that means."

"It's not a hard question. I didn't ask you to list for me the contents of the periodic table. Were you two in love?"

"I think she might have loved me. For a time."

"And you?"

"I enjoyed her company."

"And you enjoyed sleeping with her."

"Yes."

"Why did you stop?"

"Her husband wanted to come home. He insisted he'd changed; he said things would be different. It seemed to me that if I told her not to take him back, I would have an obligation to marry her myself."

"Or tell her that you didn't love her enough to marry her."

"In all fairness, I didn't want to be responsible for breaking up a marriage that might have a second life."

"Even a marriage that bad?"

"So it would seem."

"But you didn't care enough for Alice to fight for her. To make a serious commitment. You left her to fend for herself with George."

"Apparently."

My eyes were growing moist, and I tried to regain perspective. To imagine this conversation both from God's vantage point and from an angel's. I heard in my head the word *forgiveness*, and I thought about Jesus Christ's admonition to Peter: Be prepared to forgive someone not merely seven times, but seventy times seven. I might have mastered myself completely, but I was so unnerved by those last lackadaisical responses—*So it would seem. Apparently.*—that I made the mistake of asking him one more question.

"Well, then: Did you kill him? Either of them?"

"Or both?"

"Yes. Or both."

I was just beginning to wonder why Stephen wasn't answering my question and whether he would when he said, his teeth seemingly clenched in exasperation, "I can't believe you would even ask. Has it really come to that?"

I considered pressing him, but I knew by the glacial disgust in his tone that I didn't dare. Besides: I had my answer.

"There's another thing," he said.

"Yes?"

"Aaron said you might want to get some coaching from a lawyer."

"Me?"

"That's right—but only so you'll be prepared when the Vermont State Police come to interview you."

"I'll take that under advisement," I agreed. But still I didn't turn around, because I didn't want him to see that I was no longer able to bridle my tears. I didn't turn around when I told him that I thought he should go.

"Thank you," he said, misunderstanding me completely, perhaps because he couldn't see my face. "I'll return as soon as I can."

"No," I told him. "Please don't. I'd rather you didn't ever come back."

CHAPTER FOURTEEN

eople often share with me stories of the angels who have dropped into their lives and how they have been saved by them. When the tale comes via e-mail or the postal service and the writer seems to need a response, either my assistant or I will answer it. Usually it is my assistant who pens the first draft, and the year that the Haywards would die my assistant was a young Columbia grad student named Rick who once was less than a second away from qualifying for the Olympics in the four-hundred-meter freestyle and still looked an awful lot like a lifeguard. His fiancée, two years his senior, was already an assistant editor in publishing (though not at my house), and I expected that eventually Rick would follow her into the profession.

About an hour after I had broken up with Stephen—and this was, in my mind, an irrevocable break—Rick came by with some letters and e-mails from readers that were hauntingly beautiful and precisely what I needed at that moment. There were encounters that were stirring, and there were encounters that were poignant. A young soldier in Afghanistan e-mailed me that he had been driving a jeep with three comrades in a mountainous stretch of Uruzgan when a female angel stood in the path of the vehicle. He veered around the spirit and wound up careening into the grass off to the side. No one was hurt, and when the soldiers went to the spot on the road where the driver insisted he had seen the angel, they discovered an IED that would have detonated like a mine had they driven over it. Another reader shared with me that at the precise moment when her much-beloved mother expired in a hospice, an angel was sitting calmly on the mattress beside the older woman and lifted the hands of the two generations of women, one already cold, and clasped them together for a brief moment. Then the room filled with light, causing two of the aides at the hospice to race there because they feared that the building was on fire, and thus there were three witnesses to the sight of the angel gently lifting the soul from the dead woman's body and carrying it like a honeymoon bride off to heaven.

That evening I felt that I needed an angel rather badly. My despair wasn't simply that Stephen had been sleeping with someone and hadn't told me; that alone wouldn't have sent me into such a funk. People have secrets. Certainly I do. It was that withholding this particular piece of information about Alice Hayward, given how paramount the woman's life and desperately sad end had been in our brief time together, was a breach of faith that made tawdry our supposed intimacy. I was hurt: There is no getting around that detail. Moreover, it had caused me to question so much else of what he'd told me. If he could withhold this facet of his involvement with the Haywards, what else wasn't he telling me? The reality is that I suspected he really had murdered at least one of the Haywards, and so I needed to separate myself from him while I prayed for guidance and tried to understand what I was feeling.

As he did every day that he came to my loft, Rick had prioritized the letters and e-mails that were most important. Usually these were from my editor or my literary or speaking agents, or they were from journalists. But the chaos that surrounds the launch of a book had settled down, and so when I was alone that evening, there were mostly e-mails and letters from readers. Among them were those stories from the soldier in Afghanistan and the woman who had witnessed an angel cradle her mother's soul. But the one that caused me to think about what was most important in my life—what I really needed to do next—was from a fifteen-year-old girl in Ohio whose father had died a year earlier after a brief battle with brain cancer. The teenager shared with me that she was an only child and she and her father had been very close. For months after her father's death, both she and her mother had been nearly catatonic. Her mother, an accountant in Columbus, had returned to work in the small firm where she was employed, and the teen had resumed her schooling after three weeks away. But neither was functioning especially well, and separately they both had begun seeing therapists who specialized in grief counseling.

"I know from your book that angels often have real halos and wings," the young woman wrote to me in her e-mail, "but my mother and I both believe that Dr. Noel is an angel, too." I Googled Dr. Noel and found that she was a psychiatrist whose first name was Corona. Corona Noel. Is there a more perfect name for an angel? The teenager said that she and her mother were getting better now, and she wanted to know if I thought angels sometimes took on the guise of a mortal and whether she might have been correct that her therapist was a celestial being. She also wanted to know more about how I had handled the deaths of my own parents and what it had been like to see their bodies after they had died. Apparently it was soothing to her to have seen her father's face at peace after the physical and emotional agony he had endured in the last months of his life.

The e-mail, I realized, was both a responsibility—as is much of the correspondence I receive—and a message for me. This young woman, wise beyond her years, may not have met her own angel yet (though it did indeed seem possible to me that this Corona Noel had celestial connections), but I found myself contemplating the notion that she herself was being inspired by an angel. By my angel. Alone at my desk, I found myself sniffling back real tears because I hadn't seen my parents' bodies after they had died, and I grew alarmed at what I had missed. What, I wondered, had happened to them? How had they been handled and treated by the pathologist?

Moreover, I concluded that in my self-absorption—my interest in Stephen and my misguided concern for the man—I had lost sight of someone very, very important: Katie. My sister had been right that afternoon when we'd gone skinny-dipping at the funnel. I should have been focusing more on the girl. And so I looked at my calendar and I pinpointed a row of blank days. I decided I would return to Vermont and visit the newly orphaned daughter of George and Alice Hayward.

I AM NOT sure how Stephen had expected me to respond to his confession that he'd been sleeping with Alice Hayward. Had he anticipated that my heart would be so resilient that I wouldn't be hurt? I know he didn't believe that I would have an angel to care for my wounds, because he had no faith in angels at all. He had no faith in anything. But did he presume that I would—and here is a word that is too often misused by therapists and self-help gurus who believe we can be healed with mortal counseling alone—*understand*? Did he think either that I would understand that he'd had an affair with a parishioner or that I would understand his reluctance to tell me? In hindsight it was the latter that disturbed me far more. People—therapists and pastors alike—sometimes succumb to temptation and move from healing to hurting. The preacher becomes the predator. We are all flawed, and I could have forgiven that. In my mind I imagine Stephen telling me about the affair our first afternoon together on the parsonage porch. (And though the prosecutor from Vermont, at least in the early weeks of her investigation, didn't believe that that Tuesday afternoon was the first time Stephen and I had met, it was.) Or, more likely, I hear him telling me about his intimate and inappropriate relationship with the poor woman our first Saturday in my loft in the city. He certainly could have told me then. He had ample opportunities that afternoon and evening.

But he didn't.

The fact was, I realized, he was never going to tell me. He only confessed when he did because he had to: because that investigator with the state police had learned that he had been sleeping with Alice Hayward and he was a suspect in the murder of one or both of the Haywards—and now, it seemed, I might be, too.

It all left me a little sick and despairing in ways that I hadn't experienced in a very long time. I honestly wasn't sure what I found more troubling: the reality that Stephen Drew was comfortable keeping such a secret to himself or the possibility that he was capable of murder.

And as the days passed, it seemed more and more conceivable to me that he had indeed killed George Hayward. Alice? No, not really. I saw the horror unfolding in the same conventional manner as, in the end, would that state's attorney. Stephen had gone to the house that Sunday night in July and found Alice already dead and George passed out drunk on the couch. And so he had taken the fellow's handgun and murdered him.

The world is filled with human toxins—not the darkness that we all occasionally crave, but actual people who are so unwilling to bask in the angelic light that is offered us all that they grow poisonous—and you can pray for their eventual recovery and healing. And sometimes those prayers will be answered. But sometimes these individuals have been vaccinated against goodness and against angels and they are so unwilling to give an inch to their God that often they never (and I use this expression absolutely literally) see the light. As scarred and as wounded as my sister had been by the thorns that mark our paths through this world, Stephen Drew was even more seriously damaged: Unlike Amanda, he had become a thorn himself.

KATIE HAYWARD'S HIGH school was one of those sprawling two-story complexes that were built in the 1970s for durability, not aesthetics. It was designed to endure teenagers, not educate them, and so it was a labyrinth of cinder-block walls and windows reinforced with wire mesh. It smelled of antiseptic and—because the gymnasium and locker rooms were across a thin lobby from the front doors—adolescent sweat. Everything was painted a drab green, ostensibly to celebrate the Green Mountains, but I was left with no sense of foliage when I stood for a moment outside the sliding glass partition bearing the sign VISITORS SIGN IN HERE. Eventually an elderly secretary with a round face and a kind smile listened to my story and found Katie's guidance counselor, Joanne Degraff, and then Joanne escorted me to the cafeteria, where Katie was having lunch with her friends. I wasn't quite sure where Katie and I would speak and whether we would get to be alone, but Joanne had moonstone-blue eyes that were rich with understanding and compassion, and she suggested that Katie and I take a walk around the school. Katie seemed content with this plan. She had finished her sandwich, and it was a beautiful September afternoon. The leaves were just starting to change color in the hills to the east of the school's athletic fields, and there were thin ribbons of red and orange beginning to form along the peak of the distant ridge.

"My friends think you're another psychiatrist or a social worker," she said to me as we started to stroll beside the oval where the track team practiced and out toward the football field with its two long walls of wooden bleachers with peeling evergreen paint. Students on the far side of those stands were playing soccer in gym class. Katie was wearing a black T-shirt with a Chihuahua sporting a studded collar on the front and blue jeans that clung to her legs. She had used mascara and eyeliner with great enthusiasm, and I thought I might have seen the edge of a tattoo where the back of her shirt collar met her left shoulder blade. But she also looked a little lost to me, and that gave me some comfort: She was needful and frightened, and I knew that eventually her angel was going to be there for her.

"You've seen a lot of social workers?" I asked.

"Yup. And two different counselors, though I seem to be spending the most time with a social worker named Josie Morrison. But it's, like, totally okay. I get it. I know why everyone is so worried. And I know you get it."

"Thank you."

"Ginny loaned me her copies of your books."

"You read them?"

"Uh-huh."

"Well, thank you. I am very flattered," I told her, and I was.

"Ginny thought they would help me."

"Did they?"

"Little bit. Ginny said they helped her."

"Your mother's friend is struggling?"

"Yeah. She is. I don't see her a ton. But I guess she's still kind of freaked. I hear Tina's mom and dad talking."

"It's hard to lose a friend—especially in such a violent fashion. It's not as bad as losing a parent. But it is scarring. Life-altering."

She seemed to think about this. Then: "Some of those stories about angels in your books were really out there."

"Angel stories usually are."

"But you don't, like, actually believe them, do you?"

"It depends on the story. Some of them I believe. But yes, others have a significance that is more allegorical. Like a parable. That's why I include them. But I can tell you this: There is absolutely no doubt in my mind that angels are real. As real as you and me and your friend Tina. As real as Lula," I said, referring to the springer spaniel that she and her parents had gotten at the local humane society when she was younger.

It was clear that my declaration of faith had made her a little uncomfortable, and she wasn't sure how to respond. "So how long are you here for?" she asked, what I presumed she viewed as an innocuous question—her way of changing the subject.

"In Haverill? Just this afternoon. Maybe a little longer in Vermont. I don't know. I really don't have a schedule."

"Are you here to see Stephen?"

"No."

"But you will, right?"

"No, I probably won't."

"Huh. I kinda thought you two were, you know, like an item."

"For a time we were friends," I said, "but he seems to have built a wall against angels." I looked over at her, but she scrupulously avoided eye contact. The fact that we were walking and talking, I realized, made this conversation much easier for her than if we'd been sitting across from each other at one of those cafeteria tables.

"But you knew him before my parents died, right?"

"Nope. I met him the Tuesday after that happened. I read about it in the papers and saw the story on the news. And his aura seemed in such sad disrepair that I went to see him. I went to see you."

"After that happened," she said, repeating the words and nodding. "Oh."

It wasn't hard to imagine the stories this young woman had probably heard—or, in some cases, merely overheard. It broke my heart when I thought about what she was learning about her mother and Stephen through the rumor mill.

"So, then, am I, like, the reason you're here now?" she went on.

"You know, I think you are. Is that okay?"

She shrugged as she walked and folded her arms in front of her chest. The sun abruptly caught the stud in her nose, and for a split second it sparkled. "I guess. Do you have a place or something in Vermont?"

"This is so funny. I thought I would be asking you all the questions. But you seem to have turned the tables on me."

"Oh, I'm sorry," she said, her voice rising just the tiniest bit, and for the first time she actually turned to face me. She looked a little stricken.

"No, it's okay," I told her, and I was sure to smile. We were near enough to the gym class that we could hear the gym teacher with his whistle and occasional reprimands or shouts of encouragement. "I think it's just fine. And to answer your question, no, I don't have a place in Vermont. I live in an apartment in New York City."

"Yeah, I think I knew that. From your second book."

"You really have done your homework."

"Not so much," she said. A tall boy from the gym class with a great mane of yellow hair waved at her and shouted something I didn't quite hear. She made a face at him that suggested she was disgusted and then gave him the finger, but I could tell it was meant in good fun. "Sorry about that," she said to me sheepishly. "That was kind of awkward."

"It's fine."

"Since I'm already, like, asking way more questions than I should, can I ask you one more?"

"Absolutely. You can ask me as many as you like."

"How long . . ."

"Go ahead."

"How long does it take you to get over something like this?"

I wasn't surprised that she would ask this particular question, because I had discovered the first time we met how frank Katie Hayward could be. But I was nonetheless impressed. "On the one hand, I don't think you ever do," I answered. "And I don't think you're meant to. It's always going to be a part of who you are. Certainly that has been my experience. But eventually it recedes into one more of the many experiences that have shaped you. It may be the most wounding. It may be the most terrifying. But you don't have to remain wounded and terrified. I mean, I haven't found myself avoiding relationships or marriage because of how my parents' lives ended. I assure you, that's not the reason I'm single. Nor am I always thinking about how they died—what my father did to my mother and then to himself."

"Do you dream about them? I don't sleep well these days, and it's not just because I miss my own house. But when I am asleep, I have these totally freakish dreams. Not exactly nightmares. But stuff that really, really creeps me out. Sometimes I can't even go back to sleep afterward."

"Such as?"

"Well, I see what Ginny must have seen when she got there the next morning."

"Your parents' . . . bodies."

"Yeah."

"I used to imagine my mother's body after my father shot her. And my father's after he hanged himself. Even now I try to avoid those police shows on television. They always show dead bodies, and that always sends my imagination into overdrive. Sometimes when I'm channel surfing, I remain stuck on QVC—there seem to be corpses on every other station."

"And I know what I'm seeing in my dreams isn't quite right. Either it's bloodier than it could have been—I mean, the blood is just everywhere—or my mom is wearing clothes. But she was in her nightgown, right?"

"So they tell me. I wasn't there."

"And my dad's blood is all over her shirt and her jeans. I mean *all over her.* But it couldn't have been, right? Because they said my dad was on the couch and my mom was all the way across the room."

"I don't think there was any blood on your mother," I told her, hoping I could put her mind at rest.

"Did they tell you which nightgown she was wearing?"

"No. Sorry."

"Ginny said she didn't remember, either. When I asked Stephen—"

"When did you ask Stephen?" I said, not meaning to cut her off. I was surprised, given the fact he was under investigation for murder and the story had been in the newspapers, that he was still counseling her. I was struck by the casual way she had used his name just now. "Was this in July or August or recently?"

"Yesterday," she answered, and when I glanced over at her, she didn't seem unduly alarmed by the seeming urgency of my interruption. She pushed her dark hair off her face. "I saw him in Bennington yesterday afternoon. Tina drove me."

"And you asked him about the nightgown."

"I did, and he said he didn't quite remember, either. But the one he described was one I don't think she even owned. He said he thought it was a plaid summer nightshirt. But all her summer nightshirts had, like, flowers on them. Or they were solid colors. One was red. One was green. But plaid? One of her winter flannel nightgowns was plaid, but there was no way she was wearing that one in July.

I mean, back in April she had probably stored it with her winter clothes and sweaters in these tubs she keeps way in the back of her closet. Was it possible she had a plaid summer nightshirt and I just didn't know?"

It was possible. But it was also conceivable that Stephen knew of Alice Hayward's plaid flannel nightgown from their affair in the winter; perhaps she had worn it then, when they'd been sleeping together, and now, months later, he was confusing the images in his recollection. It was also possible that he honestly didn't remember what nightgown Alice had been wearing and yesterday had described for the girl the only one he could recall. "Yes," I said simply, "that's possible."

"But you don't think so. I can tell from your voice."

"What else did you two talk about?" I asked.

"He wanted to know if I was angry at him. He knew I'd heard about the stuff that went on between him and my mom, and he wanted to apologize."

"That was kind of him," I said, but something was gnawing at me. I felt far from angelic, and I was hoping that a little magnanimity would help clear my head. "So: Are you angry at him?"

"No. I really don't see the big deal anymore. At first I didn't believe they were sleeping together. I was totally weirded out by the whole idea. But now I realize they were having an affair, and I'm okay with it. I mean, my mom and dad were apart, and so she and Stephen hooked up. I mean, my dad was . . ."

"Go on."

"He was mean to Mom. I know you know that. He would hit her."

"You heard their fights?"

"Didn't you hear your parents'?"

"Yes."

"So you know how much it all just sucks," she said, and she wrinkled her nose as if she smelled something unpleasant. "So, like, what did it matter if my mom and Stephen had something? It didn't hurt anyone. It's like the two of you—who does it hurt if you two have something going on?" I considered correcting her—reminding her that *have* should be *had*. But I restrained the impulse, and she continued, "When my dad came back, things seemed to be a little better. At least for a while. They were like newlyweds for the first weeks of June. And so, maybe, my mom's . . . relationship . . . with Stephen had the potential to make things better between her and Dad. In the end it didn't. But maybe it could have."

"Do you think your father knew that your mother had been involved with Stephen?"

She turned to me, and she looked so intense that the world seemed to grow quiet. Suddenly the students at the soccer field in the distance were a television image with the volume muted. It was as if there were no birds and no breeze as we circled the perimeter of the school. "I think he found out the night they died," she said carefully. "I've thought about this a lot the last couple of days, what with all the stuff on the Internet and a conversation I had with Ginny. I sure don't think my dad knew when he came home in May. I don't think he knew at the start of the summer. I think somehow he learned what was going on when I was at the concert in Albany."

"That Sunday night."

"Yeah. Uh-huh. I mean, she had been baptized that day, and Dad didn't go. I know she was a little angry at him about that. A little disappointed. And so maybe that night they were talking about the baptism and she was talking about Stephen and it just, like, came up."

I contemplated whether confessing to an affair could just, like, come up. And while that wasn't likely, I did think that Katie's instincts were sound: It seemed plausible enough that if Alice were angry at

George for not attending a ritual that obviously meant so much to her—a ritual conducted by her former lover—it was conceivable that as the last fight of their lives escalated, she told him she'd been involved with her pastor. Perhaps she'd told George she'd loved this other man. Still, why hadn't he gone after Stephen if that was the case? Why hadn't he taken his gun and gone to the church or the parsonage after strangling his wife?

"But until he found out—if he found out," I said carefully to Katie, "the reality that your mom and Stephen had discovered each other actually made things better between your mom and your dad. For a time, anyway. That's what you're suggesting, right?"

She nodded. "For a time. Maybe because she was a little more confident. But it didn't last. I don't know. They were fighting again in July. Well, Dad was fighting."

"How do you feel about Stephen?"

"Now?"

"Yes. Now."

"That's a freaky one for me. I mean, how would you feel if you learned after your dad had killed your mom that she'd been having an affair with the minister? You might be really pissed off at the guy. You'd think, whoa—is he the reason my mom is dead? But then maybe you wouldn't go there. Maybe you'd just think how he had made your mom happy. You know, maybe your dad would have killed your mom anyway, and so you think, well, at least the minister made her happy for a while."

"But that assumes the minister did make her happy. That he didn't break her heart."

"Did he break yours?" We were almost back to the entrance to the school. My sense was that Katie had asked this quickly because once we were at the building and in the midst of the students and teachers, she wouldn't have dared. Still, I stopped in my tracks. Tentatively I put my arm around her shoulders, wondering how she would respond to my touch. But her body didn't tense, and she allowed her small frame to fall against me for a moment.

"Be careful," I said simply.

"Like, in what way? Like around Stephen?"

"Just be careful. Please. Promise me you will always keep your heart open to angels and you will always take care of yourself." Then I gave her my cell-phone number and told her to call me whenever she'd like.

HOURS LATER I found myself a little nauseous. I had just left the pathologist's office in Vermont, and for a long moment I sat in the front seat of my car in the hospital parking lot. The vehicle was steaming inside from having baked in the sun with the windows rolled up, and so I opened them all and pressed hard on the button that rolled back the moonroof. It wasn't that I had seen anything especially distressing in the mortuary—the bodies on the shelves in the walk-in refrigerator were the elderly who had passed away of natural causes that day on the hospital floors high above—and their faces looked downright beatific. They looked as if they were sleeping deeply and comfortably on their backs beneath blue hospital blankets. Rather, I think I was disturbed because now I could imagine precisely how my parents' corpses had been autopsied. I saw concretely in my mind the way the medical examiner in our corner of New York had placed each of their bodies on the slanted steel table—slanted for drainage—and meticulously described aloud precisely the physical characteristics of each of my parents. I didn't know who had gone first, but I found myself envisioning my mother's corpse on the table, since I had seen her naked in the bathtub when I would keep her company as she bathed and in the changing room of the country club. Her face, in my mind, was intact, but I knew in reality that a large part of it had been obliterated completely by the bullet. And then I saw what the Vermont pathologist had described as the Y incision: a cut in the shape of a capital Y, a wishbone with the two prongs at the shoulders and the point extending from sternum to pubic bone. The incision, the pathologist had told me, was deep—you had to cut through the abdominal wall. Then all three of these great flaps of skin were pulled back.

"The one over the upper chest," I had asked. "You pulled that back over her face?"

"That's correct," he had said calmly. "How do you know that?"

I'd shrugged. "A college course. I really know very little."

Next, my mother's ribs would have been cut apart and the anterior chest wall opened so the doctor could examine the organs underneath. Their connections to the body would be severed and each one carefully scrutinized and weighed. The intestines would be drained in the sink to see what undigested food and feces were present. The contents of the stomach would be noted. Samples from most organs would be preserved and then, in my mother's case, the organs replaced back inside the cadaver.

I thought of the names of the tools he had mentioned: Bone saw. Scalpel. Skull chisel.

"And the brain?" I wondered, because I realized abruptly that the bullet wound might have affected how the brain would be autopsied. "How would the way my mother was killed affect how the brain was autopsied?"

"Well," the medical examiner began, clearly choosing his words with care to minimize my discomfort, "what might have happened would have depended on what sorts of conversations had occurred between the pathologist and your adult relatives: an aunt and uncle, maybe, or your grandparents. A fresh brain can be difficult to study, and so on occasion it will be fixed for as much as two weeks in formalin.

It would depend upon what the officials investigating the case needed to learn."

"Two weeks?"

"Or less."

"So it was possible my mother was buried without her brain?"

"It's possible. But not likely," he said. "Not from what you've told me of the circumstances of your mother's death. It was a bullet. And your father left behind a confession."

"Of sorts," I agreed, and I sighed. For a moment I wondered why anyone had bothered to autopsy my parents, since it was painfully clear what had occurred: My father had shot my mother and then hanged himself.

But then a thought dawned on me, and I recall looking up from my steering wheel toward one of the old, Gothic buildings on the university campus adjacent to the hospital and mortuary: To the casual eye, it had also been rather apparent what had happened in the Haywards' living room back in July. But, in fact, George Hayward hadn't shot himself, and that only became clear when the medical examiner with whom I'd just met had autopsied the man's body. And so it was just as important that my parents' bodies had been examined as well.

"What color nightgown was Alice wearing when she died?" I'd asked the medical examiner as I was leaving. "I'm curious."

"I would call it a nightshirt," he'd said. "It only fell to midthigh."

"Was it plaid?"

"No," he had told me. "I'm quite sure it was solid red."

IN THE WEEKS after I had returned to New York after my brief visit to Vermont, I thought of Stephen Drew all the time. I didn't miss him, precisely. After all, as meaningful as our affair might have been, it had also been brief. But I did wonder about the ways that my intentions, which had only been kind, had led me astray. Initially I had hoped only that I could provide counsel and healing. Offer my experiences and share my access to the angels. Instead I had misread everything about the man and lost focus on the light and the wings that have guided me since that night I almost took my own life. That autumn I didn't necessarily view the fallen minister as beyond salvation. But I did view him as poisonous to the stillness and equanimity that helps me to commune with the angels. And I knew that if our paths crossed ever again, it would be extremely difficult for me to trust him.

Still, he was often on my mind. How could he not have been? After all, I'd had the Vermont State Police in my home.

Day after day I would find myself living in two worlds in my head, one I knew well and one constructed entirely from my imagination. The first comprised all of those days and nights I had spent with Stephen in Haverill, Manhattan, and Statler. I would close my eyes, and a whole cyclorama of our experiences together would unfurl before me. I would feel again the warmth of his body beside me, and I would savor the scent of the skin on his neck. I would see his eyes and the way he would listen as I spoke, with his long, beautiful fingers steepled together, almost unmoving. I would recall the stories he had shared with me and the sound of his voice—as soothing as a warm bath—and how I had believed all he'd told me.

The second world was far more abstract to me and tended to have an uncertain fluidity to it, because I was crafting it entirely from things people had told me or I had manufactured for my mind's eye. And that world was the final day—the final hours—of Alice and George Hayward. It would begin with the baptism on Sunday morning, with the images from the digital photos of the ritual that Ginny O'Brien had taken and shared with me at Alice's funeral. With the pond, deserted when Stephen and I had driven past it.

No, it would commence even before that. I would imagine Alice getting dressed in the morning. Choosing her bathing suit in her bedroom at eight-fifteen or eight-thirty. Perhaps gazing at herself in the long mirror that hung on the inside of the white closet door in her and George's bedroom. This wouldn't be vanity on her part: After all, she was about to wear that Speedo before the whole congregation, and she needed to be sure that George's handiwork was well hidden. At that moment she would have had just about twelve hours to live.

There was her emergence from the pond water itself. Roughly eleven-thirty now. She would have nine hours remaining. I would see her spooning macaroni salad onto a paper plate at the potluck (and macaroni salad is a guess founded on nothing, because no one ever said a word to me about what Alice might have eaten at that meal). Gardening in the middle of the afternoon, in the vegetable plot in the backyard, perhaps weeding among the rows of carrots and harvesting her string beans and peas. Racing to the general store just before it closed at five o'clock to buy a clear plastic container of coleslaw: her very last purchase on this planet. She now had barely three hours. Maybe three hours and a few minutes. Less time than it takes me to drive to my sister's in Statler. Less time than it took my mother to roast a turkey when I was a child. And, finally, there was her last phone call with Ginny. Strong, sisterly, protective Ginny O'Brien (now, it seemed, sad, scarred, and struggling Ginny O'Brien). There it was, her last conversation with anyone in the world other than the man who would kill her. She had only minutes now, though how many we'll never know. The medical examiner in Vermont said it was impossible to be that precise with the time of death. But it was clear that the time remaining to her would be calculated in minutes, not hours.

Still, the vision I kept returning to was this: Alice Hayward alone in her bedroom at eight-thirty in the morning as she studied her curves and her legs and her breasts in that bathing suit. Twelve hours. Half a day. That was about what she had left. What, I would wonder, would she have done differently if she had known that in half a day she would be dead? If the rules were such that there was no appeal to her predestined fate—she couldn't leave; she couldn't be somewhere else that Sunday night—but she understood that these were her last hours on earth, what conversations would she have initiated? What experiences would have mattered to her? What advice would she have shared with fifteen-year-old Katie?

But obviously she didn't know what loomed before her. Stephen insisted to me that she had known—that it was clear to her she was going to die and that he, in turn, should have done something. He said she might not have known it was going to occur that Sunday evening, but she had been confident that her death was coming soon at the hands of her husband. And, indeed, it had been at his hands.

Yet I questioned whether Alice really had seen this coming. She had fought George. Struggled. She had not gone quietly to the angels. And according to Ginny, there had been nothing in that last phone call that might have suggested that Alice was either frightened or despondent. She had even joked about George. Infantilized him on the telephone. And, of course, Alice had Katie. I knew if I had a child, that would be reason enough for me to want to carry on. Parents may commit suicide every day, but nothing I had heard or learned about Alice suggested she was depressed.

Consequently I found myself wondering if Stephen's long, desperate riffs on guilt and self-loathing were nothing but an act. *There.* That was the whole clue, he had said, that single word. Her response to her baptism. It began to seem more and more likely that Stephen had made the whole thing up: the word as prophecy. The word as message.

Oh, he might have been feeling guilty, and indeed a measure of it might have been because Alice was dead. But he hadn't killed his former lover. If Stephen Drew really was feeling remorse, it was because he had left Alice to her fate by breaking off their affair and then, months later, because he had murdered her husband.

CHAPTER FIFTEEN

When my cell phone rang, I was home, rolling a yoga mat into a tube. It was raining outside, but it was a warm, Indian-summer sort of rain, and my windows overlooking Greene Street were open. I had finished my yoga for the day, and I was as close to content as I was in those weeks: not as serene as I was accustomed to being, but through prayer and meditation I was confident that eventually my aura would lose the toxicity that was causing me to see the world through an enervating smog. I felt that my angel was with me, ensuring that I would endure this strange autumn, as I had far worse crises—spiritual and physical—in my life.

"Hi, Heather, it's me," said a little voice, and I knew instantly that it was Katie Hayward. I sat down on the daybed so I could focus on her. I asked her where she was and how she was faring. There was a ripple of anxiety in her tone, and instantly I was worried. She was calling from the bedroom that was now hers and Tina's at the Cousino family's house, and the disquiet I heard was fueled, she said, by another dream she'd had the night before and she'd been thinking about all day at school. The dream—a nightmare, really—had taken place the evening when her parents had died.

"And Lula was inside the house, and my mom and dad's bodies were there in the living room," Katie was saying now.

"Lula was inside the house?" I asked. I remembered that someone had told me that the dog had been outside when Ginny O'Brien had arrived Monday morning.

"Yeah. And she was . . ."

"Go on."

"She was drinking my dad's blood off his head. Lapping at it. Sort of nibbling at the hole where the bullet went in. Isn't that gross? I feel like I'm really sick to even think of such a thing."

"No, you're not sick at all. But remember: Lula hadn't been in the living room. It was just a dream. Lula had probably been out all night. Your mom or dad let her out before they . . . fought."

"But that's just it: They didn't let Lula out! She was a shelter dog, and she's always been a bit of a kook. Like a total lunatic. So either we walked her on a leash or we let her out when we could watch her. You know, keep an eye on her. We never just opened the door and let her out. Never. And let me tell you, she hasn't changed a bit here at Tina's. There is no way you just open the door and let that dog rock. I think it's a miracle she was sitting on the front porch when Ginny got to my house the next day."

Did Katie understand the ramifications of what she was saying? I thought she did, which would explain the fretfulness in her voice. But I wasn't sure, and so I pressed her just a bit. "Your father had been drinking. Maybe he—"

"He didn't let her out. I don't care how drunk he was, he wouldn't have let her out. I mean, like, why would he?"

"Perhaps your mother tried to leave. And Lula left then. Maybe she just ran out the door."

"No. That's what hit me because of the dream. As awful as the nightmare was, it made something really, really clear to me that I hadn't thought about: Someone else let Lula out the door that night, either on purpose or by mistake. Now, sometimes, if something has totally freaked her out, she'll just zoom out the front door. But she really does have to be totally freaked. Totally scared."

The implication, and neither of us said anything for a moment, was that whoever had killed her father—assuming that he hadn't killed himself—had let the dog out.

"Was Lula ever scared of your father?" I asked.

"No way. He treated Lula a lot better than he treated Mom."

"But she was scared of strangers, I presume."

"She was scared of men—except for Dad, who won her over. But other men scared the crap out of her. Even Stephen."

"Why do you say 'even Stephen'?"

"Well, he's, like, a minister. Isn't he supposed to be all about peace?"

"Do you think Stephen was at your house on Sunday night? Is that what you're trying to tell me?"

"They're selling the house, you know. It will pay for my college."

I repeated the question: "Do you think Stephen was at your house on Sunday night?"

"Yes."

"Why?"

"Because Lula was out."

"There has to be more to it than that."

She exhaled so profoundly that I could hear it clearly over the phone. "Remember when you called me the day after you visited the coroner guy?" she said after a moment. "You told me he said Mom had been wearing her red nightgown."

"Go on."

"I mean, I don't know if any of this is what happened. But I keep thinking about it a lot. When my mom sent my dad away last winter, he didn't take the handgun with him. He made a big deal about this. My mom didn't even want to touch it, but he insisted she hang on to it, because she was going to be the only parent in the house looking out for me. And our house is sort of isolated. Two women and all. So he left her the gun and the bullets, and then he went to go live at the lake. And Mom put the gun in one of these big plastic tubs she uses to swap out her clothes. She puts her summer clothes in them in the winter and her winter clothes in them in the summer. And as far as I know, the gun was still in one of the tubs in July, even though the summer clothes had been replaced with the winter ones. She'd kept the gun where it was. See?"

"I'm listening," I said simply.

"Well, here's the thing: I don't think Stephen ever saw my mom in her plaid flannel nightgown. Her winter one. I mean, if they were sleeping together, it was during the day when I was at school, because they sure weren't doing it when I was home at night. And so she wouldn't have been wearing her nightgown at, like, eleven in the morning or when she came home from the bank to be with him. She would have been wearing clothes. Casual clothes or work clothes. But clothes. Besides, that nightgown is sort of grungy. It's got weird tears and coffee stains. My mom really liked it. But there is no way she would have let anyone other than my dad or me ever see her in it. Especially . . ."

"Especially what?"

"I'm a virgin. Okay? I'm a virgin. But I'm not totally naïve. And if you're having sex with a guy for the first couple of times, you want to look as hot as you can, even if you're, like, middle-aged. And I know my mom. There is no way she would ever have let Stephen see her in that plaid flannel nightgown."

"And so you're suggesting he saw the nightgown for the first time when he got the gun."

"I don't know what I'm suggesting," she said, her voice growing more animated, more urgent. "But I just can't see how else Stephen could have known about the nightgown."

"Do you know if he knew the gun was in one of those tubs? Did your mom ever tell you that she'd told him she kept the pistol there?"

"You sound like a detective."

"I'm sorry. But my head is spinning a little bit. Have you told the police any of this?"

"They didn't ask me any questions about the gun. Or about Lula. And it was only when I had the dream about Lula that the whole nightgown thing even crossed my mind. See, in the dream my mom was wearing that ridiculous plaid nightgown. And that image made the rest really, really clear."

"I'm going to tell you three things," I said. "First of all, grown-ups are strange, and sometimes we get comfortable with one another pretty quickly. Your mother and Stephen were intimate in the winter. And so I wouldn't discount completely the idea that your mother wore that grungy plaid nightgown around him at some point. Then, in the midst of whatever else Stephen is experiencing right now, he confused the nightgowns in his mind when he spoke with you. But here is the second thing: You might be onto something, and you should share your conjectures with the police. I would call them myself—and if you want me to, I will be happy to. But they're going to want to talk to you anyway after that, so you might as well just pick up the phone and call them yourself. Call that state trooper who interviewed us or call the deputy state's attorney. I believe her name is Catherine. I'll get you both numbers—or Josie can. That social worker. Let them decide if there's anything to it."

"And the third? You said there were three things."

"Don't tell anyone else what you told me."

"Not even Tina or Ginny?"

"No, not even Tina or Ginny," I said. And then, because I wanted to leave nothing to chance when it came to Katie Hayward's safety, I added, "And not Stephen. Under no circumstances tell Stephen what you just told me."

"Oh, yeah," she said, "he would be the last person I'd tell."

I STARTED READING the Vermont newspapers online that autumn, peeking at them every day to see if there was any news about Stephen or any quotes from his attorney, Aaron Lamb—a name that struck me at some moments as appropriate, others as ironic. I watched to see if Katie's revelations about the gun and the nightgown would appear in the papers, but they didn't. A friend of mine who is a lawyer for the City of New York told me that unless the case went to trial, I wouldn't read about them. She said that didn't mean that the information wasn't being used as part of the investigation into Stephen Drew or that detectives weren't trying to (her words, not mine) turn up the heat on the now officially retired minister. But she said that from everything I had shared with her, unless they could link him to the gun, an indictment wasn't likely.

"But it's so clear that he did it," I told her one evening over a glass of wine at a bar at the South Street Seaport just after Columbus Day weekend. Outside, the shoes of the businesswomen and -men clattered along the cobblestones as, invariably, they chatted on their headsets and PDAs.

"Well, maybe it's clear to you," she corrected me. "But it sounds to me that unless he confesses, he's going to get away with it."

I considered calling that Vermont state trooper who had interviewed me, and periodically I found myself fiddling with his card, which, for reasons I couldn't quite pinpoint, I kept in my purse. I considered making another statement, a second one, but what more really could I say? Stephen refused to own up to his guilt to me and had told me nothing I could add. I could make sure that Katie had shared her ideas with the investigators, but there really wasn't any doubt in my mind that she had. By now they knew about the gun and the night-gown and the dog.

Stephen did try to reconcile with me that autumn, but only one time with real effort. He called twice and left messages, and he e-mailed me once asking me whether it might be possible to have a conversation. The messages were not insincere, but nor were they impassioned. They were a little chilly and a little tame. Only in one in-stance did he make an effort in which I glimpsed the iridescence that hovers like a halo amid an aura, and even that was but a passing glance. It was in a handwritten note on a piece of yellow legal paper that he mailed me. Most of the individual letters on each line were so small and controlled that I wondered if he had had a contest with himself to see how many words he could wedge onto the page. He began by reiterating how I should, at the very least, see him once more. Face-to-face. See what it felt like for the two of us to be together, see if there was a hint of the fire we had once felt in each other's presence. He had moved out of the parsonage by then and was renting an apartment in Bennington while he decided what to do next with his life. He never came right out and said that he was confident he was never going to be tried for murder, but it seemed to me that he was behaving that way. He was almost arrogant. I think he had moved to Bennington, rather than anywhere else, to flaunt his freedom before the very criminal-justice system that wanted to arrest him. Still, it was clear he didn't plan to settle there. He said the lease was short-term because he was contemplating a move to Manhattan, where he would try to find a new career. He wrote that he thought he was going to become a social worker and, if necessary, he would return to school to get his M.S.W. He claimed that he wanted to work with the homeless. He had visions of himself rolling up his sleeves and doing the sorts of work he should have been doing when he had been in the pulpit. He insisted this wasn't atonement. Altogether, it was a lot of information, and at first it felt rather formulaic to me. But then I came to a paragraph in which I saw his relentless self-control quiver: "If I make it to eighty, I wonder who will look back with me at the footprints I've left on the beach. I presume both that I will be the only one gazing at them and there will be but one set. This isn't another plea for you to hear me out (I've already done that) or a plea wrapped in the most transparent of gauze that you'll reconsider your distance; it is merely an acknowledgment that I am conscious of the tendency I have to wall myself off from others and that this inclination may not serve me well in the end." I might have been more sympathetic if he had used the word *fear* instead of the word *presume.* But he hadn't. Stephen Drew really didn't know from fear, and whatever vulnerability he might briefly or inadvertently reveal, he would mask the moment he understood what he had done.

I never responded to his phone calls or missives, until eventually they stopped coming. Like all things mortal, they simply disappeared.

IT WAS AMANDA who said most firmly that I was being ridiculous about Stephen. She came to New York to meet with a gallery owner who represented Norman's birds, and as she does always when she visits, she stayed on the daybed in my loft. That evening, while smoking a cigarette and sipping a diet soda watered down by melted ice, she told me, "You took in too much of our parents' quarrels. You're thinking too much about the fights that young girl must have seen over the years in Vermont. You're looking for a reason not to commit."

She was wearing a smock dress that fell to midthigh and a cardigan sweater that was navy blue. But I could see from her knees that she had put on a little weight. Not a lot, but some. Clearly she was in a better phase than she had been back in August. Somehow she had learned that I'd called both her therapist and her nutritionist, but she hadn't been angry with me. Her hair had regained a bit of its natural luster.

"He had been sleeping with Alice Hayward and hadn't told me," I reminded her.

"So what? Think of all the angels and devils you've slept with."

"And he killed a man."

"He killed a man who had beaten his wife for years and just strangled her with his bare hands. Not a great loss for humanity."

"I could never feel safe with him," I said.

"You spend too much time reliving our childhood and adolescence."

"Funny. I told Katie Hayward just the opposite. I told her I don't."

"And these days it's not just ours you relive. It's hers, too."

"Hers? Katie's?"

"Yup, that orphan. The kid."

I thought about this. "Actually, it's Alice I seem to think about most."

"Maybe. But I know you. You're fixated on the Haywards and you're fixated on the Laurents. You think about us. You and me and— I don't know—pick a night. Pick the night we cowered behind the living-room couch."

I sipped my wine. Here was a memory that—try as I might—I was never going to repress. I was in the third grade at the time, and so Amanda had been in the fifth. It was a weekend, probably a Saturday night. Our parents had been out that evening, and our father had just returned from driving the baby-sitter home. Both our mother and father had been drinking heavily, and there must have been an angel looking out for that baby-sitter that night, because otherwise I can't imagine how she would have survived the three-and-a-half-mile drive to her house. Our mother had kissed each of us sloppily as she had checked in on us in our bedrooms, accidentally waking us both with her awkwardness, and then stumbled back down the stairs. I remember vividly how it sounded as if she'd fallen the last few steps. Amanda and I hadn't planned to get out of our beds when our parents returned, but we had both heard the slight tumble and gone to investigate. We saw that our mother was already up. She was standing in the kitchen between the sink and the dishwasher, leaning against the counter the color of fossils. She had a juice glass in her hand, half filled with scotch. She was in her own world and didn't realize we were watching. When we heard our father pulling in to the driveway—squealing to a stop and splintering one of the wood panels on the garage door with the sedan's bumper—my instinct was to race back upstairs to my bedroom, but Amanda grabbed me by the wrist and dragged me into the living room.

Their struggle that evening was about our mother's drinking. At least that was what on the most obvious level had led our father to start in on her. On another level he had undoubtedly been angry at himself for dinging the garage door. And while I expected my mother to fight back by observing that he wasn't exactly a teetotaler, instead she brought up some woman from his office with whom, she implied, he was having an affair. In reality I have no doubt that her language was far more specific and colorful. Sufficiently specific and colorful that he said she had a sewer for a mouth and he couldn't believe he had ever once kissed it or (and Amanda insists that we have not made this up, our father really did say this) stuck his penis in it—though, again, he did not use so clinical a word as *penis*.

At first we listened in on our parents' fight from a perch atop the couch, but when we heard the rapid-fire sound of her open palm on his cheek and then the grunt as he punched her hard in (we would learn later) the abdomen, we dove over the back of the couch and hid underneath the table behind it. A moment later, our parents moved from the kitchen to the living room. Amanda and I have deconstructed what happened next any number of times in our adult lives, trying to make sense of what we heard or thought we heard in light of what we would discover later about the confusing and disturbing place where violence and adult sexuality sometimes intersected. Had our father sodomized our mother against her will that night over the front cushions of the couch? Had she asked him as he worked hard to hurt her whether he did this to his girlfriend, too? Had he told her, as the couch shoved the table against the wall and I almost cried out myself as one of its wooden legs tore a strip of skin off my pinkie, that she was a completely unfit mother and everyone would have been better off if he'd only fucked her there all these years?

There. The word that decades later Stephen Drew would insist symbolized everything for him one tragic summer and autumn.

"You know," Amanda was saying now, "those troopers acted like they suspected Norman and me."

"You? Why?"

"Well, Norman and I don't make the best presentation, if you get my drift."

"I thought they were just checking Stephen's and my story."

She chuckled and took a small sip of her soft drink. I noticed how carefully she nursed it, and I presumed this was a habit from drinking beverages that might have actual calories. I had drained my second glass of wine, and she had barely made a dent into her first diet soda. "Oh, they were. But when you meet a fellow with a criminal record who is as badly socialized as my Norman and a woman with my"—and here she paused, choosing her words carefully—"issues, you think they might be capable of anything. Anything bad, that is."

After our father had finished with our mother, he slapped her one last time on her rear, and the sound was so sharp it echoed. Later I would think his hand must have hurt, too. Amanda and I wouldn't go upstairs until our mother had lurched disconsolately into the bath-room (powder room in her vernacular) to clean up. We moved quickly but silently, because we understood that neither parent could ever know all that we had overheard. The next morning there would still be a small Rorschach of blood—a tree leaf, maybe, perhaps that of an oak—on the rug by the base of the couch, and the slipcover from one of the cushions would be in the laundry.

"I knew they thought I might have been involved," I said. "But the two of you? That's absurd."

She shrugged. "Maybe. But I can see them looking at either you or me. Let's face it: We're both pretty damaged goods."

Had she meant to be hurtful? It was possible. She knew that I didn't view myself as any more damaged than most mortals. She knew that I took comfort in the way I was held close now by angels. When I said nothing, unsure how to respond, my older sister continued, "Se-riously, Heather, just because our parents' marriage was a disaster in every conceivable way, you shouldn't assume all relationships are. My advice? Spend less time with your cherubim and seraphim. Spend more time with real people."

"You're the one living in the woods with the world's quietest man," I reminded her.

"And I'm a disaster. I'm nobody's role model, least of all yours. But until you cut bait once again on what had the potential to be a terrifically normal—perhaps even healthy—relationship, I always presumed you were doing a lot better than me."

There was never going to be anything normal or healthy about my involvement with Stephen Drew, but I was not going to argue that evening with Amanda. I remembered that Tuesday at the end of July when I had first met him: Originally I thought that I had gone to see the pastor of a small country church, because he'd seemed so lost to me in the newspaper and I presumed my history could help him.

Could help his community. Only later would I admit to myself that my motivation may have been slightly different—or, at least, more involved. On some level it was likely that I had been drawn to Haverill that afternoon by the inexorable gravity of memory. By my own fathomless scars. We may talk a good game and write even better ones, but we never outgrow those small wounded things we were when we were five and six and seven. When we were in grade school and hiding behind the couch. It's why we need angels.

And there was something else that was always going to preclude any rapprochement with Stephen: There was that small detail that he was capable of murder. I understood the justification, and I appreciated the fury he must have experienced when he came upon the scene—when he saw his former lover dead on the floor in her nightgown. I was not unsympathetic. But I also knew that I wanted nothing to do with him ever again.

PART IV

Katie Hayward

CHAPTER SIXTEEN

The fights were horrible, but the silences might have been even worse. No one could do silence like Mom and Dad. Especially Mom. We're talking plasma TV with the mute button on. It was her way of fighting back, and it just drove Dad crazy. Because the thing was, after he'd hit her, he'd be all contrite and sorry and want to make it up to her. Breakfast in bed, sit with her on the couch and watch whatever she wanted—even *Sex and the City* reruns (which he hated), if that's what was on. And that was the time when Mom was in the driver's seat. Of course, it also meant that the fighting could drag on for days. Dad would hit Mom, Mom would clam up, and Dad would go from sorry to sulking to pissed. Not a promising cycle, if you get my drift.

Now, they had friends. My dad had his buddies in the volunteer fire company and people who worked at his stores and his restaurant. I think he was probably a pretty good boss. And Mom had chums, too. Some people said Dad took away Mom's friends, and there were definitely some women he didn't want her hanging around with. That's true. But he didn't stop her from seeing everyone. Mom still had the crumblies in the Women's Circle and Ginny O'Brien—who was also in the Women's Circle but was a couple generations short of crumbly. And there is nothing that Ginny wouldn't have done for Mom. Nothing. And I guess she had her friends at the bank. But the thing is this: Even if my mom had had lots of gal pals, the last thing she wanted was for people to think that her marriage was a failure and she was, like, a total victim. A total loser—because she wasn't a loser, at least in my opinion. This was really clear when I would visit her at the bank branch on Saturday mornings, which I did pretty often by the time I was in middle school, because it was near stores and it was a chance to get out of Haverill. I saw her with the tellers and a man named Frank Albertson who was a commercial loan officer there. She was totally professional. She was completely different from the way she was at home. I wish she had known how good she was.

Sometimes I think Mom put up with a lot of Dad's worst creepiness because she was afraid if things ever got too crazy—too violent— we'd both wind up at the shelter. We came close a couple of times. Sometimes Mom talked about going to Ginny's, but we never did, because she was afraid of bringing her friend's family into our nightmare. And I think she was afraid of what people would think if things ever got totally public. Like, what did it say about her as a mom and a wife that she had put up with this crap for so long? And I guess she figured if we spent even one night with Ginny or even one night in the shelter, there would be no going back. The marriage would be over. And looking back, it's weird, but I don't think she was ready for that. Really. I don't know what freaked out Mom more: the fear that she had sunk so low that she was going to be in the battered-women's shelter with her kid or the idea that she was walking on eggshells in her own house and no one was supposed to know.

THE SOCIAL WORKERS and the therapists all wanted to know if Dad ever hit me. The short answer is yes. But it's complicated. I mean, no kid deserves to be hit, but a smart one doesn't get in the middle of some of the crap that I did. When your mom and dad are in the midst of an electrified-cage match, you steer clear if you want to keep your teeth. (That's an exaggeration. A: I have never seen a real cage match, just videos of them on YouTube. And B: I have all my teeth. My father never punched me in the mouth.) Twice I made the mistake of thinking I could save my mom alone, and both times I got swatted like one of those gross, slow-moving cluster flies we had in the attic. In all fairness, the first time Dad walloped me was a mistake on his part. He hadn't meant to. He was in one of his moods, and I don't even remember anymore what set him off, and my mom was crying pathetically. They were both in their bathroom, and I could hear them through the walls, and I was at my wit's end and totally furious with him. Maybe even furious with both of them for living the same rerun over and over and over. And so I went in to yell at my dad. I was a big-deal thirteen, and I think I was going to tell him to grow up. The scene I walked in on was really weird, because it was after dinner and he was, like, shaving. I knew he was worried that the toy store wasn't making enough money—even I knew that a shop that sold mostly marionettes and wooden puzzles in an age when everyone wanted a PlayStation or Wii was a pretty lame idea—which meant that he was a little stressed. Still, I have no idea why he was shaving. He was also pretty hammered. I'm amazed he could figure out which side of the Bic he was supposed to use on his skin. Anyway, I went in with all this determination, and my timing was just perfect. Totally perfect. He was winding up to whack Mom, who was actually on her knees and pleading with him about who knows what, and I walked straight into his knuckles as he swung them back, taking it right on the ear. And I can tell you that ears have a ton of nerves. I guess hearing cells don't. But the outer ear?

Trust me, it hurt like crazy, and my ears rang for hours. I fell against the frame of the door and then, I'm not sure how, wound up on the floor, half in the bedroom and half in the bathroom. Dad didn't even realize what he'd walloped at first. I think he thought my head was, like, the door. But my mom knew, and she just threw herself at him, leaping to her feet like a missile, which of course caused him to throw her down onto the floor beside me. And that's when my dad looked at me like, "Hello? What are you doing here?"

The other time he did hit me on purpose. It was a year later, and we had begun to figure out just how much we hated each other: I hated him for what he did to Mom, and he hated me for knowing he was a jerk and mean and pathetic. And that's the thing—I knew he was pathetic. I don't care how successful his restaurant or his stores were. My mom wasn't the loser: He was. And so he probably despised me. But, in all fairness, it was only that one time that he meant to hit me. Just like that evening he nailed me by accident in the bathroom, he hadn't hit Mom yet. But I could see where it was going. It was a Friday morning, and the bank was experimenting with casual dress on Friday, so the bankers didn't have to look as formal as usual. Mom was wearing a pair of black jeans. Nice jeans—not mom jeans. They were tight, and she looked very pretty and very young in them. My dad didn't know she owned them. Anyway, he had left early to play golf that morning, and so my mom had figured she could wear them to work. Unfortunately, my dad forgot his golf shoes, and so he came back for them and saw what Mom was wearing. His voice got that creepy, sarcastic, I'm-your-daddy tone to it. He almost sounded British when he got like that. And that was always the overture. The warm-up. You knew what was coming next. Mom and I were in the kitchen when he returned, and I was eating a Pop-Tart or something at the counter and making sure I had wedged every binder I would need that day at school into my backpack. (My backpack is always a total wreck.) Mom immediately dropped the lipstick she'd been holding in her fingers into her purse when he started leaning into her. His golf shoes had these pointy metal studs on the soles, and he grabbed one by the top and was holding it like a knife. He ordered her upstairs to the bedroom, where he told her that she was going to put on clothes that didn't embarrass her or him or his daughter.

And so I told him that Mom's jeans sure didn't embarrass me. I said I liked them and thought she looked great. He turned to me and hissed something about how this was none of my business and to get ready for school. I shrugged and held up my backpack with both hands. (And it really did take both hands, because it always seemed to weigh as much as a case of beer, which, just for the record, I only know weighs a ton because I carried them in from the supermarket when I would help Mom with the grocery shopping. In the months after my dad killed my mom, I smoked a lot of dope, but I was never into beer. Too fattening. And it reminded me too much of Dad.) I told him I was all ready for school. And so he said in that case I should go. And Mom said I should, too, and she was practically begging me to get out of the house. But I didn't want to leave her like this. To leave her to him. So I told my dad that Mom's jeans were fine and to let it go. I said he didn't want to miss his tee time. Mom was, like, babbling about how she was going right upstairs to change, she was, and she scooted around Dad so she was between the kitchen and the stairs, and she yelled back at me in a voice that was bizarrely cheerful considering what was going on that I didn't want to miss the school bus. And I thought, fuck the school bus, this has gone too far. And, in fact, I may even have said that. I can't recall for sure. All I remember for certain is my dad glaring at me and his eyes getting narrow: Think of a newt. And then, out of the blue, he rammed the toe of the golf shoe into my stomach. It didn't hurt that much, and it didn't knock the wind out of me, but it did cause me to drop my backpack and coil up like a spring.

My mom screamed at him to stop, but she didn't need to worry. He was totally shocked at what he'd done. He was stunned. Then he shook his head in disgust and said I was every bit the slut my mom was and walked out of the house with his golf shoes.

That was the only other time he hit me. And it led to the longest cold war my parents ever had. It took him longer than usual to get all syrupy and apologize, maybe because he'd never had the chance that morning to vent the full fury that was always smoldering just underneath his skin. Also, he needed to apologize to me, too, this time. Which he did. I wound up with a new iPod and a hundred bucks on iTunes. I believe it would be months before he would hit Mom again. Not till the autumn, I think. But when he started up again, things would spiral quickly through the holidays. I'm amazed it took Mom until February to find the backbone to get the restraining order and kick him out of the house. It wasn't just that he was becoming so unbearable to be around and so weirdly scary. It was that by then she had Stephen Drew in her life.

MY MOM IN black jeans? That was never going to embarrass me.

The stuff everyone found in my bedroom that awful Monday in July when they went there to get me some clothes and stuff so I didn't have to go back inside the house? Now, *that* was embarrassing. There in the chaos on my bed and on the floor were, like, a whole zoo full of stuffed animals. There was Bunny Jo and Elmo and Scraggles the Bear. There was Eeyore, for crying out loud. There were three American Girl dolls. Obviously I don't play with American Girl dolls, and I haven't since I was, like, nine. But I was never able to bring myself to put them in boxes and cart them up to the attic. Once Mom offered to do it for me, and another time she even offered to sell them for me on eBay if I wanted. But I just couldn't see Samantha and Addy and

Kirsten getting all moldy in the attic or being sold to some other family. And so they were right there in my bedroom when Stephen and Ginny and everyone else just popped in and started touching my underwear and my bras and my makeup. Yup, they saw the trolls and the rub-on tattoos in one of my drawers and my thongs and boy shorts in another. Not too weird for them. Not too awkward for me. And yes, it did feel like a violation of sorts. On Sunday it hadn't crossed my mind that I wouldn't be back in my house the next day.

They also saw the jewelry Mom had given me on Friday. A pair of earrings that were rubies and diamonds and her own grandmother's pearl necklace. I didn't think much of it at the time. I mean, I guess I was touched. It was clearly supposed to be one of those mom-and-daughter bonding moments. On Monday, if she hadn't died, we were going to put the jewelry in the safe-deposit box at her bank, because the stuff sure as heck didn't belong in my jewelry box with my ten-dollar hoops.

Of course, the grown-ups didn't bring me half the stuff from my room that I really wanted. They did fine in the needs department: They brought me, like, every pair of blue jeans and shorts I owned and about seventeen pairs of underwear. They found my retainer. (Oh, joy.) They filled a shoe box with CDs (most of which I had already cherry-picked for my iPod). It was the wants department where things were a little lacking. Shirts? None of my favorites. And way more long-sleeved shirts than I needed in July and not nearly enough T-shirts. And two sweaters I never wore (and wasn't about to wear in July or August). And none of the DVDs of my favorite shows I would watch in the summer on my laptop before going to sleep. And only about half of the things I used to keep my skin clear, as well as the totally wrong foundation.

But Tina was amazing. So were Ginny and Tina's mom, Carole. Tina shared everything she owned with me (and I mean everything), and Ginny or Carole seemed to make things magically appear all the time. It was like they could read my mind. I'm sure Tina was telling them the things I needed, but still: It was totally amazing. Ginny wanted to be a superhero and solve all my problems. I think she was okay that I chose to live with my friend, Tina, but I could also tell she was a little disappointed that I didn't move in with her family. (Sometimes Tina thought Ginny was kind of mental those months, but I reminded her that the woman had just lost her best friend.)

Still, it was incredibly nice of the Cousinos to take me *and* Lula in. I mean, they didn't have to take the dog. But they did. Lula and I weren't super close, but we became a lot closer after Mom and Dad were gone. She seemed to need me a lot more, and I guess I needed her. In the old days (and that was how I came to describe in my mind my life before that Sunday night), she had slept in Mom and Dad's bedroom. Now she slept with me in Tina's and my bedroom.

At first I felt really guilty that Tina no longer had her room to herself. But she said I shouldn't worry about it. I should view it like we were in college or boarding school and we were roommates. Tina's father was an engineer, but his hobby was woodworking, and in his basement he had a workshop that was pretty serious-looking. In August he completely redid Tina's closet, putting in all these shelves and dividers, and he built this nook with yet more shelves above her bureau. He moved out her night table and replaced her dresser with a much thinner one, and then he brought in my bed and my mattress from the old house and managed to make everything fit in the bedroom. It was cramped but not unpleasant. We both learned to fall asleep with someone else in the room. At first her younger brother and sister—Eddie was in third grade, and Emily was just starting middle school—treated me like I was dying of some terrible disease that might be contagious: They were very nice to me, but they kept their distance. They said as little as possible to me. It wasn't until a few days before Halloween, when I helped them figure out their Halloween costumes and showed Emily that she could make the mermaid thing work if she wore wheelies instead of regular sneakers (that's how they made the fish swim when they brought *The Little Mermaid* to Broadway), that they began to view me as someone who was going to be a part of their lives for at least the next two years and, in some ways, maybe forever.

Did I feel like I was imposing on the family? Totally. I almost didn't try out for the school play because it would mean weird hours and extra driving time for them, but they insisted I go for it. So I did. I tried to do as much as I could to help around the house, which in all fairness was the exact opposite of what my approach to chores had been when I'd been living at home. I think my new habit of, like, loading my plates in the dishwasher and making my bed in the morning drove Tina crazy sometimes. She would kid me that I was making her look bad, but I knew there was some truth behind the joke.

But Tina also knew since the sixth grade what had gone on in my house. I think that was when I started telling her about what a total cretin my dad was and what a jerk he was to my mom. I think she was very glad I was out of that house.

And here is one more strange thing: I'm sure Tina's parents fought. Tina told me they did. But I never once witnessed one. Not a single time. Just as I felt I needed to be on my best behavior around them, they thought they needed to be on their best behavior around me. I told Stephen this at one point in September, and he gave me a sheepish little grin and shrugged. He said it was one good thing to come out of that awful Sunday night: We were all striving to be better people. To be kind. To be gentler with one another.

IT WAS ACTUALLY Tina's idea I get the tattoo. And she got one, too, though it's so close to her hip bone that no one sees it except her boyfriend. It's also pretty small. Hers is this fantasy animal that's part horse and part dragon. A little over a year ago, her horse died. It was this beautiful Appaloosa named Maggie. The vet had had to put her down. And since Tina would be leaving for college in a couple years and her younger brother and sister didn't ride, the family didn't get another horse. But Tina missed Maggie, and so when we decided to get the tats, it was natural she'd get this mystical-looking horse that was probably supposed to be immortal.

We went to the place in downtown Rutland where Josie, my social worker, had gotten most of hers. It really wasn't a big deal. And mine hurt a lot less than Tina's, even though it's a lot bigger. The guy wasn't nearly as creepy as I would have expected. He wasn't my type, because he shaved his head and he had tattoos everywhere on his arms and neck (and who knows where else), but he was very nice. And he had great breath. He must have lived on peppermint gum.

The biggest difference between Tina's and mine is that I wanted my tattoo where people could see it. I wanted to flaunt it. So I got mine on my shoulder. My left shoulder. August still had a couple days left, and I knew even in Vermont there was at least a month when I could wear shirts with spaghetti straps. Mine is a big, blooming pink rose, and I had the artist add a stem that ran a few inches down my back and a couple of green leaves. He combined two patterns.

I picked a flower because my mom loved roses. We even had some wild rosebushes at our house. The flowers really didn't last all that long, but they were pretty. The petals were just starting to fall off when my mom died.

Anyway, my tattoo was sort of a test, I think. Just how much slack were people really cutting me? Answer? A ton. I could have gotten a tattoo of people doing it like dogs (they do have tattoos like that), and all the adults in my life would have hugged me and told me it was very elegant or I had very good taste.

MY MOM'S FUNERAL was completely different from Dad's. My mom's was packed. There were people overflowing into the choir loft and downstairs into the community room, where one of the trustees had set up a video feed. I'd had no idea how many people had cared about my mom or me—there were a ton of kids there, some of whom I thought viewed me as a total dork—and I was really touched. Dad's funeral, which we held a few days later in Buffalo, was just me and my grandparents and my aunts and uncles on his side. Not even my cousins were there for some reason. It was so lightly attended that we used this dark chapel off the main sanctuary and still everything the minister said echoed like we were in a cave. It was very creepy. As I recall, the minister talked about forgiveness and understanding, but I think most of us there were just too ashamed to pay much attention. And we *were* ashamed—at least I was. I just couldn't wait to get back to Vermont after that part of the nightmare. Anyway, Stephen and I talked a lot the three days after my parents died, and I'm pretty sure I was the first person in Haverill to know he was going to leave as soon as Mom's service was behind him.

I must admit, there were times that spring and summer, after he and my mom had stopped seeing each other on the sly, when I was seriously pissed at him. At first I told people I didn't know about their affair. But I did. Even now I'm not exactly sure who ended it. I mean, my mom never acknowledged to me that they'd even had one, and Stephen only did in a vague sort of way when I confronted him about it after my parents were dead. But I knew what had been going on. And I knew how happy my mom was with him. It was really easy to go into fantasy land, because Dad was living at the lake then and my mom was happy. I could imagine my parents getting divorced and my mom and Stephen getting married and no one using her as a punching bag anymore. I didn't think too hard about the specifics of Stephen Drew as my stepfather, because I was in tenth grade and way too old to get watery-eyed about a new family. By then I was counting the days until I could leave Haverill once and for all. But I wanted Mom to be happy.

Still, I wasn't surprised when I realized that Stephen was going to get out now, too. I knew right away he was going to feel the loss of my mom a lot more than he might have expected in those months between when they broke up and when my dad killed her.

FROM *ANGELS AND AURASCAPES*
BY HEATHER LAURENT (P. 118)

My friend Cynthia once taught me to say, "I was wrong before. I'm smarter now." They are two very short sentences, but there are few among us who are comfortable pairing them together. And yet so much of life is about growing smarter: garnering wisdom, accepting the lessons that are offered every day we walk this earth. Almost all cultures but the youth-obsessed narcissism of modern America revere elders for this very reason: With age comes acumen. With experience comes insight.

And yet so often the angel is portrayed as youthful. I am not referring to the pudgy cherubs that appear in late November like crocuses in March. But think of Botticelli's angels. Or da Vinci's. Recall for a moment the angels in any illustrated Bible. Angels in art, regardless of whether they are female or male, are vital and vibrant and vigorous. They are beautiful if they are female, handsome if they are male. Sometimes they verge on androgyny. Always, however, they are charismatic.

The reality, of course, is that angels are ageless. Eternal. Everlasting. Twice I have met with individuals who were quite sure that their angel was elderly. Not frail, mind you. But in both of these instances, the angel's countenance was lined, her eyes milky, and her fingers starting to gnarl. And both times the individual sharing this story with me was a grandparent.

CHAPTER SEVENTEEN

sually I told the police whatever I could, but sometimes I told them what they wanted to hear. It was just easier that way. And sometimes I volunteered whatever Stephen suggested I say. I wasn't nervous about that until I realized that they thought Stephen had killed Dad (maybe even Mom and Dad), and then I found myself thinking long and hard every time I opened my mouth and—what was even more disturbing for me— every time I said something Stephen had advised me to say. Tina said she was surprised I hadn't been more freaked out around the state troopers. She said after she spoke to them that one time that she didn't think she could have handled talking to them as much as I did. But I reminded her that everyone, including the police, was really, really worried about me. I was, like, the Vermont Poster Child for Domestic Abuse. I could pretty much do or say whatever I wanted. It wasn't just the tattoo. I stayed out as late as I felt like, and the Cousinos just smiled and asked if I was okay or needed anything. I cut classes, and the teachers asked me if there was anything they could do. I could have been dealing crack cocaine to five-year-olds and people would have said, "Oh, think of what happened to her parents. Poor kid." I could have been carving up kittens in the Cousinos' basement and people would have patted me on the head and asked me if I wanted a different therapist or social worker. Membership in Club Orphan has its privileges, too.

Still, I don't recommend it. I probably wasn't nearly as cool a customer as I sound now. One day I had this totally uncontrollable crying jag in the girls' bathroom at school, and, unfortunately, a teacher found me. And then some days it just felt easier not to talk at all.

Josie Morrison asked me all the time how much I missed my mom, but only once if I missed my dad. I was pretty clear about the fact that I didn't miss him at all, and that was that.

But my mom was another story. Suddenly I had all these pretend moms in my life, all these women who wanted to mother me like crazy. There was Carole Cousino and Ginny O'Brien for starters, and then there was Josie, who sometimes was the hip young mom and sometimes the badass big sister. She was better in the big-sister role, because not a lot of moms in Vermont have dreads and tats. And there were the female teachers at school and my guidance counselor, Mrs. Degraff. I got some of the best grades of my life that autumn, even though my work was pretty half-assed and my attendance was basically whenever I felt like going to class. But none of those women could even begin to fill the void. I loved my mom. I loved her so much. We had grown incredibly close in the winter when Dad had been gone. She changed. The vibe of the whole house changed. Sometimes Tina would come over and we actually baked with Mom: We made things like coconut cupcakes and pineapple upside-down cake and your basic brownies out of a box. Suddenly Mom and I weren't walking around the house like scared, silent cats, waiting for Dad to get nasty about something ridiculous. I didn't spend so much time with my earbuds in, listening to my iPod. She bought me a dock and speakers for the device, and we blared the music as loud as we wanted. She was, like, totally liberated.

Things were so peaceful that I allowed a boy who was interested in me to pick me up one Saturday night and hang around for a couple of hours before we went to a party in the village. He was a senior. He drove. Dad would never have allowed me to date a senior. He would never have allowed me to even go to a party with him. But Alan was fine, totally harmless. He was already into college by then, and we were just having a good time—which, looking back, is exactly why Dad would never have let me near him and why it wouldn't have crossed my mind to invite Alan to within a hundred yards of our house if Dad had been there.

And Mom and I could talk about Alan. We could talk about Brendan, another boy who I liked a bit, although we only hung around together as friends. (The summer and fall after Mom and Dad died, Brendan and I got a little closer, but I think that was mostly because he had spectacular dope. We didn't hook up or anything.)

It's interesting, but the two males Mom and I didn't talk about very much when Dad was gone were Dad and Stephen. One time I asked her why Dad often seemed so angry, and she said he came from an angry family. I knew what she meant: I know my grandfather. I know my uncles—all those brothers. She also said he was under a lot of pressure at work and sometimes he drank too much, and those were the big reasons why they had problems. But I could tell she was being evasive. She was suffering and didn't really get it herself.

I didn't bring up my fantasy that she might divorce Dad, but for a while in February and March there really was this out-of-sight, out-of-mind thing going on. Dad knew how pissed I was at him, and so for a while he kept his distance. But at the end of February, I got a text from him on my cell. It was a joke about something—something he'd seen on TV that he thought would make me smile. And there was something so pathetic about my dad alone at night at the lake watching crap TV that I texted back. And the next week he sent me an e-mail. Short, but with a link to a video on YouTube he thought I'd get a charge out of. Then, the week after that, he sent me a long e-mail, the first of many, and it was all about how sorry he was for being such a crummy husband, because it meant that he had always been a crummy father. But he said he was resolved to be a better person, and he said he was going to look into counseling. He always went on and on about how much he loved Mom and how much he loved me. I wasn't totally sure what to make of the e-mails and whether I should show them to Mom. I thought I might even just delete them. Mom and I had been living a day-to-day life without Dad, and it wasn't hard to imagine him gone forever. To want him gone forever. Not necessarily from my life, because that wasn't going to happen. Already he was insisting we have lunch every week or two in Manchester, where he had his stores and his restaurant. (We would do that beginning the end of March, and it would continue until he came home in May.) But out of the house forever—that sort of gone. And I feared if I showed the e-mails to Mom, it might screw things up with whatever she had going with Stephen.

In the end Dad made the decision for me about whether to show Mom his e-mails. It seems that he had been e-mailing her, too. Or, maybe, calling her. I don't remember. I just remember that one night in April when we were having dinner, Mom told me that she heard Dad had been sending me some very sweet e-mails and she was wondering if she could read a few of them. I was pretty cornered: I really couldn't say no. And so she read a couple before we had even cleared the table and loaded the dishwasher, and sometimes I wonder if this was the beginning of the end of her relationship with Stephen.

Looking back, I really wish I had just deleted them.

IF MY MOM had been into Facebook or MySpace, here's a video she would have uploaded for sure: They're at a wedding reception at some beautiful inn when we still lived in Bennington, and I was about three years old. It's New Year's Eve. I'm not in the video, because it's a pretty rockin' reception and I was home with a baby-sitter. But I love the dress my mom is wearing. It was a black-and-white zebra print without any sleeves. My mom wore a cardigan sweater over it, more likely because my dad thought it showed too much shoulder than be-cause it was cold in the ballroom. Supposedly when Mom kissed me good night before leaving for the wedding, she said, "See you next year," and I melted down like a Fudgesicle in July. We're talking near panic attack, the way Mom would tell the story. The problem was that I didn't totally get New Year's Eve yet. Once Mom explained it to me, I chilled, but I gather it was pretty gnarly there for a couple of minutes.

Anyway, they're at this inn that has pushed all the tables in this huge room against the walls so people can dance, and there are still all these tiny white Christmas lights along the ceiling and the windowsills and over the top of the glass doors. There's a good crowd, and every-body's dancing—even the bartenders, a guy and this girl in bow ties behind this long table with rows and rows of bottles and glasses. The two of them look like they're having as much fun as the people on the dance floor. Most of the crowd seems to be in their twenties and thir-ties, but there are grandparents and aunts and uncles, I guess, sitting at some of those tables. Whoever is holding the video camera must have known it belongs to Mom and Dad, because they're focusing more on the two of them than on anyone else in the room. And they are really moving. They look more than a little dorky, but I guess it's sweet that they're so into the party and so into each other. Suddenly the DJ, wherever he is, says he is going to play something slow now for all the lovers in the room. My mom falls against my dad, and the camera catches them looking into each other's eyes like they invented romance. Her fingers are on the back of his neck, and when they finally break eye contact, her head falls forward into his chest, she closes her eyes, and she has this smile on her face that looks like she is having the most peaceful and beautiful dream of her life. We're talking movie moment.

Anyway, it would have been a classic on Facebook. And it reminded me that once, a long time ago, my parents' marriage hadn't been the natural disaster that it would soon become and will look like forever to most of the world.

OBVIOUSLY I THINK a lot about what must have been going on at my house that Sunday night while Tina and I were in Albany at the Fray concert. Everyone around me seemed to be concocting whole scenes that August and September, and the only thing they all shared was this: I was lucky as hell that the band was playing a Sunday-night gig, because that's the only reason I'm alive today. The general consensus is that if I'd been home, I would have been killed. We'll never know, but I also think it's possible if I had been there, all three of us would have been alive the next morning. Maybe my mom would have kept to herself whatever it was she said that put my dad over the edge. Maybe Mom and I would have gotten the heck out of there before my dad blew up like a furnace. And maybe, pure and simple, Dad would have been incapable of killing Mom if I'd been in the house.

But everyone who talked to me had a different idea about how the fight might have unfolded, and they were all basing it on their memories of their own parents' fights—or, I guess, on their own fights with their own spouse or partner or whatever. That's the thing. We all have recollections of fighting with someone we're supposed to love, and I figured out at a really young age that what goes on when the doors are closed is anyone's guess.

Still, I have tried to piece together that Sunday night from what I know of their fights (which is, unfortunately, a lot), what Ginny told me, and what the investigators seemed to have figured out in the weeks that followed. Stephen and I talked about it a couple of times before it became clear to me that he was the last person in the world I should have been talking to.

But if I were one of those hidden cameras, here's what I think I would have seen at my house that Sunday night: I would see my mom in the doorway when Tina and I are starting down the driveway in her parents' red Subaru wagon. Tina has had her license for about three months, and even though she drives like she's about ninety years old—we're talking five miles below the speed limit, always, and she might be the only one of my friends who doesn't text while she's passing a manure spreader—my mom is worried. She has worried whenever I have gotten in the car with Tina the first half of the summer. She has no idea that even though I only have a learner's permit and am only supposed to drive a car when Mom or Dad are right there beside me in the passenger seat, I drive that Subaru all the time around Haverill. Not smart, I know. But not ridiculous, either, because the state police never patrol around here. And so I drive that wagon a lot, and I am, like Tina, a pretty careful driver.

Anyway, Mom is standing in the doorway, and she still has in her arms the big blue bowl with the peas she has plucked from the garden. Her garden. My dad and I really have very little (read: nothing) to do with it. She hasn't shelled those peas yet. Imagine Auntie Em, but still young and pretty. Remember, my mom was only thirty-eight when she died. I know that's supposed to seem ancient to a teenager, but it's not. It's just not.

So my mom waves once, and I hope I wave back. But there's no guarantee. Meanwhile my dad is tidying the garage. Organizing. I have absolutely no idea why, but that's what he is doing late that Sunday afternoon. He doesn't come out to holler good-bye to me or wave. But the last time I saw him in there, he was drinking a beer. It is at least his second bottle and maybe his third, and the idea has crossed my mind that this is trouble. When he first returned in May, he wasn't drinking at all. But at a picnic for one of his manager's birthdays in late June, he started again, and since then he has been ratcheting it up. Mom has said it's because business is a little slow and we're in a recession. When things pick up, he'll—as grown-ups put it—go back on the wagon. But when he drinks, he becomes a total jerk. This month has been three-plus weeks of Mom and me walking on glass, tiptoeing around the house so we don't piss him off any more than we seem to simply by breathing. Something about Mom's baptism this morning has ticked him off, and I've been unable to put my finger on what it is. Midafternoon I almost asked Mom if it was as obvious as the idea that the baptism involved Stephen, but in theory I don't know about Stephen, and I have to assume that my dad doesn't either.

As Tina and I reach the end of the driveway, I have a thought: Dad is puttering around in the garage because Mom never goes there except to pull out the car in the winter. It's a place where he can hang out and totally avoid Mom and me. Which, with him drinking right now, is probably a good thing for Mom. Something happened on Friday night when I was at a party in Pownal. I don't know the details, but even by the admittedly very low standards of civility my dad subscribes to, it couldn't have been pretty. How badly did he hit Mom? I don't know because I wasn't home, and almost always he hits her in places no one can see. But since Friday night the house has been especially gloomy, even on the pathetic Happiness Scale in place at the Haywards'. I think he beat her pretty badly, no doubt on the lower back.

After I've left, my mom sits down to shell the peas in that bowl.

She probably sits down near where I saw her waving, outside in the sun that is still bathing the western side of the lawn in warmth. Eventually she will rise, go back inside, and cook the rest of their dinner. She doesn't set the kitchen table, because I think they will eat on the front porch tonight. It is a balmy summer evening, and my parents always liked to eat outside on that porch. It didn't have a table, because it really was just front steps with a landing, and so they will eat that night with their plates on their laps and their drinks on the wooden planking beside them. In my mom's case, that means iced tea, in my dad's another beer.

They probably aren't saying a whole lot as they eat, because by the time they plop themselves down on those steps, Mom is a little scared and my dad is well on the way to being totally hammered. Talking to him right now is like baiting a hungry lion. Why do that? Why go there? The thing is, it could be such a great night for them. Tomorrow is Monday, her day off, and the kid is at a concert and spending the night with a friend. Wouldn't you think most parents would be having Naked Sunday together?

But not mine. Not that night.

At some point when he is done chewing a bite of chicken, his tongue clearing bits of meat from around his gums in this creepy way that reminds me of a mole tunneling just under the grass, my dad turns to my mom and says something nasty about the meal. Maybe it's as simple as how her vegetables don't taste any better than the ones you can buy at the supermarket, but with all the mulch and manure and fertilizer she uses, these ones from her garden actually cost more. Some nights this month, this has been his song. Maybe he says something about her shorts: They're too short. Too baggy. Too frumpy. Too slutty. My dad had a thing about shorts and my mom's legs—which were really very sexy for a mom. But most likely it is the baptism he has brought up, planning to use it to find a way to wound her and pick a fight. He says, maybe, that he can't believe she paraded around like some tramp in a bathing suit before the whole batch of Holy Rollers.

That's what he called the people who went to the church: Holy Rollers.

He says that everyone must have loved that: Alice Hayward, tarting around at the pond. Now, my dad wasn't a moron. He has to know on some level that he is being completely ridiculous. So why is he saying these things? So Mom will dispute him.

It was a Speedo, she reminds him, not some bikini. And I was wearing a T-shirt over it, anyway.

Oh, how lovely, he says, his voice taking on that weird, condescending, pretend-upper-class monotone. But do you honestly think that makes it better? Do you think I would prefer to have my wife parading around town like she's a contestant in a Hooters wet-T-shirt contest?

And my mom will know what's coming and that she can't win this argument. And so she backs off. But when Dad gets like this, you can only back off so far before, all of a sudden, your back is to the wall and there's no place left to go. And Mom is already hurting from whatever she had endured on Friday night when I was gone. Still, here is the problem she faces: If she disagrees with Dad, he might hit her for challenging him, but if she agrees with him, she is admitting to having dressed like a slut at her baptism, and that will be his grounds for whaling on her.

What does she say? In my mind I see her shaking her head, realizing that she should have gotten out years ago. Or that she should have gone to court when she was supposed to a week or so after she got that temporary restraining order back in February. Or she should have taken the flowers that had started arriving almost daily in May and tossed them into the compost heap. Or she should never have allowed him back in the house when he wheedled his way into a reconciliation just after Mother's Day. But that isn't what she did, and now she's looking at her second beating in three days. And so she stands up with her plate and retreats inside. I have seen her do this before: just take her food and excuse herself from the table. Or excuse herself from the table without taking her food. The upside to this strategy—withdrawal without a word—is that she hasn't said anything that he can use as a justification for his anger. The downside? She has seriously dissed him. (And when she has done this when I've been present, she has also humiliated him in front of his daughter.)

But it is often how Mom played the game, and sometimes it worked. No fighting in the night, and the next morning there would be peace on earth and my dad would apologize for being such a jerk. My guess is that is exactly what my mom does that Sunday night. She leaves him alone on the front steps and finishes eating inside. In the kitchen, reading the newspaper, maybe. Lula is sitting beside her and wagging her tail, waiting for Mom to hand her a few pieces of chicken or cut some up and drop the meat into her dish. The picture to someone who doesn't know what's really going on? It's like Mom lives alone with her dog. Except there's this teeny-tiny detail that she is scared to death her husband is about to come in and belt her.

Based on the plates that would be found in the sink and how much of the dinner had been cleaned up and put away—at some point I overheard someone saying that the bowls with coleslaw and peas both had plastic covers on them—the strategy worked for a while. I see my dad sitting on the steps, stewing. Drinking. Maybe for a while he goes back to the garage and drinks some more.

But at some point he comes inside, plops himself down on the living-room couch, and turns on the TV set. Is he watching *60 Minutes*? Maybe. Sometimes he would turn it on. But he is so drunk by now that he really isn't watching anything. And pretty quickly he conks out. Falls asleep and isn't making a sound. It's the darnedest thing: He never seems to snore. My mom once told me that the only time she could recall him snoring was when he had a sinus infection years ago. (Not snoring is also something he takes weird pride in. I actually heard him brag to people at the annual Father's Day volunteer firefighters' barbecue that he never snores. He made it sound like it was some amazing athletic accomplishment.) My mom makes that phone call to Ginny, a conversation that led lots of people to tell me that Ginny was the very last person my mom would talk to. (One time I considered reminding them that they were mistaken: The very last person my mom would talk to was pretty obviously my dad, as she begged him or screamed at him until she could no longer breathe to stop killing her.) My mom peeks into the living room, sees Dad is still out like a light, and changes into her nightgown. The red nightgown.

And then, not too long after Mom has said good night to Ginny and gotten ready for bed, Dad wakes up. Some people say he killed Mom that night because she dropped the bombshell on him that she was leaving. The fight they'd been having outside resumed, but at some point it took a new course and ended with my mom informing him that the marriage was over and she was getting out. Literally. She was leaving him. Leaving the premises. She probably didn't tell him to get out that night, because how could he? He was drunk. Maybe my mom wouldn't have cared if he'd killed his own sorry self by driving into a maple tree at sixty or seventy miles an hour, but she wouldn't have wanted him to bring some innocent person down with him. She really did worry like crazy about cars. And so she tells him that she is out the door. So long. She is going to get dressed, pack a bag, and split.

And maybe people are right and that is exactly what she said that caused the fight to go nuclear.

But maybe not. Or maybe not right away. I think she had to be driven just a little further before she would say that. When I'm trying and failing to fall asleep at night, I see it continue like this. I see my dad trying hard to get a rise out of Mom, and even if he doesn't know that she'd been hooking up with Stephen, he knows for a while they were pretty tight. And so he says something about Stephen and manages, if only by accident, to hit just the right nerve in just the right tooth—especially since, maybe, Stephen was the one who ended their affair. I've always wondered if maybe she only took Dad back because Stephen broke up with her. All those flowers Dad sent? They only worked because Stephen wasn't around anymore. I also think that's the reason Stephen felt so guilty after Mom died. The baptism? Yeah, right. He said that he felt responsible because he'd missed all these signals about how she was ready to die, but that was totally ridiculous. We're talking fairy tale. More likely Stephen felt like a louse because he'd told my mom early in May that he didn't want their thing to go public or he didn't want it to continue. Whatever. And so she takes back her own husband on the rebound, he kills her a couple of months later, and Stephen winds up feeling horrible. As he should.

Anyway, my dad is getting a beer out of the refrigerator, and he says something stupid about Stephen's sexual orientation. Among my dad's more pathetic prejudices? Homophobia, big-time. I'd heard him make cracks before about why Stephen wasn't married. And maybe that night Mom has had just enough of this lunacy, and so she tells Dad that she knows for a fact that Stephen is straight. Very. Remember, I'm not home, so the sexual volleys might be racier and nastier than usual.

The result? Dad is confronted for the first time with the news that Mom has been with someone other than him, and it is—how's this for an irony?—the leader of those so-called Holy Rollers who Dad thinks are just such total losers. Moreover, for all he knows, Mom has been with Stephen awhile. Maybe not merely when Dad was living out at the lake. Maybe before he left. Maybe even when he was living right here in little old Haverill. It's around eight o'clock at night. That old school professor's voice of his is swamped by serious rage: Mom's latest infraction isn't just wearing a top that's too revealing or forgetting to pick up the dry cleaning. She has tossed a hand grenade down the front of his pants.

You what? I hear him yelling in my head, and she repeats whatever it was that she said the first time about Stephen and her and how they'd been sleeping together. Or how they'd been lovers. I honestly can't decide the precise wording of the bombshell, because as well as I knew my mom, there were just some things we never talked about. I mean, she had never told me that she and Stephen had been hooking up. But I'm sure there is a moment when my dad can't believe what he's hearing and has her repeat herself.

And so my mom does.

And when you repeat things, you add things. The adviser for the school newspaper, Mr. Fisher, taught us that. And so I see my mom realizing that for the first time ever, she has wounded Dad, really smacked him back hard, and so she starts piling it on. She tells him whatever it was that Stephen gave her that marriage to my dad doesn't. She talks about how intelligent and well educated Stephen is (an incredibly sharp dagger for Dad, since he never went to college). Or how tender. Or how gentle. But she always brings it back to the fact that they were lovers, because she has seen that this really ticks him off.

Nevertheless, she doesn't have a death wish. I really believe that, too. I really don't think she thought for even a split second that my dad was going to kill her. Hit her? Sure. Pound her a couple of times? Hell, yes. But I am absolutely convinced that she didn't see him taking his hands and strangling her. Stephen is very smart, but he was wrong about that.

First, of course, my dad probably slugs her. For one of the only times ever, he even hits her in the face. Open hand, backhand, a fist. I don't know. No one told me a lot about what the medical examiner said about the condition of their bodies, and I don't even know if you can tell in the end whether a bruise was caused by knuckles or palm. I never asked. Heather would tell me later that she hadn't asked, either: She hadn't asked anyone what had gone down when her dad killed her mom. And she told me that she regretted that. But still I didn't ask. I mean, how could I?

So my dad hits Mom. Does she hit him back? No way. My mom was never going to hit back. Besides, she has just had the wind knocked out of her. Or she has fallen to the floor. Or she has banged into something (that seemed to happen a lot). I see her on the floor in the living room, Dad standing over her. And when she gets her breath back or she gets back in control, she says something more about Stephen. As my grandfather—my dad's dad—always says, in for a nickel, in for a dime. And Dad is thinking the same thing. *I hit her in the head and the sky didn't fall in. And my wife was sleeping with some dude I don't really like. Maybe she's sleeping with him even now.* So he beats on her some more. Whacks her in the nose.

And then—*then*—Mom tells him she's leaving. That's what I mean about having to drive my dad to that point. She had to seriously get under his skin. Even my dad needs a little motivation to wrap his hands around Mom's neck and squeeze till she's dead. I see my mom holding her nose (because he has hit her there, not because she smells something bad) and wiping away the blood that is trickling slowly over and around her lips. She straightens her back and rises to her full height (which is still shorter than Dad) and announces that he has hit her for the last time. This time there will be no backing down when the day comes to show up in court.

Which is when he kills her. He loses all control. He has his hands around her neck, and he is shaking her, maybe not realizing that this is it—that he has passed the line of all reason—but shaking her and pressing his thumbs against her esophagus. I have tried to see what it must have felt like. One time I even had Tina squeeze my neck till I said, "Enough, I get it." (She was creeped out, but she understood what I wanted to know, and so she did it.) It must have hurt like crazy. Agony. But here is that expression again: in for a nickel, in for a dime. Once you've started to kill your wife, how do you stop?

And so my dad didn't, even though my mom had to have been trying to get him to. Although I have never asked, I'm sure she fought back, if only because it must have hurt so much. She must have tried to push him away or get his fingers off her neck. She must have tried to hit him or scratch him hard enough that he'd release her, if only for a second.

And then, before he knew it, she was dead in his hands. And that's the thing about the way he killed her: One minute she was alive in his hands, and the next she was dead. One minute she was struggling, and the next she wasn't. Fighting. Not fighting. Breathing. Not breathing.

And that, in my opinion, is when my dad polished off the rest of the beers that we had in the house. He was drunk when he killed her, but not nearly as drunk as he'd be when he died.

AND YET ONLY a little more than two months before that nightmare, Mom had taken him back. Had him move in with us again. I thought this was nuts even then and told her that I thought this was a very bad idea. But it's funny how the memory works and how sometimes we just believe whatever we want. And I guess my mom wanted to believe that everything would be different.

I really wasn't all that surprised when she sat me down one night in May and said Dad was coming home. There had been plenty of signals—Exhibit A, all those flowers. And Dad had been getting goopier and goopier on the telephone, telling me that he was convinced we would soon be reunited as a family and how much this meant to him, since in a few years I would be off to college and he didn't have a lot of time left with me. (He sure was right about that one.) He had also been saying for weeks that he knew he would still make mistakes in his life because he wasn't perfect, but he was positive that the worst was behind him. (Okay, he was wrong there.) And he did sound better. Happier. He said he wasn't drinking.

But there had been signals from Mom, too. The biggest one was that sometime in the late spring something happened between Stephen and her. I don't know for sure when they first started hooking up, but I think it was before Christmas, when Dad was still living at home. And you could just see Mom opening up like one of her roses that winter. She was less nervous, more confident. She was laughing a lot more. Suddenly anything and everything could be funny. My big worry in the beginning? Dad would figure out something was up and that fight would be the sort they would eventually have in July. (I mean, I don't think I ever thought he would kill her. But I thought it would be bad with a capital B.) But in early May she started retreating again. Our dinners got quiet. She suggested we eat supper in the living room in front of DVDs of the TV shows I liked, which I knew she did when she didn't want to talk—when she couldn't cope. I had been making my own lunch for school for years, but when she was happy that winter and spring, she would insist on offering me advice: She would throw in an apple or a clementine, she would surprise me with the macaroon cookies I liked from the bakery. That changed, too. She might still be in the kitchen when I was making my lunch, but she would sit at the table sipping her coffee, not exactly a zombie, because sometimes she would be toying with a crossword puzzle, but not exactly present, either. She would be dressed for work by then, because a lot of days she would drive me to school before continuing on to the bank. And what she considered dressed for work changed, too. In the winter she had started dressing a lot cooler, especially after Dad was gone. The jeans were a little tighter on Monday, when she didn't have work, and the skirts were a little tighter the rest of the week. No more of those I'm-running-for-Congress pants suits. Sometimes she even allowed her blouses to show a little cleavage, a hint of bra. After Dad was out the door in February, it was like she had bought a whole new wardrobe. Unfortunately, those clothes went the way of her laughter as summer approached.

I asked her about this once, but she was pretty cagey. That's one thing I have learned about women like my mom: There are no people in the world who are better at keeping secrets. You want to find a good spy? Pick a battered woman. There are things they won't tell a soul. And they can really take a punch.

Anyway, Mom sat me down one evening, and I knew instantly what was coming. It was May, so the days were getting long, and I remember there were a ton of birds at the feeders. Mom had three, and they were all on the opposite side of the house from her vegetable garden, because she loved birds, but she loved her garden, too, and she didn't want the robins or the blue jays eating her seeds. And she had just planted most of the garden and put her freaky clear plastic tepees over her tomato- and pepper-plant seedlings. The tepees always looked like they belonged in a science-fiction movie or video game: You know, the way the human colony grew things on some faraway planet. We were sitting on the steps (the same steps where I have always imagined they ate their last meal together), one of us occasionally stroking Lula behind her ears. Mom sort of beat around the bush for a few minutes, asking about school and what sorts of things Dad and I had been talking about lately when he phoned or at lunch. Then she went on this riff about how complicated adult relationships are, which would have been the absolute perfect moment for me to bring up Stephen. But I didn't, and that will always be a regret I'll live with, because now I'll never know for sure what she was thinking. At any rate, I acted surprised when she said Dad was coming home, because I figured I was supposed to. Then I told her that I really didn't think this was such a good plan and reminded her of some of the worst fights they'd had in the months before he moved out. But she said things were going to be different now because Dad was going to be different now. She said this had been a real wake-up call for him and he had learned from his mistakes—which was not unlike what my dad had said to me, too, though he'd also said he was still going to make plenty of them. (Yup, that was my dad: a real lifelong learner.)

But the thing that struck me then and I think about now is this: Mom didn't seem all that happy about Dad coming home to live with us. She seemed resigned to the idea. It was like it was all a big chore that loomed before her. Something we both would just have to endure.

FROM *A SACRED WHILE*
BY HEATHER LAURENT (P. 301)

Make no mistake: Although my faith in heaven is unshakable, although I am confident in the angels that reside amongst us, I am as filled with sorrows at endings as you are. I cry at the funerals for friends I have lost, I mourn for lovers with whom, in the end, I will not have the pleasure or privilege of building a life. I grieve for the parents who have outlived their children, and I will always despair for the children who have watched their own parents break the rapture of the night with violence.

CHAPTER EIGHTEEN

When I think of that spring, the first thing that comes to mind is how easy it all was. There had been so much tension in the house for so many years that I hadn't realized how simple life could be if you weren't always waiting for the boiler in the basement to explode. And I know my mom felt that way, too—probably even a ton more than I did. There was this massive late-season snowstorm on Easter, but still Mom and I trudged up the hill in our parkas and snow boots for the sunrise service at six in the morning. Obviously we didn't expect to see the sun rise over the mountains to the east. No one did, and there were about seventy of us who made it there. (Just for the record, it was the first sunrise service I had gone to in three or four years. Usually I slept in and would stagger out of bed for the regular nine forty-five service. And the only reason I went to the sunrise service that year was for Mom.) Stephen was very funny, even though you could only hear about every other word in the gale. But about six-fifteen the wind started to slow and we could all see the sky lightening to the east. Soon there were just a few big flakes floating around, and then even they were gone. We never got actual blue sky that morning, but we could all see this great round lightbulb behind the thin shade of clouds. And that's what it was like for me when Dad was away. This big storm I had gotten used to was gone, and while there may not have been total sunshine, I could see the light—and I knew that with a little luck even that last veil of clouds would disappear if I gave it more time. And I imagine it was even better for Mom, because she wasn't being abused and she had this cool thing going with Stephen.

Unfortunately, it wasn't long after that when, for whatever the reason, her affair with Stephen began winding down. And then, a little later, the flowers from Dad started coming. It was like he knew that now was the perfect time to wedge the toe of his boot back in the door.

It's funny, but I have a childhood memory of Mom reading to me in the apartment we had lived in when I was a little girl in Bennington that I link in my mind with that spring. Mom is reading to me from *Blueberries for Sal,* which I still have, incidentally, and I'm curled up in her arms in this massive rocking chair that she told me once was the chair in which she liked to nurse me when I was a baby. I guess I'm, like, four. The chair went with us when we moved to Haverill. And one Sunday afternoon that spring when Dad was gone, I saw Mom sitting in that chair and reading a novel. The dust jacket had the same blues and yellows as the cover of *Blueberries for Sal*, and the afternoon sun was coming in through the window just the way it had that day long ago when I was curled up in her lap in Bennington. And just like that day when I was four, I felt totally at peace and totally secure. That's what that spring had felt like when Dad was gone. And that feeling, I guess, is what my dad had taken away from me for most of my life.

BETWEEN THE FIRST days of February and the last half of May, I never saw my parents together. They had a colossal fight the Sunday night after Groundhog Day. (Looking back, Sunday might have been the night they were most likely to collide. Maybe, like me, my dad just found Sunday nights totally depressing. You know, it's the end of the weekend and school and work are all you have to look forward to for the next five days. And even though my mom had Mondays off, it's possible she felt those same end-of-the-weekend blahs, too, because for the rest of the world the weekend was ending.) Nearly three and a half months would pass between the fight that led Mom to get the temporary restraining order and the day I came home from school and there was Dad at the kitchen table. I was living with my mom that whole time, but by the end of March I was seeing my dad again, either in Manchester or one time at our cottage on the lake.

I'm not sure why my dad started that fight in February. Actually, I'm not sure why he started most of their fights. There was never a good reason. Usually he was drunk, but not that Sunday night. I mean, he had been drinking. That I know. But he wasn't so drunk that he couldn't drive. After all, he got in his car and drove away on his own when Mom told him to get out. At first he'd said there was no way he was leaving his own house. He reminded Mom that her salary at the bank sure didn't cover the mortgages on the house or the cottage or the car payments. (I must admit, until that night I didn't even know we had car payments. I knew we had mortgages. But I hadn't really thought about how we might not own Dad's BMW or Mom's Accord outright.) But she held her ground. She had rolled up the sleeve of her sweater and her turtleneck so she could hold an ice pack on her elbow. Dad had, for reasons that probably didn't make any sense and certainly no longer matter, pushed her down the stairs. I saw him do it. And, worse, he saw that I had witnessed it. I think we all thought he had broken her arm. He hadn't, but despite the ice pack it would swell up like she was Popeye. She also had a bruise on her hip that was so black and blue it looked like a screen saver of outer space.

I think Dad was torn when Mom told him to get out. Should he get out, like his wife was demanding, or should he take her to the hospital? Mom would say to me later that night that his big concern was his reputation. It wouldn't look good for him if he had broken his wife's arm pushing her down the stairs. But my mom also thought it wouldn't have looked good for her, either. She would go to the hospital the next morning, just in case. But I don't think she would have gone if Monday hadn't been her day off. Still, she did get her arm and her back X-rayed. Nothing was broken. But someone at the hospital must have said something to her, because it was on the way back to Haverill that she detoured to the courthouse and got what is called a relief-from-abuse order and had the papers served to Dad before he could come home.

Dad, I assume, had thought he was just leaving for the night. And so it must have been quite the shocker when the police showed up at his little suite of offices above the toy store. I don't know what he told his secretary or his accountant or anyone else who might have been present about why a couple of policemen were there. But I'm sure he figured out something. He was pretty fast on his feet when he was sober. And, like I said, I'm sure a lot of the world thought he had left Mom, not the other way around. He was, in many people's eyes, a pretty solid catch.

Months and months later, Josie explained to me that the police had probably told Mom that they could arrest him, if she wanted. But she didn't want that. She just wanted him out. She just wanted a little peace. And, maybe, she just wanted to be with Stephen.

Anyway, she never went to court when she had the chance.

JUST AS THERE were times when my dad wasn't a total jerk to my mom, I have memories of him trying to be a pretty good dad with me.

350

(Sometimes he even succeeded.) I used to love to visit him at his stores or that restaurant of his when I was younger. He seemed extremely important, and so that made me feel important. His employees treated me like a princess. He used to do a lot of paperwork for the restaurant at a table near the door to the kitchen, because when it was quiet, he could get work done and when it was crazy busy (which sometimes it was), he could see the whole dining room and get a sense of what worked in the restaurant and what didn't. He could see how his servers moved in and around the tables. (And, just maybe, he knew that they knew he was watching, and he liked that idea. I mean, if he liked controlling Mom, why wouldn't he like controlling his employees?) I remember a couple of times doing homework there when I was in the fifth grade, and it made math and geography a lot more fun. The work wasn't hard, and I ate tons of cornbread with butter and dirty rice. And more than that, Dad seemed to be in a good mood on those occasions, and that always boded well for my mom and for a quiet evening at the house when we got home.

My dad never drank at work, at least on those times when I visited him. Even as a kid I had figured out the connection between the beer and the beatings. That doesn't excuse it, of course, but my mom used to insist that Dad loved her and things would be fine if it weren't for the alcohol. I don't believe that, personally. I know there were times when he was horrible to her when he was completely sober. He may have been worse when he'd had a couple of beers, but there was always the chance he'd be a bastard regardless of whether he'd been drinking.

I MAY HAVE been a little wild that autumn, but in late September I also got coaxed back into the church Youth Group. I liked the older man who was the interim pastor, and I liked the young woman the church had brought in as a special youth pastor. Sometimes I think they brought her in just for me. She had a stud in her nose, too, and she thought my tattoo was beautiful. Her name was Julie. She wouldn't be around long, because soon she would move on to a much bigger church in Burlington. But she was only, like, twenty-two or twenty-three, and we talked a lot. I remember the third Sunday in October really well. She convinced me to spend the afternoon helping to chaperone the little kids in Haverill who were carving pumpkins. It was the two of us and Tina and a couple of deacons in this big hay field near the center of the village. A few of the parents stayed, but most of them dropped off their kids and ran. And while a lot of the children were in the fourth and fifth grades and were helping their younger brothers and sisters, many of the kids came up to my waist and shouldn't have been allowed anywhere near knives the lengths of their forearms. And there must have been eighty children there.

A fellow in the church named Mr. Humphrey had donated the pumpkins, and he was one of the grown-ups who stayed. He was a little older than my parents had been, and his real business was this beautiful bed-and-breakfast that he and his wife owned. There seemed to be weddings there all the time. They had things like a pumpkin patch and strawberry fields and blueberry bushes, but they were mostly so the guests would feel they were staying on this working farm.

Anyway, the plan that Sunday was that each kid would carve a pumpkin and then Mr. Humphrey was going to stand up on this hay wagon and name them. He did this every year, and he was really pretty funny. Sometimes he'd give the jack-o'-lanterns names that a five-year-old would think were hysterical: Oogly-Boogly if it had massive eyes or Bobby Booger if its most obvious feature was its nose. And sometimes he would name the pumpkin after someone who had been in the news a lot that autumn, and so election years were always easier for him than other years. I mean, he wasn't Jon Stewart, but he was pretty fast on his feet. And all of the children would howl with laughter no matter what, because they were tanked up on cookies and brownies the Women's Circle had baked, and no matter what they were going to get a coupon worth a dollar at the Haverill General Store as a prize.

Counting the parents who hung around and Mr. Humphrey, who was mostly just surveying the scene like a rock star, there were about ten adults or young adults looking out for those eighty elementary-school kids. That's not a bad ratio if the ten adults are schoolteachers who know what they're doing and the young adults aren't that young. But it's not terrific if two of the chaperones are teenagers like Tina and me and two are deacons somewhere between the ages of seventy-five and death.

And then, of course, one of those two teenagers would lose it. That would be me. For about twenty-five minutes, Julie and one of the few moms who stuck around had to care for me off to the side of the field and watch me sit in the mown grass sobbing and sipping apple cider from a paper cup. One minute I would be howling like a kindergartner who was left behind on the school bus, and the next I would be unable to breathe. It was like I had forgotten how. And sobbing without breathing is no easy trick. At one point, Tina told me later, I was braying sort of like a donkey.

What set me off? It was this carving knife that a girl named Alicia was using. Alicia was, I think, five. And the knife had this brown wooden handle with rivets and this long row of ovals along the blade. The ovals didn't get smaller as the blade narrowed, they simply took up more of the blade. And for a few seconds I watched her struggle to poke the knife through the thick rind of her pumpkin, twisting it sometimes and stabbing it others. (See what I mean about what a disaster just waiting to happen that whole day was? It's a miracle that none of the kids gouged out one of their own eyes or took off one of their own tiny fingers.) She was bringing her little arm up and down, up and down, but she wasn't very strong and so the tip never punctured the pumpkin. It kept bouncing off the gourd like it was Super Pumpkin.

And that's when I had this weird image, which I realized was actually a weird memory. When I was five, I had done something sort of like that with a knife that looked exactly like the one Alicia was using. It had the same rivets on the handle and it had those same ovals along the blade. In my memory I was on the tile floor of our apartment in Bennington, a place I remembered in some ways only because of the pictures in the photo albums and a couple of old videos my mom had transferred onto a disc. And I was trying to puncture something with the knife. A basketball. I was trying to pop my dad's basketball. When we lived in Bennington and he was younger, he played pretty often with some friends at a school playground with a couple of hoops not far from our apartment. And then there was this memory: I was trying to destroy my dad's basketball with that knife, because the night before I had seen him threatening my mom. And the knife he'd been using was the very same kind Alicia was using now. It was dark out, and I'd heard a commotion in the kitchen. I came out of the bedroom, and there was my mom in her nightgown pressed up against the cabinet that held the broom and the vacuum and the cleaning stuff (all of which had these labels Mom had put on them that said something like "Mr. Yuck," so I wouldn't start guzzling the toilet-bowl cleaner), and my dad had one hand around her neck and was practically lifting her off the floor. In his other hand was the knife, and he was holding it near her cheek. He was talking in such a low voice that I couldn't hear a word he was saying, but I could tell by the tone it was pretty darn menacing. Looking back, I don't imagine he was threatening to kill her. When I think about where he was holding the point of the knife,

I guess he was only threatening to disfigure her. Scar forever that pretty face.

I must have said something, because Mom saw me out of the corner of her eye—she really couldn't turn her head—and she must have managed to mumble something to Dad. Because he turned and saw me. And when he did, he looked at the knife in his hand like he didn't know what it was or how it had even gotten there. He let go of Mom and tossed the knife on the kitchen table, and then he rumpled my hair as he started past me to their bedroom. He was shaking his head, but at what, I couldn't have said. Meanwhile my mom slid to the kitchen floor, her back still against the cabinet, and she was crying so desperately that for a minute she wasn't even able to scoot across the tile floor to me. And so I went to her.

It was the next day that I started trying to destroy my dad's basketball. I didn't have any more success with the rubber than Alicia was having with the pumpkin rind, but Mom found me before I managed to slice through an artery or cut off a leg. And that night Dad took Mom out to some fancy dinner and I had a baby-sitter. And soon after that they started to build the house in Haverill.

That afternoon at the pumpkin carving, it all grew connected in my mind: the flashback of Dad scaring the hell out of Mom, my getting medieval on a basketball, and the whole path that would lead us from Bennington to Haverill and to the two of them dead in the living room. I think that's why I lost it that afternoon. I mean, I had plenty of other reasons to lose it that autumn. But I attribute my mini-breakdown at the pumpkin carving to that flashback. Eventually Tina and Julie and that mom got me calmed down, and I returned to the carving. But I'm pretty sure no one handed me a knife, and I helped mostly by scooping out pumpkin guts for the kids, because no seven- or eight-year-old likes pulling out the cold, mealy crap inside a pumpkin.

SOMETIMES I WONDERED if Stephen saw something in Heather that he didn't see in my mom. When I try to be objective, I guess Heather was a little bit prettier, but my mom was no slouch. I mean that. And while my mom may have put up with more from my dad than she should have, at least she wasn't seeing angels in parking lots the way most people spy seagulls. And I always try to remind myself of this: Stephen did not dump my mom for Heather. If I were to guess, he and Mom had separated early in May. Stephen wouldn't even meet Heather until the end of July. Two days after my parents had died.

But my relationship with Heather, distant as it was, was weirdly complicated, too. On the one hand, I really couldn't help but see her as my mom's competitor for Stephen's affections, even though my mom was gone. What did she have that Mom didn't? And so that would make me want to push her away out of loyalty. But then there was the fact that she understood more about what I was experiencing than any of the social workers or therapists that everyone kept parading before me. She knew what it was like to suddenly be an orphan (and I am an orphan) and to feel all the time like you're an imposition. And that is what I felt like: If you're a kid without parents, even a teenager, you're always forced to depend on the kindness of other people. You feel indebted to everyone. I had known the Cousinos forever, but it's not like I was their kid. But there I was, living under their roof and eating their food and using their bathrooms. I could have lived with my grandparents in New Hampshire (for obvious reasons, my dad's parents were never really an option in my mind), but I had lived in the same village since I was six and been friends with the same group of kids for almost a decade. Does any kid really want to move when she only has two years of high school left? No, of course not. So I chose to be a nuisance.

Heather also understood what it was like to see your mom bullied by your dad and be totally powerless to stop it. Sometimes we talked about all the fights we had witnessed. It seemed like her dad would say the same sorts of things as mine and her mom would sometimes hide out in the same ridiculous world of denial. Who knows? Maybe wife beaters really are one-trick ponies. They're bullies, but about as creative as the bullies you hear about all the time these days who are my age.

And, of course, Heather was famous. Not famous to me, at least not at first. But soon I figured out that she was very well known to a lot of adults. Ginny, for instance, thought she was totally amazing. And there were at least fifteen videos of her that I found on YouTube. She had been on lots of talk shows and seemed right at home on those comfy couches with the beautiful hostesses. And I loved reading what people said about her books at the online bookstores. Some readers thought she was brilliant, and some thought she was in serious need of medication. Anyway, I would be lying if I said that her celebrity didn't appeal to me. It did. I thought it was very, very cool.

But I kept reminding myself that there's more to life than being on talk shows and having lots of clips of yourself on YouTube. There's more to life than selling a boatload of books.

And even after reading both of her books—and I read them carefully—I still didn't believe there were angels. I'd seen my mom's bruises, and there was no way I could reconcile those marks with angel wings.

Sometimes I'd wonder if she and Stephen would ever get back together. I didn't see it happening, but Tina did. When we talked about it, she said I was like that old Aerosmith song "Jaded." She was wrong (and she was wrong about the song, too, because, I think it's more about a girl who is spoiled than a girl who is totally cynical), but I understood what she was getting at. She thought Stephen and Heather would be a good pair because they would, like, balance each other out. Maybe. But it would mean that Heather would have to get over the idea that Stephen had killed my dad, and for a million reasons that's never going to happen. And Stephen? I don't know. But I think he's built to live alone.

Anyway, in the end I remained most loyal to my mom when it came to that whole weird Stephen thing. Even if by any standard my mom wasn't as hip as Heather Laurent, she was still the woman who had raised me and read to me and, until Dad killed her, was going to be there for me no matter what.

WHEN I WENT to the parsonage that Sunday night, Stephen told me to go back to Tina's house right away and he would deal with the nightmare in my living room. He told me not to tell anyone anything, not even Tina. Later, of course, I did tell Tina. I told her a ton. Not everything. But almost everything. Stephen offered to drive me to Tina's, but I told him that I had driven to my house and then to his in the Cousinos' wagon. Aren't you fifteen? he asked. I said yeah, but then he must have realized that underage driving was the least of my problems that night and sort of shrugged. I think he was in shock, too.

In all fairness, when I went from my house to Stephen's I'd figured that we would go to the police or call for help or do the sorts of things that I had seen on TV. He seemed like the right person, because even though I hadn't been real good about Youth Group over the last year and a half, he was a minister and I knew he liked me. And I knew he had liked my mom. Now, I'm not sure I would have gone to him if I'd known he would actually go to my house and, as he put it, clean things up. I mean, I thought the two of us were just going to, like, call 911. It was horrible enough for me to see my mom dead that way.

I really didn't want Stephen, who may have loved her for a while, to have to see her that way, too.

The thing is, I had only gone home after the concert to get my laptop. Tina and I wanted to be online at the same time, and that meant that we needed two computers. We wanted to be on Facebook, and we wanted to buy new songs for our iPods, and there were concert videos on YouTube we wanted to find, and so I said I would go get my laptop. It would take ten minutes. And Tina didn't even offer to drive. She didn't need to, because I was just going like a mile to my house. She just tossed me her keys from the bottom of her purse.

Anyway, after I saw Stephen, I did what he said. I went back to Tina's.

The plan, as much as there was one, was that he was going to make it look like my dad had killed himself. He reminded me that my dad had just killed my mom. And that my dad was a horrible man. Stephen didn't expect that anyone would think he'd murdered my dad. I don't think it had crossed either of our minds that that would happen. It was supposed to look just like a suicide. Whenever I saw him later that autumn, I told him I was worried he was going to go to jail. Each time he reminded me of something important: There was never going to be any evidence that he'd killed my dad. They might believe that he did it, but they could never prove it. He assured me that looking out for me now was the very least he could do for my mom. I think that was a big reason why he was still hanging around Bennington for a while. He wanted to be there for me till this whole mess blew over.

And doing something for my mom seemed to matter to him like crazy. Whenever we spoke that fall, he was like this uncle or godfather who felt this huge responsibility to my mom. I mean, he was already into Heather (and then broken up with Heather), so it wasn't like he was pining for a lost love. But he did feel this burden that he was a part of the reason my mom was dead.

He was already living down in Bennington when I told him I thought the police were starting to think I was involved. He chuckled a little bit and said he didn't think that was likely: He said he was the big suspect and to just keep reading the newspapers. But I told him I was worried because of some of the things they had been asking me, and that's when he told me to go ahead and incriminate him. He said why not? They already thought he'd done it, but his attorney had assured him that they would never be able to prove it. So, he said, throw a little gas on the fire. He said he would, too. I was supposed to call Heather, but before I did, she showed up out of the blue one afternoon at my school, and I was like a windup toy. I just let it all out, just as Stephen had suggested, and I saw right away that he was absolutely correct. She gave me her cell-phone number, and a little later I did call her and made absolutely sure that she—that everyone—was positive that Stephen had killed my dad.

But he was also right that they were never able to charge him with murder.

Of course, from that point on I also had to steer clear of Stephen. As I said, he was the last person I should have been talking to. After all, the more I talked to him, the more someone might have figured out that we were—and here is one of those great TV terms from the cop shows I watch all the time now—co-conspirators. If I was seen with Stephen, suspect numero uno in my dad's death, they might have begun to believe that I knew a lot more than I was letting on. Eventually they might even have begun to think that I was the one who had pulled the trigger.

I thought it was really ironic that we read *The Brothers Karamazov* in an AP English course I was taking that autumn. Suddenly patricide was everywhere. One day I felt so guilty I couldn't get out of bed, and Tina reminded me of what my dad had done to my mom. No one, she said, should have to see her mom the way I had seen mine that night in July. But the thing was, at first I simply thought she was passed out, too. I mean, the place just reeked of beer. I thought she and my dad were both just sleeping. But then I saw the marks on Mom's neck, and I knew what had happened. (I find it interesting that I can no longer remember her face when I found her. Really. I have a feeling from what I've read on the Internet about death by strangulation that at some point in my life I'm going to recall her eyes, and it won't be pretty—either the image that will come to me in the night or my reaction. I don't see her eyes when I think back, but something tells me they were open. Anyway, for now at least, I'm spared knowing for sure if my dad actually hit her in the face or punched her in the nose before he killed her.) And that's when I went upstairs and decided I would go get the handgun instead of my laptop.

I never did go back for the laptop, and so it would be among the stuff that Ginny and Stephen brought me the next day. When I left, Lula was pacing nervously back and forth between the kitchen and the living room. It was Stephen who had let her out when he went back, and—to be totally honest—I'm pretty sure he kicked her out because she really was lapping up the blood that was all over the place. I don't remember his exact words, and clearly he regretted like crazy what he'd started to tell me. He was trying to explain why Lula had wound up outside.

Someday, I know, he'll regret that whole, horrible night. He should have just been a pastor and called the police, but I guess he was afraid I'd go to prison. (One time he said the fact that my dad had been such a psycho might reduce the sentence, but I shouldn't kid myself: This would be no juvie offense.) If he'd been a dad himself, that's what he would have done, and maybe ten years from now we'd both be better off.

Anyway, if I live to a very old age, I know I'll have tons and tons of regrets. I mean that. But somehow I don't think putting a bullet into my dad's head is ever going to be one of them.

ACKNOWLEDGMENTS

Once again I am indebted to a great many early readers, none of whom is a literal angel but all of whom were profoundly helpful. Among them? There is the Reverend David Wood, one of my closest friends and the pastor of the church where I have worshipped most of my adult life. There is Lauren Bowerman, an assistant attorney general with the State of Vermont. This is the third time that Lauren has graciously told me what is authentic in one of my manuscripts and what is completely ridiculous.

In addition, Dr. Steven Shapiro, the chief medical examiner for the State of Vermont, helped me understand what would have happened to the fictional George and Alice Hayward after they died. Siri Rooney, the victim advocate for the Lamoille County state's attorney's office, shared with me the horrors that a battered woman such as Alice was likely to endure, as well as the resources that were available to her. Meanwhile Bridget Butler taught me about birds. Among the books that were especially valuable was Dr. Louis Cataldie's memoir of his years as the chief coroner of Baton Rouge, *Coroner's Journal: Forensics and the Art of Stalking Death*.

Other readers included a variety of friends and agents, many of whom are both, including Stephen Kiernan, Jane Gelfman, and Dean Schramm; my editor of fifteen years and one of my very closest friends, Shaye Areheart; my lovely bride of a quarter century now, Victoria Blewer; and, for the first time, my deeply thoughtful teenage daughter, Grace Experience.

I am grateful as well to Cathy Gleason at Gelfman Schneider; to Arlynn Greenbaum at Authors Unlimited; and to the whole enthusiastic team at the Crown Publishing Group: Andy Augusto, Patty Berg, Cindy Berman, Sarah Breivogel, Whitney Cookman, Jill Flaxman, Jenny Frost, Kate Kennedy, Christine Kopprasch, Jacqui Lebow, Matthew Martin, Donna Passannante, Philip Patrick, Annsley Rosner, Jay Sones, Katie Wainwright, Kira Walton, and Campbell Wharton. It really does take a village—or a skyscraper floor.

I thank you all for your wisdom, your counsel, and your honesty.

SECRETS OF EDEN
Chris Bohjalian

Reading Group Guide
by Kira Walton

A NOTE TO THE READER

In order to provide reading groups with the most informed and thought-provoking questions possible, it is necessary to reveal important aspects of the plot of this book—as well as the ending.

If you have not finished reading Secrets of Eden, *we respectfully suggest that you may want to wait before reviewing this guide.*

ABOUT THIS GUIDE

"There," says Alice Hayward to Reverend Stephen Drew, just after her baptism, and just before going home to the husband who will kill her that evening and then shoot himself. Drew, tortured by the cryptic finality of that short utterance, feels his faith in God slipping away and is saved from despair only by a meeting with Heather Laurent, an author of wildly successful inspirational books about . . . angels.

Heather survived a childhood that culminated in her parents' murder-suicide, so she identifies deeply with Alice's and George's daughter, Katie, offering herself as a mentor to the girl and a shoulder for Stephen—who flees the pulpit to be with Heather and see if there is anything to be salvaged from the spiritual wreckage around him.

But then the state's attorney begins to suspect that Alice's husband may not have killed himself . . . and finds out that Alice had secrets only her minister knew.

This reader's guide is intended as a starting point for your discussion of the novel.

1. Re-read the quotes that open the book. One is from a leading voice of Enlightenment rationalism, the other from the Bible. Samuel Johnson speaks about loss and sorrow; the quote from Genesis is about the bonds of marriage. What did you think of this unique pairing when you began reading? Now that you've finished *Secrets of Eden,* how do these quotes help shape your understanding of the story?

2. What did you think of the title before you began reading? The phrase "secrets of Eden" appears when Heather Laurent and Reverend Drew are together in New York: "He pulled me against him and said simply, 'There were no secrets in Eden'" (page 259). What do you think Reverend Drew means by that? What are the secrets in the biblical Eden? Where is the "Eden" in *Secrets of Eden*? Is it a place? A state of mind? What are the secrets in the story, and who is keeping them? What is gained or lost when these secrets are revealed?

3. Chris Bohjalian is known for writing novels with an evocative sense of place: New England, especially small-town Vermont. How does the setting of *Secrets of Eden* impact the characters? How is it vital to the story? Could these events have taken place in another landscape, another social context? Why or why not?

PART I: STEPHEN DREW

4. The novel begins from Reverend Stephen Drew's perspective. How would you describe his voice as a narrator? Is he sympathetic? Reliable? What is his state of mind? In the first few pages of the first chapter, what does Reverend Drew reveal about himself? About Alice Hayward's life and death? What does he *not* reveal? Did you immediately trust his point of view? Why or why not? What words would you use to describe him? Do you think he'd use the same words to describe himself?

5. When he recalls Alice Hayward's baptism, Reverend Drew remembers the word "there" in a poignant way, comparing the last word Alice spoke to him with Christ's last words on the cross. Why do you think this simple word—"there"—is given such weighty importance? How is it related to what Reverend Drew calls "the seeds of my estrangement from my calling" (page 13)?

6. Reverend Drew says of his calling to the church: "All I can tell you is I believe I was sent" (page 44). He then delves into a grisly description of the Crucifixion (pages 45–48), recalling the first time he studied it in high school. With what we know about Reverend Drew up to this point, how did this revelation help you understand him? Were you drawn in or repulsed by his fixation?

7. How does Reverend Drew explain his spiritual breakdown? Was there one moment when he lost his faith (Alice's baptism, her death) or was it the result of a series of events? What kind of response did you have to his breakdown? One of empathy? Curiosity? Suspicion?

PART II: CATHERINE BENINCASA

8. Before we hear from Catherine in her own voice, we see her through Reverend Drew's eyes. What is your first impression of her from his perspective? Does that impression change once you see things from her point of view? What words would you use to describe Catherine?

9. Catherine says of Reverend Drew, "the guy had ice in his veins . . . [a] serial-killer vibe" (page 106). How does this compare with how he portrays himself? Do you think Catherine sees Reverend Drew clearly based on what she knows? Is she jumping to conclusions, or making use of her intuition and the hard truths she's learned throughout her grueling years on the job?

10. At one point, Catherine says, "I know the difference between mourning and grief" (page 193). What do you think she means by this? Do you agree that there's a difference? How would you describe the reactions, so far, of Reverend Drew, Heather, and Katie to the terrible events they're faced with—as mourning or grief?

PART III: HEATHER LAURENT

11. By the time we get to the section narrated by Heather, we've seen her from both Reverend Drew's and Catherine Benincasa's points of view, and we've read excerpts from her books. How would you describe her? Do you agree with Drew that she's "unflappably serene . . . an individual whose competence was manifest and whose sincerity was phosphorescent" (page 65), or do you agree with pathologist David Dennison's take on her: "'Angel of death. I'm telling you: That woman is as stable as a three-legged chair" (page 182)?

12. Heather's section begins with her description of her first encounter with an angel: she's a young woman, lost in the depths of de-

pression, and intends to commit suicide (pages 225–232). How would you interpret this moment? What does it reveal about how she deals with the deaths of her parents? About how she sees the world?

13. Reverend Drew and Catherine Benincasa both provide graphic descriptions of crimes and crime scenes—the Haywards' and others—but Heather's memories of the violence between her parents is particularly grim. How do you react to reading these passages?

PART IV: KATIE HAYWARD

14. Ending the novel in Katie Hayward's voice is a provocative choice. What do you think of it? You've now seen her from the points of view of Reverend Drew, Catherine, and Heather—how would you describe her? Does she seem like a typical teenager? To borrow Catherine's distinction, is Katie grieving or in mourning?

15. At one point during a conversation with Katie, Reverend Drew says, "it was one good thing to come out of that awful Sunday night: We were all striving to be better people. To be kind. To be gentler with one another" (page 321). Is this true in the case of the people in this novel? Can good come out of such violence, such painful loss? How does each of the four main characters respond? How does the town in general respond?

16. Re-read the interview between Katie Hayward and Emmet Walker (pages 155–160). Think back to when you read it the first time, before you'd finished the book. Did anything give you pause? Is there anything in Katie's responses that reveals what we later find out to be true?

17. The novel ends with a revelation. Did it surprise you? How does the author build suspense throughout the novel? Can you find moments of foreshadowing that hint at the ending?

18. Part I ends with Reverend Drew saying, "If there is a lesson to be learned from my fall . . . it is this: Believe no one. Trust no one. Assume no one really knows anything that matters at all. Because, alas, we don't. All of our stories are suspect" (page 101). Do you think all the narrators' stories—Reverend Drew, Catherine, Heather, Katie—are suspect? Is one of them more believable, more reliable, than the others?

19. Pay particular attention to the minor characters: Ginny O'Brien, Emmet Walker, David Dennison, Amanda and Norman, Alice Hayward. What does each minor character reveal about the narrators? How does each move the story forward?

20. Reverend Drew remembers an intimate moment with Alice Hayward in which she asks him to "Remind me who I am" (page 99). How do you understand this need in Alice? What was she looking for in Reverend Drew? Do you think she got it?

21. Excerpts from Heather Laurent's books are interspersed throughout the novel. Look closely at each excerpt and at what comes before and after. Discuss why you think these are included, and how they impact your reading based on where they appear. Is there a literal connection between what's happening in the story and what's happening in Heather Laurent's books, or is the connection more nuanced? Does one excerpt stand out to you more than the others?

22. Chris Bohjalian's readers know that his novels often address a significant social issue. *Secrets of Eden* tackles the tragedy of domestic violence. How did reading this novel influence your understanding of domestic violence?

23. Angels are a recurring image and a major theme in *Secrets of Eden*. Who sees them? When do they appear? How are they described? How do they affect each character differently? In the end, do the angels provide an image of hope?

POCKET
BOOKS

MIDWIVES
CHRIS BOHJALIAN

On an icy winter night in an isolated house in rural Vermont,
a seasoned midwife named Sibyl Danforth takes desperate
measures to save a baby's life. She performs an emergency
caesarean section on a mother she believes has died of a
stroke. But what if Sibyl's patient wasn't dead – and Sibyl
inadvertently killed her?

As Sibyl faces the antagonism of the law, the hostility of
traditional doctors, and the accusations of her own
conscience, *Midwives* engages, moves, and transfixes
us as only the very best novels ever do.

978-1-84739-339-5
£7.99

POCKET
BOOKS

SKELETONS AT THE FEAST

CHRIS BOHJALIAN

In January 1945, in the waning months of World War II, a
small group of people begin the longest journey of their
lives: an attempt to cross the remnants of the Third Reich to
reach the British and American lines.

Among the group is 18-year-old Anna Emmerich, the
daughter of Prussian aristocrats. There is her lover, Callum
Finnella, a young Scottish prisoner of war who has been
brought from the stalag to her family's farm as forced
labour. And there is the intriguing Wehrmacht corporal
whom the pair know as Manfred – who is, in reality, Uri
Singer, a Jew from Germany who managed a daring escape
from a train bound for Auschwitz.

As they work their way west, they encounter a countryside
ravaged by war. Their flight will test both Anna's and
Callum's love, as well as their friendship with Manfred –
assuming any of them even survive.

978-1-84739-340-1
£7.99

POCKET
BOOKS

THE DOUBLE BIND
CHRIS BOHJALIAN

When Laurel Estabrook is attacked while out riding her bike
one Sunday afternoon, her life is changed forever. She
begins work at a shelter for the homeless and there meets
Bobbie Crocker, a man with a history of mental illness and a
box full of photos he won't let anyone see.

When Bobbie dies suddenly, Laurel discovers that he was
once a successful photographer, and her fascination with his
former life begins to merge into obsession, not least because
some of the photos are of the very same forest trail where
she was attacked and nearly killed.

Laurel becomes convinced that his photos reveal a deeply
hidden, dark family secret. Her search for the truth leads her
further from her own life and into a cat-and-mouse game
with pursuers who claim they want to save her.

978-1-84739-193-3
£7.99

POCKET
BOOKS

These books and other **Simon & Schuster** and **Pocket Books** titles are available from your local bookshop or can be ordered direct from the publisher.

978-1-84739-339-5	**Midwives**	**£7.99**
978-1-84739-340-1	**Skeletons at the Feast**	**£7.99**
978-1-84739-193-3	**The Double Bind**	**£7.99**

Free post and packing within the UK
Overseas customers please add £2 per paperback.
Telephone Simon & Schuster Cash Sales at Bookpost
on 01624 677237 with your credit or debit card number,
or send a cheque payable to Simon & Schuster Cash Sales to:
PO Box 29, Douglas, Isle of Man, IM99 1BQ
Fax: 01624 670923
Email: bookshop@enterprise.net
www.bookpost.co.uk

Please allow 14 days for delivery. Prices and availability
are subject to change without notice.